A Dream of Destiny:
Children of the Fates

P. H. Townsend

First published 2025
by Rowanvale Books Ltd
The Gate
Keppoch Street
Roath
Cardiff
CF24 3JW
www.rowanvalebooks.com

A CIP catalogue record for this book is available from the British Library.
ISBN: 978-1-83584-123-5
Ebook ISBN: 978-1-83584-124-2

Grateful Acknowledgments

Mum, for always being there.

To my wonderful family, near and far, for their continued love and support.

H and Craig, for keeping faith.

My wonderful editor, Ellie, and to Alice, for bringing the cover to life. And everyone at Rowanvale Books for their tireless work in bringing *Children of the Fates* to you, the reader.

And most importantly, a heartfelt thank you to all those who have joined the adventure. You have made a dream come true.

P. H. Townsend.

The old gods were jealous.

In their lust to taste all of the fruits mortals possessed, a hybrid race was created: half god, half human.

They were called demigods.

—from the book *Mortal Gods* by Hesiod, Senior Elder of the Order of Disciples

CHAPTER ONE

GUESS WHO'S COMING TO DINNER

Jacen was gone. Pandora's coffin, taken from the safety of her tomb.

The huge wall of fog had lifted and the Followers, led by the devious Mr Tripp, were now only a speck on the horizon.

***

Three ships glided through the water, heading directly for the island. Rapidly, they closed in on the beach.

From the pinnacle of the stone steps, four teenagers stared out toward the deserted, ghostly decks. Was this a rescue party? Or a new menace to be faced before they could escape this nightmare?

Kyle and Josh Michaels sped to the clifftop that over-looked the beach and the harbour. There, they could hide among the tall trees and keep a lookout, while Mira Alextopolis and Jo Loris hurried back through the bronze gates and along the moss-ridden pebbled path toward the palace.

Narrow rays of light illuminated the great hall. Silence lay within. And yet, Mira couldn't help feel that someone, or something, was watching from the shadows. This wasn't the physical presence she'd felt outside her bedroom window, or even aboard the ill-fated cruise ship—the sensation she was now experiencing was more… supernatural.

To make matters worse, Jo was breathing heavily and staring down at her own feet. "This wasn't here before, Mira." She pointed shakily to the ground.

Mira looked to the symbol embedded in the marble floor: a hooded cloak encased inside a large circle. Strange, ancient writing was engraved around its circumference. She, too, could not remember seeing it—and she had got up close and personal with the stonework when Peter tossed her around like a rag doll, right before he'd carried her brother away from her.

Mira dropped to her knees, desperate to see if the inscription gave any clues as to where they truly were and, more importantly, who had originally occupied the island. She brushed away the leaves and dust that had blown into the hall during the night and ran her finger along a narrow channel running through the emblem's centre. A warm, light snuffle of air brushed against her hand. Mira held her breath. She was kneeling upon a gateway.

"Should we find a way to open it and see where it leads?" Jo asked, her eyes once again wide in anticipation.

Mira silently shook her head. She had no intention of opening the gateway or venturing inside. Its very presence sent a cold, uncomfortable stirring through her entire body. Instead, she took a tight hold of Jo's arm and hastened her through the secret tunnel that led out to the arched stone bridge. But even when they were standing once more in the bright sunlight, Mira was compelled to look back over her shoulder and into the dark recess of the corridor.

There it was again, that feeling of foreboding. Even if they were lucky enough to escape the island, one day, she would have to return and see for herself what lay beyond the mysterious doorway.

Nearby, the huge body of the wolf lay lifeless on the ground, a spear still protruding from its bloodied mouth. Mira winced at the scene once more. She'd always been a strong advocate against the killing and torture of any animal but now had to admire Pyrrha for the ordeal she had gone through to defeat such a wild beast.

Together, Mira and Jo slipped past its giant frame, afraid that, at any moment, it would magically come back to life and attack. But then, and adding to Mira's already frazzled nerves, Jo doubled over and clasped her hands to her head.

This action spurred Mira into scanning the ground for any symbols that may have magically appeared. But there was only the large pool of blood and scattered chunks of the wolf's flesh.

"Are you OK, Jo?"

Jo slowly removed her hands from her face. There was fear in her eyes, but also deep regret. "Yes… Don't worry, I'm not going to attack you. It's just… things are starting to come back to me. They are not…"

Jo hesitated for a moment and appeared to gaze into nothing. "…pleasant images," she said finally.

That can't be good. "Like what exactly?"

Jo bit down on her bottom lip. "I remember what I said and how I acted at the tomb. I am truly sorry. It's just, when I went with Josh to get oil, there was this high-pitched scream. Then came the terrible cries of pain and unbearable suffering. I—I lost consciousness. Josh said he did, too. But I know he was just saying it to make me feel better. Anyway, when I awoke, I was overwhelmed by this voice in my head. It commanded me to kill you and Jacen, but also—and I'm ashamed to say it—it promised that all the riches on the island would be mine. That I could finally get out from under my parents' strict, Victorian ideals. Break free from the constant arguing concerning my sexuality. I tried to ignore it, fight it, but the more I fought the more intense the voice became until—you know, I, umm... threatened you with a sword."

It wasn't exactly comforting. But Mira didn't want to alarm her further, so said, "It doesn't matter now, Jo. Pyrrha did say there's something about this island that makes people go a bit... la-la."

"But why did it affect me more than the rest of you? What is wrong with me?"

Jo began to sob, and Mira placed a gentle arm around her shoulder in an attempt to give her friend some comfort. She had to allay Jo's fears if they were all going to escape the island together.

"There's nothing wrong with you. Whatever voice you heard, it went for the strongest with everything it had, that's all."

Jo wiped her teary eyes. "I'm not the strongest, Mira. But thanks—thanks for trying to cheer me up. Now I just need to make up for my terrible actions."

"If you feel up to it, there is something you could do for me, actually. Could you shed some light on something that's been bothering me?"

"What do you need?"

"Pyrrha told me that she killed Linus because he wanted to open the tomb. Can you confirm that? Did he give any indication what he was planning to do?"

Jo was quick to answer. "No. When I left the chamber in search of treasure, everything seemed OK with the both of them. And Linus, he seemed ready to do anything to stop what was going to happen." Her eyes narrowed. "Why would Pyrrha have saved his life if he was a threat? If you ask me, something just doesn't add up with her story."

You're right about that, Mira thought.

***

They had reached the top of the embankment. Pyrrha was finally conscious and struggling to escape the bootlace bonds Kyle had placed upon her.

"What the hell are you two playing at?" she snarled.

Mira angled the sword toward her but remained silent, while Jo untied the cords from around their captive's feet.

"Answer me, Mira. I demand to know what is going on!" Pyrrha insisted.

Mira wanted to scream, pound her hands into Pyrrha's chest and beat some answers out of her—who she really was, for one. But she needed to remain in control.

Best if you allow Jo to speak, she convinced herself.

"Nothing you need to concern yourself with," Jo said, pressing a dagger close to Pyrrha's throat. "But if you would be so kind as to tell us where you hid your boat, it will save the time of me having to beat the location from you."

Maybe letting Jo speak first hadn't been the wisest decision. She was relieved when Jo shot her a sly wink.

Pyrrha again refused to cooperate. A simple nod from Mira, and Jo roughly swung Pyrrha round to face the palace. With the tip of her blade pressed to Pyrrha's back, Jo forced her hostage toward the secret tunnel that would lead back to the tower.

Mira headed to the clifftop where Kyle and Josh were still watching the approaching ships.

"How long before they get here?" she asked.

"I'd say ten minutes if they park up on the beach," said Josh. "Maybe twenty if they get into rowing boats. Then they'll be walking right past us, and the 'guess who's coming to the dinner party' will finally be answered. I think we can safely say it isn't the navy, or any lifeguard service. I've never seen any type of rescue boat that looks like these. To be honest with you, they look like they've been pieced together from various other ships by some crazy engineers."

"All we need to know is that they've come for Pyrrha." Mira tried to harden her voice, but couldn't keep a tinge of fear from creeping in. "Her eyes ignited seeing those, what you call, weird-looking ships."

Josh blew out his cheeks. "OK, if you're certain... Talking of the mysterious Amazonian warrior goddess, any luck in her revealing where her boat is hidden?"

"She won't say. I suspect it's underneath the tower. It has to be. It's the only logical place. Jo's taking her there now. I just hope Rachel has already found a way to get to it. I don't think we're going to have the time to get the location out of Pyrrha if I'm wrong."

"If its torture you want, I'd leave it to Rach," said Josh. "She'll scare it out of her in seconds. I'll just need to wind her up a bit first, that's all."

Mira had to smile. Rachel Hayes did have a temper that could scare even a lion at times. She recalled how, in a fit of fury, Rachel had knocked one of the Followers unconscious when she'd thought that Josh had given up to them at the tomb. But when Mira looked to Kyle, her expression quickly changed. From the moment the ships had been sighted, he'd remained silent and apart from her. She placed her hand on his shoulder, hoping for just a smile or a simple word of encouragement. But Kyle didn't respond, and time was against them. Reluctantly, she turned on her heels and followed after Jo to the great hall of the tower.

The fire was still burning in the hearth, but there was no sign of Rachel.

"Rach?" Mira called, then, when there was no response, "Rachel!" more urgently. The name echoed back at her.

Jo propelled Pyrrha across the marble floor and forced her to sit at the long table.

After a few minutes of blind panic, searching every room, Mira's worries were finally put to rest when Rachel appeared, out of nowhere it seemed, with a huge, beaming smile across her face.

Mira exhaled a sigh of relief upon seeing her best friend unharmed. "Any luck?" she asked.

"Oh, yes. You were right. Pyrrha's boat was in another hidden chamber beside the sunken ship. Now, as soon as you reach the bottom of the stairs, there's a narrow corridor *behind* the steps that will lead you to it. Take a lamp with you, though—it's a dark passage."

Mira took a lantern from the wall and handed it to Jo. "Take Pyrrha down to the boat. Rachel and I will get some supplies. Be careful, she's trained to kill."

"You're making a big mistake. I'm here to help you!" Pyrrha shouted, before disappearing down the narrow staircase.

"We're taking her with us?" Rachel asked, her eyebrows raised high.

Mira looked to the chair at the table where Jacen had sat only the day before. She held back her tears. "For now."

CHAPTER TWO

ESCAPE

Two rowboats had landed. Six figures dressed in hooded garb similar to what the Followers had been wearing strode up the beach toward the steep stone steps.

Tucked behind a large tree on the clifftop, Kyle and Josh held their breaths, waiting for the menace that was lurking unseen under the sand, and which had taken the life of Barry Cutter, to strike. But the faceless group reached the top of the staircase safely.

Kyle and Josh weaved through the trees to the nearest building and hid inside.

"Do you think they know where the secret entrance to the tower is?" Josh whispered.

"How should I know?" Kyle peered out through the open window. "But if they start heading this way, I'd say yes."

The hooded group were now standing at the open gates, in deep conversation.

"The Followers were dressed in black," said Josh, "but this lot are in—oh, what colour would you call it?"

"Aubergine," said Kyle.

Josh squirrelled up his nose. "Must be the light screwing with my eyes," he mumbled, and slyly, he, too, took another look. "If you say so... Do you think the colours could be some sort of ranking system in their order?"

Suddenly, one turned and looked directly at the building Kyle and Josh were now occupying. The brothers swiftly dropped to their knees.

"Again, how should I know?" Kyle said through his teeth, then peeked back up over the sill. The group had turned and were disappearing along the path to the palace. "All I do know is that we need to get to the tower and get the hell out of here. They give me the creeps. At least they're gone for now."

Josh threw back his head, closed his eyes and pressed his hands into a steeple. "C'mon, let the screaming begin," he prayed.

Kyle cast a wary look at the beads of sweat on Josh's brow. "Are you alright?"

"No. I want to get as far from this place as I possibly can. When I went to get oil with Jo—don't laugh—I saw these terrifying shadows appear along the walls of the building where we first discovered the smell. It was like something out of a horror movie, Kai. As we were about to leave, the temperature suddenly dropped dramatically. I've never felt that cold in my life. And there were these voices. At first, it was sweet-sounding. Like, like little children playing, or when Mrs Roberts wanted us to pay attention to her in English class—"

"When she wanted *you* to pay attention, more like," Kyle corrected him.

"OK, me. But the way she would softly talk—even you have to admit that Mrs Roberts could have made anyone, even Mum, do what she wanted, right?"

"I guess," said Kyle. "But where is this heading?"

Josh lowered his eyes. "One particular voice kept telling me to get Jacen to the tomb. But even though deep inside my gut I knew it was a bad idea, I began to agree with it. Was it like that for you?"

Kyle nodded.

"Good. Sorry, I don't mean good. What I mean to say is, at least it wasn't just me hearing it. Anyway, just when I was about to give in to it fully there came these other voices. It was horrible. Cries of pain and unbearable suffering. It was so intense I thought I was going to pass out. Jo actually did. What I'm trying to say is, I think this island is, or was, one great sacrificial arena, and I'm afraid that if we don't leave soon, then we may end up joining those voices."

Kyle shook his head in disbelief. "So, why do you want the screaming to start?"

"Whoever those hoodies are—the Followers or these mysterious Disciples that Pyrrha claims to be a part of—I want them to feel what I did. Maybe then they'll understand to leave things well alone. To leave us alone." Josh leapt to his feet. "You know, it's not going to take them long to find that the tomb is empty. If Rachel hasn't found Pyrrha's boat, we're in a lot of trouble. Look, I reckon we take one of their ships." He grinned, his eyes once again twinkling. "The speed they got here means they're fast. If we're lucky, we can catch up with Mr Tripp and get Jacen back."

Though he was impressed with Josh's instant switch from fear to heroism, Kyle couldn't believe what his brother was planning to do.

He shook his head. "Josh, do really think they have left the ships unguarded?"

"Not the big one, but there are two littler ones." Josh beamed. "If we swim around to that one at the rear, we could take it, sail around to the sunken one under the tower, pick up the girls, and Jo, and be gone before they know it. What do you think?"

Kyle held his hands firm to his side to keep from cuffing his brother across his head the way his mother would often do. *Yet again, he hasn't thought this through.* "How many have gone through the gates?"

"Err… six?"

"Then do you really think the not-so-small boat you're pointing to is only manned by the same six people that have entered the gates? In fact, do you really think they are stupid enough to have left any of the boats empty?"

Josh pressed his lips together. "Fine." He pouted. "Pyrrha's boat it is. But I've told you many times before, Kaiboy: sarcasm is not your thing. Looking pretty is what you bring to the group. Mine is planning and coming out with cocky wisecracks the audience loves. Rachel's the muscle. Jo's the know-it-all who cracks under pressure and turns even nuttier, while Mira is the shy, passive intellectual who finds her inner strength and becomes a total badass. You know, like Sarah Conner in the first, and for me personally, *only Terminator* movie worth mentioning—*Hasta la vista, baby.* God, how corny can you—"

Kyle slammed his hand over Josh's mouth. More hooded figures were running up the steps. At first, Kyle thought they were going to follow the others through the bronze gates, but when they began to head in their direction, he dragged his brother through the backstreets toward the building with the secret tunnel.

***

The stone tile was replaced at the entrance to the tunnel, and Kyle and Josh ran until they reached the tower where Mira and Rachel were gathering the last of the supplies.

"Did you find it, Rach?" Josh wheezed. His eyes were wide in anticipation.

"I did." She winked.

The last of the crates were taken below the tower to where Pyrrha had hidden her boat. But when Jo appeared from inside the cabin, alone, her eyes still red from crying, Kyle felt his heart drop to the pit of his stomach. "Where's Pyrrha?" he asked, scanning the area, fearing she had escaped.

"Taking another nap," said Jo flatly while lifting one of the crates of food.

Josh rolled his eyes. "Taking another nap? Who is she, Sleeping Beauty?"

"Yes, she's taking a bloody nap!" Jo snapped. "She managed to remove her bindings and went for me, OK!"

"And what happened?"

"Luckily for me, Rachel was behind her and bonked her across the head." Jo shrugged.

Josh cast Rachel a wary look. "Told you, Kaiboy. She's the muscle. Remind me never to piss you off, Rach."

Rachel's eyes narrowed. "When aren't you pissing me off, Josh?"

***

All the crates had been loaded onto the boat. The sunken ship could have sailed straight out to the ocean, if it could still sail at all, but this wasn't an option. The hidden chamber had no visible access to the sea. Jo had to guide Pyrrha's vessel with great skill through a narrow, underground, winding tunnel, careful to avoid detection.

When they looked back, they found the route they had just exited by was now nowhere to be seen.

"The wall is an optical illusion." Josh beamed. "How clever is that!"

From the depths of the ocean, the great wall of fog, once again, began to ascend high toward the heavens.

"Keep taking it slow, Jo," Josh added. "The mist may cover our escape, but we don't want the sound of the engine to give our position away."

Jo nodded in agreement. Yet, when a high-pitched wail, the same as she and Josh had heard before, sounded behind them, she engaged the throttle fully forward without hesitation, and with the roar of the motor echoing out, she sped them far from the island as quickly as she could.

CHAPTER THREE

INTO THE UNKNOWN

The open ocean was thankfully calm. With no sign of land, nor any other vessels for that matter, Mira's and Jo's full attention was on the sea charts, and Kyle sat at the stern staring up at an empty sky, so Josh entered the cabin to see if Rachel, at least, would speak to him.

The inside was arranged in two parts. A small kitchenette and dining area, where an unconscious Pyrrha was tied to one metal leg of the table, and opposite, a two-seater couch that could be pulled out into a bed. A smaller room at the rear had two bunks separated by a small side dresser and lamp.

Josh took a seat on the sofa beside Rachel. There was a large kitchen knife gripped tightly in her hand and a steely glare fixed upon their prisoner. Josh began to wonder if it was safe, or wise, to say anything. But he'd always found it hard to sit in silence.

"Do you think we can catch Mr Tripp's ship, Rach?" he whispered.

"We're not going after him," she said flatly. "We're following Mira's lead. She said it would be crazy for just the five of us to go after him. He's too well protected. She's right, it would be suicide."

Reaching inside his jacket pocket, Josh pulled out his last Mars bar, split it in two and handed Rachel half. "So, we're going home to get the army then, right?"

"No. Didn't you listen to Mira back on that island? She believes that Jacen is safe, so she's going to find answers."

Josh kept his eyes on the knife. A bead of sweat trickled down his forehead.

"Righto… Look, I swear I'm not trying to wind you up, but does she know where exactly she's going to find these answers?"

Rachel's expression softened. "I don't know, sweetie. She hasn't said. I guess she will let us know when she's ready. Like I said, I would gladly go after Jacen now, but I trust that Mira knows what she is doing, so I'm going to follow my best friend until she says otherwise."

Josh sat back and chewed on his favourite chocolate bar. He pointed to Pyrrha. "I still don't get why we're bringing her with us."

"Because we don't know what her real intentions are yet. Better to keep an eye on her. Which, I'm trying to do now."

"Yeah, but why don't we just throw her overboard?"

"Ask Mira."

"But—"

Rachel's expression took a turn for the worse. "Ask Mira! I would be more than happy to do it!"

Josh took the hint and forced the last morsel of chocolate down. "O…kay, then."

He waited a moment, watching Rachel's knuckles turn white as she gripped the knife even tighter.

"So, umm… what do you think about all that's happened, then?"

"I'm trying not to think about it—and neither should you, Josh Michaels. Now, I need to keep an eye on her, so no more questions. God knows what is going to happen when she *does* wake up!"

For once, Josh knew it would be safer for his arm (Rachel's favourite target), to remain quiet. He left the cabin to join the others on deck.

Stepping out into the bright sunshine, he took a deep inhale of the fresh sea air. Kyle was still sat at the stern, now staring at the deck beneath his feet, and Jo still at the wheel, but now she was waving her arms around and muttering, "I don't know which way to steer." Josh decided to join Mira at the bow for what he hoped would be a less stressful conversation.

"Hello." He sidled up to her with a smile. "Umm, so, ah, where are we going then?"

"To find my father," said Mira calmly, her eyes firmly fixed on the maps laid out across the deck.

"Oh, right. Off to find Dad. Yeah, of course we are. Err… and why exactly are we doing that?"

Mira didn't blink. "He knows what is going on."

Josh tried to remain upbeat. "At least one of us does, then." He laughed. "So, err, do you know where he is?"

"Not yet."

Josh opened his mouth, but Mira held her hand over it. "Before you ask, I know Jacen is safe. Trust me, if he wasn't, I would be heading after the Followers right now—I promise you that," she said, and removed her hand.

"OK, then. Err—don't mean to keep on, but any idea where we are now?" he said, trying his best not to show any of the panic he was feeling.

"No. But Jo believes we are in the Mediterranean and not the Atlantic," she said, flipping to another chart.

Josh sucked on his top lip and slowly nodded his head.

Mira's cheeks reddened in annoyance. "Ask what you want, Josh."

"OK, umm… here goes. If we're not going after Jacen, I'm assuming you know where they are taking him?"

"No. But someone does."

Josh waited for more of an explanation, but when none came, he quickly moved on to his second question. "Right, not going to get *persifik* about it… OK, question two—why aren't we throwing Pyrrha overboard? She lied to you and then killed Linus."

"Did she kill Linus? Or was it the wolf? All I saw was his blood-soaked shirt. As for Pyrrha, I get the feeling she knows where Jacen has been taken. That's why we have to keep her alive. And it's *specific*, Josh. Not *persifik*."

"Noted… Ha, I always wondered why my teachers would mention the ocean when telling me to be more *persifik* with my answers. Specific, makes sense now." He laughed, hoping to lighten the mood. "So, do you know if Pyrrha really is a Disciple now, or a Follower, or a Potential, or just part of a group of homicidal maniacs? Because the team of hoodies that landed were wearing similar, err, uniforms. Except that the Followers were in black and that new group that turned up were in, umm, tangerine."

Mira finally looked him in the eye. "I'm pretty certain she is a Disciple, but not convinced enough as to what her real intentions are for me to untie her yet. And I saw what they were wearing. It was aubergine. Tangerine is orange."

Josh blushed. "Yeah, I know. I meant, umm, aubergine."

As Josh began to stroke his chin in thought, Mira added, "Aubergine is kind of a deep purple, Josh."

Josh exhaled a deep sigh. "Oh, right. I thought my eyes were playing tricks when Kyle said…" He could sense Mira's patience was wearing thin. "Not important. Anyway, do you think I should try and see if I can get the truth from her?"

Mira's gaze returned to her charts. "If you think you can, then be my guest. But you saw how she handled a weapon. Don't give her any opportunity to get the jump on you."

Josh felt an inner spark—maybe he could actually be of help here. "Okey-dokey, will do." He turned to Jo. "This last question is for you, Jo. When the heck did you learn how to drive a boat? And how in the hell would you know we are in the Mediterranean?"

"My father taught me. And it's not rocket science, Josh." Jo glowered. "You have a control throttle that propels the boat forwards or back, and a steering wheel that guides the rudder in the direction you want to go. That's about it. And I don't know why I know it's the Mediterranean, I just do. And for future reference, it's the *Pacific* not the *Persifik* Ocean."

Mira and Jo were united in their silence. Josh took the hint and, afraid to say anything else, joined Kyle at the stern.

The island was now only a dot on the skyline. An icy tingle suddenly rippled through Josh's body. A feeling that they were being followed—but not from the island they had just departed. He searched the horizon in all directions but saw nothing. Not wanting to alarm Kyle, he smiled at his brother as he sat beside him.

"You OK, Kyle?" he asked chirpily. *Because you don't look fine to me...*

"Yeah, thanks for asking. You OK?" Kyle asked, refusing to look him in the eye.

Josh looked out at the rolling waves. "Am I OK? Hmm... Good question. Let's see. Well, Rachel's in a bad mood with me. Mira's now in a bad mood with me. Jo looks ready to kill me—but what's new?—and when Pyrrha wakes up, no doubt she's going to be in a bad mood, probably with me. I don't know, Kai, I really don't fancy my chances of surviving this trip."

"Why do think I'm staying back here?" Kyle said in an offhand way.

"I know we're going to look for Mira's father," Josh continued, "but do you have any idea where exactly we are now? I can't believe we've drifted into the Med like Jo reckons."

"Not a clue," Kyle replied, "but Mira will figure it out and let us know, I guess. Or let you know. She hasn't told me we're going to look for her father."

Josh nodded. *Has something happened between them?* he wondered.

Not wanting to risk making Kyle surly as well, he thought of something else to talk about. "I wonder what Mum and Dad are doing now. Holding a street party, no doubt, in celebration of getting rid of me." He laughed, happy that Mr Tripp had told them their parents were safe, but when Kyle looked away, Josh's smile soon faded.

"Are you sure he was telling the truth?" said Kyle coldly. "The Followers could have them locked up somewhere, and when they find out that they need Mira to open that sarcophagus, they could use them to get us to betray her."

"I won't betray her, and you certainly would never betray her," said Josh.

"I already did once. Deep down, I knew that opening those bronze gates was wrong. I talked her into it anyway…"

Kyle closed his eyes and covered his face with his hands. For the first time, Josh could see how deeply affected his brother was.

"You came through for her in the end, like I told her you would," he said, and gave Kyle a gentle punch in the arm. "That's what matters."

"I think, when we reach land, it would be better to leave me behind," Kyle mumbled.

"Don't talk like that!" Josh snapped. "She needs you. Are you really gonna leave her to deal with all this?"

Kyle shook his head. "No, I won't leave her until she asks me. But what if the Followers have Mum and Dad hostage?"

"Then, God help them," said Josh. "You know what Dad is like when he loses his temper. And if they upset Mum, they won't have to open Pandora's box to see death or destruction—she'll be the one performing it on them."

This brought a smile to Kyle's face—Josh's, too. He couldn't remember the last time he'd seen Kyle express anything other than anger. But as he lay back on the deck and placed his hands behind his head, content that he'd at least brought one of his shipmates some comfort, a dark cloud appeared and blotted out the sun. Suddenly, a gust of wind rose up out of nowhere and began to swirl around the boat.

Josh leapt to his feet. "Oh, what now?!"

CHAPTER FOUR

A RISING STORM

The ocean swell was making it harder for Jo to steer. When the boat began to roll from side to side and twist and turn violently, furiously, she relinquished her hold of the wheel. The sun had just departed behind the horizon, and Kyle and Josh could see lights in the distance, appearing and then disappearing as they rode the waves. Suddenly, a light turned on in the cabin, revealing their location to whoever was following them. Josh ran inside and quickly turned it off. Before he could return to his brother, however, Rachel pulled the blackout shades over the cabin's portholes, turned the light back on and instructed him to sit.

"I'm not leaving her in the dark!" She pointed at her now fully conscious prisoner. "I've also decided that we, the two of us, shall take turns to watch over her. We'll let Mira sleep. She must be exhausted. And leave Kyle and Jo alone; they have enough on their hands as it is with this rising storm without you winding them both up."

Before Josh could even utter a word, Rachel kissed him on his cheek, entered the bedroom, climbed onto the bunk opposite Mira and pulled the cover over her head.

Refusing to look Pyrrha in the eye, Josh pulled out his phone and, finding he had a signal, began to type away furiously. Only minutes later, though, the battery died, and without a charger, he tossed it aside.

He could feel Pyrrha's steely gaze upon him. Finally, he relented and looked up.

"See something you like, or want?" she said. Her hard stare had now become a soft smile.

"How could you lie to Mira like that?"

"I didn't lie. She's got it all wrong," said Pyrrha. "Listen, I understand her being cautious, but think about it, Josh, if I was a 'Follower', they would have found me and taken me with them, right? There's no way they would have left a potential witness for the Disciples to find."

Potential...? He thought of Lyssa. The hairs on his arm stood to attention. "But they did leave you. And do you want to know why? It's because they don't care about you. They have what they want. Look, we know you lied. You're not Mira's aunt, so you might as well admit to being a Follower. Or are you really a Potential?" He smirked.

Pyrrha smiled back. "You got me there, Josh. I can see there's no fooling you. No, I'm not her aunt. I only told her that because I didn't want her to open the tomb. But, I give you my solemn word, I am not a Follower. As for these 'Potentials', I have no idea what you are talking about."

There was a moment of awkward silence. Eventually, she broke it. "So, your surname is Michaels, then?"

This caught Josh off guard. "Yeah, what of it?"

"It doesn't matter." Pyrrha wiggled her bound body against the leg of the bolted table until she was sat upright. "Look, Josh, I feel a little embarrassed asking you this, but you do like me, right? Cos—because I really like you."

Josh leaned forward. "What do you want, Pyrrha?"

Pyrrha fluttered her eyelashes. "What if I promise you that if you convince Mira to let me go, I will do anything you want?" she whispered.

Josh's eyes widened. "Anything—anything I want?" He smiled. "You would do that for me?"

"Josh, sweet Joshy, I think you're really cute and funny." Sultrily, she bit her bottom lip. "If you do this for me, you and I can be together, if that's what you want. Rachel is nice, but wouldn't you rather be with someone who doesn't slap you around just because what you say isn't always right? You want a *woman* who will take care of you. Who will always please you. And Josh, we may not have much time left on this earth, and I would rather spend my last moments with you holding me. I mean—holding each other... Oh, don't make me say it. You know what I mean?"

Josh took a big gulp of air. "Really? That would be so cool. But—but if I was to untie you, how would we, umm, you know, get 'jiggy with it', with Rachel and Mira in the bedroom, and my brother and Jo just outside?"

"Trust me, Joshy, what I know and what I can do, they will never know. I'll take you to heaven and back." She winked with a seductive smile.

Josh leaned in closer. "You are really beautiful, Pyrrha. And I have no doubt you would send me to heaven... But there would be no coming back for me, would there? Look, I can be stupid at times, I know that, but I've seen too many movies to know that as soon as I untie you, you'll snap my neck and kill everyone before my corpse hits the floor. And for your information, I would rather spend my last minutes with Rachel slapping my arm into oblivion than be with someone who tries to manipulate people into getting what she wants. So, if you don't mind, I'll decline your generous offer."

Pyrrha lowered her head and quietly laughed. "I must be losing my touch. And there I was thinking that you really liked me. You certainly couldn't keep your eyes off me back at that tower. Look, my offer still stands—because I know what you really want. But you have to know it's what I want as well. And I always get what I want. You'll see."

"No, you're alright, thanks. I have one crazy woman in my life—actually, two, if I count my mother—and that's more than enough for me."

Josh smiled, and lying back on the couch, he began to whistle quietly to himself.

***

When Rachel awoke an hour later and spied Josh's phone on the arm of the sofa, she delved into her bag to retrieve her own. "Damn it! Still no signal!"

"That's funny," he replied sleepily. "Mine worked OK."

Rachel's eyes lit up. "Your phone works?"

"Not now the battery has died. Hey, you haven't got a charger in that bloody bag of yours, have you?"

"No. I left it in the cabin aboard the cruise ship—your fault for rushing me. But your phone did work?" she said excitedly.

"*Yesss.*"

"Did you call your parents, or the police, or the coast-guard?"

A blush crept onto Josh's face as he chewed the inside of his cheek. "Um, no. No, I didn't. Sorry."

Rachel sidled up closer and dug her nails into his leg until tears shone in his eyes. "What did you do, Josh?"

"I—err, checked, um… Talk till You Drop."

Rachel's nails dug deeper. "You did tell someone about our situation, though, didn't you? Tell me you did that, at least."

Josh was now biting his bottom lip to stop himself from yelping. "I forgot. I was having a rant at Lisa Gale and Albert Wallis."

Rachel released her vice-like grip, closed her eyes and buried her head deep into her hands "About what, may I ask?"

Josh took a moment to allow the relief from the pain to travel through the rest of his body. "Lisa just happened to mention that the cost of everything had gone up in the shops, so, I kind of sarcastically thanked her. I just said how lucky we are to have her point it out, as obviously no one else does any shopping anymore or, if they do, they're too stupid to have noticed for themselves."

Rachel was breathing heavily again. "And Albert Wallis?"

"He said he was eating a chocolate cake he'd made himself filled with peanut butter, marmalade and Skittles, and he thought it tasted nice and was thinking of going on *MasterChef*—I know, I know. I should have rung someone. But c'mon, every bloody time you go on that site there's someone putting pointless crap on it. Like… *Hey, everyone, it's like so sunny outside*—I know. I do have windows in my house… *Hey, everyone, I have an important newsflash! I can't like believe it! I'm so like in total shock, like! There was just an advert on the TV for Easter eggs, and it's only September!* Really, that's what was so important? By the way, I do have a calendar, thank you. And if you hadn't noticed, they're advertising Christmas in June, so not much of a shocker that Easter would be advertised *way* too early next. If we allow the marketing nutjobs any more freedom, they'll have us celebrating Halloween in May and lighting bonfires in July before long."

Rachel was now nose to nose with him. "Anything else?!"

"Yes—my favourite one of all was from Julie Wilkinson John: *Hey, everyone, I'm like so totally tired. Should I like, go to bed now, like?* I mean, get a freaking life, people! You don't have to message every little thought that comes into your head, you know!"

Rachel's right hand was now clenched like a coiled spring, ready to be unleashed. "I know why you didn't call for help. You're secretly loving all this, aren't you?"

Josh opened his mouth, but no words came out.

"Answer me, damn it!"

He needed to escape. He looked at Pyrrha. Rachel, still scowling, followed his gaze. He took his chance and, sweeping from the cabin, leaving Rachel's rant behind, climbed the short steps to the top deck. There, Jo was holding tightly to the rail, glaring out at the rising waves, leaving the controls unmanned.

"Are you nuts?!" he said, taking hold of the steering wheel.

"Yes, Josh. I'm Alexander the Great nuts," she shouted back.

"You're not going to let me forget that, are you?" he said, ruing opening his mouth.

"No, Josh. I'm not. And why are you bothering to steer? Until Little Miss Premonition tells us where we're going, there's no point!"

Josh left Jo alone, angrily rubbing her hands together, and climbed down the steps to sit with Kyle, who was still watching the lights following in the distance.

"What was Rachel shouting about?" Kyle asked.

"When isn't she shouting?" Josh smirked. "But you'll never guess what..." Trying to stop himself from sniggering, he moved closer. "Pyrrha, the warrior goddess, offered herself to me. You know, if I would release her."

Kyle dropped his head. "How long did you think about it before realising she would kill you?"

"I knew straight away. I'm not a complete moron, you know."

Kyle was no longer listening. Josh wheeled his head around to where his brother was looking.

The lights appeared to be gaining on them.

Kyle rushed up the steps and grabbed the wheel, frantically attempting to turn their boat.

The wind and the waves were steadily becoming more aggressive, and salt-water spray covered the deck. Jo was mumbling something incomprehensible. Suddenly, she sank to her knees.

"She's reliving the moment the cruise ship sank," said Josh. "Look—the fear in her eyes! She can't stay out here."

Kyle lifted her to her feet and ordered her inside the cabin.

Josh took her place at Kyle's side.

The wind howled as if a million wailing banshees were chasing them as the boat ploughed through the tumultuous waves.

"We should try and find land," said Josh. They only had a small rubber dinghy on board; if the boat sank, it would mean curtains for them all.

"We have to wait until Mira knows where to go!" Kyle cried above the rising wind.

"Bottom of the bloody ocean, if the weather gets any worse—that's where we will be going!" Josh yelled back.

As heavy rain began to lash, and Kyle refused to leave the wheel, Josh returned to the cabin. But as soon as he entered and found the girls glaring daggers at each other, he quickly returned to his brother, feeling safer outside than in.

"You know when Dad goes for long drives on his own, I completely understand why he does now!" he screamed. "If the tension gets any worse in there, it's going to be like watching the girls play hockey in school—violent as hell!"

The wind and rain whipped at their tired bodies. When it became impossible to see anything, and too dangerous to remain outside, Kyle unbuckled his belt, tied himself to the wheel and ordered Josh to enter the cabin, close the door tight and somehow keep everyone's spirits lifted.

"Calm the girls?" Josh's shoulders slumped. "I'll say my goodbyes now then, shall I?"

***

Inside the cabin, Mira was still asleep, and with Jo refusing to try and sleep, and Rachel still silently glaring at Pyrrha like a spider waiting for a fly to enter its web, Josh searched the cupboards just so that he could be as far as possible from this ticking time bomb.

"Remember what I said, Joshy," said Pyrrha, smirking at Rachel. "You don't want to disappoint the prom queen if the time ever comes, do you?"

Rachel tilted her head to look at him. "What's she on about, Josh?"

Sweat, not rain, dripped down Josh's brow. He took a step back toward the exit but then saw a pack of playing cards tucked away at the back of the cupboard. "Well,

well. What do we have here?" He waved the pack in the air, desperate to change the subject. "OK, Pyrrha, I think it's time for a bit of honesty. Now, is this really your boat, or another of Mr Tripp's?"

"Josh, what is she talking about?" Rachel asked again. Her cheeks were now blood red and her piercing green eyes scarily narrow.

He gulped. "Don't you want to know why she has a deck of playing cards first?"

"No, Josh. I don't. Millions of people have playing cards. Now, what is she on about?!"

"OK, but you have to promise me you won't lose it first."

"Josh!"

Startled, he took another big gulp of air. "OK, OK. She said she would basically… turn me into a man? If I convince Mira to let her go. So, if you all don't mind, I'm going outside now to tie myself to something because I don't fancy having to swim to Egypt or Turkey or wherever the hell we're really going."

Before Josh could open the door, Rachel yelled for him to stop. "If you don't want me to tell everyone what you did, Joshy, I strongly recommend you get your arse over here… now!"

She grabbed his hand and pulled him into the bedroom. Awakened by the shouting, Mira got up from the bunk, left the room and slid the door closed behind her. Rachel pushed Josh onto the bed.

"Now, don't be jealous—I turned her down flat, Rach," he said nervously.

"Josh, lie back," she growled.

He took yet another big gulp of air. "We're not going to—you know—are we?"

"No, Joshy, we are not," she said through gritted teeth. "I want you to give me a cuddle, because if I stay out there with her, I will do something that I *won't* regret!"

THE HEAT IS ON

Mira slipped past Jo and Pyrrha and took a bottle of water from the mini fridge.

"You know, Pyrrha…" Jo leaned in close to the woman, but still spoke loud enough for Mira to hear. "If you had offered yourself to me instead of Josh, I would gladly have let you take me to heaven. Better to have your neck snapped than drown. But, sadly for you, I'm nobody's second choice and so you'll never have the pleasure, will you?"

Pyrrha stared at Jo. "How did you know?"

Jo pointed to an air vent behind the table that led to the upper deck. "Your voices carried." She smirked.

Cherry-faced, Pyrrha quickly turned her attention to Mira. "Look, let's just find an island and wait for the finish, shall we? They have your brother now, so it won't be long before it's the end of everything."

Mira sat on the sofa beside Jo and slowly peeled away the sealing strip on the bottle cap. She took a sip. *I wanted to believe you, Pyrrha, so badly.* "First, why don't you tell me what's really going on?"

"I've told you everything I know." Pyrrha's jaw was clenched. "And now the prophecy is about to be fulfilled, thanks to you and your brother. So just release me and I'll take my chances in the dinghy!"

Mira shook her head. "I don't think so. You still have a part to play. And this isn't the end, not by a long way."

"Jo, you're smart enough to know this *is* the end, aren't you?" Pyrrha pleaded. "Please, will you talk some sense into her?"

Jo stared at the table. "Well then," she said, "until the storm eases or we can see where we are going, how about a game of bridge, or poker? It's going to be a long night."

Pyrrha didn't answer. Her eyes were now wary.

Mira also recognised the signs. *Oh, not again! This is all we need—Jo goes nutty again.* "Are you sure you're feeling alright, Jo?"

"Yes, I'm fine. Everything will look better in the morning, you'll see." Jo beamed.

The table of charts was cleared away, and after ensuring that Pyrrha was still firmly tied to the leg of the table, Jo sat and dealt the cards. Feeling uncomfortable with Pyrrha silently staring at her, Mira reluctantly joined her.

***

It was a long night, but with each hour that went by, the storm eased, until they could hardly feel the boat moving at all.

As soon as the sun had risen, Mira stepped out onto the deck beneath a clear blue sky. Kyle, who had remained at the wheel the entire night, untied himself and joined her. After he'd spent the previous day ignoring her, at first Mira didn't know whether to say anything, but when she saw his blood had seeped through his T-shirt, she thought, *To hell with feelings*, and lifted his shirt to inspect the knife wound that had been cruelly inflicted by Lyssa. Surprised to see that it was already almost healed and that the swelling around his eyes, inflicted by Peter, had dramatically reduced overnight, she gently stroked his cheek.

"Have you always recovered this quickly? From the amount of blood on your shirt, I was expecting something far worse. You can hardly see it now. I don't think you'll even have a scar."

Kyle took her hand, gently. "I know this is going to sound strange, but I've never been injured before."

Her eyes widened. "What—never?"

Kyle shook his head. "There's something I need to ask you…" Mira could feel his hand trembling. "We haven't spoken since we left the island, and it's my fault. I'm so sorry for getting you to open the gates, and if you want me to go when we reach land, I will. And I understand if you do want me gone—I don't know what the voices could make me do if they come back. But I need you to say it."

Mira lifted his chin with her finger and looked deep into his eyes. Her heart fluttered. It was like seeing him for the first time.

"I wanted to open the gates and the tomb at one point." She smiled. "Look, there's nothing to forgive. You were there for me and my brother when we needed you the most. You broke the connection to whoever was speaking to you, and I truly don't think it will be able to influence you again."

"You don't know that for certain. I don't know it. What if the Followers have my parents and threaten to kill them? Who's to say I won't betray you once more?"

Mira had to allay his concerns. "Because you have those fears, I know that you won't."

Kyle leaned in to kiss her, but Mira pulled away. She didn't mean to. She wanted him to hold her, tell her everything would be OK. She wanted to fall deep into his kiss. But her brother was missing. "I can't—"

Kyle took a few steps back. "Oh, right. I see... I understand."

She tried to reach out to him, but the cabin door opened, and Rachel and Josh emerged, ruining her chance to explain. Mira forced a smile. "Morning..."

"I still think it is dangerous keeping Pyrrha on board, Mira," said Rachel, looking back into the cabin.

"I agree," said Josh.

"Why?" Rachel snapped. "Do you think you won't be able to resist her and you'll get to have your naked party before she kills you, is that it?"

"I told you, the only party I want is with you in Africa in lion territory at night." Josh backed away, covering his arm, before the lightning strike of her hand could connect.

This was the last thing Mira needed right now, more arguing. "Rach, I told Josh yesterday that I think she also has a part to play. Now, there's something I need to tell you three—and only you three. I don't think Jo is up for more bad news at this moment—"

Before she could continue, Kyle's jaw dropped and he ran toward the stern.

"They've found us again!" He pointed to the large ship riding the waves behind them. "Get Jo!"

***

The engine was started and Jo quickly steered toward a group of small isles.

"Looking at the size of their ship," she said, "we're shallower in the water, so they'll have to go around. It might give us time to keep ahead of them and, if we're really lucky, lose them. But Mira, you have to figure out where the hell we need to be going."

"That's not the ship that was following us yesterday," said Josh flatly.

"How do you know?" Rachel asked. "They all looked alike."

"The one following us yesterday was different," Josh insisted before joining his brother at the rear.

Mira closed her eyes and silently prayed to be shown where they had to go. But with no visions appearing, she joined Jo at the wheel. The ship was gaining on them.

The isles were within reach and the larger vessel was slowing down. Jo expertly steered the boat through the narrow channel where the ship could not follow. But when they once again reached clear, open water, the shortcut had not secured them as large a lead as Jo had hoped.

The pursuing ship was once again bearing down upon them. Kyle tried to usher Mira inside the cabin, but she refused to leave his side, as did Rachel. Josh, however, had other ideas.

"You need to hide, Rach," he insisted. "If we're taken hostage, we need someone the authorities back home will listen to, if they're going to come rescue us, right?"

Reluctantly, Rachel agreed. She hid under one of the bunks inside the cabin, and Josh placed pillows from the sofa in front of her, and then did the same to the other bunk, making it look as though they were stored in there, then ran back outside.

Jo was desperately trying to outmanoeuvre the larger vessel, but it moved in right behind them. When gunshots were heard, Kyle, sensing Jo's apprehension, took over the wheel, while Josh dragged Jo down the steps and into the cabin.

Kyle attempted a sharp turn, hoping to double back—the pursuers couldn't perform the same tactic. But a sudden loss of power told him that the engine had been struck, and as the boat came to almost a complete stop, all he could do was watch as the ship pulled up alongside.

Armed personnel were on the deck. Some aimed their weapons at the teens, while others quickly boarded the boat. Thanks to Pyrrha having watched everything unfold, Rachel and Jo's hiding places were found in a moment. Hoods were pulled over the teens' heads, and they were dragged onto and through the larger ship until they heard a door unlocking. Silence ensued. Then, the hoods were removed.

Relief; they were all together. But they were now inside an empty, windowless room.

Without a word, the guards left and closed the door behind them.

"Don't know why they bothered with the hoods, I could see everything through them anyway," said Josh, as the clasp of the lock shut.

Rachel was trembling. "Do you think they are going to kill us?"

"No, everything will be fine," said Jo chirpily.

Josh grimaced. "Are your batteries finally starting to fail you, C-3PO? You're acting really weird. You're being even more weird than usual!"

"No, everything is fine, Joshy," said Jo. "What could possibly be wrong…? Oh, except that I got on board a ship that sank. I got lost at sea. I ended up on an island where I witnessed a wolf—the size of a small car, mind you—kill a man I'd tried to save. I went mad for treasure. I've taken part in the kidnapping of a woman who professed to be Mira's aunt, but isn't. I've now been locked in a cell by some very scary, heavily armed, crazy religious cultists who believe that a fictitious woman is trapped inside a coffin and will wipe us all out if released. And then, to top it all, I'm now trapped, for God knows how long, with a person who never takes anything seriously and who thinks I'm the one who's acting weird! And I am not a bloody robot, Josh!"

"That's it, Jo," said Josh, patting her on the shoulder. "Better to release the stress with friends, that's what my mum always says."

"Oh God… Can someone please shut him up and tell me what's really going to happen?" Jo yelled, throwing her hands behind her head, beginning to hyperventilate. She caught her breath. "Just look at the weaponry those creeps had when they boarded Pyrrha's boat! They had enough firearms to start another world war. When will they see that it's *them* that's the real threat to this planet! Can't the sensible people of this world just stand up and say, NO MORE! And then destroy every single life-destroying weapon…! Look, I'm sorry about your brother, Mira—truly I am—but I just want to go home!"

Mira's heart sank. She looked to all the faces silently staring back at her. Did they all feel the same way? Her pulse began to *thump* rampantly through her chest. She was afraid to ask but realised it was only fair. If they did indeed want to go home, she would have to understand. She wiped the sweat from her clammy palms. "Is that what the rest of you want?" She held her breath.

"No!" said Rachel. "I'm not going anywhere until we get Jacen back safely, and if finding your father helps us achieve it, then I'm with you until the end!"

"I feel the same way," said Josh.

Mira looked to Kyle. She hadn't had time to explain why she'd rebuffed his attentions on Pyrrha's boat. Would he now want to leave her?

He smiled. "If you trust me, then I swear I won't rest until Jacen is back with us."

Mira had to take a moment to compose herself. "Are you sure?"

Kyle looked confused, as if she'd actually asked him to go. "Yes, of course."

Mira could sense his, and the others', sincerity. Only a week ago they were all strangers. But here they were, ready to fight alongside her to the bitter end.

"Then, when they come for me, Jo," she said, "I'll try and negotiate a way to get you home."

Jo lowered her head. "I'm sorry. I feel ashamed. I'll stay and help. You all had good reason to leave me back on that island, but I know none of you even considered it. If I can truly be of help in getting your brother back, then I'm happy to go on with you."

Mira placed her arm around Jo's shoulder and pulled her tight against her. But with the gentle sway of the boat as it began to move again, all they could do was sit in silence, fearing what lay in store for them next.

CHAPTER SIX

NOT ANOTHER ONE

Due to the bright lights in the cell, the temperature had risen so dramatically that it felt like a sauna.

How much longer will this torture last? Mira thought, wiping away the perspiration trickling down her temple. She looked to Kyle, who was sat with his head lowered onto his raised knees and his eyes closed. Gently, she lifted his hand to check his watch. It had been two hours since they had been locked up. *Remain calm, Mira. If they wanted you dead, they would have done it already.*

She looked to Kyle's watch again. "It's your turn," she said, tapping Rachel's leg.

Rachel rolled onto her knees and crawled to the rear of the hold, where Jo was taking her turn by the vent blowing a light breeze of air.

"How much longer are we going to be kept in here?" Jo asked, taking Rachel's place beside Josh.

Mira could hear the distant tramp of approaching footsteps. "Not for much longer." She gave an encouraging smile, but her stomach was turning somersaults.

The door was unlocked and two hefty, uniformed men stepped inside.

"You," said one, pointing to Mira. "Come with us."

Kyle stood up, blocking their way to her. "Where are you taking her?"

"Step aside. The captain wants to see only her," said the second guard in a more forceful tone.

Josh joined his brother. "And what if we say no?"

Both guards unclipped their holsters and placed a threatening hand on their sidearms.

Josh retook his seat. "Okey-dokey. You made your point."

Mira placed her hand on Kyle's shoulder and nudged him aside as she stepped past. "I'll come quietly, but only if you allow cool air inside this hothouse."

One guard slowly reached out to a switch on the wall outside. As the vent began to introduce cold air, Mira followed them out into the passageway.

Mira was led up three flights of stairs and into the captain's cabin, where she was forced to sit in a chair. Pyrrha was already there, talking to a man of considerable size with thick, grey, curly hair and a long, dense beard.

That's in desperate need of some care and attention, Mira thought absently.

While waiting for the interrogation to begin, Mira spied a group photo on the desk. In it, Pyrrha was beside the man stood before her, along with four additional figures. She didn't know why or how, but she sensed that even though they didn't look alike, they were somehow related to one another. Strangely, it brought her some comfort, looking at their smiling faces.

That was, until the man, whom she assumed was the captain, thrust his hands down upon the table and leaned menacingly across the desk.

"Do you know what you have done?" his deep voice rumbled.

As the giant of a man stared down upon her, Mira lowered her gaze to her feet. But a fire had been ignited inside her gut, and as it rose into her chest, she raised her head and glowered back. "We didn't do it on purpose! And just so you know, I've been through too much to be scared by the likes of you, so you can cut the intimidation act, cos it won't work on me! Now, unless you're going to kill us, let us go this instant!"

The man took a step back, as though she had struck him in the face. A brief moment later, he'd composed himself. "No. I want you to witness what will now happen to this world."

"Trust me," said Mira, "nothing is going to happen."

"And how do you know that?" Pyrrha glowered at her. "The Followers now have what they need."

Mira shifted her contempt from the man to Pyrrha, who was studying her closely. "Let's just say I know. Now, let us go, I have a brother to rescue."

"That is out of the question," said Pyrrha. "I'm sorry, but Jacen is out of your reach—and your old life is over."

Mira was confused. "What good would there be in going anywhere if he"—she pointed to the captain—"wants me to witness the end?"

Pyrrha gave a nod of her head, and the man left the room. She reached over the table and patted Mira's hand. "He gets a little dramatic at times. The stress of being a captain can be hell. Now, listen to me. I'm sorry I lied to you. I thought telling you I was your aunt would stop you and Jacen from entering that place and that you would come back with me to the safety of our sanctuary, peacefully."

Mira narrowed her eyes. "Who are you really?"

"I *am* a Disciple, sworn to protect the tombs," Pyrrha answered, sitting back in her chair.

That's what I saw in Pandora's crypt. "As in, more than one, I take it?" Mira had to remain calm.

Pyrrha leaned forward. "Yes. I can see that you already knew that. What have you seen, exactly?"

Mira smiled inside. *Ah! The wheel has turned. You fear what I now know.*

Problem was, Mira didn't fully understand what she'd seen, in neither her dreams nor the flashing images that had appeared to her inside Pandora's crypt. As she was thinking of them, one in particular jumped out, as if someone else had chosen it for her.

"What is the purpose of the vase that was placed upon Pandora when she was entombed alive?"

Pyrrha's brow furrowed. "In ancient times, as part of the funeral ritual, the priests would remove the brain, the heart, liver and kidneys and, in extreme circumstances, the eyes of the dead and place them inside a vase. They were then placed outside of the sarcophagus—"

"I didn't ask that," Mira interjected. "I said, what was the purpose of the vase that was placed *inside* Pandora's coffin?"

"The Pharaoh," Pyrrha continued, "forbade such an act happening to his wife. Tefnut, an Egyptian goddess, and whom the Greeks called Artemis, told him in a dream that if he was to desecrate such a wonder of nature in that way, he would bring forth her wrath not only upon him, but the whole of Egypt. That not a living soul would survive. So, Pandora's body was skilfully prepared in another, secret way and then wrapped with bandages. Her beauty preserved, they believed, for all time. The priests, however, did insist that a binding agent had to be placed over her body."

Mira frowned. "What sort of binding agent?"

49

"Mystical herbs and whatnot," said Pyrrha. "I'm not really sure. The ancient Egyptians' knowledge of protection spells has been lost over time."

"Don't you find that odd?" said Mira. "If she was wrapped up and unable to move, *why* was there a need for a binding agent?"

"It was to stop anyone else from releasing her if the coffin was ever opened. An extra insurance policy, I suppose."

That makes no sense. Try again. "Then tell me why the exact same thing was done to Epimetheus." Mira waited for Pyrrha to answer, but instead, Pyrrha simply stared back. "I know that he was locked away by your people, the Disciples. Before you ask, I recognised the robes your people were wearing back on his island as the same from my… dream."

Pyrrha's eyes widened. "Yes, the ancient Disciples locked him away. They had to. After they moved Pandora to that island, Epimetheus, in his fury, began hunting them down—killing them, in point of fact—as he searched for her location. He even went after the Pharaoh of Egypt. During the assault on the pharaoh's palace, he was captured and placed inside a coffin, much like Pandora's. But it was taken far from Egypt and hidden away inside a sepulchre."

Mira thrust her hand forward to stop Pyrrha from saying any more. "If he was such a threat, then surely the humane thing to do was simply imprison him? And not in the same way as was done to Pandora?"

Mira could see that Pyrrha was thinking on how best to answer.

Pyrrha lowered her gaze. "I agree wholeheartedly with you, Mira. But according to our records, he was not someone that could be simply locked away behind bars. He was much too powerful, and had many allies."

"Then the merciful thing would have been to kill him quickly!" Mira spat.

Pyrrha raised her eyes. "Many mistakes were made. That is why we now have to ensure that we do not make another by allowing the Followers to release Pandora. No doubt, she, too, will want to find and release her true love."

Mira was confused. "You don't actually believe he could still be alive, do you?"

"If Pandora is alive, why not him? It is written that his last words were in prayer to one of the gods of old. Those that came before the Olympians. If they were to keep him in a deep slumber, then come the day Pandora was released, he would awaken and bring destruction upon my order. But you don't have to worry, he is safely hidden away."

A dark thought suddenly struck Mira. She took a deep breath. "But if what you're saying about my brother and me is correct, and we are his descendants, how do I know that your order won't do the same to us as they did to him? OK, maybe not bury us alive, but, instead, lock us away in some... other godforsaken place?"

Pyrrha took both Mira's hands into her own. "Because I give you my word I will not allow it. Please, Mira, things are different now from what they were back in the old days. We only want to protect you. You have to believe me."

"How can I believe you when you are obviously still holding something back from me?"

Pyrrha released her hands, stood up and began to pace the room. "I want to tell you everything, but after everything that's happened, perhaps it would be better if you hear it first hand from my leader."

"And why should I trust this leader of yours?"

"You'll see," Pyrrha replied simply.

Seeing that Pyrrha was not going to tell her what she needed to know, Mira decided to change tactic. "At least tell me if it is my destiny to open Epimetheus' tomb, as it was my brother's fate to open Pandora's."

"No. I mean—I don't think so... No."

With Pyrrha still refusing to make eye contact, Mira sat back in her chair. She followed Pyrrha's slow, thoughtful gait back and forth. "You don't know, do you? You're just as much in the dark as I am."

Pyrrha finally stopped pacing and stared back. "Epimetheus' tomb is safely hidden away," she said with more confidence. "And you are now safe."

Mira casually looked about the cabin. "If you're sure that Epimetheus' tomb is safe, I guess it's safe."

Pyrrha's eyes narrowed. "What's that supposed to mean? You go on about how I'm holding back information. What exactly do you know, Mira?"

"I don't know anything, that's the point. Look, all I'm saying is that I wouldn't be so sure that the Followers don't know of its location, that's all. There was another ship following us, OK?"

Pyrrha's frown deepened. "What other ship?"

"Josh saw a different vessel following us. Come to think of it, where are the other two that came with this one?"

"They remained behind to do some... research."

"Research on what? Oh. Was it the screaming by any chance?"

Pyrrha stared back, unblinking. "Screaming or singing?"

"We heard screaming just as we left. And Josh and Jo heard it when they went in search of the oil."

Pyrrha excused herself. Her expression told Mira that she truly hadn't heard anything. But when she returned moments later, her frown had vanished. A smile had appeared in its place. "No one aboard this ship heard any screaming. And the ship that you saw took another route. Now, please believe me when I say you don't have to fear us. I want to protect you."

Mira began to wonder if she had truly heard any screams. Could it simply have been a mass hallucination, after everything they'd been through?

"If you want me to trust you," she said, "then, as a show of faith, tell me the truth. Did you really know my father?"

Pyrrha shuffled in her seat. "Yes, but only from afar, I'm afraid. I was forbidden to converse with him. But I would sneak looks while he studied. Truth is, I always felt sorry for him. If my order had paid more attention, then maybe he wouldn't have left. And before you ask, no, I don't know what he read to make him want to leave."

Mira didn't blink. "And who was Lyssa? She said her real name was Lyssara, and that she was from a group called the Potentials. Who are they?"

"They are... decoys, to keep the true descendants' identities safe. We have other sanctuaries where they are hidden."

"You have innocent people locked away?"

"You misunderstand," Pyrrha was quick to answer. "They are well cared for. Look, the Followers have been searching for Pandora's descendants since the beginning. To keep you and your brother's bloodline safe, my order set up decoys. No other order knows that, mind you. When the comet arrived, the leader of one particular sanctuary asked for permission to kill Lyssa to stop Pandora's curse from ever happening. The request was denied. But I'm guessing Lyssa must have overheard. How she found out about you and Jacen and how she got aboard the cruise ship, I doubt we will find out now. She must have thought that killing you both would free her."

Mira felt sick at the thought. "The fear Lyssa must have been feeling… I can't blame her for wanting to kill us. And that explains why she basically kept to herself. Why she was always surly with everyone. Why I couldn't connect with her on a personal level. Why none of us could."

"It was a tragic mistake," said Pyrrha. "And I swear to you, we do not kill the innocent where I come from. We swore to protect the descendants of Pandora, and that is what I will do until my last breath."

"So, what will happen to the other Potentials, now that my brother and I are known?"

"It doesn't matter now, does it?" said Pyrrha solemnly. "Now that the Followers have Jacen, all we can do is try and survive what is to come." Pyrrha turned her back and stared out the window.

Against her better judgement, Mira suddenly had an overwhelming need to share her knowledge. She blurted it out. "The Followers can't open the sarcophagus. It requires a second key. The first could only open the outer tomb."

Pyrrha stood motionless. Her eyes unflinching. "How do you know?"

Confused as to why she'd said it, Mira had to take a moment to compose her thoughts. "Let's just say I know. But if the Followers find out, they are going to spare no expense in trying to find it."

Pyrrha again began to pace the room. "Then we have more time to get your brother and Pandora's coffin to safety. Do you know where the second key is hidden?"

Mira didn't trust Pyrrha enough yet to disclose that she already had it. "I'm sorry, I don't. That's why I need to find my father. I have a feeling he does."

Pyrrha stared out of the porthole. "Then, as soon as we arrive at our destination, I shall send people to try and find him. But you must stay with us until the comet has gone."

Doubt crept into Mira's mind. "And those that are with me, what happens to them? You can't leave them locked in the hold—they've proven they didn't want the tomb open. Can they go home?"

Pyrrha's focus remained firmly on the outside. "No. Not yet. If the Followers were to get their hands on them, then they would use them to get to you. But they have already been taken to other quarters. I must insist, though, that you stay in the cabin, and before we arrive at our destination, for everyone's protection, you must all be placed back in the cargo hold." Finally, she turned to face Mira. "Now, before I take you to them, there is something I need to show you."

As they left the captain's cabin, Mira could sense there was a struggle playing out within her captor. *She's itching to tell me something.* Mira only hoped that she would get the opportunity to find out the whole truth before something else unexpected happened.

CHAPTER SEVEN

LAZARUS

Mira was led down a flight of stairs and to a room across a corridor. When Pyrrha opened the door, Mira was so surprised at what she saw that she almost fell back into Pyrrha's arms.

"Linus?!"

He was lying face down unconscious on a medical bed. Stitches had been applied to his left arm and lower back.

Mira turned to Pyrrha. "How? I thought you killed him."

"I thought I had, too. But somehow, he managed to escape the wolf," said Pyrrha, glaring down at him. "My people found him staggering along the beach. His wounds are life-threatening, but do not feel any sympathy; he plotted his mother and brother's deaths."

Mira had to fight to regain her breath. *Hang on. Is this divide and conquer?* "No," she said. "Something dragged his brother under the sand on the beach. Kyle and Josh saw it. And his mother didn't make it off the cruise ship, as far as we know."

"I'm sorry, Mira. He admitted to breaking the lock on the cabin door so that his mother couldn't get out. And when you arrived on the island and the voices began, he made a deal: if he convinced you to get inside the gates, she would deal with his brother, and, as you know, she did."

"She... You mean, Pandora?"

Pyrrha raised an eyebrow. "Who else could it have been? The gods wouldn't have helped. Not even Artemis, who forbade the priests from removing her organs. Not with what Pandora has become."

Mira didn't know why, but she felt that it wasn't quite that simple. She had a nagging suspicion that there was someone, or something, else at play.

Pyrrha closed the door to the medical room and led Mira down another flight of stairs into a long compartment that provided housing for some of the soldiers. In the centre of the room was a large, round table with chairs tucked neatly underneath. Bunks were laid out either side of the cabin where Kyle, Rachel, Josh and Jo were already sat, and to Mira's surprise, there was a window providing a view of the world outside.

Ah, that's why Pyrrha wants us back in the hold before we dock. So we can't see how we got there.

"Don't worry, nobody will disturb you," said Pyrrha, stepping back into the passageway. "Until we get to where we need to go, everyone is to remain on duty."

The door was locked behind Mira, and Rachel was the first to run forward and hug her.

Keeping her voice to almost a whisper, Mira sat the group around the table. All except for Jo, who insisted on remaining by the window. Mira brought them up to speed with the information Pyrrha had shared with her.

Rachel was the first to respond. "Another bloody tomb now?" She grimaced. "And he was buried in the same way as Pandora? I'm sorry, but I just don't buy it. For it to have happened to one of them, yes, maybe, but to the two of them?"

"The punishment was called a… Hyundai, if memory serves," said Josh.

A loud *urgh* came from the direction of the window. "That's a car manufacturer. Idiot." Jo's voice trembled with fury as she stomped to the table. "And that word, Hom-dai, I'm pretty sure was made up simply for *The Mummy*, Josh!"

"Actually," said Josh, calmly, "in Egypt, the practice of burying someone alive was all too common back in the day. If someone committed a murder, let's say, they would tie the culprit to the dead person for three days and then bury the murderer alive, along with the corpse."

"Whatever it's called," said Rachel, "it's all the more reason for us to keep as far away from this group of religious nuts as possible and get help from home to rescue Jacen."

"That what's I think, too," said Josh. "If this Epidural character is out for revenge, best we leave them as soon as possible. Cos who's to say that once we arrive at… wherever the hell they're taking us, they don't just lock us all away for good and forget about rescuing Jacen altogether, now they know it requires a second key."

"That's what I thought at first," said Mira. "And it's Epimetheus, Josh. An epidural is… Never mind. Look, I don't trust Pyrrha completely, but she could have had us killed, or we could still be locked in that sauna. And she did seem sincere about getting Jacen back. Look, to be honest with you, I'm still trying to process everything I saw in Pandora's tomb. But it is clear that there is more to what happened to her than just being locked away…" She shivered at the thought of what Pandora had endured. "Listen, we can't do anything at the moment, especially with the armed personnel on board. I think we should just stick with them for now. But there's something else you should hear."

When Mira revealed that Linus was still alive, Josh threw his hands to his head. "Are you kidding me? This is quickly turning into an episode of Hollywood Housewives."

"I have to admit, I never really trusted Linus," said Kyle. "Then again, I don't think I'm one to judge anyone now."

"None of us are," said Rachel. "We all wanted to get Jacen to that place, but in the end, we fought against doing it."

Jo huffed. "Excuse me—I never wanted to get Jacen there."

"No, you just wanted to kill everyone for treasure," said Josh, and leaving his seat, he threw himself down on one of the bunks.

"OK, point taken." Jo slunk onto another bed further away from him. "I'll just keep quiet from now on."

"And you didn't want to take Jacen to that tomb either, Rach," Josh added. "In fact, it was only us boys, to our shame."

The cabin fell silent.

***

An hour passed before Pyrrha finally brought them all food. Rachel had to initially be restrained from attacking her, but once Pyrrha had apologised for her attempt at seducing Josh, Rachel, sensing everyone's hunger, allowed them all to tuck in.

"Don't have any Mars bars for dessert, do you?" Josh grinned.

"No, we don't," said Pyrrha curtly. "Now, I have some news. When we get you safely situated, we are going to try and get Jacen back, but it's going to take time to do it right."

Kyle's jaw hit his chest. "You know where he is already?"

"Yes—I mean, maybe," said Pyrrha. "There are three possible locations, hence why it will take time. Each place is a fortress. But if we *can't* get to him, then our best chance to reach him, we believe, is when the Followers perform a ceremony that must take place in Egypt. The exact same location where the curse was placed on Pandora. We know precisely where that is. Lucky for us, the Followers don't."

"Yet," Josh added.

Mira's eyes widened. "He's right," she said nervously. "And what if the Followers have already discovered they need the other key? Who knows what they will do, or have already done, to Jacen?"

"They won't harm him, I promise you that," said Pyrrha. "And if they have discovered the location, which is highly unlikely, then we can only hope the comet disappears before they find out about the second key. Their chance will be gone and they will then let him go."

"What if they don't?" said Rachel, her eyes ablaze.

Pyrrha took Mira's hand. "I promise you now that I will not stop until he is back with his family."

Kyle paced the room, all the while casting wary looks toward Pyrrha. "So where are these three places, and how do you know about them?"

"We know because they are our enemy, Kyle," Pyrrha replied. "And it is always wise to know your enemies' locations. The Followers have three major enclaves. One in London, one in Rome, and one somewhere in Greece but we have yet to discover where exactly. Now, have any of you dreamed of the location where Jacen may be being kept?" She raised an eyebrow. "If you have, it will speed up this whole process."

"Hang on," said Kyle. "Before we left for the cruise, the news stated that rebel forces were in Paris and Madrid. And then Cardiff, Edinburgh and London were attacked. It wasn't the Followers, was it?"

"Yes. We believe they were looking for Mira. Now, before you ask, my sanctuary is well hidden. You shall be safe, I give you my word."

"I don't understand," Kyle continued. "From what the reporters were saying and showing us, it looked like more than just Follower attacks on sanctuaries. Militaries were fighting each other."

"The Followers' numbers are vast, and they have people in high places of government. Their ultimate goal is to destabilise every country first and, when the time is right, bring forth Pandora's curse. As I told Mira, they believe that they will be saved and there will be a new beginning."

"Looking at the state of the world, a fresh start doesn't sound like a bad idea," said Kyle.

Silence hit in the room. All faces turned toward him.

Pyrrha stepped toward him, her face twisted by aggression. "Have you seen what a plague can do? I have, and it is not something I wish to see ever again!"

Before Kyle could respond, a giant thud came from beneath the boat. The ship violently tilted. Pyrrha stumbled from the room, locking the door behind her.

Sat with her knees tucked up to her chin, Jo wrapped her hands around her head. "It's the beginning of another storm, isn't it? I'm going to drown! I just know it!"

Josh scrambled to his feet and scurried to the window. "No, it's not a storm," he said, looking out. "But I hope it isn't what I think it is."

"What do you think it is?" said Rachel, gripping the table.

"Godzilla," Josh whispered. "Or the white death."

"I'm sorry, the white what?" Jo squealed.

"The great white shark… Jaws."

"I was thinking it was coral we'd hit." Rachel scowled. "But thank you, once again, Josh, for making me want to go to the toilet!"

Jo threw her hands down onto the bed. "They don't hunt in the Mediterranean, Josh! They're found in warmer waters like the Pacific, Atlantic and Indian oceans."

"Ha!" Josh scoffed. "Actually, they can swim and munch in most waters if the food source is good, Miss Know-it-all. They have a kind of built-in thermostat that runs through the length of their bodies. When they swing their tails, it regulates and controls their body temperature. I guess it's like an internal hairdryer that's able to keep them warm in cold waters and cool in hot. And if the scientists and eco-warriors are correct and the oceans *are* warming up, then why not great whites in the Med?"

Kyle shook his head. "That was a small wooden boat it attacked in *Jaws*, Josh. This is by far a bigger vessel and constructed of thick steel."

"Yeah, but remember the third one? That was thirty-five feet in length."

"Josh, there are no thirty-five-foot great white sharks!" Jo shrieked. "It's the beginning of a storm, I just know it!"

"And there are no wolves the size of small cars," said Josh. "Oh, wait, there are."

CHAPTER EIGHT

A DESCISION OF FATE

For an hour, Mira, Kyle and Rachel remained glued to the window, watching the ocean. Jo, breathing heavily, once more had her forehead pressed tightly onto her raised knees, while Josh paced back and forth humming the *Jaws* theme. That was until Pyrrha pulled the rug from him.

"We think it was coral we hit," she said. "Strange that our sonar didn't pick it up. Luckily, there doesn't seem to be any damage."

"See, I was right!" said Rachel.

"Godzilla or a thirty-five-foot great white shark..." Jo spat. "What an utter pleb you really are, Josh!"

Josh shrugged. "Pyrrha said it could have been coral. But if it isn't Godzilla or Jaws, who's to say it's still not a megleedon?" he persisted.

Jo emitted another exasperated huff. "Megalodon, Josh. Not *megleedon*. And they definitely don't exist now. Moron!"

"Fine, have it your way. Don't say I didn't warn you."

As Pyrrha was about to leave, Mira pulled her to one side. "How is Linus doing?"

"He should make a full recovery. That is, until he is put on trial for what he did," Pyrrha replied plainly.

"Are you sure it wasn't just the island that turned him crazy, like Joanne Blackbeard over there?" said Josh, straining his neck to listen.

Jo groaned. "Johanna, if you must know."

"Even if the island did affect him," Pyrrha replied calmly, "Linus planned and executed his mother's murder before getting there. I'm sorry. He *must* be punished for his crimes."

The group fell silent. Mira could see by their expressions what everyone was thinking. She was thinking it herself. She felt sick inside. "And what punishment is he likely to get?"

"He took two lives in the worst possible way. He shall receive the same."

Josh scrunched up his face. "And which would that be? Drowning in water or suffocating in sand? Either way, I don't ever want to see it again, thank you. Once was enough."

"Hear, hear," Kyle added.

"He shall suffer both," said Pyrrha.

Again there was silence. But all judgemental eyes were upon Pyrrha.

"How can you do both?" Rachel finally asked.

"We have fine doctors. First, he will be drowned and then resuscitated. Then, he will be buried alive, and that will be that."

Rachel looked away and joined Josh at the window. "Oh, now I'm really sorry I asked."

Mira glared at Pyrrha. "Then you are no better than him! In fact, you're a hypocrite!"

"So, what would you do, Mira? Put him in prison for a couple of years then release him and say, *'Do not do it again, you naughty boy'*?" Pyrrha replied. "We've heard about your laws and the courts that enforce them. They are a joke. How many have been released only to steal or kill again and again and again!"

The thought of Linus' fate twisted the increasing knot in Mira's stomach. Again, she had to speak up. "I know the judicial system needs looking at, but what if he *didn't* do what you say? What if he *was* possessed when he did what he did and, oh, too late, you've killed him?" She sighed deeply. "Look, can I see him first, please? I need to hear it for myself, from his own mouth."

Pyrrha took a moment, then said, "I don't think that would be wise. He will say anything to save himself."

"You said he admitted to it," Josh pointed out. "Doesn't sound like someone trying to save himself."

"Exactly, and after everything that happened on that island, I think I can tell a lie by now," Mira pressed. "And does it really matter? You've already passed sentence on him. Look, I would just like to see him before you kill him, that's all."

Pyrrha's gaze fixed on Mira. "I'll see what I can do," she said, and with a nod of her head, she slipped through the doorway and once again left them alone.

When the door was locked, Jo curled into a tight ball on her bunk and closed her eyes. With Rachel and Josh standing at the window, silently peering out, Mira decided to take a seat at the table. She needed to think.

Could Linus truly be the monster Pyrrha has made him out to be? Have they drugged or tortured him into saying the things they wanted him to say? And how would Pyrrha have known what he did to his mother?

As if he'd sensed her quandary, Kyle sat down beside her. "Do you think Linus is innocent?" he asked.

Mira shook her head. "I truly don't know what to think. That's why I need to look him in the eye, to be sure."

But when she laid her hand on his, Kyle pulled it away.

"Are you OK?" she asked, stunned.

Kyle looked at the floor. "Yeah, fine," he said simply and rose from his seat to leave her alone.

What was bothering him? "Hey, it's me. You know you can tell me, right?"

"I think you made your feelings toward me pretty clear back on Pyrrha's boat."

"Pyrrha's boat...?" Mira's eyes suddenly widened. She'd forgotten. "Oh, no, no, I didn't mean to pull away—with Jacen missing—"

Kyle doubled over and cupped his face in his hands. "How could I be so—oh God, I'm sorry, I thought...?"

Mira reached out and stroked his hand. "Kyle, there is nothing to be sorry about. I'm with you. Until the end of time, or until you get locked up for life for finally killing Josh."

And as they both looked at Josh, they started to laugh uncontrollably.

Josh, who had been scanning the horizon, spun around. "Hey, what's so funny?"

"Not a thing..." Mira continued to chuckle.

"Then, does anyone still have their phone on them?"

"Why?" said Jo. "Are you planning on calling Jason Statham to help us against your megleedon? Huh... Megleedon."

"It's pronounced megalodon, Jo." Josh smirked. "And if I had Jason Statham's phone number, yes, I would call him. He'd be more of a help to us than you are at the moment. But for your information, Johanna, I wanted a phone to see if I could download a compass app to see where the hell we are. But I have to admit, I was then gonna take a photo of you and send it to that new show that's starting on TV this Christmas. Another *Punk'd*. It's where people prank their friends or family while secretly taking their picture. It's called, *Oh, Look! I've Peed My-self*."

The arguing entered another bout, but just as Mira was about to finally lose her temper with the pair of them, Pyrrha walked back into the room.

Rachel quickly stepped forward and hushed the group. "Did you bring my bag with you?" she asked, wide-eyed.

"Yes, and it will be returned to you shortly," said Pyrrha. "But without the phone, sorry. The Followers will no doubt have your numbers and will be attempting to trace them."

Rachel released a sigh of relief. "Screw the phone. As long as I have the bag, I don't care."

Mira had to smile. *Everything is going to hell, and yet as long as she has her bag, Rachel is fine. What a marvellous sense of priorities she has.*

"Mira, Linus is waiting, if you are ready," said Pyrrha, and motioned to her to leave.

CHAPTER NINE

TRUTH OR LIE

Mira entered the medical room. Linus was awake and sitting up. But his hands and feet were securely strapped to the bed.

Pyrrha and the medical team departed, and Mira quietly lifted a chair from the corner of the room. She could see the straps holding him firm to the bed but still sat well out of his reach. As she stared at the floor and tried to think on how best to broach the subject, Linus spoke first.

"Go ahead and ask." His voice was hoarse.

She leaned forward slightly. *Here goes...* "Did you do what they say you did?" she whispered.

For a brief moment, as Mira looked into his face, she prayed he would shake his head and deny it. But when he answered simply "Yes", she felt sick.

"Did Pyrrha or the captain put you up to it?" She was desperate to remove any responsibility from his shoulders.

"No, they haven't put me up to it."

"Then, why, Linus?" She lowered her tone. "Why? How could you?"

Linus looked away. "I could say it was because of the way they treated me, or that I was possessed. But I won't lie, not to you. I guess the real reason is because I'm just plain evil. And whatever they have planned for me, I deserve."

Unprepared for his honesty, Mira blinked back tears. "If you really were evil, Linus, then you wouldn't think you deserve what they have planned." She hesitated. "Actually, have they told what they are going to do to you?"

She feared his answer.

"I've been given a fair idea," he said. "Probably for the best, don't ya think?"

Was this an act? "Linus, what you did can never be forgiven, but nobody should go through what you will suffer, so please, beg for mercy and ask to be locked up. Please, Linus, beg for your life!"

It took only a moment for Linus to think about what she had said. "What if I had locked the door to your parents' room or set Jacen up to be taken by that thing in the sand? Would you still be happy for me to beg and just be locked up?"

Mira couldn't answer him. Her thoughts went to her brother. If Linus had sacrificed Jacen, she would have killed him the moment she found him in the medical room. She now felt the hypocrite.

She rose from the chair, looked at him one last time then knocked on the door to be let out.

But before she left, Linus called out to her. "I would never have done it to *any* of you. And please, tell the others, if they are with you: up until, you know... tell them it was the happiest I've been in a very long time and I'm sorry I let you all down."

The thought of what was going to happen to him set Mira's insides churning again. She wanted to turn and face him. But what could she say, now that he'd admitted it? She didn't look back, and closed the door behind her.

"As you can see, he is not possessed or drugged," said Pyrrha as she led her back to the quarters. "He must be punished."

Mira couldn't answer. Her anger toward Pyrrha, and now herself, was choking her.

CHAPTER TEN

THE REALITY OF WAR

Apart from toilet breaks, the small company was kept inside the cabin. Once Mira had shared Linus' mental state and his confession to his crimes, surprisingly, nobody had much to say.

As the silence persisted, Rachel and Josh sat close together on his bunk and held each other. Jo and Mira, still sat at the table, voicelessly stared into space.

In a bid to escape some of the tension, Kyle decided to stand by the window. But as he watched the rolling ocean, he spotted smoke billowing in the distance. As they got nearer, a bombshell struck in the pit of his stomach. He opened the window to peer out.

"You'd all better come and have a look at this," he called out.

Devoid of any enthusiasm, everyone stood up and joined him. The moment they saw what lay before them, the group let out a loud gasp.

A line of merchant vessels was burning furiously. This was the first time the company had witnessed the inhumanity of the war they had left behind. With no sign of any survivors, the ship slowly navigated through the carnage.

"What the hell do these monsters think they will truly accomplish attacking innocents?" said Rachel. "Has society regressed this much?"

When they were finally clear of the wreckage and once again presented with a clear horizon, everyone took a seat at the table. Rachel's bag was returned when food was served, and before Pyrrha could leave again, Kyle called her back.

"How long before we get to where you're taking us?" he asked.

Pyrrha averted her gaze and refused to answer. Instead, she asked Mira to leave the room.

Kyle rose from the table. "Hey! I asked you a question! How long?"

"You are not the leader here, Kyle. From now on, I give the orders, you take them!" said Pyrrha, following Mira from the room.

With that blow to his self-esteem, Kyle slumped onto his bunk.

Josh was quick to join him. "I know I said to be calmer with people, but she was way out of order. Let her get away with it and she will walk all over you."

Kyle ground his teeth. "I should have hit her in the mouth then, is that it? Is that what you're asking of me?"

"Hell no! And you know exactly how I feel about that topic. Michelle Forbes' father used to beat her mother, remember, the coward... If she'd only told me sooner, then maybe I could have gotten my hands on him first and Michelle's mother would still be alive and Michelle wouldn't now be serving a ten-year jail sentence for killing him—"

Kyle threw his hands up. He'd forgotten how close Josh and his friend Michelle had been. He, too, had been shocked to discover what had truly been going on behind closed doors, but it had made him understand why Michelle asked to join Josh in the boxing gym. He also remembered how deeply affected Josh was when Michelle, who was two years older, received her jail sentence.

"I know. I'm sorry, Josh. I didn't mean to imply—"

"I just meant be smarter than Pyrrha," Josh interjected. "You can get a lot of info when you know what buttons to press."

Kyle was again amazed at how Josh could simply switch from anger to calm. It was something he wished he could do. "Yeah, well, I'm not like you, Josh. What you see is what you get. Besides, Mira should be the one to ask the questions from now on; she's a better leader than I was. And before you ask, I'm not sulking. She proved it back at the island."

Josh raised his eyebrows. "What the hell are you on about?" he said. "OK, enough of this *leadership* crap. We work best as a team. But I can see that your head is still screwed up, so, as your teammate and your brother, leave it to me from now on, yeah? You did enough for all of us and went through hell. Take a timeout, come back refreshed." He smiled.

Kyle's head was aching, and not wanting to discuss what he was truly feeling, he threw his arm around his brother's shoulder and gave it a squeeze.

***

Mira was taken out to the top deck. As she stood at the railing, more ships burned in the distance. She began to panic.

"Is there any news on my family? How bad is it on land?" she asked. "Is my home still there? Is anything still there?"

"We have received no reports of your family at this time, I'm afraid," said Pyrrha. "But there are rumours that a ceasefire will be agreed shortly. For how long, who knows." She placed her hand lightly on Mira's shoulder. "I'm sorry, I know this is hard for you, but once you're safe, then we can concentrate on finding your parents and getting your brother back. But remember, even if the comet leaves, you and Jacen will still not be safe if you leave my sanctuary. Your children and your children's children will never be safe from them."

Mira looked at Pyrrha in disbelief. "Children? Who says I want children? Are the Followers stupid enough to think that I would ever have children after this? Or that my brother would? If we survive this, it all ends, and if we are the last descendants, then that will be that!"

"Mira, if the Followers catch you, they will force you to have children, and when your brother is old enough, they will do the same to him, too. So, you see, for your protection, you have to stay with us. Both of you will have to stay with us, and if you choose not to have a family, then fine, and the same will go for Jacen."

"What about the other Disciples? What if they want to kill us? If Lyssa's group wanted us dead, then who knows who else does?"

"They don't know where we are. I told you, no sanctuary knows our location for safety reasons."

That sounded fishy to Mira. "But my father does. What if the Followers have him prisoner, and he tells them? What then?"

"You shall be taught how to defend yourselves. But even if they have your father, he wouldn't tell them. He would die first. Besides, he has built up a resistance to any drug that the Followers may use on him, and he's been trained to endure many forms of torture. It is something we've all had to do."

Mira couldn't believe Pyrrha was foolish enough to actually believe what she was saying. "No one can withstand torture forever, you must realise that?"

"Mira, I promise, you don't have to worry about that." Pyrrha smiled. "Now, I brought you out here because I have a sensitive matter to discuss... How well do you actually know these friends of yours?"

Mira felt her stomach muscles instantly clench. "Well enough to know they will not stop helping me until Jacen is safe. Why?"

Pyrrha looked to the horizon. "I have just received news that greatly concerns me..."

CHAPTER ELEVEN

CLASH OF A TITAN

Mira was taken back to the cabin. At just the sight of her friends, she knew in her heart Pyrrha had to be mistaken.

"Your information has to be wrong," she whispered to her.

"When we get to where we are going, we have something that will scare the truth from them," said Pyrrha. "Until then, keep your wits about you, and please don't say anything, not even to Rachel. All our lives could be placed at risk."

The door was once again locked. Mira looked around the cabin. Kyle was standing by the window, staring out at nothing, and Josh was trying to teach Jo his sleight-of-hand trick.

Mira sat on one of the bunks. She felt exhausted and just wanted to forget everything Pyrrha had told her. She longed to sleep and dream of pleasant things, to escape this new nightmare. But then Rachel joined her.

"So, what did she want to speak with you about?"

Mira ached to tell her. "I'm so sorry, Rach, but it looks like you'll all be coming with me for the foreseeable future."

"I told you, I'm with you until we get Jacen back and until you can go home, too. I'm sure Kyle and Josh feel the same way—"

"What about, Jo?" Mira interjected. "We both know she's not going to last much longer without having a total breakdown."

Rachel looked over her shoulder, checking Jo wasn't listening. "Yeah, she's really surprised me with how quick she went from being the strong-willed, robotic know-it-all to the quivering wreck she is now. Same goes for Kyle. What's up with him? I've noticed that you two don't seem as close as you were. And there's no way a few days ago Kyle would have put up with the way Pyrrha spoke to him earlier. It's like he's turned into Peter. The Peter before Mr Hyde showed up, that is."

Mira tried to be diplomatic. "They went through a lot, Rach. The voices that Jo and Kyle heard must have been really bad, by the looks of it."

"Josh heard it, too, but you don't see him sulking. So, until Jacen is back with us, they're both going to have to just suck it up, aren't they?"

"Give Kyle time, Rach. He will come back stronger, I'm sure of it."

"Fine, but if he doesn't come back and Pyrrha is lying about saving Jacen, then I say we unleash Josh on the both of them." Rachel smiled. "Pyrrha will soon want rid of us, and Kyle will be back to yelling at him in no time."

***

Everyone had a fitful, dream-free night, and when breakfast was served, Pyrrha brought fresh, military-style uniforms for them all to wear.

The morning passed slowly, prompting Rachel to finally erupt and start pounding on the door, demanding to be let out.

Trying his best to ignore the racket, Kyle directed his attention once more to the outside, and once more to something in the ocean that brought fear to them all. The ship's alarm bell began to sound, and everyone clambered to the window.

As the waves crashed over the side and covered the deck, from out of the depths, an enormous hump attached to an unseen creature broke through the water. Five bone spikes as tall as a ship were splayed out along its spine, layered with a thick, leathery skin, and as it began to circle, the ship was caught in a vortex.

Josh let out a yell. "OK, Jo, you were right! It's not a megalodon. But if that's not Godzilla, then there's only one more thing it could be… Have any of you seen *Clash of the Titans*? And I'm talking about the classic original."

Dour, frightened, but also angry faces glared back.

"OK. Let me put it another way," Josh quickly added. "Do you all know the story of Perseus and Andromeda?"

"I do," Jo squawked. "But what's your bloody point?!"

"I think my point is obvious. The gods are pissed we left that island and have sent the kraken to deal with us."

Gunshots and screams rang out from the decks above. The bullets fired had little impact upon the monster, other than annoying it further. The creature suddenly banked hard, colliding into the ship's side, and everyone was thrown across the cabin.

Kyle banged furiously on the door to be released. Josh attempted to climb through the window, but the ship was struck again and the impact tossed him back into the room.

Suddenly, the ship picked up speed and the stern was lifted clear of the water. Josh clambered back to the window, only to see something else that brought panic.

"You have got to be kidding… Not the bloody fog again!"

Everyone desperately held on to each other as, once again, the ship was immersed in a corridor of darkness.

Jo began to freak out. "It's taking us back to the island, isn't it?" She threw her head in her hands. "I'm going to go mad again!"

As Mira and Rachel held her tight between them, the ship emerged into the bright sunlight. Whatever was waiting for them, Josh could see that it was not their island.

"Look, Jo. There's no beach, or huge walls and gates. There's rows of trees massed along the shoreline and—"

Before he could finish his sentence, the immense creature released the ship. Realising what they were being propelled toward, Josh yelled for everyone to take cover on the mattresses.

The ship smashed against the shore at high velocity. Trees that were standing tall along the edge of the bank were cut down like butter beneath a knife, and branches flew past the window. The ship came to an abrupt stop.

After a brief moment of silence, there then came the familiar sound of the door unlocking. As they waited to see who would appear, fearing that if Pyrrha was dead the captain would take it upon himself to end their lives in a fit of anger, the group formed a tight huddle.

Slowly, the door opened. But it wasn't the captain. Instead, standing in their way to freedom, blood seeping from a new wound to his head, was Linus, now dressed in the same uniform worn by the crew. Everyone remained rooted to the spot.

Linus took a step back. "I'm sorry for what I've done, but I can't take it back. I also can't let them do what they said they were going to do to me, because I'm a coward. So, I have to see if I can get off this boat and take my chances wherever we are now. But I still consider you all my friends, so I would suggest that you also leave, and I wish you all the best. And again, I'm so sorry."

He turned and ran, leaving them staring after him. Mira cautiously led the others out only once she was sure he'd gone, disappeared into the ship. The lights in the passageway were flickering wildly now, and the group had to feel their way to the stairwell. When they finally spilled out onto the deck, Pyrrha and the crew were scrambling out of the water.

Mira noticed a familiar shape disappear among the trees. *Good luck, Linus.*

"Well, here we go again," Josh called out. "At least there doesn't appear to be any sand, but if any talking badgers come to greet us, then I'm staying in the cabin."

"For goodness' sake, Josh. They were beavers, not badgers," said Rachel. "And I for one would be delighted to see them at this moment in time. Cos this all feels like I've walked through a bloody magic cupboard!"

When everyone was finally out of the water and the captain had pulled his troops together into a tight huddle, Pyrrha joined Mira by her side.

"Should we, or I, be worried?" Mira asked, refusing to remove her gaze from the huge bushy beard still giving orders.

"I told you, we are not murderers," Pyrrha replied. "But truth be told, I think we all need to be worried now."

Mira looked to the high trees further up the shore. "Do you have any idea where we are?" Pyrrha didn't have to answer. As if a light had turned on inside her head, Mira suddenly realised she knew exactly where they were. Her heart made a run for her throat. "This is where Epimetheus is buried, isn't it?"

Pyrrha closed her eyes and nodded. "I think so. Say nothing to the others. Panic is the last thing we need right now. And remember, we don't know who we can fully trust yet."

At first, Mira had to agree. But as she looked to each of her friends, deep inside, she knew she could trust them. If they were willing to put their lives at risk for her and her brother, then, if they asked if she knew why they had been brought to this new island, there was no way she was going to lie to them.

CHAPTER TWELVE

HERE WE GO AGAIN

A small patrol of Disciples was sent into the forest, others high into the trees to act as lookouts. Mira and the other teens, however, were led back aboard the ship and onto the bridge to await Pyrrha.

"I know I'm not a celebrity, but get me the hell out of here!" Josh cried out.

"And can someone please bring me my bag?" said Rachel to the guard stationed outside the door. "It's in the cabin."

"For goodness' sake, will someone staple it to her hand, please?" Jo yelled. "And if we're going to be kept in here, can someone please bring me a book to read and earphones so I don't have to listen to any more of Josh's bullshit?!"

"I know," said Josh, hopping on the spot, "to pass the time, how about a game of hide-and-seek? You go first, Jo. I'll count to ten billion and then come find you—not!"

"How's about you just hold your breath for a count of ten billion, Josh!" Jo spat back. "Oh, that's right. You can't keep that gob of yours shut for even a paltry minute, can you?"

Rachel leapt to Josh's defence by threatening to punch Jo into the next week, and with Kyle sat silently staring at the floor, Mira's blood was finally at boiling point.

"Enough!" She flipped. "Haven't we all learned what happens if we start arguing among ourselves? We are all we've got. Now reel it in!"

Surprised by Mira's harsh tone, Josh and Rachel went to one corner of the room to calm down, and Jo to another. Mira took a seat by Kyle.

"Now I know how you must have felt, leading them back on the other island," she whispered.

"Sometimes it's better to allow them to let off steam, and as you can see, Josh is a perfect stirrer." He winked. "Trust me, he knows what he's doing."

Mira looked to each of them. *He's right. By the looks of it, Rachel and Jo are now thinking of the predicament we're in, and not their dislike for one another.*

But her respite was short lived. As the patrol emerged from the treeline and Pyrrha headed toward the bridge with a serious expression, the mood quickly turned anxious. Everyone prepared themselves for bad news.

"This island is far larger than the last, but there's not much out there," Pyrrha said upon entering. "We're going to set up a base on the other side of this forest. But I would ask if you could remain in your cabin until the tents are set up. Now, you have all endured a lot, so try and get some rest tonight. Guards are patrolling at all times, so you don't need to worry."

"Did you hear that, everyone?" Josh laughed. "We were just attacked by the kraken, but we don't need to worry. Does that mean when the camp is set up, we can have a barbecue?"

Jo rolled her eyes. "Urgh, a barbecue. How common can you get?"

"Do you mind telling us where we are exactly?" Kyle asked, ignoring them.

Pyrrha deflected the question. "We managed to get a call out to our people and give them our location before we hit the fog, but it will be a few days before they get here."

"I didn't ask that," said Kyle. "But I'll try again. Where are we?"

Again, Pyrrha avoided the question. "Don't worry, we have enough food and water, so there's no need to concern yourselves over that at least."

Kyle flew out of his seat. "Fine, don't tell us! You can even ignore me. But Josh is right—that thing out there will destroy whoever you ask to come and rescue us, or us, if we try to leave. Don't you think we need to find out why it brought us here first, or who sent it?"

Once again, Pyrrha refused to answer, but before Kyle could rant at her again, Mira placed her hand on his shoulder and silenced him with a slight shake of her head.

"Right then," said Pyrrha. "Now, if there are no further questions or sarcasm, I'll see if the cabin is still in a fit state for you to use." And briskly, she exited through the door.

"That was odd," said Rachel. "Why won't she say where we are?"

"Probably hasn't got a clue and doesn't want to look unprofessional," said Jo. "Hey, do you think they know about Linus yet?"

"Would she have told us if they did?" said Kyle. "That patrol probably found him anyway and…"

Mira gently squeezed his hand and, again, he fell silent.

"Mira, do you have any idea why we are here?" Jo asked.

It was the moment Mira had dreaded, but she'd made a promise that if asked, she would not conceal it. "Epimetheus' tomb is on this island," she said flatly.

"Oh, that's just great," Josh huffed. "Well, let's hope there are no artefacts, otherwise sleep with both eyes open. Especially with Captain Barbossa over there," he added, motioning to Jo, but before she could say or do anything, Rachel had already slapped him on Jo's behalf.

As they watched another patrol set out and the sun begin to descend, Pyrrha appeared and instructed them all to go back to the sleeping quarters. With an armed guard behind her, nobody argued.

Jo immediately climbed under the covers on her bunk, and with Josh and Rachel cuddled up together on another, Kyle and Mira remained by the window, staring out at the stars.

"So, Epimetheus' tomb is on this island. Were you ever going to tell us?" Kyle whispered.

"I thought it best not to," Mira replied.

"Why? Don't you trust us? Trust me?"

Mira sucked in a breath. "Of course, I trust you. But we've been brought here for the same reason we were taken to Pandora's, I reckon. I had hoped that Pyrrha's people would come and rescue us before you found out. I'm sorry, I should have told you." She shook her head. "Look, do you think we should just get it over with? Opening it, I mean? Or should we try and find a way of escaping? Maybe Josh and Rachel are right and we should go home and get help from the government to get my brother back, because I don't think I'm going to find my father now."

Kyle's whole body tensed. "No, I'm sorry. You were right to keep it to yourself. I can't advise you. Whatever I say, I will end up wondering if the advice has come from me or something else occupying my body. But what I will say is that whatever you want to do, I'm with you."

Mira sensed a change in him. It radiated from his very core. She pulled him in close.

"What's truly bothering you, Kyle?"

He held her tightly. "Nothing," he murmured.

It was definitely not nothing. "C'mon, you can tell me."

"I'm just tired of all this," he said. "As soon as Pyrrha tells you the truth about Epimetheus, suddenly we end up on the island where he's buried—bit convenient, don't you think?"

"I guess," she said, but she sensed that wasn't the only thing that was worrying him. Still, judging by his body language, this wasn't the time to press the issue.

As Kyle climbed onto a bunk, she joined him. Their bodies entwined, Mira closed her eyes, exhausted.

CHAPTER THIRTEEN

THAT'S A NEW ONE FOR THE BOOKS

Mira awoke with a jolt. Automatically, she reached for her phone, but it was no longer with her, lost on the previous island. She looked to Kyle's watch and was relieved to see for once it wasn't 3 a.m. But her deep breathing had also awoken Kyle. As he opened his eyes, Mira became aware that the others were also wide awake.

They gathered around the table, and without even saying a word, she sensed they had all had the same dream.

"Right then, that's a new one for the books," said Josh, wiping away the globules of sweat from his brow, "and so allow me to be the first to say it: there is no bloody way I'm leaving this ship now."

Rachel was shaking. Mira leaned across the table and took her hands into her own. "What did you see beyond the waterfall, Rach?"

Rachel threw her arms around Josh and shook her head.

"The tomb is beyond," Jo said, trembling. "But there's something in that place that makes the other island appear like... Disneyland."

"Euro, California or Florida?" said Josh.

"Does it matter, Josh?" said Rachel, finally able to speak.

"Well, I love them all, but for me—"

"Josh, it doesn't matter," Kyle interjected, giving him a *shut the hell up* look. "I have to say, though, if what I just experienced is anything like what really happens when you drown, I'm staying here as well."

Mira's heart raced. "You were pulled under the water?"

Kyle nodded. "Can't seem to remember what it was now, though."

Rachel's lips quivered. "How could only Jo and me enter Epimetheus' tomb, Mira? You and Jacen are descended from his line with Pandora, not us."

"Perhaps Pandora's children had lots of kids and there are more descendants than were first thought," said Josh. "Do you think Pyrrha knows more than she's letting on?"

Mira nodded. "Yes. I'm waiting for her to make a slip-up before confronting her. But there's something else you need to hear. Back at Pandora's crypt, I saw three tombs—"

Before she could continue, there was a knock on the door, and Pyrrha entered.

"Is she bloody telepathic or just really bad at timing?" Josh whispered.

"Our scouts have reported that *thing* is at the other end of this island at present, so now is the time to get the ship back in the water," Pyrrha told them. "We have a winch and there is a rock that we have tied the steel wire and pulley to, but it would be better if you all leave the ship and stand well clear."

***

Pyrrha waited for everyone to leave. But as Josh, the last of them, was about to walk past, she threw her arm across the door, blocking his exit. She leaned in close, her moist lips almost touching his.

"You look like you've had a nightmare," she whispered. "Is there something you want to tell me, Joshy?"

Josh backed away. "No, not really. A bit of indigestion, that's all. Now, if you don't mind, excuse me."

"OK, but if you need to talk, my tent is always open to you." She smiled.

Josh was now completely baffled. "What the hell are you on about?"

"Later, when we are alone." She winked.

Josh pushed past and, without looking back to see if she was behind him, sped through the ship.

When the boat was finally in the water and the anchors were dropped, Pyrrha led the group along a small corridor through the trees. Exiting through the same stone arch they had all witnessed in their dreams, they came out into an open field filled with long grass and dense patches of ferns tall enough to hide a large, prowling animal. An area of land had been flattened for the military-style tents.

Inside their tents, they found foldable beds with blankets and pillows already waiting. Mira, Rachel and Jo were given a tent to share. Kyle and Josh were given another.

"Five hours until the sun comes up, so try and get some rest," said Pyrrha. "Two guards will be patrolling, so no wandering off. They have been expressly informed to shoot anything and anyone that dares to wander too close to the camp, or *away* from it. And yes, I'm talking to you, Josh!"

Jo pointed to the arch. "Any idea what those hieroglyphs mean, or who put them there?"

Pyrrha didn't even turn to look. "I don't, sorry. It's a dead language."

"I know what it probably says," said Rachel gloomily. "Turn back. This place is cursed and no good will come from you being here…"

"Or maybe it simply says"—Josh grinned—"please do not feed the animals and keep to the pathways at all times. Put all rubbish in the bins as you will be fined for any litter that is left behind. Welcome to Paradise Island, and we do hope you enjoy your stay."

Mira stepped forward and placed one hand upon the cold, hard surface. "It says, '*Those that seek knowledge shall only find death eternal…*' I… I can't make out the rest, I'm afraid."

Pyrrha's eyes were wide. "How can you read it?"

"My stepfather was an expert in ancient languages." Mira half smiled. "Surprising what you pick up when you watch and listen closely to someone studying."

Josh clapped his hands together. "Right then, anyone for a game of poker before bedtime?"

With a shake of their heads, the others headed into the tents.

Before Josh could follow his brother, Pyrrha took hold of his arm. "Come to my shelter if you feel scared. My sleeping bag is nice and snug." She winked.

Confused and weary, Josh dropped his head and loped to the tent.

"I'm not going to drown or get eaten by a kraken—Rachel will kill me long before then," he muttered. After tying the flies of the tent closed, he climbed into his sleeping bag—but kept a watchful eye on the flap for the rest of the night.

CHAPTER FOURTEEN

MYTHS AND LEGENDS

Josh stayed awake the entire night. He watched the narrow beam of dawn's early light creep under the tent and listened to the soft ruffle of movement through the long grass outside. Suddenly, a shadow appeared under the flap. He gripped the sleeping bag tightly around him and hoped that if it was Pyrrha, she wasn't as strong as his mother.

Slowly, the zip began to glide in an upward direction. Thick beads of sweat formed on Josh's brow, and his heart pumped furiously as though someone had attached it to a faulty, repeating defibrillator.

Up and up the zip continued to climb, until finally, the cover flew open. Before even seeing who it was, Josh threw the sleeping bag high over his head.

"What's the matter with you?" said Rachel, taking a seat on the edge of his bunk.

"Nothing—this sleeping bag is really hot, that's all," he said, scrambling out.

Rachel huffed. "No wonder you're hot; you're fully dressed."

"Yeah, because we're on another strange island," Josh moaned. "Look, I don't want to be fussing about looking for my clothes and boots if something bad happens, do I?"

Mira sat down on Kyle's bunk and shook her head. "Josh, there are two armed guards outside. I'm sure if anything happens, you'll have plenty of time to get dressed. Not only that—"

"Oh, yeah," Josh interrupted. "You've obviously never seen the movie, *Ninja Assassin Seventeen: The Naked Tent Attacks!*"

"Josh, if ninjas are on the island and get past the guards, then it won't really matter if you're dressed or not, will it?" said Rachel. Her eyebrows then rose. "Do you normally sleep naked, then?"

Josh emitted a dramatic *Grrr*. "Sometimes… But look, if I'm going to die in a strange place I'd just rather be fully dressed, that's all. And my advice is for all of you to do the same!"

After they'd exited their tents, the group scanned their surroundings.

To the east and south-west of the island there appeared to be nothing more than high, unclimbable cliffs. And to the north, a mountain range so high that its peak, which was rising out from wisps of grey cloud, was covered in a thick blanket of snow.

Josh blew out his cheeks. "Forget *Ninja Assassin Seventeen*, this looks like a good place for a *Jurassic Park* movie."

Lowered eyes and bared teeth turned toward him en masse.

"Did I say *Jurassic Park*? I meant to say… err, Never Never Land," he corrected himself, before turning his attention to Pyrrha, who he could see talking with the captain. "Hey, what do you think that's about? She doesn't look too happy."

As they tried to listen in, Jo sleepily appeared from the girls' encampment. "What's going on?" she yawned.

"A T. rex was spotted near the camp last night," said Josh seriously. "Probably just after the stegosaurus that was also seen wandering about."

Rachel lashed out, striking Josh's arm before Jo could answer.

Jo was now fully awake. "Oh, no… Do you think that *thing* has taken the boat?"

"I guess we can ask her now," said Kyle, motioning to Pyrrha, who was walking toward them.

"Is everything OK?" Jo gulped. "Nothing wrong with the ship, is there?"

"No, nothing like that," said Pyrrha. "One of the guards was caught asleep on duty, that's all. He's been confined to the ship on washing-up duty as punishment. Which reminds me, that tent over there has breakfast waiting for you." She pointed to the largest one.

Once Pyrrha had vanished into the treeline, Josh was quick to scoff, "Did anyone actually believe that?"

"Why shouldn't we?" said Rachel.

"Because I took a good look at all her guards when we landed, and they don't seem the type to fall asleep on duty. I think something bad happened during the night."

Exasperated, the company entered the mess and, taking seats away from the guards who were still eating, poured themselves some soup and began to eat.

***

Breakfast was finished. But there was no sign of Pyrrha returning to the site.

They had been warned to remain near the camp, but Jo's moaning that she needed to stretch her legs was enough to make Mira relent and begin to lead the group across the open field. When they were quickly stopped and brought back to the tents by two guards, and then Josh demanded their wardens to tell him exactly what there was to fear on the island, other than Epimetheus' burial ground, Mira decided that *enough was enough*, and they would all go back to the ship to look for Pyrrha.

The group arrived at the shoreline. Initially, they were unable to see the ocean monster, so their spirits lifted, but their hopes were quickly dashed when Pyrrha joined them from the bridge of the ship.

"Trust me, it's there. The lookouts see it surface now and again," she said, glancing up to the guard high in the tree.

"How the hell has something that big never been reported?" Kyle asked. "I can understand those giant wolves never being seen, on an island protected by thick fog, but a creature that size roaming the open seas?"

"The wolves are seen all the time where I come from—my order breeds them," said Pyrrha casually.

"Breed them for what, babysitting?" Josh quipped.

"Security. And they, unlike you, obey. We never thought that, after our order left them there on the island, they would have survived all this time. The isolation must have turned them savage."

"So, how did they get beyond the wall?" Mira asked. "I thought you said when your order came for Pandora's children, the gates were already locked?"

"The walls were built by my people. They left two secret entrances so that only we could check on the safety of the tomb. When the island vanished, the wolves must have found a way in and got trapped because, when I arrived, rocks had sealed up the one entrance and the other you have to navigate by sea to reach, as you well know."

"That must be how the Followers got in then," said Josh. "Looks like not all your info is kept secret."

"OK, that explains the wolves, but what about that thing out there?" said Kyle, pointing to the immense spiked spine once again ploughing through the water.

"Do you know the stories about Perseus and Hercules?" Pyrrha began. "Jason and his Argonauts, who went in search of the Golden Fleece. Theseus and the Minotaur he faced and killed in the maze?"

Everyone nodded their heads in unison.

"They are all true. And there are things still out there in uncharted places you wouldn't believe. The gods of old are real, children."

Rachel snorted through her nose, "Maybe all those stories were based on real people, but you can't expect us to believe that Zeus, Poseidon, Hera and all the other mythological gods were real? We have a fair idea now how the Earth and the universe were really created. You ever hear of the big bang theory?"

"Oh, that was a great show," Josh said with a smile.

Rachel swung a fist and caught Josh's arm in the sweet spot. "I wasn't talking about the bloody show, Josh!"

Pyrrha stepped into Rachel's shadow. "And who created the big bang, Rach?"

"Touché," said Rachel, rubbing the inflamed mark on Josh's arm.

"I know what you are going to ask next," said Pyrrha. "I can see one of you is champing at the bit. You want to have a look around the island. So, I guess I will have to tell you the truth—the guard I spoke of didn't fall asleep. Something came for him in the night. So, I wouldn't advise wandering off until we know what exactly *is* on this island. I didn't want to tell you, but knowing how you lot like to run around—and yes, I mean you, Josh—I guess it's better to let you know now."

"I knew it," said Josh under his breath. "Welcome to Jurassic Park: Part Twenty-Five everyone; the visual effects can't get better than this."

"If that's the case," Jo squeaked, "then our easy-to-tear-apart tents are not going to keep out whatever took the guard. So, if you don't mind, I'll stay on the ship. It's big enough for me to exercise."

But as she strode toward the bridge, the creature surfaced again, sending a giant wave crashing upon the bank. Jo hastily walked back to the safety of the group.

"The tent will be fine." She smiled.

"Look, Pyrrha, they're not stupid," said Mira. "They all know what is on this island. Trust me, none of them want to go anywhere near Epimetheus' resting place."

Pyrrha let out an exasperated groan. "You've all had a dream, haven't you?" A quick snap of her fingers, and two armed guards appeared. "Then, I'm afraid that until rescue arrives, you will all have to be locked up."

"That won't be necessary," said Josh. "According to the dream we had, I'll be the one to open the tomb."

Pyrrha shot a look to Mira. "Is he telling the truth?"

Mira hated lying, but she trusted Josh, even though she had no clue why he of all people would offer himself up to be locked away. "He is," she said, pinching her leg.

"That's impossible."

"Why is it impossible?" Mira asked. "It's obvious that all of us here were saved from the storm for a reason. It seems to me we are all distantly related to Pandora and Epimetheus somehow, right? You said it yourself, they didn't come together straight away."

The creases on Pyrrha's forehead deepened. "Very well," she said, and with a motion to one of her men,

Josh's arms were pulled behind his back and his hands tied. "I'm sorry, Josh. It's for your own good."

"Sounds good to me." Josh smiled. "OK, let's go then."

Once Josh was escorted aboard the ship, Pyrrha pulled Mira aside as they walked back to the tents. "Do I need to lock Kyle up as well?"

"No. You know he won't go there."

"Fine, but answer me this, why was Josh happy to be locked up?"

Mira hesitated. *She knows it's not Josh who can open the tomb, I can see it in her eyes. But she's not entirely sure who can now. Is she trying to see if I will give Rachel and Jo away?*

"Oh, right," she said. "Well, he did say earlier that he felt safer on the ship than in a tent."

Pyrrha's eyes narrowed. "If you say so. But please, Mira, don't make the same mistake on this island that you did on the last. There are things here even we don't know about, except for in vague writings that were handed down to our order. Now we are letting you have some freedom around the camp. Don't make me lock you all up."

Mira gave a simple nod of acknowledgement, and when Pyrrha disappeared back into the forest, she took another look at the guards high in the trees. A shiver slithered up her spine.

They're not safe up there. Should I warn Pyrrha?

But Rachel slipped her arm under hers. "We can't leave Josh all alone," she said, staring back up at the cabin.

Kyle threw his arm around Rachel's shoulder. "Let me tell you something about my brother." He smirked. "Our mother would lock us in our room whenever he played up—"

"Why would you be locked up as well if it was just him acting up?" Rachel interrupted.

"She wouldn't discriminate, and I guess deep down she hoped that I could talk some sense into him. But, as you can all see, nobody can tell Josh what to do. Anyway, she would lock us in, and he would time how long it took before she came back and unlocked the door. After a few times of Mum doing it—yes, it was regular—he would listen to her walk downstairs, then climb out of the window, shimmy down the drainpipe—which, I might add, was directly outside the living room where both my parents would be sat watching television—go wherever he would go and, every time, make it back just as she returned to unlock the door in the hope sense had been regained. Trust me, that window will be even easier for him to climb out of, despite the long drop."

"Didn't you ever go with him?" Mira asked.

Kyle shrugged. "No, I would just lie on my bed and read."

A warm glow fluttered inside Mira. "So, that's why Josh did it then, because he knows he can get out whenever he wants to."

Rachel was also smiling. "Deep down, you don't have a choice; you really have got to love him."

***

The morning passed slowly. After lunch, and a lot of badgering from Rachel, Pyrrha finally relented, and with two armed guards accompanying them, the group were allowed to walk across the field and climb the steep grassy bank.

A deep valley stretched out before them and, at its base, a wide, fast-flowing river that led back to the ocean. Beyond, to the north-west of the island, was another forest, within which they could just about make out some sort of stone structure. To the north-east, in front of the mountain range, a huge statue stood tall. But the real reason they had ventured this far remained unseen—there was no sign of either the town nor the sepulchre they had all dreamed of.

"Do you really think the boats that are coming for us are going to be able to get past that thing out there?" Kyle asked, staring intently at the river.

"Now that we have the ship back in the water, and with any luck nothing too much wrong with it, then when the boats arrive they will create a diversion and hopefully, yes, we should be able to leave here," said Pyrrha. "Oh, unless you know something that I don't?"

Mira could see Kyle was hatching a plan of some sort. Not wanting Pyrrha to lock him away, too, Mira took her arm and started to head back toward camp.

"I need to ask you something," she whispered. "Something that's been playing on my mind."

Rachel and Jo walked on ahead toward the tents, and while Kyle tried to bond with the guards, Mira and Pyrrha dropped back.

Checking that they were out of earshot, Mira pulled Pyrrha closer to her. "How do you know it's only those three locations where Jacen may be kept?"

"They're the ones that are best protected," said Pyrrha. "You see, we have spies in their order who reported extra troops arriving at those sites."

Mira began to panic. "If you managed to get spies into their order, don't you think they have their own in yours? I mean, it only makes sense. Otherwise, how did they know about the secret entrance back on that last island?"

Pyrrha stared at the ground ahead. "I don't know how they knew about it," she said quietly. "But I can assure you they don't have spies in our order. That is something we take very seriously. It's your friends that bother me. In fact, I think it's time to have a little chat with some of them. I'll start with Josh, now that he's alone—"

"I'm sorry, Pyrrha. Even if what you say is true, confronting the others at this moment is not a good idea," Mira insisted. "And don't underestimate Josh. He's not as stupid as he makes out."

Pyrrha took a deep breath. "Then keep a close eye on them. But don't let them go looking for Epimetheus' tomb, at all costs. As for Josh—don't worry, I know how to get the truth from him. He's only a man, after all."

As Pyrrha headed toward the ship, Mira followed Rachel and Jo into their tent, where she had to hold herself from yelling at the top of her voice.

"Surprise," Josh whispered with a big grin on his face.

Mira immediately grabbed a hold of his collar. "Pyrrha is going to the ship right now to see you, so get your arse back there before we're all in the doghouse!"

As Josh scrambled out through the rear of the tent, Rachel stamped her foot. "Why does she want to see Josh?"

Mira couldn't answer. She was desperately trying to think of a way to delay Pyrrha.

CHAPTER FIFTEEN

SWEET JOSHY

Josh weaved through the trees and ferns on his way back toward the ship. But as he neared the shoreline, he saw the lookout in the tree was closely monitoring the route he needed to take. A solution to this problem was suddenly provided when Mira caught up with Pyrrha and noisily pulled her to a stop. The guard, yawning loudly, switched his attention to the girls instead. It was the perfect opportunity to slip onto the ship unnoticed, but Josh's curiosity was now piqued. He slinked through the ferns to listen, but in taking his time, he missed what was said. And more worryingly, Pyrrha had turned on her heels and was making her way to the ship in haste. He had to get back.

Still aware of the watcher in the tree, Josh took a detour and, once clear of the guard's sight, ran as fast as he could to the rear of the vessel. Quietly, he climbed up the anchor chain and over the railing, jumped up to the window, leapt in toward the bunk and landed just as he heard the door unlock and the handle turn.

"Hello, Joshy," said Pyrrha on entering.

Josh lay on the bunk, trying to hide the fact that he was completely out of breath. But when Pyrrha locked the door, loosened her ponytail and gave her hair a seductive swish, he inhaled deeply.

"Oh, no," he said under his breath.

"Alone at last and nowhere to run," she said, dimming the light. "Now, I think it's time to have our talk, don't you?"

Sweat was pouring from Josh's forehead, and when Pyrrha sat on the end of the bed, he took another big gulp of air. "Now, Pyrrha, you don't want Rachel to find out about this, do you? For one, she will kill you without a second thought. Trust me, I've seen—and felt—a little of what she can do when she's angry. Secondly, she will kill me, and I don't want to die. And thirdly—what in God's name are you on about?"

Pyrrha leaned in close. Josh tried to slip off the bed, but she blocked his escape with her arm.

"Look, Pyrrha, I'm flattered," he said, wiping the river of perspiration from his face, "but this is wrong. I'm with Rachel."

"But Josh, don't you find me attractive anymore? Isn't this what you've always wanted? You used to stare at me all the time on the other island." Her sultry tone and the way she was stroking his knee was making it hard for Josh to think clearly.

"Did I? Must have been the island's influence then. You know, like Jo. She went Alexander the Great nuts for treasure; I must have gone bananas for a beautiful woman... I mean, women." *Well done, Josh. How not to put fires out!*

"See, I knew you thought I was beautiful. And I promise this will be our little secret." She pressed closer to him and began stroking his hair. "But first, I need you to answer my questions truthfully. Only then can you have what you desire most. Now, whose side are you and your brother really on?"

Josh attempted to back away, but the bunk was against the wall. "Whose side?" He gulped. "OK, is the same thing that was mind-screwing us on that last island now talking to you?"

Pyrrha slinked closer. "Why are you really with Mira?"

Josh threw himself forward off the bed and stumbled up, putting distance between them. "I'm not with Mira. Hello, I'm Josh, not Kyle. He's the pretty one." For the life of him, he couldn't understand why Pyrrha would be making a move on him. "And I've told you: I'm with Rachel! Now, cut it out!"

"Tell me about William Tripp then?" Stretching out across the bed, she batted her deep brown eyes at him.

"Mr Tripp…? OK, you're not making any sense. Did you bump your head when we hit the shoreline?"

Pyrrha slipped off the bed and slowly approached. She pressed her body against his, pinning him to the wall. "I told you, Josh. I like you. Now, tell me about your relationship with Tripp?"

Josh felt his head was about to explode. "I have no relationship with Mr Tripp. Why the hell would you think that?"

"He taught you that card trick you performed on Pandora's island. I saw you do it to his minions. And a little bird told me that Kyle was awfully keen to get him to safety when the ship was about to sink."

Josh's blood began to boil. "Yes, Mr Tripp taught me a card trick. My uncle Trevor taught me to swear in four different languages, so what? Look, my brother and I had no idea he was head of the Followers. And all Kyle was concerned about was getting *everyone* to safety… Wait, how do you know he taught me the card trick?"

"The driver that took you to the dock was one of us. He was sent to keep an eye on Tripp. He saw how close you were with him. And we had our people on board that cruise ship watching everything that went on. Before the ship sank, they contacted my order, who were able to forward the information to me."

Suddenly, her warm breath was brushing his neck. His earlobe was being nibbled. "Don't be angry with me, Joshy. I know you want to protect Mira now, but can you tell me more about what Tripp has got planned?"

Josh was furious that she'd even imply he was working for Mr Tripp. He decided to turn the tables on her. He slipped one hand round to the base of her back and pulled her closer. "You know what, Pyrrha? You're right," he whispered. "You are very beautiful, and I would be stupid to miss an opportunity like this. And like you said, it will be our little secret, right? So, let's get to the fun stuff, and then I'll answer all the questions you want."

Pyrrha released herself and took a step back. Josh kicked off his boots and unzipped his jumpsuit, pulling it down to his waist. Slowly, he inched toward her.

Pyrrha's jaw hit her chest as she backed away. "Josh, what are you doing?"

"A deal is a deal, Piri-Wiri." He grinned. "I've been told what a great kisser I am, so come on, take me to heaven, and I'll answer all the questions you want. You want to try a bit of Joshy? Here I am. I can't deny the chemistry between us any longer…"

He puckered his lips, and, her bluff called, Pyrrha turned on her heels and left the room. Moments later, she returned, but before she had a chance to yell at him to put his clothes back on, Josh was already waiting with his arms wide, ready to welcome her.

"Ah-ha, I knew you couldn't resist me. Come on then, get some Joshy. I'm young, I'm fresh and I'm ready!" And, waving his arms in the air, he let the suit drop to the floor, leaving him standing in only his socks and underwear.

As Josh waddled toward her, Pyrrha blinked furiously and, without saying a word, swept from the room, slamming the door behind her.

"And don't sneak out tonight!" she hollered through the door. "My people have orders to shoot you!"

Josh returned to his bunk, grinning. "Try it on with me, will you…? Right then, Joshy, time to find out what's really going on, methinks."

With his jumpsuit zipped and his boots back on, he watched Pyrrha, still shaking her head, leave the ship and head down to the seafront, where the captain and crew were pulling salvage from the water.

The coast clear, he opened the window and crept out.

CHAPTER SIXTEEN

TAKEN

The sun had set on another day. The moon was rising, and Mira and Kyle were standing outside the tents, watching the comet burn slowly across the autumn sky.

As a chill wafted through the trees, Kyle slipped behind Mira and wrapped his arms around her to keep her warm.

"Funny how a simple ball of rock brought us to this," he whispered. "Maybe we should stay here till it's gone and then go in search of Jacen?"

Mira glared at the fiery asteroid of doom, silently cursing its arrival.

"There's something I need to tell you, Kyle. And for now, only you should hear it."

Kyle turned her to face him. "It would be wise if you didn't tell me. Keep what you know to yourself. I'll back any decision you make." He smiled.

That wasn't what was worrying her, but perhaps he was right. Best she remain quiet for now.

"You know," she said instead, "with everything that's happened, we haven't really talked. I mean, talked about things other than the mess we're in. I know you like architecture, but I know so little else about you."

Kyle pulled her closer. "What do want to know?"

Mira hesitated. *Damn it! He's willing to tell me about himself, and I can't think of anything to ask. He's waiting. Oh God, say something!*

"How about you tell me more about yourself," he said, "and I'll try to think of something you might want to know about me?"

Mira's mind was in meltdown. It was as if she couldn't remember anything of her life before the start of the holiday. "Umm… Umm…"

"Can't think of anything, can you?" He laughed. "Nor me. OK. How about we start off small… What's your favourite colour?"

That was easy. It was the colour she'd seen at the start of the voyage. Her chest began to heave as she gazed into his eyes. "Turquoise. What's… what's, um, yours?"

His lips were almost touching hers. "Violet."

He placed his hand on the small of her back and held her firm. His eyes seemed to penetrate her very soul. This time, Mira didn't pull away. She couldn't. She didn't want to. And then his lips met hers and all her worries suddenly drifted away. She wanted it to last forever. But then, as quickly as their lips had come together, Kyle pulled away. For a moment he stared ominously over her shoulder.

"Is something wrong?" she asked and turned her head to see what had grabbed his attention. She saw nothing.

Kyle closed his eyes tight and gave a shake of his head. Mira felt her cheeks flush, the first touch of a familiar wave of frustration and anger.

Oh, is this your childish way of getting your own back? But as she watched him tremble, she bit her lip. *It's definitely not that. Fine, if he won't tell you… Then again— what are you doing, Mira? Your brother is missing and all you seem to care about now are Kyle's strong arms and soft lips!*

"What is it?" she asked again. "Oh. Are you hearing voices?"

Kyle released his hands from her waist, opened his eyes and smiled. "Sorry. But I think we should…" He stopped mid-sentence. His eyes were wide again, focused, unflinching.

Are you looking at me, or…? Mira glanced behind her again. *There's nothing there?*

"We should go inside," he said, and lifting the flap of her tent, he entered.

Mira wanted to drag him back out and shake him. His flip-flop of emotions was giving her a migraine. Just then, a rustle came from the forest. Fearful of another wolf appearing, she regained her breath and composure and entered the tent just as Josh slipped through the rear.

Not now, Josh! I need to have it out with your brother once and for all! she silently fumed.

"It's only me," said Josh glibly. "So, what's up?"

Mira took a deep breath. There was lipstick on his neck. "Nothing is up." She blocked Rachel's view and hugged him, while wiping away the lipstick. "I guess you're here because Pyrrha has brought you up to speed?"

She had told Rachel why Pyrrha had wanted to see him and hoped that Josh could see it etched on her face.

Josh simply stared blankly back at her. "Sorry—on what?"

Rachel's lip started to curl. "About not saying a word to anyone that you can open the tomb, or that there's a second key?"

Josh scrunched up his face. "But, I can't open it…"

Rachel edged closer. Her eyes became narrow and scary.

Mira knew that look. "What did she actually say to you, Josh?"

"Uhh… At first she wasn't making any sense, but when she sat on my bed—"

Rachel stamped her foot and stood nose to nose with him. "She sat or lay on your bed? What the bloody hell went on?"

"Oh, no, no, no, nothing happened, honest. She thinks me and Kyle are—"

Rachel stalked around him like a cat with a mouse. "She thinks you're what, Josh? Cute? A toy boy? Boyfriend material? What? Do you fancy her now? You obviously have a thing for older women!"

"Look, nothing happened." Josh gulped. "And I don't fancy her. I think she looks like—um—what's her name, from *The Wizard of Oz*?"

"Glinda," Jo said with a wink, and taking a seat on the bed, she rested her chin in her hands, wiggled her bottom to get more comfortable and, smiling widely, waited for the fireworks to begin.

"Yes, that's it. Glinda."

Mira sighed and wondered whether to put a stop to it there and then. "Glinda was the good witch, Josh. The pretty one."

"Well, they were all pretty hot," he said.

Even Mira was confused now. She loved the film dearly and for the life of her could not imagine even Josh finding the green witch attractive.

"You're thinking of *Oz the Great and Powerful*," said Kyle. "Not *The Wizard of Oz*."

Josh's jaw hit his chest. He tried to recover. "No, I meant the wizard one. Remember the green witch that melts when a glass of milk is thrown at her?"

Jo smirked. "Water, Josh. It was water."

"Does it really bloody matter, Jo? She melted, didn't she! All I'm saying is Pyrrha looks like the green witch.

With her long, pointy nose and…" He paused, considering. "In fact," he continued, nodding his head toward Jo. "I'll go one better. To me, she looks like one of the flying rodents."

"Monkeys, Josh. They were monkeys."

Josh closed his eyes and lowered his head. When he offered his arm up to Rachel, for once she didn't slap him. Instead, she did the one thing everyone now knew was far worse. She folded her arms tightly across her chest, sat down with her back to him and crossed her legs, ready to embark upon another marathon sulk-fest.

All was silent within the tent. Kyle was again massaging his temples. Jo was smiling at Josh, who had placed a pillow over his face to block Rachel's furious glare. Mira began to wonder why she wasn't on the ship sailing after her brother alone.

Excusing herself, she slipped out of the tent. There she found Pyrrha and her guards staring fearfully up at the night sky. Her heart rate increased. "What is it?" she whispered.

"Don't know, yet," said Pyrrha. "We heard sounds, like the flapping of wings, but we couldn't see anything. Look, you should go back inside, just in case."

Mira's dream came flooding back. "Are you sure it was flapping wings?"

"That's what it sounded like." Pyrrha stared at her questioningly. "Why? Is there something you need to share with me?"

Mira thought quickly. "No. I mean, yes. I thought I heard it, too. Earlier, I mean, when you left to see Josh. But I couldn't see anything either. By the way, what did he have to say?"

Pyrrha paled. "We'll discuss it another time. For now, I believe he at least doesn't know anything."

Pyrrha led her back to her tent. Without thinking, Mira opened the flap wide—and was relieved to find Josh had already made his way back to the ship.

Not wanting Kyle to be alone in his tent, Mira insisted he stay with them. The day had been warm, but at night the temperature had dramatically dropped. Nervously, as Mira climbed into her sleeping bag, she asked Kyle to join her.

He shook his head. "You sleep. You deserve it. I'll keep watch." He smiled.

Mira pulled the sleeping bag tightly around her. She thought of the kiss. But as her eyes slowly drifted close, Jacen came to mind once more.

If I can't find Dad, I will find another way to get you back, she promised.

***

Mira didn't know how long she'd been asleep, but when she opened her eyes, Kyle had dozed off. There was a sudden *whoosh* outside, like the fluttering of many wings overhead. Against her better judgement, she unzipped the tent and crept outside. The guards who had been patrolling were nowhere to be seen. Cagily, she stepped across the dew-covered grass, cautiously scanning the night sky. There was nothing to see but darkness.

She crept closer to the other tents. There was no sound within any of them. Suddenly, it occurred to her that Pyrrha and the crew had left them on the island. Panic rising within her, she ran toward the ship. When a gunshot and high-pitched scream echoed out, she increased her pace.

The ship was still anchored ahead, but before she could feel relieved, the alarmed expressions of the crew brought her to a sharp halt.

"Get back to your tent!" the captain yelled. "And don't come out till we say it's OK to come out!"

This was the second time he'd spoken to her like a misbehaving child. Mira ignored the order and ran to Pyrrha's side instead. "I heard a gunshot and scream—what the hell's happened now?!"

"Whatever it was, it's taken another lookout," Pyrrha said. "So, we're going to keep everyone out of the trees from now on. But you should go back—in fact, how did you get past the guard?"

"Guard? What guard?"

The sudden realisation that she'd left the others alone hit the pit of her stomach like a torpedo. Without a moment's hesitation, she ran back to the tents as fast as she could, with Pyrrha close behind.

To her relief, Kyle, Rachel and Jo were still asleep. Not wanting to disturb them, Mira and Pyrrha made their way to Pyrrha's own tent.

"There should have been a lookout patrolling," Pyrrha growled. "Did you see or hear anything?"

"I heard the flapping noise for a moment, that's all. But there were no screams or sounds of any struggle until I got to the treeline—and that was the guard you said got taken," Mira said, while keeping a watchful eye to the heavens.

Pyrrha quickly inspected the other tents. Finding the off-duty guards still asleep, she let out a sigh of relief. "At least they're still here."

She ducked into her tent, and when she returned carrying a handgun, Mira took a step back, fearing what Pyrrha had in store not only for her, but the others still resting.

"Right, Mira, it's time to show you the basics of how to use one of these," she said, removing the gun's magazine and chambered bullet. "You were right. Tomorrow, everyone gets full weapon training. But for tonight, I need you to keep watch on those three."

After a quick tutorial, Pyrrha then strode to the other tents. "Best get back inside. I'm going to wake the others. It's my fault this happened. I pulled one of the guards away to keep an eye on Josh. From now on, nobody walks outside alone."

With the pistol firmly in hand, and casting one more cautious look to the stars, Mira returned to her tent.

CHAPTER SEVENTEEN

RULE BREAKER

Josh watched the captain pull his men together for a short lecture and made a note of the route the new patrols were taking. But then came a gentle tap on the door. When Pyrrha entered the room, he waited for her to speak first.

"Just checking you're OK," she said harshly.

"What's going on?" he grumbled.

"Nothing you will be concerned about. But I'll tell you anyway. Thanks to you running around, one of my people is dead!" she snarled.

"Because of me?"

"I had to pull one of the guards off watching the others in order to keep an eye on you. Did you really think I was unaware you were in the tent with your friends earlier? That I wouldn't notice Mira trying to delay me?"

"I'm sorry. But if you hadn't locked me away, I wouldn't need watching, would I?" he said. "Look, I don't know what's going on with you, and I don't care what you've been told, but let's get one thing straight, shall we? I am not with the Followers, and neither is my brother. I am not interested in you, so cut the flirty act! And unless I'm your prisoner, I can go wherever the hell I like!"

Pyrrha took a step back. "Let's say I believe you... answer me this: are you really the one that can open the tomb on this island?"

"Does it really matter? Look, I won't go to that place. I'm still having nightmares about the last playground we visited, thank you. And I'm pretty sure the others don't want a repeat performance of *An American Werewolf in London*. Now, what's really going on?"

Pyrrha's gaze was still loaded with mistrust, but also confusion. "It doesn't matter."

"No, come on. Why is there a wasp in your underwear? What have my brother and I done for you to stop trusting us so suddenly? C'mon, this isn't about Mr Tripp at all, is it?"

"It's 'bee in your bonnet', Josh." Pyrrha groaned. "Look, forget about it. And I apologise for my behaviour. When we get to our destination, I'm sure all will be set right. Now, we have to work together if we have a chance of leaving this place alive, so please, do me a favour and don't sneak out again tonight. Tomorrow, you can rejoin the others."

She left. Josh sat on the edge of his bunk and listened to the click of the lock. A devilish grin spread across his face.

***

A ray of light appeared under the flap of the tent. Mira lowered her gun when, a moment later, Pyrrha appeared and motioned for her to step outside. But then Pyrrha saw Josh curled up asleep on the ground next to Rachel.

"Does he ever listen to anyone?" she said in a low growl.

"Rachel, and that's about it," said Mira, also shaking her head at him. She handed back the gun. "I know I said we all needed training, but I hate these things. Once, on a holiday to France, I saw the police gun down someone. He probably deserved it, but…"

Pyrrha pressed it back into her hand. "It doesn't matter if you hate them, it could save your life."

She led Mira outside. "Right then, you now know the basics, but you need to be fast and precise when reloading, and you need to ensure that when the target is in sight, you remain calm. Control your breathing and keep both eyes on the target. Don't shoot at just anything."

Mira studied the weapon. "Fine," she murmured. Then, she met Pyrrha's eyes. "Before we start, I saw the lipstick on Josh's neck. What did he tell you?"

Pyrrha flushed. "It's not what you think. I swear. But either he doesn't know anything of what I revealed to you, or he's more intelligent than I gave him credit for. Either way, as I told him, it doesn't matter now. When we get to our destination, the truth will come out. We have something very special at the sanctuary that never fails to encourage people to talk. Now, get your friends. We don't have much time, and I only want to do this tutorial once."

Wearily, Mira made her way toward the tent. She pondered upon what Pyrrha could possibly possess that would prise the truth from someone, but her thoughts were brought to an abrupt standstill when Rachel threw open the tent flap. Mira knew what Rachel was thinking. It was written clearly across her face. Anticipating that her best friend would act first and ask questions later, she intercepted Rachel to give Pyrrha room to manoeuvre out of her reach.

Unfazed by Mira's attempt to block her path, Rachel swiftly placed her hands around her waist, lifted her up and placed her back down well out of the way.

"From now on," Rachel growled, standing nose to nose with Pyrrha, "stay away from my boyfriend!" She grabbed one of the handguns that had been laid out on a portable pull-out table and, to Mira's relief, stomped to the target range that Pyrrha had set up.

Hearing Rachel's raised voice, Josh lumbered out of the tent next. "Best not use live ammunition, Pyrrha. Otherwise, we're both done for."

Pyrrha closed her eyes. Her cheeks were once again bright red. Mira again wondered what had truly happened between her and Josh. But this was clearly not the time to ask. Instead, when Kyle and Jo made an appearance, she gave Pyrrha a nudge to start the training.

***

Pyrrha spent the entire morning showing them, first as a group and then on an individual basis, how to correctly hold, aim, load and unload each of the weapons she'd brought. Once she was confident that all of them could handle the firearms proficiently, she then took the weapons away, assuming that boredom had already infiltrated the group. She was immediately met with a loud groan from the company.

"What's the point in showing us if we can't have them?" Jo complained.

This statement took the group by surprise. Jo, like Mira, had also expressed, vehemently, a dislike of the use or ownership of firearms.

"They are only to be used in an emergency," Pyrrha replied gruffly.

"Any sign of the guard who was supposed to be guarding us?" Mira asked, not wanting to hide it from the others.

Pyrrha shook her head.

"What's happened now?" Rachel and Jo asked in unison.

"Three guards were taken by something last night. Mira watched over you, but from tonight, you'll sleep on the ship."

"With that thing out there in the water? That's crazy!" Rachel shrieked.

As they were about to head for the ship, Jo called the group back. "You know you said that there were no signs? I think you need to check this out." She pointed to the long grass near to where she was standing. "If I'm not mistaken, it looks awfully like blood to me."

Pyrrha examined the blades of grass and followed the droplets of blood. Mira soon realised that they appeared to be heading in the direction of the large statue to the north-east. But the trail soon petered out, and Pyrrha insisted they all follow her back to the ship. Mira felt the knot in her stomach growing. She took one last look back to the grassy hill, and beyond to the huge statue.

If that is where the temple lies, how long before I get taken there?

CHAPTER EIGHTEEN

SHADOWS OF THINGS TO COME

The mood on the bridge was sombre as the teens watched Pyrrha lead her diminished group of soldiers back through the forest.

"Wonder if we will ever see her again?" said Josh, leaning across the control console and resting his hands on his chin.

Rachel tightly folded her arms. "Oh, and I bet you would be really sorry not to see her again."

"Oh, for Pete's sake," Josh groaned. "Of course I'll be sorry if she doesn't come back. Captain Blight might just take it upon himself and kill us all," he said, clearly agitated that he was not going with her.

Jo, who had been staring solemnly out toward the ocean, turned her head sharply toward Josh. "Don't you mean Bligh?"

Josh blew out his cheeks. "Bligh? Who's Bligh?"

"The captain of the ship, the *Bounty*." Jo waited for Josh to show some sign of recognition of the name. When it didn't come, she slapped her hand hard on the back of the captain's chair. *Mutiny on the Bounty?* Don't tell me you don't even know that?"

"No, he means Blight," said Kyle. "He was our PE instructor in school. A complete psycho who made us call him 'Captain' instead of 'sir'."

Josh shook his head. "No, I was referring to that mutiny guy. He was a complete nutjob, too, wasn't he? Killed all his passengers or something? But I forgot about Blighty. Nice one, Kaiboy."

"Captain Bligh didn't kill the passengers or something," said Jo, slapping her forehead. "That's it. Kyle, I'm going to ask you again. Was your brother hit a lot as a child?"

"No, it's only been lately." Kyle eyed Rachel's hand.

Jo shook her head. "Well, if we ever do get home, Josh, I suggest you visit your doctor."

"Don't have a go at him!" Rachel snapped. "If it wasn't for him, I would be dead. And if it wasn't for him making me laugh, then I would probably have killed myself having to listen to you all the time, Miss Bloody Boring Know-it-all!"

Josh grinned. "I make you laugh?"

"Shut up, Josh, I'm speaking now. And don't think I've forgiven you for allowing Pyrrha to sit on a bed with you! Now, Little Miss Smarty-pants, any more cracks about my boyfriend and you'll have me to deal with, OK?"

Jo backed away to the corner of the room. "OK, OK. Sorry, Josh."

"It's OK, Jo. I know—"

"Shut up, Josh! I've made my point!" said Rachel, dragging him to the other side of the room.

Mira, who had been listening quietly, slammed her hand down on the console. "*Enough!* Jeez! How many times do I have to say it? If we start bickering between ourselves, it will provide this group we are stuck with an advantage over us. We have to hold it together. We beat the last island and we shall beat this one. But only if we are united as one!"

Rachel and Jo reluctantly mumbled their apologies, but Mira had already turned her attention to the ship's controls. "Jo, do you think you could drive this thing? There appears to be a lot of buttons. More than were on Pyrrha's boat, at least."

Jo gingerly got to her feet and studied the layout. "Yes. It has a steering wheel and throttle. The only real difference is that this ship also has a joystick to direct extra rudders, it seems. You know, to move the ship sideways. But what's the point if that thing is still out there?"

"Because," Mira answered calmly, "if they don't come back, we may have to make a run for it, that's all."

Jo's breathing quickened. "Have you had a vision, or a dream?"

Mira shook her head. "No, but that reminds me—did any of you dream last night?" She scanned her friends' faces in anticipation.

"I didn't," said Jo.

"Nor me," said Kyle.

Josh also shook his head, but Rachel was silent. Kyle nudged Mira's arm.

Mira quietly prompted her again. "Rach, did you dream?"

"Yes, I dreamed, but I don't want to talk about it!"

Oh, here it comes, Mira thought. "Why not?"

"Because—because it wasn't very nice!"

Rachel swung open the door to the bridge and marched out. Swiftly pursuing, Mira attempted to grab her arm but missed.

"Rach, what was it?" she called out after her. "We need to know."

"No, you really don't!" said Rachel, continuing to storm ahead.

Mira followed her to the cabin, and when Rachel flopped down on one of the beds, Mira shuffled the guard, who was looking around in his lockbox, out of the room, telling him they were going to take a shower.

The door closed, and Mira turned back to face Rachel. *OK, she's my friend, but I have to be firm with her now!* She took a deep breath. "Rach, if it's bad, we need to be prepared."

Rachel dropped her head onto the pillow. "It wasn't about this bloody place. I dreamed that I was married to Josh. It's a couple of years from now. Everything is peaceful. But then, out of the blue, word comes that there's a book we need to find. Before we can retrieve it, however, we all get separated. A battle ensues and... and some of us get taken hostage. There's a long bridge—deep underground. Fire and brimstone are around us. Like the picture of Dante's Inferno. But there is also a great ocean. I can see hundreds, no, thousands of different faces, but I only recognise some. There are screams of pain and suffering. Then you show up. You have a book in your hand. But they won't listen to you. And—and we are then forced to watch as innocent people are sent to their death in a swirling pool of lava."

Mira froze. Rachel had just described what she had seen in Pandora's tomb. She wiped the perspiration from her hands. "That's what I've seen... But what was the book?"

Rachel sat up, but one of her legs trembled. "I have no idea. But it seemed really important. You were holding it aloft and waving it around."

With this hanging over their heads, as well as the uncertainty of what they could be facing on the island, Mira knew she had to say something positive. She took a seat next to Rachel and held her hand. "I think these dreams and visions are a blessing, Rach. Someone or something is helping us. Preparing us for what could happen. Now that we're aware, we can do something about it. Make sure it doesn't come to pass." She forced a smile.

Rachel threw her arms around Mira's shoulders and began to laugh. "You're right. Me, marry Josh! Ha! That's never going to happen."

Mira rose to her feet, but when Rachel placed her hand onto the pillow to steady her, she felt something hard beneath. Slowly, she slipped her hand under the pillow until her fingers made contact with the object. Rachel's smile turned to a snarl as she swiftly revealed her discovery.

"Look! The crafty git has got a gun already. I thought I saw Josh pick something up off the beach when we landed! Right, then, if things do get back to normal, I now have this to kill him with when I'm in my forties and he leaves me for a cheerleader half my age."

Mira laughed. "I doubt he'll ever leave you, Rach. He slept on the floor beside your bed all night like a little watchdog. He knows what he's got. He won't cheat."

When they arrived back on the bridge, Rachel flopped into the captain's chair and turned her head away from Jo, who still had her head lowered as she bit down on her fingernails. Mira joined Kyle and Josh at the window.

"See, if we go now, even though we have a short window of time, we should be able to slip through," said Josh.

"But what if there are guards in among the trees?" Kyle whispered back.

"Nah, I counted them when we arrived." Josh winked. "There were sixteen, including Pyrrha and the captain. Four have gone missing, four are with Pyrrha, there's four patrolling the shoreline, and the captain is keeping watch just inside the treeline. There was also a woman Pyrrha pulled from the water when we landed—Laurie, I think she called her—and a man who must be a scout, because I haven't seen him come back since, either."

Kyle grimaced. "This Laurie could be with the scout, or perhaps she was taken by those things as well. What really concerns me is where they are exactly. The possibility of bumping into Pyrrha's group when, or if, they return… I don't know, Josh, it sounds too risky."

Mira stepped between them. "What's going on?"

"Josh still thinks we should go have a look around the island and get our bearings, just in case," said Kyle.

"Are you nuts, Josh?" said Rachel, and leaping from her seat, she unleashed a mind-blowing slap to his arm.

It wasn't just Josh that winced this time. Everyone, it seemed, felt the full force of her blow.

"*OUCH!*" Josh cried, rubbing his arm. "Listen, you mental case, the more we know about this place, the better chance we have of surviving. I'm not suggesting that we go anywhere near that sepulchre, temple, crypt-type thingy, but when have our plans to not do something ever gone right?"

Rachel's eyes were still daggers. "But we don't have any weapons to defend ourselves—or do we?"

Mira knew exactly what Rachel was hinting at. Would Josh own up to having hidden the gun under the pillow?

He grinned. "Last night, I watched Pyrrha put the weapons away in her tent in a locked box, and I saw the code that she entered."

"You were in her tent?!" Rachel screeched.

At that precise moment, Mira quickly grabbed Rachel's bag with the loaded weapon inside off her shoulder.

"*No, nooo,*" said Josh, backing away out of her reach. "I just thought if something happens to her, it would be good to have access to the weapons. That's all, I swear."

Rachel prowled around him. "Did you watch her get undressed?"

"*Jeez*, no—what do you take me for?" Josh pleaded. "Besides, she didn't get undressed. I don't think she ever bloody sleeps. Ah, no, that came out wrong. She left the tent and went back to the ship and that's all she did, I promise—"

"Josh, stop talking. Please, stop talking," said Kyle, massaging his temple.

"I found the gun, Josh!" Rachel cried.

Josh was now wide-eyed. "What gun?"

"The one you hid under your pillow!"

Jo stood up. "I'm sorry, it was me. I found it on the beach. I was going to tell you, but after my performance on the last island, I figured you would all panic if you knew I had it. Look, I'm happy for any one of you to keep it, except Josh. We need someone mature who won't use it needlessly."

"And if we are sharing secrets," said Mira, "to be honest, Rach, Lassie there"—she inclined her head toward Josh—"didn't go into Pyrrha's tent. Not in the sense you're thinking."

"How do you know?" Rachel said, still eyeing Josh's inflamed arm.

Mira felt relieved that she could unburden herself of this to her friend.

"Last night, when Pyrrha gave me a gun, I went back outside and took a walk around the camp. When I came back, I saw her enter her tent. I also saw Josh sneaking a look inside before quickly entering ours. He was there only for a brief moment, Rach. Definitely not long enough to watch her get undressed."

"See, innocent again." Josh grinned. "Now you have to admit I'm right about taking a good look at this island. Our lives may depend on it."

"I'm not sure," said Mira. "If we get caught, we'll definitely all be locked up."

Josh paced the room. "OK, I'll go alone. Pyrrha knows that I will, and then at least the rest of you won't be in any trouble."

"No," Rachel snarled. "If you go, I'm coming with you."

Not wanting anyone to go—and a little shocked Kyle hadn't tried to stop them or volunteered to do it himself—Mira was about to attempt to dissuade them but was interrupted by Jo.

"For once, I have to agree with Josh," she said. "I want to go as well. I know I never believed any of you, and I know what I did back on the last island, but since I saw that thing out there in the sea and had that weird dream… I think we are meant to go to that crypt. I don't know for sure, but I get the feeling we aren't going to be able to leave otherwise."

Jo was clearly scared—but was she right? Would it be better to get it over with?

"So, do we all go or just us three?" Josh asked finally.

Mira stood by the window and gazed out at the forest. "We all go. But let's leave it until tomorrow. We'll go at first light. I don't fancy wandering around in the dark again."

CHAPTER NINETEEN

CAN'T STOP THE FEELING

It was late afternoon when Pyrrha returned. After a brief discussion with the captain, she entered the bridge. Mira knew immediately by her body language that the news wasn't going to be good.

"We've had a good look around. Unfortunately, there's no sign of my people or anything else, so we definitely stay on the ship from now on," said Pyrrha, looking each of them pointedly in the eye, making it clear this was an order not a request.

"You're not going to leave them out there, are you?" Mira asked, surprised.

"There are no tracks. What else do you suggest we do?"

"Keep looking until you do find them," said Josh.

"It's too risky," said Pyrrha firmly.

"Can I at least go and get the pack of cards from the tent?" said Jo. "Otherwise, it's going to be a long night waiting for your friends to save us."

Pyrrha's personal guard escorted Jo back to the tent while everyone else, now very hungry, were taken back to the cabin.

As Rachel and Josh once again whispered sweet nothings together, Mira and Kyle stood at the window, awaiting Jo's return.

"What do you think about what Jo said?" he asked her.

"I don't really know. It's nice that she finally believes us, but can she truly be trusted? She didn't inform us about the gun straightaway. Then again, if the last island has proved anything, we're not going to leave this one until she—and Rachel, by the looks of it—do their thing. Look, I know you said you don't trust your own thoughts, but what's your gut instinct?"

"I'm starting to think that either we're causing all these bad things to happen despite our efforts to prevent them, or that we've never really had any control to begin with," he said. "Perhaps scoping the island, as Josh suggests, *is* the right move. If we can get rid of these flying things and find enough food and water to last us until the comet goes, maybe it would be better to just stay here. Without you, the Followers can't open the coffin, and now that we know who can open the one here, we could ensure everyone's safety by avoiding it. But look, I've told you—whatever you want to do, I'll back you."

For a brief moment, the thought of staying did sound appealing to Mira. *If Mum and Dad and Jacen were here, and with Kyle by my side, would it be so bad?*

But the thought of Jacen, scared and alone, quickly helped her come to a decision. "We have to leave. I need to get Jacen back." Then, another thought came to her. "Although—as I've already said, it's obvious we're here for a reason, right?"

Kyle nodded.

"What if we've been brought here to release the very thing that can stop Pandora? If they were meant to be together, maybe their love will lift the curse?"

Kyle smiled softly. "I don't think this a Disney fairytale, Mira. I can see no happy ending when it comes to Pandora, sorry."

"OK, then what if we can find another way off this island and then use this tomb's location as a bargaining tool to get Jacen back? We take the contents out first, of course."

Kyle stared out of the window. "Do you really want to take the chance in opening the tomb? Besides, the Followers would want proof first, before giving up Jacen... OK, you want my opinion, I say we check the island first, then see how things pan out. Like I said, I don't think we have much say anymore on what is going to happen."

Mira nodded and rested her head on his shoulder. But despite everything, she still believed that releasing Epimetheus was the right thing to do.

***

Dusky shadows crept along the shore. There was still no sign of Jo returning, and panic was taking hold of the group once more. As Rachel banged at the locked door, Josh climbed out of the window and headed through the treeline, making his way for the tents. When Kyle made no attempt to follow him, Mira mounted the sill instead, but had to immediately jump back down and close the window when she heard the lock on the door being opened.

It was Pyrrha. "They never made it to the tents, and it's getting too dark to send a patrol," she said, clearly agitated. "But I promise, at first light, we will go looking for them."

"That's too late," said Mira. "She could be miles away by then if one of those things took her."

"I'm sorry, but I can't risk losing anyone else, and—" Pyrrha scanned the room. "Where the hell is Josh?"

"Umm…" Rachel thought quickly. "He needed the loo and there was no one outside to unlock the door."

Pyrrha stormed to the window and slapped her hand on the pane of glass.

"He's gone back to the tents to look for her, hasn't he?"

"No, no… Oh, what the heck. Yes," said Rachel, with a shrug.

"I have to give it to you, Rach," Pyrrha growled, "if he was my boyfriend, I would have killed him by now!"

Dread was now searing through Mira's chest. "I'm going after him," she said sternly. "Give me a gun and I'll go alone."

"No, you won't. I'm going, too!" said Rachel.

Pyrrha hesitated for a moment, then handed over her weapon. "Fine. I know you'll just climb out after him, and I don't have anyone to watch over you lot now. Mira, it will be just the two of us that go to look for them—agreed?"

Rachel stamped her foot. "Then leave the bloody door unlocked this time, because I'm not climbing out of a window to go to the toilet or peeing in that shower!"

As Mira was about to leave, Kyle pulled her back. "I'll go. Mum will kill me if I don't." He gave her a half smile.

At last, he was making a comeback. Mira felt some relief at that.

***

When Kyle and Pyrrha arrived back at the campsite, neither was surprised to find Josh running in and out of the tents.

"She's not here, and the pack of cards is still in the tent," he called out to them, "so we know they didn't get this far."

Just seeing his brother lifted one great weight from Kyle's shoulders. "We know."

"So where do we start looking, then?"

"We can't go now, Josh," said Pyrrha. "It's too dark to see or track anything."

Josh finally snapped. "I'm not going back till I've found her!"

Better do something, Kyle thought. *Mum will kill me if I let him go alone. Even she knows there's no stopping him once he gets an idea inside his head...* "Josh, listen to me, just this once. I promise, as soon as the sun comes up, I will go with you, and we won't come back unless she's with us. But if you go now, you're on your own. I mean it this time, and you know that will break Mum's heart."

Josh's eyes filled with rage. "Swear to me, Kaiboy! As soon as the sun comes up, we look for her."

"I swear," said Kyle, stepping away. He'd only seen his brother completely lose his cool twice before, and it wasn't a pretty sight.

Pyrrha threw her head back and closed her eyes. "Then you're going to need a weapon."

"I got one already, thanks," said Josh, holding the gun aloft before disappearing back through the trees.

Kyle could feel Pyrrha's eyes boring a hole into the back of his head. "Don't look at me like that," he said. "You've had a couple of days with him—I've had him all my life."

Pyrrha entered her tent. When she returned with a bag full of weapons, Kyle laughed out loud. "You know he'll discover where you hide them, don't you?"

"I swear, Kyle, if he so much as touches this bag, I will break his bloody neck," she growled, storming past.

***

Kyle entered the cabin and handed out guns to Mira and Rachel. Pyrrha left the room, but this time she left the door slightly ajar.

"Right, do we give it five or ten minutes before setting off?" Josh asked, peeking around the door to make sure nobody was listening.

Kyle's jaw dropped, incredulous at his brother's bravado. "We just agreed when the sun comes up?"

"Oh, I thought that was for Pyrrha's benefit. Look, it will be too late by morning. I say we all go now?" Josh looked to Mira and Rachel for support.

"I agree," said Rachel. "I would hope if I got taken that you would come after me straightaway."

"She's right, Kyle," said Mira, heading for the door. "We can't leave Jo."

Outvoted, Kyle stomped across the room. "Fine, so where do we start looking?"

"I think you know the answer to that already, Kaiboy." Josh grinned. "We go to the sepulchre."

ACT II

CHAPTER TWENTY

THE SEARCH FOR JO BEGINS

After a brief deliberation, it was agreed that Josh, the escape artist, should lead the company out through the ship. A small number of guards were patrolling the shoreline, and Josh watched them for his opportunity. When he saw it, he motioned for the others to follow.

The group kept low, as Josh instructed, and once they were clear of the rear of the ship and into the forest, they made their way out into the open field.

But the sound of flapping wings suddenly descended upon them.

They darted back into the trees, hoping the dense foliage would hide them. Warily, they looked up. This time, they could just make out human-like forms flying and swooping above.

"I know what they are," Josh whispered, closing his eyes. "Did you see the horns? They're called herpes."

"For goodness' sake, Josh! Even I know it's pronounced harpies!" Rachel scowled.

Josh flashed a look to where Rachel was crouched among the tall ferns surrounding the trees. "That's what I said. Anyway, Pyrrha is right. These things do still exist."

"Oh, I don't fancy running across open land with them flying about," said Mira.

The creatures were now no longer in sight, but as the group edged out of the forest, the sound of gunshots began to ring out. It was coming from the ship.

Kyle turned back toward the forest. "We have to go back and help."

"No, now is our chance," said Josh. "If those things are attacking the boat, then it gives us time to run to that other forest we saw!"

Mira inhaled deeply. *You have to take charge again.* "He's right, Josh. We can't just leave—we have to help them."

Josh threw his hands in the air. "What about Jo? We can't leave her!"

"We'll have a better chance in the daylight," said Kyle. "It looks like these things only come at night."

Josh turned to leave. "OK, you all go back, and I'll go look for her then!"

"Why are you so keen to find her?" Rachel asked, pulling him back. "She likes women, Josh. Not men—and certainly not crazy boys!"

Josh's mouth fell open. "What? *Jeez*, no—I don't like her in that way. It's just, with Linus being a psycho, Lyssa and Peter dead… I can't lose another friend. Oh my God, I just called Jo my friend."

I have to stop him, Mira thought. *Say something!* "I don't think it's her fate to die on this island, Josh," she blurted out.

Josh stopped and slowly turned toward her. "How do you know?"

As Mira struggled to bring herself to say what she'd seen in Pandora's tomb, Josh began to stride ahead. Reluctantly, Mira called out to him. "Because—because I've seen what happens to her, alright!"

Josh turned back. There was an intensity in his eyes she hadn't seen before. "What do you mean, you've seen what happens to her?"

This is it, you have to tell him. "Back at the other tomb, I told you I saw things. But please, let's leave it at that."

Josh's eye began to twitch. "No, no way! Have you seen what will happen to us as well?" he fumed, prompting Rachel to stand between them. "No, Rach, I want to know. I mean, she's wanted to tell us. Now's her chance."

Mira dropped her head. She knew at that moment, if she didn't tell him, then she'd lose Kyle and Rachel's trust as well. "Fine, I'll tell you. But when we find Jo, you can't let her know. Deal?"

***

Josh and Rachel stood together, mouths ajar. Kyle, on the other hand, just quietly stared at her. Mira held her breath, anticipating that all three would turn their backs on her.

"That's mental," Josh gasped. "Why would she do it? After what happened on the last island, she'd be crazy to attempt it again. Are you sure?"

"Kyle's dream of the storm came true," said Mira. "The island I saw came true. So, yes, I'm pretty sure."

Josh's glare softened, and before Mira knew what was happening, he'd thrown his arms around her, squeezed her tight then turned back toward the ship. "I hope you're right and wrong at the same time."

The gunshots were growing louder, and as the group exited the treeline, they saw Pyrrha firing a machine gun into the air. The gunfire was having no effect on the creatures above. Their large, leathery wings were repelling the bullets, protecting their feathered torsos with ease. Instead of trying to help, the group ran back aboard the ship, entered the bridge and watched from behind the thick sheet of glass.

For the next ten minutes, the creatures swooped and zigzagged in tight formation, testing the ship and crew's defences and reactions. But when the captain called out a change in orders, commanding the guards to form a circle, the creatures struck before they could.

CHAPTER TWENTY-ONE

MISSED OPPORTUNITY

The flying menace were gone. One guard had been taken, high into the night sky. Another lay injured, blood seeping from the open wound on her leg. As the remaining guards formed a line of defence on the deck of the ship, Pyrrha and the captain assisted the wounded soldier to the medical room. Everyone on the bridge took a nervous seat, all except for Josh. His gaze was firmly fixed on the forest. The desperation in his eyes revealed not only grief, but inner rage.

"Mira, I'm sorry I got angry," he said sombrely. "But we should have gone after Jo when we had the chance."

Rachel was shaking. "Did you see what they did to that poor man? They tore him in two." She gagged. "What is wrong with us? We should be hiding somewhere. Are we becoming desensitised to everything that's happening around us?"

"Hiding from it won't help us, Rach," said Josh. "Best get used to it."

Rachel slammed her hand against the window. "I don't want to get used to it. I don't want violence to become just a normal thing in my life, thank you!"

Mira knew she would have to calm the group if they were going to go look for Jo. "Look, they killed that man straightaway. And now you know it's not Jo's time to die and that we can prevent it from happening. This will all stop once we get away from this place. So, from now on, only positive thoughts, everyone. We will get Jo back. Look, it's getting light out. Those… things… will probably be asleep soon."

"Yeah, let's hope it's not on a full stomach," said Josh.

***

The sun rose into a cloudless sky. Pyrrha finally entered the bridge, followed by the captain.

"What were you lot planning to do?" he growled. "Don't deny it, I saw you out on deck!"

What he had seen was them returning to the bridge.

Rachel shot from her seat. "Don't you take that tone with us! We thought we could help, that's all!"

"You can't help," the captain replied, equally aggressively. "Their skin is like dragon hide. I hit one of those things square in its chest with my Remington. It didn't even slow it down."

"I'm not surprised, if you only tossed your electric shaver at it," said Josh.

The captain's eyes bulged with murderous intent. "SHOTGUN! Here we are, trying to protect you, putting our lives on the line… Look, if you can't do what you're told, why should my people put their lives at risk?"

"Yeah, well, next time we won't try to help, then," said Rachel, "and I'm sorry for your people, but just so you know, we didn't ask for any of this."

Pyrrha attempted to escort the captain from the room. "I'm sorry, too," she said. "But we can't afford to lose any more of us. From now on, we all stay on the ship and wait for rescue."

"I'm not staying here!" said Josh. "Jo's my friend!"

"Friend?" Pyrrha snorted. "You're always hurling insults at one another."

"So?" said Josh. "That doesn't mean I'm going to leave her to get eaten. I say we look for her, and then your people won't get hurt. Right, Kaiboy?"

Kyle's head was lowered, staring at the floor. "Just do what they say, Josh."

"You know we can't allow you to go," Pyrrha said, scowling. "Open the tomb and it's sure to be the end of us."

"I say we lock them in the cargo hold. There's no way out of there," said the captain, looking back over his shoulder.

Time was being wasted, and Josh had had enough. "Yeah, I'd like to see you try, Thanos!"

It was as if Josh had antagonised a bull. With a loud snort, the captain turned on him and, stretching to his full height, stomped forward until he was standing in front of Josh.

Josh didn't move. Instead, he stood his ground and stared up into the blazing furnace that was now glaring down upon him.

"Oh, wait," said the captain, the veins in his neck popping. "You're just the little boy with a big mouth—"

Before the captain could say another word, Kyle got to his feet and stepped between them. "Get away from my brother!"

The captain shot him a threatening glare. "Ah, the real tough guy finally makes an appearance. Well, what are you gonna do, boy?"

But it wasn't Kyle who responded to the threat.

"Not him." Josh smirked. "Her."

The captain turned his head to where Josh was pointing. When he saw Mira with her gun aimed directly at his face, his jaw dropped and his whole body shrank.

"Now listen to me, little girl, you don't want to pull that trigger, do you?"

Slowly, Pyrrha inched toward Mira. But Pyrrha hadn't considered Rachel's reaction.

"Let's not allow things to get out of hand, shall we?" said Rachel coolly, her own gun pointed to the back of Pyrrha's head.

A river of sweat poured from the captain's brow. Slowly, he raised his hands. "I told you it was a bad idea to give them weapons."

Pyrrha held out her empty palms as a gesture for everyone to calm down. "Mira, I promise you won't get locked up, but you know what will happen if you enter that place. None of you will be able to stop yourselves from opening it. And we have writings that tell us that the dangers in this place are worse than the last."

"We stopped ourselves the last time," said Josh. "But if you think we're going to leave Jo behind—our friend—think again!"

The standoff dragged into a silent eternity.

"Pyrrha, what if you come with us?" Mira asked finally. "If any of us so much as tries to open the tomb, then you can, you know... shoot us?"

Pyrrha threw the captain a sideways glance. With a slow nod of his head, reluctantly, Pyrrha agreed.

"But if you're not back when the rescue boats get here," said the captain, "then you're stuck here forever!"

CHAPTER TWENTY-TWO

MISCONSTRUE

After an hour, preparations were complete. Each member of the search party was given a backpack filled with food and water, and Pyrrha led them through the forest and past the tents.

"So, where have you looked, then?" Kyle asked.

"We got as far as the river," said Pyrrha. "But there are things in there making it impossible to cross. To the south and west of this island there is only the ocean, so we shall follow the fields to the east and see if there is anything else around. If not, then we'll head north for the river and see if there's a crossing further upstream."

The company walked for a few hours, but after seeing nothing but high cliffs and long grass, they all sat and took a break.

"Wish I had a—" Josh began.

"Oh, don't say it," said Rachel.

Josh wheeled his head around. "What? I was only going to say I wish I had a camera right now. No one is going to believe all this if we ever get home."

Rachel looked down bashfully. "Oh. I thought you were going to ask for a Mars bar," she mumbled. "So, err, Pyrrha. Who is that monument dedicated to?" She pointed to the statue rising above the hills in the distance.

Pyrrha gave only a fleeting glance. "I don't know. There were many gods that were worshipped. It could be any one of them."

Mira sensed that Pyrrha did know who it was, but she suddenly wanted to know something more important. "Why was Epimetheus buried here? Why wasn't he buried at your sanctuary, where you could keep an eye on the tomb?"

Pyrrha didn't respond. Instead, she just kept rummaging in her backpack.

This ruffled Mira. Why wouldn't she just answer a simple question? Mira knew she'd have to be tactful if she was to get a positive response. She gently placed her hand on Pyrrha's arm. "You want us to trust you, right?"

Pyrrha sighed. "This is where the Disciples originate from. When Epimetheus was locked away, the... the great flood came. Many Disciples were killed. Those that survived moved on. Some went to Egypt, others to a more secure location. But those that chose to stay to keep guard..." She paused.

All eyes were now upon her.

Pyrrha rose to her feet and pressed on. "Come on, best not waste any more daylight."

Josh looked around the group. "Is it just me or, when she said, *those that chose to stay*, did anyone else get the impression she actually meant 'were *forced* to stay'?" he asked.

No one responded, yet as they followed behind Pyrrha, Mira could sense they were all thinking the same thing as Josh. What else had Pyrrha possibly misrepresented?

After another two-hour trek, following the huge wall of rock, the company finally detoured, heading for the river and a forest of densely populated firs. It was then

Mira felt they were being watched. Noticing Kyle's body tense, she took his hand and pulled him close.

"Do you think it's Linus?" she whispered.

"Maybe," he said, trying not to be obvious as he scanned the area.

Josh popped his head between them. "Or it's a giant bear."

Rachel's head quickly appeared next. "Why a bear, Josh?"

Josh pointed. "Cos it's a bear."

The group followed his finger. Deep among the brush, a huge brown bear was scraping at the bark of a lone maple tree, searching for sugary sap as two of its cubs foraged for rowan berries.

"I don't want to go any further," said Josh. "There could be more of them deeper in."

Pyrrha indicated a narrow path leading down between the trees. "Look—the ancients that lived here probably used it to avoid the forest."

And following her lead, the company entered the ravine.

"Lucky we were upwind," said Josh. "Bears go protective nuts when they have cubs. I wouldn't want to face an angry mother—I have enough of that at home."

"Bears are meat eaters," said Kyle, "so there must be wildlife. But why haven't we seen any?"

"Probably learned it's safer to stay hidden," said Mira, now thinking that those prey creatures were right.

Finally, the pathway levelled out, and it was then the group realised how deep they had travelled. Glacial potholes had created natural amphitheatres all around them. Everyone stared in wonder as the sun glinted off the rock faces. The different shades of moss were creating a magical lightshow of various colours.

At first, there appeared to be no way out of the gorge, but the company pushed on, following the sound of water running alongside the rocks. They came to a narrow gap in the wall of rock just wide enough to crawl through. Once through, and after a steep climb, it wasn't long before the group was once again standing in open fields.

The wide river was in sight, but still there was no sign of a crossing in either direction. The company again sat and ate on the rubble of what had once been fully formed buildings. All except Kyle. He stood at the water's edge, his focus on the murky depths. It was only when Mira slipped her hand through the crook of his arm that he stepped away.

"What is it?" she asked.

Kyle glanced back to the group. Josh and Pyrrha were in an argument about whether it would be safer to go back to the ship and get a dingy. Rachel was trying to mediate between them.

Kyle whispered, "I can feel something watching us deep below the waterline. I fear it's going to change everything. But there's something else…" He again looked back over his shoulder. "I don't think Rachel and Jo are the reason we're here. I believe it's only me this island wants."

"Why do you say that?"

Kyle pulled her closer. "I think I've been here before? I know for a fact this river leads into another one further on, and there's a wooden bridge. How would I know that? I haven't dreamed of it—only the town and the sepulchre. Should we ask Josh and Rachel if they're having the same feelings?"

Mira shook her head. "They would have told us already. Especially Josh. But I have something to confess. Since we landed, I've had this constant fear that I'm going to end up at the sepulchre at some point, whether I like it or not." A thought struck her. "Hey, maybe your ancestors came from here and what you're experiencing are past memories, like I had with Pandora. But if you want my advice, wait and see if they have anything else to show you. No need to panic Rachel any more than she already is."

Mira led Kyle back to the group, where the argument was coming to a conclusion.

"Before you get any ideas, Josh," said Pyrrha, "for the last time, the lifeboats are not for taking excursions. Now, let's carry on, there has to be a crossing at some point."

Ensuring that there was no trace of food left behind that could attract the bears or any other wild animal, they carried on following the river until they saw a wooden bridge ahead.

Mira and Kyle shared a glance. Mira could sense his anxiety growing again.

They crossed one at a time and headed onward, up a steep, grassy hill. From the top, they looked down into the valley below, where they could see deer and bighorn grazing.

"Ta-da," said Josh. "There's your wildlife, Kaiboy."

The group ambled down the hill, keeping as far from the herd as possible, and after crossing more open ground, they came to another river and another wooden bridge.

Pyrrha crossed first. "We need to hurry," she called back. "If there is no sign of Jo soon then it would be best if we turned back. We cannot get caught out in the open after dark."

Rachel and Josh crossed next, but when Mira and Kyle followed, Mira noticed that Kyle's pace was now almost a crawl.

"Are you alright?" she asked.

"I feel tired, weak… It's like something doesn't want me going any further."

Suddenly, Rachel called back to them. "C'mon, slow-coaches—the town is just after the bridge. You can rest there."

Pyrrha's eyebrows shot to the heavens. "How do you know that?"

"Oh—um—just a guess." Rachel smiled. "If there's a temple thingy, then there should be buildings close by, right?"

Pyrrha waited for them all to catch up before unleashing her anger.

"Before we go any further," she snarled, "let me be blunt. You are not going into the sepulchre and that's final, understood?"

"But what if Jo's in there?" said Rachel.

"I will go alone. I need you lot to keep this one here out," she said, pointing to Josh.

Josh laughed. "Why only me?"

Pyrrha's beady eyes turned to him. "You can open the tomb, that's why."

He stroked the nape of his neck. "Oh, yeah, right. But you'll need someone to go with you as backup, surely?"

"If I need help, I'll call," she said, and again looked to everyone with fire in her eyes. "And if anyone has a problem with it—tough."

***

They had reached the edge of the town that Rachel had referred to earlier.

On either side of the wide street at the town's centre stood Hellenic-looking, stone buildings arranged in a half-moon formation. It appeared to be deserted.

When they approached, without warning, a grey cloud descended, obscuring the sun.

"Looks like it's about to pee it down," said Josh, flatly.

This prompted deep groans from everyone.

"Right, stay here, and I'll see if there's somewhere we can stay in case it does," said Pyrrha, and she ran on ahead.

"I know we don't trust her completely, but someone should have gone with her," said Kyle.

"Why?" Rachel said, coldly. "She can handle herself."

"She's right," said Josh. "Now's our chance to get inside the sepulchre and see what we're dealing with."

But as the last word left his lips, the sky darkened further, and a cold, cruel breeze whipped past. With the faint sound of flapping wings approaching, and no sign of Pyrrha, the teens ran to the nearest building to take cover.

Mira's heart pumped rapidly. "So, they can come out in the daytime just as long as the sun is obscured," she whispered. "Did anyone see where they came from?"

"Probably out of the crypt. All bad things seem to come out of the places we need to get to," Josh whispered back. "Hey, you don't think this is all a set-up?" he suggested, his eyes bright with the thought that maybe he'd uncovered something that would benefit them.

All eyes were now upon Mira. She had to think quickly. "If Pyrrha wanted us dead, she could have done it plenty of times and she wouldn't have given us weapons. I say we give her the benefit of the doubt. For now, at least."

"I didn't mean Pyrrha," said Josh. "I'm talking about you-know-who. The gods."

Mira shook her head. "If they are setting us up, then going to the tomb is a bad idea. We would be effectively carrying out their wishes."

"In that dream we had," said Kyle, "did you see the harpies, or whatever they are, beyond the waterfall inside the sepulchre, Rach? I don't remember seeing them before we reached it?"

"No, I didn't see them," said Rachel. "But there is something far worse in there, so let's pray Jo isn't beyond the waterfall, shall we?"

"Would you mind clarifying what *is* beyond the waterfall, Rach?" said Josh. "Cos it could be a sure way of keeping me out."

"All I know is that it's really big. Huge, in fact. But I couldn't say what it is exactly. It's like two enormous heads, but I can't make out what they are."

"I don't know about the rest of you, but I'm sold," said Josh.

"You are not going in there," Kyle scoffed.

Josh grinned. "Oh, I'm going in, but I'll be more cautious now."

When the flying creatures had gone and the sun had reappeared, finally Pyrrha found them.

"I'm so sorry," she puffed. "They came so quickly, I couldn't get back to you. We should be safe if we keep quiet." She then led them into an empty building.

"Did you see where those things came from?" Mira asked.

"Yes, they came from the direction of the temple."

"See, I told you," said Josh.

"And you're happy to be right about it?" said Rachel. "Oh, I don't want the last time Jo and I spoke to have been an argument."

Tears welled in Rachel's eyes and Josh threw an arm around her. "Don't worry about it, I'm sure Jo is fine. She either sent them fleeing with one of her interesting stories about comets or dream patterns or, if I know Jo, she's probably got her own throne by now and has them working for her."

Mira couldn't help but be impressed with the way Josh handled terrifying situations and again wondered what had happened to him to make him so resilient in times of peril.

"So, Pyrrha, are you going to check out the temple or what?" he said, interrupting her thoughts.

Pyrrha sat with her back to the wall. "I'll go in the morning," she said, closing her eyes.

"Bit early for sleep time, isn't it?" Kyle asked. "You do know the sun has come back out?"

Pyrrha kept her eyes closed as she pointed to the shadows in the room. "It's too late in the day now to get there and back. I should have paid more attention to the sun's location. Now, I'm going to leave it up to you who stays awake now, and who stays awake later, but we need lookouts at all times."

CHAPTER TWENTY-THREE

PEEK-A-BOO

After a brief discussion, it was decided that Mira and Kyle would try and sleep first. Rachel and Josh agreed to keep a lookout.

The town was in almost complete darkness and as quiet as a graveyard. But when Josh peered out, he spied a human form ducking across the street and into one of the other buildings.

Josh took a step out to gain a better look, but Rachel yanked him back inside.

"You're not going anywhere, Sunshine. Your wandering-off-on-your-own days, from this very moment, are over for you."

"But I think I saw Linus," he said, and pointed across the street.

As Rachel looked toward the dilapidated building, Josh began to get excited.

"Should we take a look?" he whispered.

Rachel gritted her teeth. "No. We can't leave the others unguarded."

"OK then, should I go take a look?" The irresistible urge to investigate was becoming overwhelming.

Rachel stared back incredulously. "What did I just say, Josh? Besides, you're not leaving me unguarded!"

"Oh, come on, I'll only be a couple of minutes." He grinned, hoping his persistence would wear her down.

Rachel's lips were pursed and her cheeks had started to turn purple. A clear indicator to Josh that he'd overstepped the Rachel tolerance line.

Slowly, he began backing away. "OK, OK, no need to get murderous on me, we'll stay here." He thrust his hands into his pockets, looking like a little boy who's been told not to enter a sweet shop by his mother.

***

Three hours later, Kyle and Mira awoke and joined Josh and Rachel at the entrance. Rachel told them about seeing Linus, making sure Pyrrha couldn't hear her.

Mira peered out to the building Rachel had indicated. "Are you sure it was Linus?"

"Not a hundred per cent. But who else could it be?" said Josh. "If you let me go take a look, then we'll know for certain, won't we?"

"No, it's our turn to sleep," said Rachel, and pointed to the back wall.

"But I'm not tired."

Rachel's look terrified even Kyle. "Josh! Take a bloody nap!"

"Fine, I'll take a bloody nap." And with his head lowered, Josh stormed back inside and sat against the wall.

Mira gave Rachel a pat on her back, while Kyle stared open-mouthed. "How do you do it? I've never been able to get him to do anything. Nor Mum and Dad, come to think of it."

"You just have to be firm with him, that's all," Rachel said with a smile, and left to join him.

"I hope to God they get married someday," Kyle whispered.

Mira looked at Rachel and laughed as if she had remembered something.

Kyle couldn't see the funny side. "What? See how he behaves when she's with him, it's like magic."

As Rachel snuggled up and Josh wrapped his arm around her, Kyle again hoped that one day, for his own sanity's sake, she would take him off his hands.

"Did you dream?" Mira asked.

"No. I wonder if we all need to be sleeping at the same time, like when we first arrived?" Kyle whispered, before peeking out around the entrance, thinking he'd heard some movement.

"Then, why didn't we dream last night? I mean, the night before? You know, with the clouds blocking out the sun one minute and then plunging us back into darkness the next, I'm starting to lose track of which day it is," said Mira, squeezing his hand tightly.

Kyle looked across the room to his brother. "I know what you mean. But as to your first question, it wouldn't surprise me if, while the rest of us were asleep, Josh was already looking around the island."

***

When Pyrrha awoke shortly after, Kyle saw his opportunity to find Linus.

"I'm sorry, but I need to pee," he said. "I won't be long."

"Don't wander too far, and make sure you cover it over," said Pyrrha. "Don't want those things picking up the scent."

Once he was out of sight, Kyle sped toward the rear of the building that Josh had seen Linus enter. Cautiously, he crept inside and navigated through the rooms until he could see a figure kneeling down and peering out of a small crack in the wall.

"Look, you'd better find somewhere else to hide, because if Pyrrha sees you, she's likely to kill you," he said, still feeling anger toward Linus for what he had done to his mother and brother.

Linus spun around. His face was as white as a sheet. "Oh man, you scared me. Look, I had to find one of ya—you're heading in the wrong direction if you're looking for Jo."

"How do you know about Jo?" Kyle asked warily.

"I saw those flying things carry her away. There are two different kinds. The ones that passed over here earlier, well, they're real nasty, but the ones I saw carrying Jo, I think they're different."

The hairs on Kyle's arm stood to attention. "What makes you think that?"

"She didn't seem distressed. I know you don't trust me, Kyle, and you have every right not to, but Jo was my friend and I'm going to see if I can get to her. I just thought you should know. And if you do go, follow the river back the way you came, but keep to this side of the bank and then make for the pyramid. Trust me, you can't miss it."

Kyle hands were now clenched. "Linus, you'd better not be lying to me."

"I'm not, I swear. Just stay away from this temple. I thought of seeking refuge in there and only just managed to get away from those red-eyed demons. I also got the feeling that there are things in there, man, and not necessarily alive. Look, just get Jo and get as far away from this island as you can, please!"

Then Linus left, and Kyle didn't stop him. He was left with his thoughts.

Can I trust him? He looked sincere. But he looked sincere after getting his brother killed… No. That was another look. There was something else behind his eyes then. So, what to do…? Get Jo back, alive.

When Kyle returned, Pyrrha was waiting outside with her arms crossed. "Took your time. I was about to come look for you," she fumed. "Where the hell did you go?"

"I had stage fright. Last thing you want is to be abducted when you're peeing. I'd never live it down if Josh found out. And I agreed with you about leaving a scent, so I went somewhere else."

Kyle went back inside and sat with his back to the wall in order to escape Pyrrha's look of mistrust and an impending interrogation. He pondered on what Linus had said and wondered how he could check out his story without raising Pyrrha's suspicions.

Suddenly, something else occurred to him. A thought that caused his hands to shake. If there really was a pyramid, he began to suspect that—just like the river, bridge and gorge—he'd seen it before.

CHAPTER TWENTY-FOUR

PLAN B

Just before dawn, Kyle, who had returned to guard duty, heard the distant undulation of wings overhead. He nudged Mira's arm, and they both peeked out of the building and watched the creatures fly toward the sepulchre.

"Oh, thank God, they're not carrying anyone this time," Mira said, visibly relieved.

"And the sun should be coming up soon," Pyrrha added. "We'd better make an early start if we're going to get anywhere today."

"I've been thinking as well," said Kyle. "You were right about bringing Josh with us. It was a bad idea. If that place is what you say it is, he could be a handful if he cracks. But I also don't want to leave Jo if she is in there... I say we send Josh and Rachel back to the ship, you go and check out that tomb, and Mira and I will wait here for you?"

Pyrrha shot him a suspicious look. "You really think that Josh will go back? I thought you knew him better than that."

"If Rachel goes back, trust me, Josh will do what she says."

"OK, but I think it would be better if you and Mira came with me," said Pyrrha. "But only to the outside. I thought of what you said, too. It would be better to have backup if needed."

Kyle knew he now had to think up a plan B, and fast. As Mira and Pyrrha headed into the street, he went to awaken Josh and Rachel.

"Listen, I spoke with Linus—" Kyle abruptly stopped speaking. He could hear footsteps approaching. "Damn. Josh, just this once go along with what I say and follow my lead," he whispered.

As Rachel and Josh, looking tired and bewildered, unsteadily got to their feet, Pyrrha entered the room. "Are we set?" she asked rather briskly, in expectation of a positive response.

"It would be better if you went back, Josh," said Kyle. "Pyrrha's right. This is the worst place you can be right now. Rach, can you go back with him, and we three will go on and find Jo?"

"No way! I'm coming," said Josh. "She's my friend too!"

At least Josh's stubbornness made it seem authentic.

"Josh, I think we need to go back," said Rachel. "Actually, I *want* to go back. My stomach doesn't feel right…"

Thank you, Rach, Kyle thought.

"No, we're coming with you!" said Josh, pushing past his brother. "And the fresh air will do you good, Rach. No good will come from staying on that bloody ship all the time."

Kyle nervously looked to Rachel, imploring her to get Josh away from here.

"Fine—I'm going back on my own then!" Rachel shouted after him.

Josh stopped in the doorway to the building. His shoulders slumped. "Fine. I'll take you back," he replied, clearly conflicted and frustrated.

Kyle released an inner sigh of relief.

Josh and Rachel waved goodbye and headed off toward the river. Kyle ran back along the street after Mira. But as Pyrrha stuck close at his side, he began to suspect that she knew what they were up to.

Just as they reached the middle of the long street, he subtly checked that Josh and Rachel were out of sight, then turned sharply and began to make his way back toward the river. "I'll have to catch you up," he called back. "I want to give Josh my father's watch just in case I don't make it."

And before Pyrrha could stop him, he increased his pace.

There was no sign of Rachel and Josh at the river. Kyle ran across the second bridge just in time to see them crossing the field in the direction of the first bridge.

"Where the hell are you going?" he said, gasping, as he caught them up.

"You said go back." said Josh.

"I just meant until Pyrrha was out of sight."

Josh looked at him blankly.

"You know what, never mind. As I said, I spoke with Linus last night and he says he saw a different kind of those flying things heading toward a pyramid the other side of the river. Now, I don't know if we can trust him, so keep your wits about you. Better if you two check it out while Mira and I keep Pyrrha busy. If Jo is OK, take her back to the ship and wait for us to return. But—and I stress this—if it looks too dangerous, then the *both* of you go to the ship anyway, and when we get back we'll then sneak away and get her together. We're gonna check out this sepulchre and return to you as soon as possible."

Without waiting for an answer, Kyle hugged them both then ran back toward the town, hoping he wasn't now putting their lives at risk.

***

Pyrrha led the way to the end of the street and up another grassy hill. Ahead, the monument stood as tall as a high-rise. Below it, to the right, was the entrance to the sepulchre.

"It looks more like a temple than a tomb," said Mira warily.

As they drew nearer, they could see the four huge columns of a colonnade, smaller in size than the one built out of the rock face on the first island.

"You know, maybe this wasn't a good idea after all," said Kyle. His breathing was heavy, his head and hands slick with sweat. "My vision is blurred, and I can hardly breathe. It's like I'm suffocating."

Pyrrha instructed them to stay where they were while she ventured on, climbing the steps and disappearing inside.

Mira pulled Kyle away. "We need to go back," she whispered. "Whatever this place is, the closer we get, it's making you sick. Hopefully, Josh and Rachel have found Jo and are doing the same."

"We can't leave until Pyrrha comes back," he said. "Plus, we have to make it appear as if we need to get in there to save Jo, and not to raise Pyrrha's suspicions any more than they already are. In fact, maybe we should follow Pyrrha in now, better to see what we *may* face later?"

"You can't go," said Mira. "Just look at you—you look terrified!"

Kyle shook his head. "I'm not terrified. It's just… I have all these emotions running through me, but I know they're not my own. I feel desperation, anger and sorrow, all at the same time. Something bad happened here, Mira. And I'm not only talking about what happened to Epimetheus."

"Pyrrha did say that a great flood came through here," said Mira. "Maybe those that died have left some sort of… spiritual presence?"

"It wasn't the flood. Or the great battle that was fought here…" Kyle's eyes widened. "I think Josh is right. Those of Pyrrha's order that stayed behind didn't have a choice in the matter." He dropped his head into his hands.

"You stay here, and I'll go look," Mira insisted, leading him back to the hill.

As Kyle sat against the grassy bank, Mira ran to the steps, where Pyrrha came to meet her.

"It's empty inside, except for what appears to be a long table. An altar of sorts. I'm sorry, but there's no way through. There's only solid rock. It does appear to be more of a temple than a tomb."

"If those things did come from here, there must be another way in," said Mira. "Maybe from above?"

"If that is the case, we don't have the proper climbing equipment to scale it." Pyrrha frowned. "I'm sorry, Mira, but if Jo is in there, we can't get her back."

Though she knew Jo wasn't in there, Mira still insisted she enter.

Inside was, as Pyrrha had said, empty except for a long, stone table. Where there had been a passage deeper into the tomb in Mira's dream, now there was only a solid rock face.

Maybe it's a secret door and it will appear if Rachel and Jo stand in front of it? she thought.

As Mira studied the altar, she thought back to what Jo told her about the last island and the screams she heard when she went looking for oil with Josh. "This table looks like it was made for—sacrificial purposes?"

Pyrrha ran her hand along the smooth surface. Finding perfectly drilled holes at either end of the plinth, without saying a word, she knelt on the ground and reached under the table.

Mira was now even more perplexed. "What is it? What can you see?"

Pyrrha pushed herself to her feet. In her hands were two worn leather straps. "Your theory about this being a sacrificial altar…" She grimaced. "I think you're right."

Mira grabbed Pyrrha's arm, and they both left. But as they made their way back to Kyle, Mira took another look back to the temple. Overhead, another dark cloud was looming, and an overwhelming feeling of certainty engulfed her.

It's not just Kyle you want, is it? When will I be seeing the inside of you?

CHAPTER TWENTY-FIVE

A GENTLE STROLL ALONG THE BANK OF THE RIVER

Josh and Rachel strode along the riverbank. While Rachel seemed happy to talk about what she would be doing at that moment if she was home, or just anything to keep her from thinking about where they actually were and the conundrum they were now facing, Josh, in contrast, was very quiet. The rolling hills seemed to stretch on for miles ahead, and the sun had sunk low enough to gleam off the snow-covered mountaintop. And they were approaching a section of the land where the grass was tall and thick enough to hide a Bengal tiger. Would he see it coming in time?

Get a grip! he thought. *Tigers are native to Asia.* His neuroses took over again. *But what else could be hiding in there?*

It was then that Rachel's voice brought him back from his intense meanderings.

"Are you going to answer me or not?" she snapped.

Josh took a dramatic inhale of breath. He had completely switched off listening to her jabbering when he'd thought he'd seen movement in the grassland.

"Yeah, of course," he answered. "I was—err—just thinking about how best to respond."

"It was simple question, Josh," said Rachel. "Do you believe what Pyrrha told us about the old gods being real?"

Josh breathed an inner sigh of relief when a small bird flew out of the grass.

"I've always believed there was something out there," he said. "Aliens, maybe, that crash-landed thousands of years ago, and finding that they were superior to us, simply took on the mantle of gods."

Rachel nodded in agreement. "I've never believed in God. The school I went to rammed religion down our throats so much that, in the end, I found everything they were saying to be a contradiction. But what you just said actually makes a kind of sense."

Josh shrugged. "Perhaps the government will finally release information to the general public—slowly, so we don't have another panic like they had in 1938 with that radio broadcast of *War of the Worlds*. But don't count on it. For all we know there could be gods that look exactly like their statues or what's portrayed in the movies. But whatever's really out there, I do know this: it's sadistic and it likes to take a very large dump on my head on a regular basis. Look, can we talk about something else, please?"

Rachel smiled, threw a hand through the crook of Josh's arm, and they both continued on.

They seemed to have walked for hours, but fortune smiled upon Josh when Rachel spied a deer drinking. It was a relief to have a break from listening to her pontificating about the pros and cons of wearing strappy shoes while walking on sand.

"Aw, look at that." She smiled. "I never thought I would see one for real."

"Yeah, cute," said Josh, now keeping a watchful eye out for bears. "But where there's deer, there are things that eat them."

"Thanks, Josh. Just what I needed to hear."

"Just being realistic, that's all."

They pressed on, but when Rachel expressed her wish for Mira and Kyle to be with them, Josh felt a little hurt. He released his arm from her grasp and came to an abrupt stop. "Why? Don't you feel safe with me? Don't you trust me?"

Her eyes widened. "Yes, of course I do, sweetie. I just meant that when we are all together, I don't worry as much. That's all…"

Josh noticed her taking a breath. *Oh no,* he thought, knowing that there was no escape—he was going to have to bite the bullet and deal with another grilling.

As usual, Rachel didn't disappoint.

"We might as well deal with the elephant in the room," she said. "What's up with your brother?"

He grimaced. "What do you mean?"

"Back on the cruise ship and Pandora's island, he was more your 'take charge, don't mess with us' type of guy. Now he seems disengaged. He's reluctant to make any decisions. In fact, he doesn't seem to want to do anything. In comparison, Mira has stepped up incredibly. Even with her brother missing, she hasn't fallen apart like I think I would have if my sibling had been taken from me. You know, when I first met Mira, she wouldn't say boo to anyone, but now she has a sense of drive and control I envy. I wouldn't want to get on the wrong side of her, if and when she finally loses her temper completely."

"Kyle went through a lot. His body took a beating. That's all it is," Josh assured her. "Don't worry, he'll be back to bossing us all around soon enough." But deep down he, too, was feeling the same concern. *Will he actually come back to his old self?*

"So, no regrets staying with Mira?" Rachel then asked.

"No. Why, have you?"

"No. Although I do think Jo should go home. It's just, after what happened on Pandora's island, I was wondering if Kyle had said anything about leaving us?"

Josh let out a short chuckle. "You don't know my brother like I do. He took a beating, yes, but that will only spur him on even more now. He's stubborn that way. Besides, I've never seen him this ga-ga over a girl, ever. He would follow Mira into the pit of Hades."

"Not quite the answer I was looking for, Josh, considering what we've been told. But that's good." Rachel smiled. "And you will definitely stay, too?"

"Hell yeah!" Josh whooped. "This beats going to school any day of the week."

For the first time in days, Rachel let out a chuckle. "You know, you're the only one of us that has remained the same person since this all began."

"How so?"

"Haven't you noticed? Look at Jo for starters. She's no longer the strong-willed girl we first met who stood up to Barry, took care of Ted, the first one to approach Pyrrha. Now she's more like… Shaggy or Scooby Doo. And Kyle, as I've already said, is no longer Jean-Claude Van Damme, but Mira is… kind of."

"And you?" Josh asked.

Rachel's smile vanished. "Haven't you noticed the change in me?"

"No. Not really. At least my arm doesn't think so. Do you feel you've changed then?"

Rachel took a moment. "Yes. I have changed, if you must know."

Josh prepared himself to run from yet another of Rachel's speciality swipes. "In what way?"

But she just let out a long sigh instead. "I haven't killed you yet. That's a start. Before the holiday, I would have ripped you to shreds for some of the things you do and say, and not thought twice about it. Maybe these islands are having an effect on me," she said, and walked on.

Josh waited a moment before following, considering what Rachel had said. But with another look to his arm, her favourite target, he shrugged and ran after her.

When he'd caught her up, suddenly, a stag appeared out of the long grass and approached the river. Not wanting to disturb it, again they stopped and watched it drink.

"Oh, he's a handsome fellow," Rachel whispered and reached for Josh's hand. "It's really heartwarming and relaxing, watching them drink, isn't it?"

Before Josh could answer, there was a huge eruption from the water. The stag was grabbed around its neck by giant jaws and dragged squealing into the murky deep. The animal's blood sprayed directly into Rachel's face.

Frozen to the spot, she began to scream. "Please tell me it's not in my hair!"

Josh's eyebrows reached for the sun. He could only gape.

"Is it in my hair?!" Rachel repeated.

Josh wiped the blood from her face with his sleeve. "No, you're alright, your face took the brunt of it," he lied, trying not to look at the red streak through her blonde locks.

"What the heck was *that*?" she cried.

Unsettled, Josh looked to the blood-curdled water. "I have no idea, but I'm not getting any closer to find out." He pulled Rachel further away from the bank. "Like I said, where there's deer, there's always things that eat them."

Now keeping a very wide distance from the river, they reached the brow of a small hill. Finally, they could see the pyramid Linus had promised, just ahead.

"It looks more Mayan in design than Egyptian," Josh pointed out.

"It looks scary, whoever built it," said Rachel. "But answer me this, Josh. How do you know this pyramid looks Mayan and not Egyptian, but get things like megalodon and Hom-dai wrong?"

Josh broke into a huge grin. "I knew it was megalodon. Just like I know Hyundai is a car manufacturer. I just like winding Jo up, that's all. And you have to admit, when I say these things, it does kind of stop her from freaking out."

Rachel's eyes narrowed. But the side of her mouth turned up. A kiss on his cheek, and no more was said on the matter.

Huge oak, beech and ash trees circled the immense base of the structure. In front of the pyramid was a man-made, rectangular lake, lined with willow trees. Their long branches cast a perpetual shadow over the crystal-clear water.

As Josh and Rachel approached the edge of the water, Linus appeared from inside the entrance of the pyramid, a stone gateway that looked like it had been made for giants.

"Where's Mira and Kyle?" he called out.

"They've gone on to the sepulchre!" Josh answered. "Making sure Pyrrha doesn't get her hands on you!"

"Sepulchre… I thought it was a temple." Linus shrugged. "Look, I'm sorry, but this is where they took Jo. There's an entrance at the top where they flew her in.

I've been inside, but it's too dark to see where you're going. Look, I don't expect you to trust me, so, if you want, I'll go back in alone and try to find her."

"No, we'll come," said Rachel. "But if you're leading us into a trap, it won't be Pyrrha killing you, it will be me!"

Josh cast a wary look at her. "You can be awfully scary at times, Rach. You know that, right?"

Linus raised his head. "Fair enough, but like I said to Kyle, Jo is my friend, too, and she was good to me. And I don't want to sound rude, but is that blood in your hair, Rach?"

As Rachel knelt at the edge of the lake and stared at her reflection, Josh slowly backed away. "Now, don't get mad, Rach. I didn't tell you because… because, well, I'm stupid. But I think it looks really sexy. You look like you could be a superhero. Captain Marvel, huh, eat your heart out."

Without a word, and to Josh's relief, Rachel simply rose to her feet and began to navigate the stepping stones that crossed the water to the entrance.

Josh, instead, began to climb one of the trees.

"What the hell are you doing now?" Rachel called out.

A branch snapped and dropped to the ground. Josh removed a knife from his rucksack and proceeded to trim the foliage. Then, using the lighter taken from his pocket, he burned the tip until it looked like the nib of a pencil.

"Now we can mark the walls." He winked and, equipped with the small torches they'd brought, and Rachel holding tight to his arm, cautiously, followed Linus inside.

***

A long tunnel led inside the pyramid, and at each intersection they came to, Josh marked the wall with a number and an arrow pointing the way to the exit. Small chambers were spread out throughout the complex. Inside, they could see wicker burial caskets stacked one on top of another.

"Oh, great," said Josh. "Looks like this place is one big, indoor cemetery. You don't think…" But noticing Rachel narrowing her eyes, he didn't finish what he was going to say.

They didn't know how long they had been searching, but when they arrived back at the first marker, they proceeded, undeterred, along another winding tunnel. Finding no chambers or crossroads to lead them astray, they finally came out into the centre of the complex. As daylight streamed in from the wide, rectangular opening above, Josh ran his fingers across strange, blackened grooves along the walls.

"Is it just me or do they look like scorch marks?" he said excitedly. "It's like they were made by huge blasts of electricity." His eyes widened further. "Hey, you don't think…"

"Zeus, casting thunderbolts?" said Rachel.

Josh lowered his head. "No need for the sarcasm," he said, sulkily. "But even you have to admit it does appear that way, doesn't it?"

Rachel shook her head. "No, it doesn't. And it doesn't look like Jo is in here. I think we should go back to the boat."

But Linus had spotted another tunnel hidden behind an ancient stone statue. He forged ahead. "We can't give up yet!"

Rachel looked the statue up and down. "Is it me, or does this remind you of someone?"

Josh rolled his eyes. "Brad Pitt, by any chance? When he played Achilles?"

Rachel brushed the dust from the plinth, revealing markings beneath. "I was going to say Kyle."

Josh looked up at the face again. "It doesn't look anything like Kyle... For starters, it's smiling."

"I know it isn't Kyle, silly. I just meant the physique and the hair are similar. Damn it, the writing is faded. Did the gods have their own islands?"

"They did," said Josh. "They were like ancient Richard Bransons. Zeus, before he became supreme ruler, ruled over Crete. And Aphrodite came from Cyprus."

Rachel groaned. "I should have known you would know where the hottest goddess came from..."

With Linus no longer in sight, they continued on. Feeling suddenly cold, Josh drew his pistol and kept it close to his side.

They hadn't walked far when they caught up with Linus, who had stopped at the entrance to another tunnel. Ahead, something scratched and scurried, and a ruddy yellow light that looked suspiciously like a burning fire flickered behind a large pillar. Slowly, the trio entered the chamber.

CHAPTER TWENTY-SIX

THE BEARDED MAN

Pyrrha led Mira and Kyle back through the town and across the bridge. As the sun was now low in the west, Pyrrha picked up her pace.

"We'll follow the river this time," she called back. "It should save us a lot of time. I just hope we make it before nightfall."

Pyrrha smiled, but Mira could sense an undercurrent of nervous tension. "Do you think the rescue boats have come?" she asked, recalling the captain's threat to leave without them.

"If they have, Sherme won't leave us behind," Pyrrha replied lightly.

"Are you sure about that?" said Kyle. "He seemed pretty ticked off before we left."

"Unless he wants to explain to my father what happened to me, he would not dare leave without us. He's my older brother, you see. Actually, he's the eldest."

Mira was taken aback by Pyrrha's sudden revelation. "How many siblings do you have?"

"Four. There's Sherme—you've already met him. Then there's my brother Paul. I have a sister, Neith. Next in line is Ross, and the youngest, me, complete our happy band. They were all adopted, mind you. Until I arrived, my mother thought she couldn't have children. Oh, and of course, my father is also a guardian to—"

"Are they soldiers like you and the captain?" Mira cut in.

"Neith isn't, but the rest are. When we get home, I hope I can introduce you." Pyrrha smiled. "They haven't been home in the longest time. In fact, I can't remember the last time I saw them. Anyway, now that you are with me, they will come."

She cast another anxious look to the sky, at the dark clouds threatening to eclipse them, and insisted they should run back to the ship. But as Mira picked up her pace, Kyle suddenly pulled up, clutching his calf. Mira called out to Pyrrha to stop.

"You'd best go back without me," Kyle said, writhing in pain. "It's an old rugby injury. I thought I felt a twinge when we climbed that last hill."

Pyrrha's anxious expression was replaced with a look of dread as she once more looked to the darkening sky. "We'll carry you," she said.

Kyle pushed himself to his feet and tried to walk forward. "No. I'll only slow you down, and we'll never make it back in time. I'll go back to the town and rest up in that place we stayed in. I should get there before it gets too dark. But you need to go back and ensure that Josh doesn't come looking for me."

Pyrrha looked back in the direction of the town. "You can't stay there alone."

Mira threw her arm under Kyle's shoulder. "He's right, Pyrrha. You have to go back to the ship. I'll stay with him," she insisted. "We have guns to protect us."

Pyrrha took one last look at the sky. "Then you'd best make a move. But stay inside that building—do not go wandering!"

Pyrrha tossed them extra ammunition clips and left at speed. Mira helped Kyle limp back toward the town. But once Pyrrha was a speck on the horizon, Kyle grabbed Mira's hand and started to run.

"You mind telling me what all that was in aid of?" she called out.

"I have this feeling that Josh and Rachel haven't gone back to the ship," he replied. "We have to get to the pyramid. I think they're walking into a trap."

They had reached the second bridge, and the gloomy grey clouds had extinguished the last rays of light. Although everything appeared calm and quiet, Mira again sensed they were being watched. "Do you get the feeling we're not alone?" she whispered.

Kyle shot a look to the statue of the god, and gasped. "We're not," he said, and pointed to what he could now see.

Mira's heart flew up into her mouth. High in the night sky, the creatures were setting out on another hunt.

Their only option for cover was in the town. They bolted inside the nearest building, with only moments to spare before the creatures flew overhead.

***

Hours had passed. Mira opened her eyes, sure she could once again hear the heavy flapping of wings. She went to nudge Kyle awake, but his eyes were already open and firmly on the entrance.

Both crept to the open doorway and peered out to see the harpies returning, carrying another screaming guard.

Mira gasped. "We have to help her." She swiftly turned to leave the safety of the shadows.

Kyle was quick to pull her back inside. "We can't. We'll have to wait till the sun comes out. You heard what Captain Grumpy said. His shotgun didn't even graze them. So, I seriously doubt these pistols will fare any better."

Mira knew he was right and reluctantly nodded in agreement. "Do you think Josh and Rachel have found Jo and are simply waiting, too?" she whispered.

"I hope so. But knowing Josh, he's probably come up with some mad idea of how to get back to the ship."

A sudden thought caused Mira to catch her breath. "Perhaps we should make a run for the pyramid now. If Josh and Rachel are walking into a trap, now that those things have taken that guard to their nest, it should give us the time we need to get there." It was then that she noticed Kyle's wide-eyed expression and that his knuckles had turned white as he gripped the frame of the door. "What is it?" she said, fearing his response.

"They know we're here."

Mira slowly peeked around the door frame. Her insides flipped. The creatures had landed in the centre of the street. Slowly, they began to split up and enter more buildings.

Mira's heart was pounding. "We can't stay in here— it's only a matter of time before they find us. Should we—should we try and make a run for it?"

But when she turned to Kyle, he was nowhere to be seen. Mira cast another despairing look to the street. The creatures were closing in on her location.

At first, she couldn't move. She couldn't even call out to Kyle. But as she steadied her nerves and slipped her fingers into her pocket to retrieve her weapon, a hand suddenly gripped her shoulder. She clamped down on her instinct to yell out, not wanting to reveal her location to the enemy. She held her breath and slowly turned round to face the owner of the hand.

"I've found a place to hide," said Kyle. "There's a trap-door in the floor that was hidden by an overturned table."

Without needing to be asked twice, Mira climbed down the rickety wooden ladder. The latch pulled closed, and to ensure it was tightly shut behind them, Kyle then tied the hanging rope around a hook to hold it secure. Mira turned on her torch and found they were in what may have once been a larder. There was no way out but the trapdoor. She turned off the light and drew her gun.

Desperate to steady her trembling hands, Mira slowed her breathing as Pyrrha had taught her and aimed at the hatch.

"If the rope is on the inside"—she struggled to get the words out—"then the original occupants must have built this place to hide from those things as well."

Kyle pressed his finger to her lips.

She held her breath.

The silence was deafening, but it wasn't long before it was broken by the sound of huge claws scraping across the stone floor above their heads.

Mira strained her neck to look through the small cracks of the hatch. At least one of the creatures was standing directly over it. Slowly, she slid the safety on her handgun to the red dot that would enable it to fire.

Again, there was silence above. Mira was sure she could hear Kyle's heart, a steady beat as opposed to the rampant thump of her own. At one point, she could even swear she could hear the pulse of the creature quicken.

Then, a narrow ray of blue, silvery light pierced through the hatch. Instinctively, Mira and Kyle edged back into the darkness, just as a demonic, red eye appeared.

The creature scanned all before it. Bright light radiated from its irises, focused like a laser beam searching for its target. Suddenly, it spied something, and with a high squeal of excitement, one of its talons reached down through the broadest crack. Slowly, the razor claw began to cut through the rope.

Mira prepared to fire. But Kyle was once again frozen.

Mira reached out with her free hand, but she didn't have time to prod him into action. The rope was severed from the hook.

Mira braced herself to squeeze the trigger. But then she heard a distant gunshot and a loud, painful screech, and then the sudden flap of wings.

Shakily, Mira released her finger from the trigger, and along with Kyle, she pressed her back against the stone wall and finally exhaled.

"You were hearing voices again, weren't you?" she asked.

Kyle avoided the question. "You don't think that shot came from Josh or Rachel, or even Pyrrha, do you?"

Mira was finding it hard to swallow. "I don't think Pyrrha would have got here this quickly," she said. "And if Josh and Rachel did find Jo, and haven't returned to the ship, I doubt they would have made it here this fast either. At this moment, I just hope those things don't come back. The wolves were scary, but did you see that thing's eye?"

Kyle nodded. "It's like your nightmare. I guess it could have been that guard they were carrying that fired the shot?"

"I was just thinking the same thing," Mira said, feeling guilty for not at least trying to save the woman. But there was nothing they could do for her now—she'd seen how many of those creatures had flown overhead. Instead, she rested her head on Kyle's shoulder. "You know what, I wish I would wake up to find that this was all a dream and that I was really back home or sitting in the coffee house in the high street as I did every morning before school, happily reading a book."

"I don't," said Kyle vehemently.

Mira lifted her head. "Why on earth not? You're not becoming like Josh, are you? Rachel is convinced he's having the time of his life."

"No, I'm not becoming Josh. But if this is just a dream, then it means I've never met you, and if that is the case, then I don't want to wake up." He looked into her eyes, smiled and began to laugh. "Thank God Josh wasn't here to hear me say that. That was *way* too corny, right?"

She smiled back, happy that, for the moment, Kyle was back in the room and appeared to be his normal self. "Maybe, but only a little corny."

Afraid to move, she rested her eyes, but a thought had been permeating, "Do you believe what Pyrrha told me—that Epimetheus was locked away for killing Disciples?"

Kyle took a moment. "I guess. I know I would do anything to get you back."

"But what if I had become a plague that could wipe out all life on earth?"

This time, Kyle took but a moment to reply. "Even then."

He smiled and rested his head back against the wall. Mira snuggled in closer and closed her eyes. But another thought then came to her. She couldn't believe she hadn't thought of it before.

The moon has a cycle of twenty-nine and a half days, yet we only see it fully for three. If we were on Pandora's is-

land for three days, and we've been on this island for another three, how is it we can still see it in all its glory?

She sat back up and posed the question to Kyle, who still had his eyes fixed firmly on the hatch.

"I was just thinking the same thing," he said. "I guess for now, all we can do is wait for the answer to present itself. We have other more important things to worry about."

Mira dropped back into his arms. He was right; there were more important issues they needed to deal with first. Like getting out of this building alive and finding the only other people they truly cared about.

***

Hours had passed. When Mira opened her eyes and found that the room was still in darkness, she reached for Kyle's hand. She'd forgotten that he'd given his watch to Josh, and his wrist felt bare without it.

She could feel his eyes upon her. "Did you manage to sleep?" she yawned.

He shook his head. "One of us needed to be awake in case that thing came back."

Mira looked up at the hatch. There was no longer a single ray of light beaming through the larger crack the harpy had made. Now they were in almost complete darkness.

"How are we gonna know when it's morning?" she asked. "You gave your watch to Josh, and I don't fancy opening the door till then."

"If the light of the moon got in through the small crack, I'm sure the sun's rays will be able to get through that larger one," he said.

She nervously laughed. "Yeah, but what time does the sun strike the room? And what if it's cloudy? We could be in here all day."

"Then at the first sign of any source of light, we run like hell, no matter what time of day it is."

Mira looked anxiously again to the only exit. There was silence above, but she had to check. Slowly, she got to her feet and climbed the ladder. Her hand trembled as she eased open the trapdoor.

CHAPTER TWENTY-SEVEN

ALIVE AND WELL

Josh edged further into the chamber toward the fire. Linus was just ahead of him, and Rachel was close behind, holding tightly to his belt. It was then that Josh heard a familiar voice: a trembling squeak of a voice.

"Linus, is that really you?"

As Linus ran past the flames, Josh looked to Rachel, and with her approval, cautiously, they followed.

Through the smoke, Josh recognised a silhouette. Before he could say anything, however, Rachel swung her hands to her face and ran forward. Josh couldn't help but smile as Rachel and Jo embraced.

"How the hell did you find me?" Jo asked, laughing and crying at the same time.

"It was all down to Linus," said Josh, patting his back.

"Have they hurt you?" Rachel asked, looking around as if she was half expecting to see the creatures crawl out from some hidden crevice.

Jo wiped away her tears. "No. They brought me here and then left."

"So, did you build the fire?" Josh asked, watching the smoke disappear into a narrow hole in the roof above. "And how did you get the smoke to do that?"

Jo pointed to a chain hanging from the ceiling. "The man who built it showed me what to do. When I heard noises coming this way, I filled this room with smoke, hoping it would hide me."

"Go back," said Josh. "What man?"

"The man that was here," said Jo. "Said he had things to do, but he would be back later."

Rachel shot Josh a wary look. "Was it someone from the ship?"

"No. He said he landed just after we did but wouldn't say why or how he got here."

"Do you think he's one of the Followers?" Josh asked.

"No idea. I was just glad to see a human being." Jo laughed.

"I'm sorry, but who are the Followers?" Linus asked.

"Doesn't matter," said Josh. "But whoever this guy is, let's get the hell out of here. Pyrrha said the rescue boats should be here soon."

"We can't," Jo insisted. "Not until morning. The man said to only go out in the daylight."

"Obviously he doesn't obey his own rules then, does he?" said Josh.

"Look, before we go rushing out there, what happened to you exactly, Jo?" asked Rachel.

"We had just got to the tents when those things came out of nowhere. They had the guard that was with me away in seconds. When more came for me, these other flying monsters came and fought them off. Before I knew it, I was in the air and then here."

"Harpies. They're called harpies, Jo." Josh winked.

"Are you sure now?" said Rachel. "Not herpes?"

"I said harpies last time, you just misheard me. Probably had your mind on something else—like that bloody bag of yours."

A little chuckle, and then Rachel's hand lashed out.

"*Jeez*, you keep hitting me there and it's gonna fall off!" Josh cried out, rubbing his arm.

Linus clapped his hands together. "Oh man, I really missed this. You two are so funny." But then, seeing Rachel's expression, her lips tight, her eyes narrow, he slumped, his gaze dropping to the floor. "I'm sorry—if you want, I'll go," he whimpered.

"No, Linus. Unlike you, I won't send someone to their death!" said Rachel harshly.

Linus refused to make eye contact. "I deserve that. Look, if it's OK with you, I'll go at first light. I can't come back with you anyway, and perhaps the man Jo spoke of will help me?" His tone was now one of desperate hope.

"Do you think that's wise, Linus?" said Jo. "What if he's a Disciple and knows Pyrrha but just hasn't seen her yet? Do you want to risk it?"

Linus' head dropped even lower. "You're right. Looks like I'm screwed then. If you don't mind, I'll stay till the sun comes up, then I'll be on my way someplace else." And slowly, he raised his head and revealed teary eyes.

"Stay as long as you like," said Rachel coldly. "We're the ones that are leaving."

Linus looked to the ground again. "Oh. OK. Thank you. Now, if you don't mind, I'll stay by the fire just for tonight. I haven't had a wink of sleep since we landed."

Linus curled up on one side of the fire, and with Rachel insisting they stay until the sun rose, the rest huddled together on the other side.

"We can't leave him here; he'll die," Josh whispered, rubbing the nape of his neck.

"He'll die for certain if Pyrrha sees him," said Rachel, not showing any signs of concern. "And besides, it's his own fault. No, he's on his own from now on."

Josh bowed his head. "He found Jo. That has to mean something to you."

Rachel stroked his cheek. "Josh, when he saves a billion people, then maybe I'll... No, he killed his mother and brother, he deserves all he gets. I'm sorry, I know you thought of him as a friend."

"Hey, don't get me wrong, I agree he deserves to be punished, but are we any better if we leave him here?" And as he laid his puppy-dog expression on her, Rachel closed her eyes and threw her head back.

"Fine! If that man comes back before we leave, and he isn't a Follower or a Disciple, put in a good word for him, Jo."

Rachel curled herself up into a ball and closed her eyes. But as Josh tried to get up, she pulled him back down.

"Jeez, I guess it's my bedtime as well. You're worse than my mother," he whispered.

Josh sat beside Rachel and listened to the crackling of the fire. And although the rest of the group appeared to settle, he kept his eyes firmly fixed on the only way in or out.

CHAPTER TWENTY-EIGHT

FAREWELL AND GOOD LUCK

Mira opened her eyes. Sweat was dripping from her brow. When she had ventured a look outside only an hour earlier, the terrifying shriek of a harpy as it flew overhead had convinced her to return to their place of safety and try and rest. But she'd had that dream again, the same one as on the first night on the island. This time, she hadn't succumbed to a watery death. This time, she'd managed to successfully navigate the large pool inside the sepulchre.

Feeling Kyle stir, she asked, "Why do think we were able to get across the pond and beyond the waterfall this time?"

Kyle's forehead shone with sweat, same as hers. "Damn it. There I go, saying one of us should stay awake, and like an idiot, I fall asleep..." He shook his head, then addressed Mira's concern: "Like I said, I think this place has something to do with me... Did you see me? I saw you, and yet when I called out, you ignored me."

Mira was also confused. "Yes, I saw you. But it was the same for me when I tried to speak with you." She hesitated, then added, "Did you see all the skeletons? It looked like they had all just lain down and died en masse. And what about the harpies hanging from the trees with their throats slit?" The vivid memory of the hanging bodies caused the knot in Mira's stomach to twist again.

Kyle wiped his forehead with his sleeve. "Yes, I saw. But where were you when that misty hand came out from the tomb?"

Mira took a moment to recall. "I was there. But I seemed to be watching from a distance. One minute you were standing beside Josh, yet when Rachel and Jo were opening the tomb, you suddenly vanished. And I didn't see the hand this time." She was aware that her breathing had become laboured again.

"Oh, right." Kyle frowned. "Are you sure you saw Rachel and Jo open it? Cos I didn't."

Mira's thoughts started to swirl. She was feeling a little panicky. "I—I think so. Although, now that you mention it, I can recall seeing their faces at the tomb, but I didn't actually see them opening it. But I didn't see you open it either… Hey, maybe this island is playing tricks with us. What do you think?"

"If that is the case, and it's Rachel or Jo who opens Epimetheus' tomb, then I just hope that the third tomb you saw is not waiting for me and Josh." He rose to his feet. "Cos I don't think I can take another bloody island."

A ray of yellow light streamed through the crack from the room above. Kyle crept up the ladder and nudged the hatch open. They clambered out, and as soon as Mira was clear, Kyle closed the hatch and replaced the table to hide it.

After ensuring the street was deserted, they left the building and headed for the river. But as they hurried along the route Linus had given, eager to see their friends, both knew what the other was thinking. Was anyone still alive?

***

Rachel and Jo silently glared at one another. Worried that something bad was about to happen, Josh stepped between them.

Rachel pushed him to one side. "So, who opened the tomb with you, Jo?"

"I was going to ask you the same thing," said Jo, without any emotion.

Josh looked to the two of them. "I'm just glad I actually made it inside the crypt this time, by the way, and thanks for asking. But from what I saw, you both opened it. Don't you remember?"

"No. I saw Jo open it. I definitely didn't," said Rachel.

Jo frowned. "But I saw you open it, Rach."

Both girls looked to Josh. "Are you sure it was both of us you saw?" they asked in unison.

Josh took a moment to recall. "You were both definitely standing by it, but then, so were me and Kyle. Mira was strangely stood at the entrance just watching us. Wait… I remember you were holding the key, Jo." He paused. "You know what—come to think of it, I'm not sure either of you did it now. It just seemed to open on its own. Although…" He paused again. "Did either of you see the two small, shadowy figures lurking by the tomb?"

Rachel and Jo didn't answer him, just exchanged a look.

"Oh well, no matter." Josh smiled. "But you were definitely holding the key, Jo. Now, I think it's best if we get out of here and find Kyle and Mira."

He hoped that Rachel would have changed her mind in the night, but to his disappointment, she walked straight past Linus on her way to the exit. *Come on, Rach, have a heart.*

"Take care, Linus," said Jo, kissing him on his cheek. "If you do decide to stay, when that man returns, just tell him I've gone back to my ship."

Rachel and Jo left the chamber, and Josh took one last look at Linus staring helplessly into the fire.

"Hey, Linus," he called out. "Don't give up hope. The way things are looking, we're going to be stuck here, too. And remember, time can be a great healer."

But just as he was about to leave, Josh's gaze drifted back to the smoke.

Rachel reappeared and nudged his arm. "Are you coming or what?" She looked to where he was staring. "What is it? You seem awfully interested in the fire, Josh. Have you never seen smoke before?"

Josh ignored the sarcasm in her voice. "Look at the position of the fire and then to where the smoke is escaping." He pointed. "It doesn't look like a chimney, does it? In fact, unless you were specifically looking for it, you wouldn't even know it was there."

Rachel stared glumly at the disappearing fumes. "So, what are you saying? The man is a habitant of the island?"

Josh shook his head. "No. I'm saying this man landed on the island, came straight to this place and built a fire in the right spot where the smoke wouldn't fill the chamber unless the chain that Jo was holding is pulled."

Rachel's eyes widened. "Oh, I see what you're saying. So, he could be a Disciple, because Pyrrha told Mira the Followers knew nothing of Epimetheus."

"Which begs the question: if he is a Disciple, why hasn't he revealed himself to Pyrrha?"

"Oh, great," said Rachel. "Yet another thing to worry about."

Josh followed Rachel out of the pyramid, and as he stepped across the stones of the lake, he suddenly spied, high above, among the branches of the trees, the creatures hanging upside down like bats. He couldn't explain why, but he knew that this wasn't going to be the last time he would see Linus.

Jo was already following the route of the river back toward the town, and as Josh and Rachel caught her up, they could just make out the figures of Kyle and Mira walking toward them in the distance.

***

Once they had all updated one another with their adventures, Mira's heart was racing. "It could have been that man who fired that shot then," she said, "and not the guard."

Kyle shot a look over his shoulder, back toward the town. "I have to go back. If she's still alive, I couldn't live with myself if I left her there to die."

A warm glow rose inside Mira. This was the Kyle she'd fallen in love with.

"I'll go with you," she said.

"I'm going with you, too," said Josh, eyes wide with excitement.

"You can't go," said Jo. "If Pyrrha thinks you're there, she'll kill you."

"She's right, Josh. I'll go with Kyle," said Mira. "You three go back to the ship and tell them we're looking for Kyle's watch that Josh dropped earlier."

"I haven't dropped any watch," said Josh.

"I told Pyrrha that I was giving you Dad's watch to take back to the boat in case we didn't make it," said Kyle. "I needed an excuse to tell you what Linus said."

"But you didn't me give me Dad's watch," said Josh.

"I know I didn't give you *Dad's* watch," said Kyle. "I gave you my watch." And reaching into Josh's pocket, he pulled it out. "I slipped it in, because if I'd said, 'Don't lose it', you would have lost it, like the last watch I told you to take care of."

"That was nearly five years ago," said Josh, rifling through his other pockets to see if anyone else had hidden their possessions on him. "And you know I had thin wrists back then. It wasn't my fault it slipped off—"

"I handed it to you to keep safe while I played rugby, and because you had forgotten your kit, you were meant to stand and watch the game. But what did you do? You sneaked off and went swimming with it!"

"Oh, brother," said Josh. "Like I've already said, that was five years ago. And it was a cheap watch anyway—"

"I cycled a whole year in all weathers delivering newspapers to save up for it!" Kyle seethed.

Rachel stepped between them. "This is getting us nowhere. Now, what if Pyrrha comes looking for you?"

"We should be making our way back before you even reach the boat," said Kyle confidently.

"Unless she's already out looking for you—umm, us," Josh added.

"Why do you say that?" said Rachel. But then her shoulders dropped. "Oh, she's coming now, isn't she?" When she turned around and saw Pyrrha and two of her guards making their way toward them, she groaned even louder. "Why did I bother asking?"

"Have you lot got a death wish?" Pyrrha cried out.

"Charles Bronson, 1974," Josh was quick to reply.

Pyrrha blinked once, took a step back and, with her mouth ajar, blinked again. "I'm sorry, what?"

"Charles Bronson. He starred in *Death Wish* in 1974, I think. I saw it on TV last year. It's no *Godfather* or *The French Connection*, but it wasn't bad, to be honest with you."

Everyone stared at Josh in bewilderment. Pyrrha turned to Kyle and lowered her voice. "Is he adopted, by any chance?"

Kyle simply shrugged and shook his head.

"Well, thank goodness you're all OK," she said. Then, as an afterthought, added, "Oh, and Jo, I'm happy you're here, too, of course," before quickly marching off. "Let's get back to the ship before something else happens," she shouted over her shoulder.

"Back to the ship again?" Josh wailed. "I'm getting tired of walking back and forth, you know! I feel like an elastic band. Look, the smart play is to set up camp in that town. We can fortify a building against the harpies, and it's far enough away from the kraken. In war you move forwards, not back."

"Any news on when the rescue boats will come?" Mira asked, ignoring him.

"Not yet, but they can't be far away now."

"Look, Pyrrha, we think the guard that was taken last night might be still alive back at that town," said Kyle. "We heard a gunshot. Mira and I were going to check it out."

"No, it's too dangerous." There was a fiery intensity in Pyrrha's eyes. "Even if it does seem your leg has miraculously got better." She scowled. "Now, if what I was taught is correct, you don't want to know what those things have done to her—"

Rachel ran forward and blocked Pyrrha's path. "Are you telling me that you knew about those flying things all along and didn't have the decency to warn us?!"

"And what if that woman is still alive?" Mira asked, confused as to why Pyrrha wouldn't at least check.

"Then she would be here now, wouldn't she!" said Pyrrha. "And I did expressly warn you not to go wandering off. And if Pelenna had done what *she* was told, she wouldn't have got taken. I didn't know about the flying things, I swear. They were just… stories."

"Whatever," Rachel growled. "But if Pelenna is still alive, are you really going to leave her behind without at least checking?"

Pyrrha closed her eyes and took a deep breath. "Fine. I'll go look. But I'll go alone—"

"No offence, Pyrrha," said Rachel through gritted teeth, "but I'm nobody's prisoner. If I want to go, I'll go!"

Mira, now also annoyed, added, "Me too! And if I die, then all the problems go away—they won't be able to open Pandora's sarcophagus!"

Worn down by the persistent whining and arms flailing about her, Pyrrha relented. She instructed her guards to accompany the others back to the ship, conceding to allow just Kyle and Mira to join her.

***

It was another two hours before the rescue party was walking back along the main street of the town. As they headed in the direction the mysterious gunshot had come from, Pyrrha suddenly stopped, leaned back and looked to the sky.

"Seriously, Kyle. I don't mean to be rude, but was your brother adopted?" she asked.

"I've been asking my parents that question for years," said Kyle. "But my mother keeps showing photos of us in her arms just after we were born."

"He plays a lot of physical sports then, lots of hits to the head, yeah?"

"He played centre in rugby, but no one could catch him. He then took up boxing, but truth be told, he never got hit. He was that good," said Kyle, smiling with pride.

"Must be the way Rachel hits his arm then. The trauma of it must go to his head."

"Speaking of Rachel," said Mira. "She has a point. How could you believe that all the stories of the ancient heroes aren't just fables—that Pandora and Epimetheus are locked away waiting to be released so they can place a plague on humanity—and yet doubt that these flying creatures existed?"

Pyrrha closed her eyes and took a deep breath. "I didn't doubt—I lied. I just didn't want Rachel on my case. She's becoming scary."

"You keep lying, and yet you want us to trust you," said Kyle calmly. "I don't know how things work where you come from, but that's just not how it's done."

Pyrrha slowly opened her eyes. "And I don't like what you did. Feigning an injury. I was worried all night. I'll tell you what, Kyle, from now on, if you can all do as I ask, then I will answer your questions truthfully. But as we are running out of time, how about we just look for Pelenna and then get back to the ship before we end up on the bloody menu as well?"

They continued on in silence, but after searching every building, there was still no sign of Pelenna. Pyrrha looked to the position of the sun.

"You know as well as I that the days are shorter here, so we're going to be cutting it fine as it is. I'm sorry, but we have to go back now," she insisted.

Pyrrha walked on ahead at pace. But as they neared the end of the street, Mira suddenly caught sight of a figure peering around one of the buildings. The man had a bushy beard and shoulder-length hair protruding from a thick woollen hat.

Mira was about to warn Kyle. But when, out of the blue, the man turned and gave her a soft smile and raised a finger to his lips, motioning for her to remain quiet, to her own surprise, Mira found she did what he wanted. Somehow, she had a feeling that he was going to help them. She simply smiled back.

Clear of the town and forest, Pyrrha was increasing her pace with every step, and Mira and Kyle had to jog to catch her up. Once the tents were in sight and the last rays of sunlight vanished, they found they were running full pelt to get aboard the ship before they became the victims of another attack.

Rachel and Josh were already on the deck, waiting anxiously for them, and as they entered the bridge, Jo surprisingly leapt from her seat and gave them both a hug.

"Did you find anything?" she asked, but with Pyrrha standing behind her, Mira shook her head. She wasn't going to mention the man she saw, especially after Pyrrha had lied.

"So, what's the plan if those things come tonight?" said Josh, peering out of the window.

"You will stay in the cabin, under armed guard if need be, while we watch from here," said Pyrrha. "Last night, they didn't try to enter, and if that stupid girl hadn't tried to be a hero by running outside and shooting at them, she would still be alive, too. Now, do I need to have you watched, or for once can you all just stay put?"

Everyone agreed, but Pyrrha's gaze was firmly locked on Josh.

He smiled. "No need for me to go out now that we've found Jo."

Only once a guard had escorted them back to the cabin and she was sure there was nobody listening, Mira quietly told them about the bearded man.

"Jo, did he tell you anything at all about why he was here?" Mira whispered.

"No, and to be honest with you, as I told Josh and Rachel, I didn't really care. I was just happy to see a human being."

"And those creatures didn't hurt you at all?" Kyle asked.

"No, they saved my life."

"Maybe they know you can open the tomb and were going to take you to it," said Rachel, resting her chin on her hand, only to then bolt upright. "Oh God, they could come for me next! I mean, any one of us?"

"And have to deal with you slapping them? C'mon, they're not that stupid, Rach." Jo laughed. "Besides, I had the key in the dream, so it's obvious I open the tomb. I think you'll be fine."

Kyle rubbed the sides of his nose. "Wait... So, you did open it then?"

Jo nodded.

Kyle turned to Mira. "I guess you're right. This place is playing with us."

Before anyone could ask what he meant, Pyrrha entered, this time with microwave meals.

Kyle rolled from the bed. "No sign of those things yet then?"

"No. They're smart enough to know they're not getting through quarter-inch steel doors."

"They will if they have a plasma torch," said Josh, eagerly tucking in to his sausage and mash potato. "Burn a hole straight through, that will. Or if they have a lightsaber."

Pyrrha cast her gaze upwards and, with a shake of her head, swiftly left.

"I have to give it to you, Josh. You certainly know how to get rid of her." Rachel giggled.

"What do you mean? I was going to ask if she wanted to play a hand of cards before bedtime. You know, to be polite."

Rachel closed her eyes and took a deep breath.

"I was kidding." Josh leaned over and kissed her cheek. "She may not know how to play poker, and that would've been rude then."

Rubbing his slapped arm, Josh waited for the rest of the group to sit and then finished his meal in silence.

CHAPTER TWENTY-NINE

AN UNDERSTANDING

Halfway through dessert, Mira noticed Jo's eyes suddenly narrow, and she begun to chew the inside of her cheek. Mira hoped she didn't have more bad news for the group.

"Hey, Mira, you don't think that could be your real father out there, do you?" she asked.

Oh, thank goodness. "No. I think I would know my own father when I saw him. Besides, my father is pasty-faced, like me. The man I saw had a lovely golden complexion—"

"Perhaps it's a suntan?" said Josh. "He could have been living all this time in a hot climate. Remember when Uncle Trevor came back from his holiday in Dubai, Kaiboy?"

Kyle nodded.

"Until the redness had cooled down, everyone thought he'd holidayed on Venus. But then he was like a bronze statue."

Mira began to wonder. *It* has *been six years. Maybe Josh is right?* How good a look at him did she get, anyway? And with that long hair and beard, he would certainly appear different... *Could it really be him?* A feeling of excitement rose up through her body.

"Perhaps your stepfather hired him to find you?" said Rachel. "Think about it, if it was your father, surely he'd have made himself known to you?"

Mira's insides fell flat again. "Yeah, you're right. Back on Pandora's island, inside the crypt, I saw myself with my real father. It was the night he left us. Standing behind him was my mother and stepfather—and, now, when I think about it, there was another man lurking in the shadows. Hey, maybe it's him?"

"Are you planning to go and see him?" Josh asked.

Mira stepped to the window and cast a worried look to the forest. "I was contemplating it. But if he's out there with those things flying about…" She paused. *Time to reunite the group.* "What do you lot think?"

"I think you should speak with him at least," said Josh. "If you want—"

"Oh, no. *You* are not going out there tonight!" Rachel declared. "In fact, nobody is going. I don't think my nerves will suffer any one of you disappearing again."

"I agree," said Jo. "And if you don't mind, I think I'll have an early night. Sleeping on a stone floor has done nothing for my back."

Jo went to bed, and while Josh joined Rachel on top of a bunk under the window, Mira stayed with Kyle at the table.

"I don't want to sleep tonight," he said, keeping his voice to a minimum.

"Nor me, but with everything that's happening, as Jo said, we're going to need our rest." She stroked his cheek and looked into his puffy, sleep-deprived eyes. "And you definitely need a proper sleep. Not the short naps you've been having."

"I'll sleep when we are away from this place," he whispered. "Now, do you really think we can trust that man you saw?"

"I don't know. Do you think I should at least go and speak with him? Jo said he had a boat, and it won't harm to have another escape route if needed."

Kyle looked to Jo's bunk. "He could be a Follower. Maybe that's why he didn't hurt Jo."

"How would he know she can open the tomb? We haven't told anyone outside of this room what we know, and Jo said she didn't tell him. Besides, it could still be Rachel that opens it. Or both of them. In the dream, the Followers take them both away, remember?"

"What if he's from the same order as Lyssa?" Kyle asked, burying his head in his hands.

Mira gently placed her arm around him. She sensed the pain he was feeling, reliving the moment when Lyssa had tried to kill him.

"You may be right," she replied, rising from the table. "OK, tomorrow, I want you to follow me. Keep a distance, though—we don't want to spook him. But if he tries anything untoward, shoot him. Now, let's get some rest." She kissed him softly and tried to take his hand, but Kyle just smiled politely and told her he wasn't tired.

Reluctantly, Mira fell onto her bunk and stared at her friends, who had finally settled into a slumber. With an ache twisting her insides, she closed her eyes and silently prayed that the bearded man had come to help them.

***

Kyle checked his watch. Only two hours had passed since Mira had gone to sleep.

All was quiet around him, except for the muffled *pup-pupping* from Jo as she slept. He slipped out of the room and climbed the steps to the bridge. In the light coming from the various LEDs on the control panel, he could just make out Pyrrha and the captain standing at the window.

Pyrrha turned her head toward him. "Couldn't you sleep?"

Kyle rubbed his swollen eyes, pulled out a chair and sat down heavily. "No. Any sign of those things?"

"They're in the trees, waiting for one of us to venture outside."

"Yeah, they think we're stupid," said the captain. He pressed his forehead to the glass. "But, peek-a-boo, I can still see you."

Restless, Kyle stretched his arms and neck. The captain left the room, claiming he was going to check on the radio operator in another part of the ship, and Pyrrha took a seat opposite Kyle.

She gave a half smile. "Has your brother taken another moonlit walk tonight?"

"No. He can act stupid at times, but trust me, he's street-smart, always has been. But he's loyal as well, so you can't blame him for going after Jo," said Kyle, feeling proud of his brother again.

Pyrrha nodded. "This may sound strange, but I like him, and his loyalty to his family and friends."

Kyle almost fell back off the chair. "So you *do* like him?"

"Yes." Her eyes widened. "No. Not in that way. I mean, even though he drives me insane, there is nothing deceptive about him. He says it as it is." She flushed. "But I—err—oh, what the hell. He told you what happened, didn't he?"

"You tried to seduce him into cutting your bonds on the yacht. Yes, he told me."

But Pyrrha's expression told him that wasn't what she'd meant, and remembering that Josh had tried to tell them something before Rachel had lost her temper in the tent got him thinking. *What did he say? "Pyrrha thinks me and Kyle are…"*

"That wasn't it, was it?" he asked. "Is there something you want to ask me?"

Pyrrha leaned forward. "You tell me, Kyle."

As her eyes looked deep into his, the hairs on Kyle's neck stood to attention.

"You're wondering if I—that is, we, my brother and I—will betray Mira, aren't you?"

Pyrrha sat back. "I have my concerns, yes… Not that you or your brother would admit it, of course."

Kyle studied her closely. "OK, if we're putting our cards on the table, truth be told, I also have concerns about you. But let me put your mind at ease first. I will kill myself before betraying her. I would die protecting her. I will die protecting my brother, Rachel and Jo. Josh, on the other hand, would die protecting any of us, and that includes you and your people. Now, would you do the same for us? For him? What is your real agenda, Pyrrha? What do you really have in store for us at this sanctuary of yours?"

Pyrrha lowered her head. "My only concern is for Mira, if you want the truth. And yes—I, too, would die to protect her. And if you are truly sincere about her, then you have nothing to fear from me, or from my order."

"Then I guess we have a common cause. Now, unless there's something else you want to ask me here and now, let's just concentrate on getting the hell off this island, shall we?"

There followed an awkward silence before Pyrrha left her seat and stood at the window. "Then we'll say no more about it."

When the captain re-entered the bridge, Kyle spun around in his seat. "Is there any news on rescue?"

The captain hesitated. Then he looked at Pyrrha and said, "No. There appears to be another fog bank moving toward the rescue team, which could cause a delay."

Kyle at last felt a little joy. "You do have signal on this island, then?"

"Comes and goes, but mostly goes, I'm afraid," said Pyrrha.

"What do we do if they don't come for us?" Kyle asked. Pyrrha and her brother exchanged a look, and Kyle repeated, "What happens if they don't come?"

Pyrrha shrugged. "They will come. But if they don't, as I told Mira, when the comet goes, hopefully that thing in the ocean will follow and then we can all leave."

Kyle had a thought. "That river we passed that leads into the ocean—couldn't your friends come for us that way?"

The bridge went silent for a moment. Kyle could see Pyrrha was at least considering it. "One of our scouts said they saw that thing circling the island, but that could help us if we cause a diversion," she said. "If we pretend to leave from here but get on another ship on the river…" Pyrrha looked questioningly to her brother.

"That might work," he said. "Nice one, boy."

"Yeah, you may not want to travel too far up it, though," said Kyle. "Josh and Rachel said they saw something big. Could be a crocodile, or something else, but it took a stag straight under. And you know how big they are. And just for future reference, my name is Kyle, not boy."

The captain stroked his chin. A look of respect appeared upon his face. "OK, Kyle. How far up the river did they see this croc?"

"Not sure, you'll have to ask Josh or Rachel."

"It's not just piranhas in there, then," said Pyrrha, staring out through the window.

"In that river? Surely not," said Kyle.

"When we first got here, one of the scouts saw one," said Pyrrha. "That's why we wouldn't cross. And I don't mean a little one. This was a mutant. Large enough to take a very large chunk of flesh. But if there's also a croc, that could explain why we haven't heard from our scout."

Another one possibly gone! Kyle's brief moment of relief evaporated in an instant. "So, what are you going to do?"

"Obviously, go looking for him tomorrow," said the captain, throwing his hands behind his head in frustration.

The room fell into silence again. Kyle got up to return to the cabin, finally feeling he could sleep. But he wasn't to be that fortunate. As he was about to leave, he caught a quick glimpse of a harpy as it flew past the window.

Slowly, he pulled the gun from his pocket and tapped Pyrrha on her shoulder. "We've got visitors."

CHAPTER THIRTY

TERRORS IN THE NIGHT

Kyle glared out of the bridge window. His blood turned cold as five harpies emerged from the treeline. They paced back and forth along the shore, sniffing the air around them.

Everyone on the bridge froze.

Suddenly, one harpy turned its attention directly toward Kyle.

Its keen, yellow eyes held him transfixed, and Pyrrha had to physically pull his head away from the creature's hypnotic stare.

"Get back to the others," she said in a low, commanding tone. "Prepare them for what I think is about to happen!"

Free from the harpy's control, Kyle bolted from the room and sprinted back to the cabin, only to find it was not as he'd left it. The company's new home was in darkness, and Kyle knew he had definitely left the light on. Instinctively, he raised his gun in defence.

Although darkness had never frightened Kyle—his optician had once informed him that his pupils were able to expand more than normal, allowing more light into his eye and enabling him to see in most dark conditions—he still edged into the gloom. Rachel was no longer lying beside his brother. Jo's bunk was also empty, and to make matters worse, the window was open. Knowing it was shut when he'd left, Kyle hurtled across the cabin to close it. But, from out of the cover of the trees lining the cove, he saw one harpy approach.

At first, the creature resembled an old woman, but when its features appeared more fully in the light of the moon, Kyle could see stumpy horns protruding from its forehead, and a mouth brimming with short, razor teeth.

Kyle reached for the handle, all the while keeping his attention on the creature stalking silently closer, but the piercing yellow eyes and the rank smell from the creature's hellcat mouth, even from a distance, caused him to fumble.

Swiftly, the harpy boarded the vessel. Using its talons like a rock climber's pickaxe and crampons, it began to scale the next tier up toward the window. Kyle remained rooted, frozen in fear.

The harpy was in striking distance. It lunged with lethal, sharpened claws. Instinctually, Kyle threw out a punch in defence and caught the harpy squarely on the nose. As it recoiled, he finally managed to lock the window tight.

He stepped back into the darkness of the room. The creature, now recovered, pressed its hideous face against the glass. Its forked tongue lapped at the smooth surface. Then, to Kyle's dread, it began to pick and pick with its razor claw at the rubber seal holding the pane in place.

Kyle inched toward Mira's bed, keeping a careful eye on the creature outside. But with his focus firmly fixed its the long, spindly talons, he didn't see the shadow inside the room steal to his side until it was too late. The butt of a gun struck the side of his head.

Kyle's body immediately crumpled. His head slammed against the metal bedpost. He raised a hand to his brow. Blood trickled down his arm, and an intense pain shot across his forehead. But still he forced open his eyes. He'd expected to see one of Pyrrha's troops, or even the captain, standing over him, but instead, he was shocked to see Rachel, and even more so, Jo, holding guns firmly in their hands, disappearing back into the shadows.

Kyle frantically wiped the blood from his eyes and tried to get to his feet. But this time, when Rachel struck out with a clenched fist, darkness finally enveloped him.

***

Kyle had no idea how long he'd been unconscious, and when he awoke, it felt as if it was from a bad dream. He lifted his head from the floor and looked despairingly to the window. Once again, he was thrust into a nightmare; he saw two harpies carrying Rachel and Jo high and away into the night sky.

He stumbled to his feet, only to realise that two more had slinked inside the cabin and were skulking at Mira's and Josh's bedsides.

He reached for his gun and fired. But his vision was still blurred, and the bullets missed his targets.

The harpies turned their attention to him. Unleashing long talons from their lank hands, the harpies advanced. Kyle staggered back toward the door. But he knew he wasn't going to make it to the passageway. And when one harpy feigned an attack from the front and the other struck from the side, all Kyle could do was thrust out his arms to protect himself and wait for the fateful impact. But it never came.

To Kyle's relief, Pyrrha appeared and turned on the light. The sudden blast of intense electric light sent the creatures backwards, each pulling its wings around itself to hide its eyes. Her weapon drawn, Pyrrha fired, but the bullets only ricocheted off the monsters' thick, leathery hides. They swept back across the floor and dived through the open window, then they, too, disappeared high into the darkness of the night.

Kyle looked to his brother's and girlfriend's bunks.

"Josh! Mira!" he called out.

There was no answer from either of them.

Why won't they wake up? His head began to hurt again.

"Kyle! Close the window!" Pyrrha cried, and he was jolted back to what was really important at that moment.

While Pyrrha went to secure the rest of the ship, he stumbled to the window and locked it tight, and with no further harpies appearing, and Mira and Josh still in a deep sleep, he lumbered from the room, floundered along the passageway and, after slowly navigating the stairwell, again entered the bridge.

Kyle's insides ached and his head felt thick and woozy. Blood was trickling down his neck. Outside, he saw the creatures entering the forest and felt a fresh flash of rage and the urge to follow. Suddenly, he felt a hand on his shoulder and was swiftly relieved of his weapon.

"Take a seat." The slow, calm whisper came into his ear. "Orders left by Pyrrha. No one is to go outside. Now, we need to see to that wound—"

Kyle shooed the guard away, wiped the blood onto his sleeve and flopped into the captain's chair.

Gradually, his vision began to clear. He retrained his eyes by first staring at the console in front of him, then the deck outside. When his sight had fully returned, he could just make out the approach of more flying fiends swooping through the sky.

"Give me my gun!" he ordered the trooper who had confiscated it.

"I can't," the guard answered. "Pyrrha's orders."

One harpy landed right outside the window. At first, the creature appeared the same as the ones who had taken Rachel and Jo, but then Kyle noticed it had red eyes and a slightly wider mouth.

The guard instantly retreated behind the captain's chair. "I'm no fighter," he said. "I'm only the bloody chef!"

Kyle watched the harpy approach the window, then, slowly at first, then faster and faster at a rhythmic tempo, the creature began to beat its wings against the glass. When a hairline crack appeared, Kyle sprang from his seat.

"Now will you give me my gun?" he asked the cowering guard behind him.

It was then that Pyrrha, the captain and another two guards entered the room. Before Kyle could warn them of the threat outside the window, the harpy lurched forward and discharged a high-pitched screech.

The imploding glass forced everyone to dive for cover.

***

Silence ensued. Kyle slowly raised his head from behind the captain's chair. There was no sign of the harpy. But as he pondered why it hadn't taken its chance and attacked, there came another high-pitched scream, echoing along the corridors of the ship.

As the captain leapt through the shattered window after the creature, and Pyrrha followed close, Kyle realised that it had not intended to attack at all; it had only been there to cause a diversion.

Suddenly, Kyle's only thought was for those he'd left in his cabin. He wrenched his gun from one of the remaining guards and once again sped back through the ship.

The door to the room was closed. Again, Kyle knew he'd left it open. Slowly, he entered. The frame of the window had been dislodged, and glass was splintered across the floor, but Mira and Josh were still lying on their bunks.

He inched forward. It was then, out of the corner of his eye, he saw, lurking in the shadows, the red eyes of a harpy. Its focus firmly on him. He removed the safety on his gun.

Kyle and the harpy stared at one another in a silent standoff. He reached for the trigger just as the creature began to back out of the window.

"If you're willing to leave without a fight, I'm not about to start one," said Kyle.

But just as the harpy was almost clear of the room, it caught its palm on the splintered frame. It bared its razor-sharp teeth in a hiss of pain. Without thinking, Kyle sprang into action. He ran forward and, forcing his gun firmly into the harpy's mouth, he pulled the trigger.

The harpy was dead. Its lifeless body sprawled against the window, preventing any more of its kind from entering the room. Kyle ran to Mira's side, lifted her into his arms, and carried her to the cargo hold.

He secured the door and returned for Josh. But his brother was too heavy to carry, and Kyle had to drag him off his bunk, along the corridor and then down the stairwell. Once Josh was secured safely inside the cargo hold, Kyle ran back to the bridge, but with no ammo left in his gun, he could only watch as more of the red-eyed harpies swooped from above to land on the deck outside.

Immediately, the guards began to panic. Strangely, Kyle no longer felt any alarm, nor fear, so, sensing the guards' anxiety, he calmly moved to their side.

"Aim for the mouth," he instructed. "Trust me, it kills them."

With renewed confidence, the guards stepped forward and raised their weapons.

The standoff once again felt like an eternity. But just when it looked like the creatures were about to retreat, another harpy, larger in size, landed in front of its kin, and as its fierce cry pierced the bridge, the demons attacked.

Muzzle flashes from the barrels of the guns illuminated the room, and three of the creatures lay dead. But as the guards reloaded, the larger harpy squealed an order to its comrades, and the remaining beasts quickly took flight and retreated into the trees.

Instructing the guards to remain on the ship, Kyle leapt out of the shattered window, ran down the plank and through the forest to the tents. He could just about see Pyrrha through the gap between her personal guards, knelt over her unconscious brother.

Instead of joining them, Kyle rushed into her tent and found her lockbox. He entered the code Josh had given him, removed the last machine pistol and returned outside.

The moon cast a supernatural glow over the scene below, and Kyle could see in the distance the dark shapes flying back in the direction of the sepulchre, carrying yet another victim.

"We'll be going into the place now, whether we want to or not," said Pyrrha wearily, watching her men carry her brother back into the forest.

"Why now? Why not when the others were taken?" Kyle asked, shocked at how expendable she considered the guards.

"They all knew the risks that we're facing," she said. "But it's his wife, Laurie, that was taken this time. She's no soldier. He didn't want her to come, but she insisted. She told him he couldn't travel without a doctor aboard."

They returned to the ship, and once Pyrrha had locked the captain away in his room, Kyle headed back to the cargo hold.

"What the bloody hell am I doing in here?" said Josh, rubbing his eyes. "Oh dear, I haven't started sleepwalking again, have I?"

"No, Josh, you weren't sleepwalking," Kyle snapped. "But you bloody well wouldn't wake up when I needed you, would you!"

"What do you mean?" Josh coughed. "When was this?"

"Half an hour ago!"

Josh's eyes widened. "Oh, wait. I remember now. I woke up and heard scratching at the window. When I opened it to see, a bloody harpy spat in my face, and when Mira came behind me to grab me away, it spat again, hitting us both, the filthy bugger. But it then flew off and... Oh, dear. I remember us feeling really tired and then I heard gunshots, but I couldn't wake up. I swear."

"You opened the freaking window!?" Kyle yelled.

"Umm, yeah."

Kyle had to hold himself back from strangling his brother. "Who did you think was going to be outside, Josh? Daenerys Targaryen just popping by with Drogon for coffee and a Mars bar?!"

Josh placed his hands over his ears. "Why are you shouting? I'm standing right beside you." Then he grinned. "Oh, but wouldn't that be so cool if she did?"

Kyle clenched his hands into fists. *This is it. The day I finally kill him!* He took deep breaths. "Josh, those *things* came and took Rachel and Jo, and the captain's wife—I mean, the ones with red eyes took the captain's wife, but the yellow eyes who took Jo the first time have taken her again. But this time, they took Rachel as well!"

"They got my Rach?" Josh sniggered. "Oh boy, are they in trouble now."

Kyle had to take a step back. "Josh, did you just hear me? They have Rachel!"

"Yes, I heard you," said Josh. "But they didn't hurt Jo, so Rachel should be fine. And as long as they don't upset her, the harpies should be safe, too. Now, if you'll excuse me, I'll just simply go and get them back." Josh attempted to get to his feet, but when he found he couldn't move, he held out his hand. "Err—couldn't pick me up, could you, Kaiboy? I seem to be having a little trouble." He laughed again.

"Are you drunk?" Kyle asked, holding the collar on Josh's jumpsuit and sniffing his breath.

"It's some sort of toxin," said Pyrrha, appearing from behind.

Kyle's feelings of anger instantly changed to extreme concern. "Lethal?"

"No. One of our guards got hit in the face—but don't worry, she made a full recovery soon after. That is, until she was foolish enough to run outside and get taken."

Are you having a laugh! "Thanks, Pyrrha! Good to know! Anything else you feel like sharing with us?" Then it struck him. "What if it was this toxin that made her do it?" He looked to Mira and Josh. "Hey, we'd better keep these two locked away."

Pyrrha agreed. "We'll put them in my cabin. There are no windows, and it would take a bomb to break down the door."

Kyle lifted Mira into his arms and carried her to Pyrrha's cabin, while Pyrrha assisted Josh.

"The effects should hopefully wear off soon," she said, gasping as she struggled to lever Josh onto the bed.

But as she locked the door, they could hear Josh calling after them. "For God's sake, Pyrrha, don't tell Rachel I was on *your* bed. And don't tell Kyle I'm on a bed with… err, oh, it's Mira." He laughed.

Kyle closed his eyes, trying his best to ignore him. "He seemed fine when I opened the cargo door."

"Yeah, Pelenna was OK when we found her, but within minutes she couldn't stop crying, and then in a fit of anger she ran outside. I guess the toxin affects everyone differently."

Kyle took a moment to compose himself. "So, what's the plan now? How are you going to get her back with no climbing equipment to get into the sepulchre?"

"My brother will scale that wall. He's an expert climber," said Pyrrha, reloading her weapon.

Now you tell me! "And yet you were willing to leave Jo when you thought she was inside!" he fumed. "And what are you going to do in the meantime, while Captain Grumpy is in the sepulchre? Boil the kettle and have a cup of tea?"

"No, Kyle! We are going to rescue Rachel and Jo. They will get me inside." Pyrrha leaned in close. "Oh, don't look so surprised. I know full well that Josh can't open the tomb. As soon as I saw that Jo was alright, I knew it was her. How, I don't know—yet. But seeing as they've got Rachel as well, I can only guess it's two-keys time again, just like Mira and Jacen—"

Her steely glare suddenly drifted over his shoulder. Kyle turned to see what had grabbed her attention. Her ruse worked. She snatched the weapon from his hand and ordered him back to the cargo hold.

"I'm sorry, this is just in case you decide to leave without me," she said, pushing him inside.

"And Mira? What the hell happens to her while you're away?" said Kyle, kicking the bulkhead in frustration. Yet again he'd allowed someone to disarm him.

"She'll stay here under guard. Don't worry, thanks to you, we know where to hit those things now."

Locked inside and with no way out, Kyle sat cross-legged on the floor and stared helplessly at the door. He could only pray there wouldn't be another attack that night.

CHAPTER THIRTY-ONE

IMPOSSIBLE MISSION

Mira turned on the sidelight and rolled unsteadily off the bed. She was still feeling the effects of the harpy's toxin and could only watch as Josh searched the cabin for a way out. Initially, he tried the door. Then, spying a vent big enough to fit through, he picked up a butter knife from the table and began to remove the screws holding it in place.

"What film did you see that in?" she asked, steadying herself. "*Mission: Impossible*, by any chance?"

"Might have been *Escape from Alcatraz*, or some other prison film like it," Josh said with a smile.

"What's your plan, then?"

"I think I heard Pyrrha take Kyle away to the cargo hold, so, we go and get him first. Then we need to find some weapons before rescuing Rachel and Jo."

Mira's chest felt tight from the toxin. "Shouldn't we wait for Pyrrha first?" She coughed.

"No. What she's got planned is a big no-no!" He removed the last screw.

Mira let out a deep sigh. "Why? What's she got planned?"

"No time to explain," said Josh, pulling out the grate. "Right, I need to climb through here and see if there's a way out."

A sense of foreboding suddenly overcame her. "No, Josh. Look, this is all getting out of control. It's going to be impossible. What if the pipework is smaller inside and you get stuck? Listen, can we for once just sit tight and not rush into doing something stupid, please?"

"Hey, I know what I'm doing. And you of all people know nothing is impossible. Now, I need you to trust me. Can you do that?"

Seeing his face full of hope and trust gazing back at her, Mira reluctantly nodded. Josh gave her a cheeky wink and a smile as he squeezed his body into the narrow tube.

"Rachel's right—you really are enjoying all this, aren't you?" she called out after him.

Josh didn't respond as he disappeared into the darkness, but to Mira's frustration, she could hear the theme tune from *Raiders of the Lost Ark* being hummed.

***

It had been twenty minutes since Josh had wriggled off into the dark. Mira dropped to her knees and was met with a silent blackness as she peered through the opening.

Suddenly, she felt a blast of warm air and guessed this vent provided the air conditioning for the room—although why it had been set to blow warm air had her confused, as the cabin was already a sauna. She began to panic. But just at the moment she was about to enter the duct herself, Josh suddenly reappeared out of the darkness, sweat dripping from his forehead and a look of great concern etched across his face. Mira braced herself for the bad news.

"Bit of a problem," he said, grabbing the butter knife. "You may want to stay in here until I can open the door."

Oh, this can't be good. "Why, what is it now?"

"This ducting leads to a steep drop," Josh said, panting. "But at the bottom of the shaft, someone has retrofitted a motorboat engine with what looks like large, and very sharp, steel blades attached to it—"

"Why would they do that?"

"The air-con unit must have been damaged when we crash-landed. Problem is, if they turn it on, then all they'll do is blow warm air."

"But I can feel warm air blowing now."

"That's just the heat coming from the engine room. Someone just opened the door and left it open. Now, as I was saying, at the moment, the fan isn't moving, but if someone is foolish enough to turn it on and we fall, then our *Strictly Come Dancing* futures will not be looking too bright."

Yup, it's bad! "Why would someone turn it on, Josh? It's like a bloody sweatbox as it is," she asked, holding her head in her hands.

"Err… Maybe they're expecting the weather to change? Or maybe Pyrrha knows what I'm doing and is waiting to turn it on just to teach me a lesson." Josh shrugged.

"So, why are you going back, I dread to ask?"

"Because halfway down there's another route, which may take me to the cargo hold or, if we are lucky, into another room where the door isn't locked."

"And if it doesn't lead to a way out? Which, knowing our luck, it won't."

"Then I come back."

With one last smile, Josh took a deep breath and crawled back into the vent until Mira was left staring into the silent abyss once more.

***

Josh had reached the drop. Slowly, he lowered himself onto the duct's thin bracing bar. Taking care not to drop the knife, he balanced above the fan blades and began to undo the screws on the vent that he hoped would lead him to his brother. But the sound of voices in the distance suddenly increased in volume, and Josh realised that all that was between him and whoever was now occupying the room below were the large blades and the larger motor under his feet. He had no choice other than to stop and listen.

"I think its mad going after Laurie," said one male voice. "Even Pyrrha believes she's dead. We should wait until that thing out there in the ocean begins to circle the island, then sail the ship out to open waters and floor it back home."

"They don't leave anyone behind, you know that," said another male voice. "I say we should have gone after the others with all the ammo we had at the start and stormed that damn tomb, then done what you said."

"Yeah, well, they're probably all dead by now. We've got the girl, so I reckon we leave now. I signed up with Brann out of loyalty to her. Not to fight the Followers or those damn creatures from Hell. Especially in this heat!"

"The problem is the rest are loyal to Pyrrha. If you want to disobey her, on your head be it. Now come on, best get back before she notices I'm not on duty."

"Then just give me one minute," said the grumbler. "I can't sleep in a sauna, you know that."

At the sound of the door closing, Josh proceeded to remove the last screw. But as he began to shift the grate, without warning, he heard the door close a second time and then felt the shuddering vibration as the fan kicked into life.

Startled, he lost his balance, and with one hand preventing him from falling into the steel blades, his other hand holding the grate and only one foot on the narrow shaft, he found he was unable to move. And to add to his woes, he was prevented from calling for help by the three screws he was still biting down on in his mouth. He was afraid to drop them—they could turn into tiny, lethal projectiles if caught in the steel blades.

The fan was spinning at a tremendous speed, and Josh could feel his grip beginning to slip. He anticipated the worst and closed his eyes. But just as his last two fingers parted contact with the grating, he felt someone grab his collar. Mira's outstretched hands were now holding him back from the blades—and from certain amputation.

"Now that's what I call great timing." Josh winked.

Careful to drop the grate to the side of the fan, when both his hands were secured on the ledge, he took a brief moment to control his trembling legs, then pulled himself up and through the vent.

The only light to guide him was provided by the string-like rays streaming through the vents. When he came to a junction, not knowing which way led to the cargo hold, he took a screw from his mouth and spun it.

"Tip is pointing right—then right it is," he said, wiping the sweat onto his dusty sleeve. But then he remembered what had happened the last time he'd taken a right turn. It had led to him and Rachel running for their lives from a giant wolf.

"O…kay. Maybe left this time."

Josh shimmied over a few more vents until he finally came to a hatch. Gently, he lowered the door and peeked out. Fridge-freezers, ovens and a large table strewn with cooking utensils confirmed to Josh that he was indeed above the galley. Briefly, he waited for any sounds of movement. Then, when he was sure no one was coming, he dropped down to the floor and used a broom handle to push the hatch closed and hide his escape.

Josh approached the exit but heard voices heading his way. Spotting a dry-store cupboard, he shot inside and closed the door. But with no locking mechanism and no place to hide, all he could do was stand still and wait.

Josh heard the galley door swing open and surmised by the voices that there were only two people in the room. When the handle of the cupboard door was turned, Josh threw his hands in the air in surrender and closed his eyes.

"Nothing in there but boxes of tinned fruit," Josh heard one voice call out—the same discontented man he'd heard only five minutes earlier.

"What? Who the hell likes tinned fruit?" asked another. This voice Josh didn't recognise.

"Pyrrha likes them, the captain likes them, and about a billion other people like them," replied the grouch. "Anyway, I thought we came for chilled beers. This heat is killing me, and the fan Sherme ordered to be fitted has only intensified the warm air circulating from the engine room. I did warn him. Anyway, now that those flying things are gone, I need a beer, or twenty."

"OK, OK, I just thought I'd see if they had any chocolate as well."

"They don't have any, I've already checked. Now what do you think we should do?"

"We follow Pyrrha's orders. She's our superior."

"Only because her daddy is important and the captain is her brother. She doesn't know how to lead. Look at how that kid runs around her. He wouldn't get away with it if Captain Brann was in charge. That's who I signed on with. Now, I reckon if Sherme doesn't wake up soon, we take our chance in the fog and get the hell away from this island. What do you say? Are you with me?"

There was a moment of silence. Josh opened his eyes and pressed his ear to the door.

"No," said the second voice eventually. "And you're mistaken about Pyrrha. I've heard the others and how they speak about her. She's definitely not one to be trifled with. I know we were not born to this life like the rest of them, but I do know this—they take their beliefs and the chain of command very seriously. They would all give their lives for her. Besides, Captain Brann asked us personally to keep an eye on things. Now, if you're planning on betraying Pyrrha, then leave me out of it. Brother or not, I'm not facing you-know-what when we get to their sanctuary."

"Don't believe those rumours," the discontented man scoffed. "They use it as a scare tactic, that's all. Now listen, Brann asked us to sail them home, not fight some damn creatures that belong in a Peter Jackson movie. And for your information, I wasn't planning on going to their sanctuary."

"Are you nuts?" the grumbler's brother cried. "We have to do what Captain Brann wants. Because of you, we now have to live under her protection from the Followers, whom you cheated—"

"I never cheated them. I won fair and square. It was that Tripp psycho. He pulled some card trick in the last hand, the underhanded bastard. And instead of accepting an IOU for cash, he hustled my business from under me. What the hell would he want with a bakery in the middle of Athens anyway?"

"You lost *our* company that father left us, you mean. I knew it was only a matter of time before your gambling cost us everything. I should have insisted before father died that he put the company in my name. Look at what's happened to us. You've lost our business, our home, and to top it off, you then went and torched the place with Tripp's people still inside and put us on his damn hit list. Now you have your beers, so let's get back to work. And no more talk of betrayal or you'll end up getting us both killed."

The handle of the door was released, and when Josh heard the outer galley door close, he let out a huge sigh of relief and turned on the light.

"Great. Not only do we have harpies and a kraken to deal with but a soon-to-be deserter, if I heard right. And who the hell is this Captain Brann?" he whispered to himself.

He eased open the door as quietly as he could and peered out into the passageway. With the way clear, he sped to the cargo hold.

Relieved to see the door was only secured with a slide bolt, Josh pulled it open to be met with the sight of Kyle sat with his head in his hands. Josh instantly swept his brother up off the floor and encased him in a bear hug.

"Right, Mira is waiting for us, so we'd better hurry before Pyrrha knows I'm gone," he said, loosening his embrace.

Kyle was wide-eyed. "How did you…? I mean—I saw her lock the door to her cabin. How in the hell did you get out?"

"Easy." Josh winked. "I crawled through the ducting, just avoided being chopped into pieces by a big fan— thanks to Mira—climbed back up the ducting, crawled through more ducting, dropped through a hatch into the galley and ta-da, here I am."

Kyle's eyes widened further. "What…? You know what, never mind. So, how are you going to open Pyrrha's cabin to let Mira out if Pyrrha has the key?"

Josh hadn't thought of that. "Umm… I don't know. One thing at a time, yeah? Unfortunately, it may mean Mira will have to follow my route." Impatiently tugging at Kyle's arm, he led him toward the stairwell, and all the while, Kyle shook his head in amazement.

Once they reached Pyrrha's cabin door, Josh gently gave it a tap. With no response from within, he whispered through the keyhole. "Mira, it's Josh. Umm, I don't want to alarm you, but I'm not Lyssa, so I can't pick the lock. You'll have to follow the same route I took. Now, when you get to the junction, take a left turn and that will bring you to a hatch above the galley. But be sure to shut it back up with the broom handle after you've dropped to the floor…" He pressed his ear tighter to the door, trying to hear her response.

"OK, Josh," said Mira, appearing behind him.

"How did you? Never mind, well done." Josh smiled, amazed that she'd already worked out her escape route. "OK, now stick close and do what I do."

"Where are we going exactly?" Kyle asked. "Cos it's still dark out—you know that, right?" Answered only with a grin, Kyle lowered his head and followed Josh along the alleyway.

CHAPTER THIRTY-TWO

TRUTH WILL OUT

The trio had made it to the stairwell without being seen. But Mira and Kyle were then taken aback when Josh, instead of climbing the staircase that would take them outside, suddenly altered course.

"Hey, we need to go up!" Kyle whispered.

"No, we need weapons first."

"But the weapons locker is near the bridge—I saw it earlier—so where are you going?"

"Ladies' shower room."

"What?" said Mira. "Have you finally lost your mind completely?"

Josh entered the room and reappeared only a moment later with a bag thrown over his shoulder.

"That's the bag Pyrrha filled from her tent," said Kyle, and he let out an exasperated groan. "How the hell did you know where it was?"

Josh's grin widened further as he patted Kyle on the shoulder and started his ascent of the stairs. "Trade secrets, my son," he called back.

As the trio reached the top deck, they found two guards standing in the doorway to the bridge.

"So, Houdini, how do we get past them?" said Kyle.

When Josh didn't respond, Mira gave him a sharp dig in the ribs. "Josh!" Her tone was low but fierce.

"What?"

"Are you listening?"

Josh looked around. "Listening to what?"

Mira's hands were now clenched. "To what your brother just asked you!"

"What? He didn't say anything to me. I heard him talk to someone called—err—Houdini, but I just thought he was hearing voices again and I didn't want to listen. You're always telling me it's rude to listen in on Mum and Dad, Kai."

"I'm asking you now," Mira hissed, "so please listen. How do we get out, Josh?"

"Easy," said Josh. "We open the door and walk through."

Sensing Kyle was ready to strangle him, Mira stood between them. "Josh, what I mean is, there are guards on the door that we have to pass, and without shooting them, how else do we leave?"

"Through the door," he said again. "Weren't you listening?"

She now wanted to strangle him herself. "What bloody door?!"

Shaking his head in amusement, Josh eased open a hidden wood-panelled door beside her. "This door." He pointed. "It takes you straight through to the outside," he said, and disappeared into the darkness.

Mira scratched her head. "Tell me, Kyle. How in the bloody hell does Josh know where everything is? He's either been with us or locked up. And this doesn't even look like a bloody door."

Kyle shrugged. "You're asking the wrong person."

"You know, it's only the fact that he saved me that I don't strangle him myself."

Kyle's eyes widened. "Saved you? When was this?"

"When I opened the window to see what the noise was outside, a harpy lunged for me. Josh pulled me clear but got spat in the face for his effort."

Kyle frowned. "He said that he opened it."

Mira shook her head. "No, why would he say that? It was my fault." She turned her attention to Josh as he opened another door to the outside. Finally, it dawned on her, the reason for Rachel's fierce, possessive attraction to him.

The weapon bag was tossed to the shore, and as Josh climbed over the side railing, Mira and Kyle followed suit and dropped into the water.

Soon after, they reached the part of the forest where the ferns were higher and denser.

"As I've already pointed out, I'm getting really tired of coming back and forth to this bloody ship," said Josh, pushing ahead. "Screw setting up camp in the town, we should have gone to the bloody tomb in the beginning and been done with it."

Mira had to agree.

The sun's warm rays beamed through the trees, and as the way forward was clear, they pressed on without looking back until they had reached the fast-flowing river. They picked up the pace while giving the murky water a wide berth. They stopped for a rest once they reached the bears' forest.

"This is where I last saw that man," said Mira.

"What, that man?" said Josh, and he pointed to a figure approaching through the trees. "Crocodile Dundee?"

Mira turned her head. Although the man was now wearing a long, crocodile-skin coat and a cowboy hat, instead of the woollen one she'd seen him wearing the day before, his brown beard tinged with grey, his light hazel eyes and bronzed skin were the same.

"That would be him, yes."

Kyle reached into the rucksack on Josh's shoulder, grabbed a handgun and aimed it at the man.

"Mira, tell him to put it away," the stranger growled.

Mira unconsciously took a step forward, surprised to hear her name. "I'm sorry, do I—do I know you?"

"I should hope so; I'm your uncle." The man smiled.

Mira's heart stopped for a second. "I'm sorry. Who… Who did you say you were?"

"Your uncle," he said, and tilting his hat, he revealed a mass of curly, greyish-brown hair. "Your stepfather, Daniel, is my brother. I was at the wedding. You called me Uncle Tan?"

Mira couldn't breathe and stared silently back.

"Hello?" said the man, waving his hand in front of her face. "Hmm… Perhaps you know me by my full name." He pulled a wallet from his inside pocket and passed Mira an ID card. It had a photo and read *Tandigo Sing*. "I prefer Tan."

"G'day, mate," Josh said with a grin. "How are things down under?"

Tan stared back. "Why would you think I was Australian?" he said. "I don't sound Australian, do I?"

"OK, my bad. Umm, how's this—Howdy, pard'ner."

"Oh, I sound Texan now, do I?"

Josh hung his head. "No. It's just your hat and coat make you look… Never mind."

Mira shook her head at Josh and handed Kyle the card. Josh leaned over his brother's shoulder and burst into laughter as he saw Tan's full name for the first time.

"What's so funny, boy?" said Tan.

Josh bit his bottom lip. "Nothing. Sorry, don't mind me. It's just, err, umm, your sweat is beginning to smudge the fake tan you've got on your face." He sniggered. "Have you thought about using a sunbed instead?"

"It's not meant to be a suntan, boy!" Tan growled. "It's called camouflage." He pulled a rag from his pocket and promptly wiped his face to reveal a pink complexion. "And tanning beds are extremely dangerous, boy. Don't you read the newspapers?"

Josh spun his head in all directions. "Do you see a corner shop around here that sells them?"

Kyle nudged his brother's arm, hoping he'd remain quiet. "If you *are* Dr Alextopolis' brother," he said, keeping his finger firmly on the trigger of his weapon, "How is it your surname is Sing?"

"Same mother, different father." Tan winked. "C'mon, children, it's the twenty-first century. Do we really need to be having this talk?"

It was the wink that prompted Mira to finally recognise the man standing in front of her. During her mother and stepfather's wedding, Tan had kept a close eye on Jacen the whole day, entertaining him with games of peek-a-boo, hide the nose and, Jacen's favourite, the case of the disappearing-reappearing eye. Mira felt her chest tighten, and tears spilled through her eyelashes at the thought of her brother. "Yes, I remember you. How the heck did you find us?" she said, hugging him.

Tan took a moment. "Plain and simple luck. When the rescue helicopter retrieved Daniel and your mother, he called me…" He hesitated.

Mira sensed he was holding something serious back. She swallowed hard.

"What is it?" she asked. "Are my parents OK?"

"Yes, they're fine." Tan half smiled.

"Are our parents alright?" asked Kyle.

"They were the last time that Daniel saw them."

"What the hell is that supposed to mean?" said Josh.

Tan shuffled his feet. "There's something you should know…" He hesitated again.

"Oh, just get to the point!" Kyle growled. "This week has been hell enough as it is!"

Tan looked him square in the eye. "Righto… But let me start by saying that you've been missing for longer than a week."

"That's how we can still see a full moon, then," Kyle said. "But if the cycle of the moon is almost thirty days, that means we've been missing…"

"Three years," said Tan. "Give or take a month. For all intents and purposes, you are now all considered to be lying at the bottom of the ocean."

Silence ensued. It was as if Mira and Kyle had been struck by a thunderbolt.

Josh simply grinned. "Cool. No more school."

"How… How is that possible?" Mira gaped, holding on to Kyle's arm to keep from falling over.

"You tell me." Tan shrugged. "I spent three years searching for that fog bank Daniel described, but I could never find it. Then, one day, when I had given up all hope, I was compelled to go back, and lo and behold, there it was. Problem was I couldn't get through the damn thing. Then, out of the blue, I saw a ship leave with a young woman steering and another desperately looking at some charts. A hunch, I followed. I tried flashing my lights to garner your attention, but then your boat suddenly began making erratic movements and then vanished when the storm picked up. When I saw another boat heading in the same direction, I took a chance and followed it. Unfortunately, when they took you aboard, I was too far back to intervene. When I did finally catch up, that giant of a thing out there in the ocean almost gave me a bloody heart attack. As it tossed you ashore, I came around the island and managed to land."

"Oh, so it was you following us," said Josh. "Wish we'd known sooner. I could be home now watching *The Traitors* with a bucket of chicken nibbles. Unless... is it still on?"

"Is that all that concerns you, Josh?" Kyle growled. "That *The Traitors* is still on? Not the fact that, somehow, we were on that island not for three days, but in actual fact, three years?!"

Josh blew out his cheeks. "With everything else we saw and went through, why not?"

"Hmm, it is written that the island was special," said Tan.

"Wait. You know about the other island?" Mira asked. Her heart was racing, and her mind quickly went to the Followers.

"Of course." Tan smiled. "Every Disciple knows of it. Daniel and I, in our youth, went searching for it. Never found it, mind you. So, what was it like?"

"Wow," said Josh. "I did not see this coming."

Mira took a deep breath and another step back. "Are you saying that my stepfather is a... Disciple?"

Tan scratched his beard. "Hmm... Guess I should have waited for him to come clean to you first really, shouldn't I?"

"But if you are a Disciple, why haven't you revealed yourself to Pyrrha, or any of the others?" asked Kyle.

"And how did you know there was a chimney in that Mayan pyramid thingy?" said Josh.

"It is not Mayan," said Tan. "The Disciples construct-ed it. I knew of the chimney because I have been trained to look for such things. Now, listen, the sun—which, may I say, is acting really strangely on this island, considering where we are in the world—could be setting shortly, so let's not get caught out in the open. I know a place in the town that's safe where you can ask all the questions you want. But I also have questions for you."

"What do you mean, the sun is acting strangely?" Kyle asked.

Tan looked surprised. "Haven't you noticed the different times it rises and sets?"

Blank faces stared back.

"This time of year, we should have at least fourteen hours of sunlight. But on this island, we're only getting eight, and that's if we're lucky."

Josh raised his hand. "And what part of the world are we actually in?"

Tan's smile faded into a frown. "We're in the Mediterranean, aren't we?"

"You don't really know, do you?" said Josh.

Tan chewed his cheek. "To be honest with you, no. We were in the Med, but then the Aegean. To be honest, my instruments kind of went haywire before I left the last island."

"So, you've never been to this island before?" said Mira.

"No, no I haven't."

Mira was now on guard. "So, how come Pyrrha knows about this place, but you don't?"

"Her order is the oldest, and sadly they don't like sharing all of their information with the rest of us. Smart of them, but it can be a bit of a pain. Look, we don't have much time, so please can we go to my shelter before those flying banshees come and use our bones to clean out our flesh from their teeth?"

Tan led the way through the forest and to the town they'd been to before. As they approached, Kyle quietly handed Mira and Josh pistols, which they pocketed.

Tan directed them through to the main street, then took a sharp turn into a narrow alleyway, leading them to a building with a trapdoor inside. All four then started to climb down the ladder, descending into blackness once more.

A portable light was turned on. Mira, who had hesitated on the ladder until she was sure it was safe to continue, motioned for Kyle and Josh to join her. Once everyone was inside, Tan then climbed back up the ladder, closed the hatch and locked it tight.

"This was the safest one I could find," he said, tapping the door. "Really thick wood. It will be hard for those things to break through. Now, first things first, are you hungry?"

"No, thank you," said Mira. "I really think you should tell me everything first. Are my parents—sorry, are *our* parents really safe?"

"Yes, yes. They're all safe," said Tan, squatting down onto the floor. "Now, make yourselves as comfortable as you can."

Mira sat with her back to the wall, and Josh took a seat on a fishing stool, but Kyle remained at the base of the ladder, watching the hatch. When Tan reached inside his rucksack, Kyle quickly aimed his weapon at him. "I would be very careful what you decide to pull out if I were you," he snarled, releasing the safety.

Tan slowly revealed a flask. "Take it easy, Quick-Draw McGraw." He smiled. "Do you mind if I have a coffee first, before I begin?"

Kyle watched as he poured himself a mug. "Fine. But no more sudden movements," he warned.

Tan took a big gulp of his coffee then slowly placed the cup and flask beside him. "Now I'm ready." He winked.

CHAPTER THIRTY-THREE

TRUST

The portable light was placed in the centre of the group. Tan blew his nose and cleared his throat. "I'm assuming by now you know all about us, right? The Disciples, I mean?"

"Pretty much, and we know about the Followers, too," said Mira.

Tan's eyes widened. "Oh, right. That makes things a little easier. But what do you know about your real father, Mira?"

"Only that he left us in the middle of the night. And the little bits that Pyrrha has shared with me. He was raised by the Disciples, but one night, after visiting a library, he left. Seems he has a habit of doing that. Leaving without warning in the middle of the night."

Tan's eyes drooped. "Don't judge him too harshly, Mira. He left so that you and your family had a chance of a life away from all this madness. Something he never truly had."

"That worked out well, didn't it?" said Josh sarcastically.

Tan cast him a steely glare. "As I was saying… When your father, your biological father, left the order, my brother and I were given the task of finding him. It was

Daniel who succeeded in doing this. I somehow ended up in some godawful place filled with rotting fish, where the people spoke only—" Suddenly he stopped, aware of the row of pale faces staring back at him. "That doesn't matter. Anyway, my brother had tracked him and—"

"Wait," Josh interrupted. "Dr Alextopolis tracked him? I thought he was a doctor?"

"I told you, Dr Alextopolis is a professor of archaeology," said Kyle.

"No, you didn't."

"Look, my brother is gifted at many things." Tan's glare intensified. "Now, if you don't mind, may I continue?"

Josh mimicked closing a zip across his mouth.

"My brother Daniel," Tan continued, "and your father, Mira—they became close friends. When Daniel revealed that the Followers had discovered where your father was hiding, Elijah decided that your mother should take you and your brother away. He didn't want a life on the run for you, too. As my brother had grown close to you all, he left our order and swore to protect you. I chose to never disclose his whereabouts, obviously for the love and loyalty I have for him.

"Now, I hadn't seen Daniel since the wedding to your mother, but then, out of the blue, he called me and told me what had happened. At that time, I was investigating the disappearance, possible murder, of a Potential at another sanctuary. Unfortunately, I had to shut it down permanently, if you know what I mean. I wasn't sure about the ones you travel with now, so I watched and followed you. But when those flying things came for you, I had to improvise, so I fired a shot, checked they hadn't attacked you and then hid myself in here until they were gone."

"Did you see what happened to Pelenna?" said Kyle. "The guard they'd taken?"

"She's dead."

"Are you sure?" asked Josh.

"Unless she can survive without a head," said Tan. "Yup, I'm pretty certain."

Silent grimaces stared at the ground.

"You mentioned a Potential," said Mira eventually. "Was her name Lyssa?"

"No, Lyssara." said Tan.

"That's what Lyssa said her name was," said Kyle, finally lowering his gun. "Lyssara Charmaine."

Tan's eyes narrowed. "That's who I was looking for. She was with you? Well, well. Where is she now?"

"Dead," said Josh flatly.

"Oh, right," said Tan. "Did she say anything to you about why she left her order?"

"No," said Kyle. "All we know is that she wanted to kill the one who could open Pandora's tomb. She tried to kill me, but I had to…"

There was a long pause before Tan finally said, "Kill her?"

Kyle's complexion turned even paler. "I didn't want to, I swear, but—"

"You didn't kill her, Kyle. Remember that!" Mira snapped.

"I stabbed her. It wouldn't have mattered if Mrs Mooney plunged her dagger into Lyssa or not. I saw the life leaving her eyes."

"You had to," said Mira, shifting her gaze back toward Tan. "Otherwise, she would have killed you, me and my brother."

"Damn fool," said Tan, scratching his beard. "What the hell was she thinking?"

"Before we get to that," said Mira. "If my father—sorry, stepfather—was part of the Disciples, surely he knew of the Followers, right?"

"Of course, he did."

Mira hesitated for a brief moment. Her next question could potentially break her heart. She took a deep breath. "Then why did he allow us to go on a cruise ship swarming with them?"

Tan's mouth fell open. "I'm sorry? Are you saying the Followers... were aboard the ship?"

Mira's hands began to shake. "Not just on it—they owned it."

Tan blinked furiously and shook his head. "I have no idea why he would do such a thing. He never mentioned them. He just said that the ship had been caught in a storm and that you were lost at sea."

Mira felt sick just thinking of it again. "Then how did you know to go to that island to find us?"

"Daniel told me that the last time he saw you, you were entering a fog bank so high that it touched the heavens. He gave me the last coordinates he'd seen you at, and so that's where I went. Look, I can see where your reasoning is taking you, but I promise, Daniel is not a traitor. He risked his life in staying to protect you. In fact, he was going to come himself but sadly has developed severe seasickness since the sinking."

"Or maybe the Followers made him an offer he couldn't refuse, and that's why he betrayed her?" said Josh.

Tan glowered at him, the shadows around his eyes deepening.

Mira's hand jumped to her gun, ready to draw it if Tan struck out at Josh. "He's right, Tan," she said. "Makes complete sense when you think about it."

Tan gave a long exhale. "Mira, do you really think your mother would have betrayed you, too? She knew all about us, and the Followers. Please believe me, my brother and your mother would lay down their lives for you. But I will get to the bottom of this, I swear."

There was another moment of quiet reflection until Josh broke the silence.

"So, if Lyssa was a Potential, why would she want to kill Mira and Jacen? Did the order sanction her to do it?"

Mira smiled inside. That was the question she'd been about to ask to see if Tan and Pyrrha's stories matched.

"No," said Tan simply.

"How do you know?" Mira asked. "And if they didn't, why then did you erase them? That's the term, right, for killing people—erase?"

"Hmm, I can see where this is going," said Tan. "When the comet arrived, there was a big meeting between all the Disciple orders. This particular one, let's say, expressed a wish to have all the Potentials killed and end the threat for good. It was voted down. But I was asked to keep an eye on them anyway. When I arrived to remove Lyssara to another sanctuary and found that she was missing, I questioned one for information. They were still going to kill her and were also planning to kill all of the other Potentials. How she found out, escaped the sanctuary and got aboard the cruise ship, that's something I can't answer. And now that she's dead, we'll have to assume she's taken the truth to her grave."

Mira swallowed hard. "You said it was voted down. Did any of the other orders vote to kill the Potentials in their care?"

"Not that I'm aware. Only the one that resides no more upon this earth," Tan said. "I came from the order at Rhodes, and I can assure you they will not allow it.

And from what I have seen and heard, neither will the ones you are with now."

The room fell quiet again. Mira could see the silence was becoming unbearable for Josh as he squirmed around on his stool.

"So, err, you met Jo, then?" he said, proving her right.

"Yes, and when I returned, I met a young man who told me you had come for her. And before you ask," he added, raising his hand, "he also told me the reason he didn't go with you."

"Yeah, that's not important right now," said Mira, who had been thinking hard about her mother and why she'd have kept this from her. "Do you know where my father is now, my real father?"

"No, I don't. Sorry."

"Then can you take us to rescue Jacen when we get Rachel and Jo back?" Josh asked.

Tan frowned, the creases on his forehead deepening. "What do you mean rescue Jacen? And get Rachel and Jo back?"

"Yeah, the Followers have Jacen, and the flying grannies that took Jo to begin with have kind of snatched her back," said Josh, "but they've taken my girlfriend Rachel now, as well."

"The Followers have Jacen? Damn it!" Tan slapped his hand down on the hard ground. "I'd hoped that you had him hidden away aboard your ship and that was why I hadn't seen him. And you say those things have taken Jo and Rachel this time? Great, I'd thought when they didn't harm Jo they were on our side... So, the red-eyed ones that have been taking those guards are obviously here to keep anyone out of the sepulchre. Back home, we have wolves to do that, but here we have flying banshees," he said, shaking his head.

Josh held his hand up. "If you want to be precise, they're called harpies."

"More like bloody herpes, the damage they do," said Tan. "OK, before we go any further, first things first— tell me everything that's happened."

Mira silently eyed him.

Tan sighed and added, "I'm happy you're cautious, all of you. Now, will this make you all trust me?" He handed over his gun.

Mira placed the weapon inside her jacket and pondered upon his question for a moment. Unable to accept Josh's theory that her stepfather would have betrayed her and her brother, she explained everything to Tan, right from the start of the holiday: the dreams, the storm, the boat that conveniently appeared to take them to the island, to Jacen being taken by the Followers.

All throughout, Tan's eyes were wide. "Right then. Some good news, but mostly bad," he said. "Let me think... OK, let's see if I've got this right. Without you, Mira, coffin number one can't be opened because it needs another key. So that's good news. But they still have your brother, and when they find out about the second key, then it could be bad news not only for him but also you, as they will come looking. I can't allow that to happen.

"Now, the two that can open this tomb and coffin are here on the island already, but the yellow-eyed vermin have them. If what I'm now thinking is right, they are going to bring them to the sepulchre at some point to open the tomb, so that's more bad news. And you say that Pyrrha and Sherme are going to try and get in there to rescue Sherme's wife, Laurie?"

Mira nodded.

"Then that's just bad for them." Tan gave another shake of his head. "What to do? What to do? First, you lot are a priority, so we get your friends, and I take you somewhere safe. I'll then contact my order, and we'll go and rescue Jacen and deal with every Follower we find, then the problem is solved." He smiled, sticking out his chest and nodding confidently.

Mira refused to allow herself even a sprinkle of hope. "Um, sorry to spoil your plan, but Pyrrha said that they have secured Jacen inside a fortress—"

Tan threw his head back and snorted. "Pish, posh. Let me tell you something... Nothing is a fortress. Anything can be breached," he added, tapping his chest and grinning. "Do you know exactly where he is?"

"Pyrrha said that there are three locations. London. Rome. And there's one somewhere in Greece. Now, the vision I had back at the other island showed me he was in Egypt. But in my dreams lately—I think it is under the Parthenon in Athens."

"Under the Parthenon you say? Inside the Acropolis...? Oh, right, maybe a bloody fortress then." An expression of extreme concern appeared briefly on his face. "What crafty beggars they are. Who would have guessed there was a secret lair buried under the Parthenon? I was pretty sure it wasn't London. The order we have there has a lot of influence in the country, and we'd have heard. As for Rome, well, the Followers know we watch it closely, as it's their biggest sanctuary... Righto. I think it would be best to wait until they take Jacen to Egypt." As if sensing Mira's concern, Tan quickly added in his best booming, heroic tone, "But, I promise, I will rescue him and kill all the Followers responsible for his kidnapping."

"I have a question," said Kyle, who had been quietly, and intently, listening.

"Oh, the strong, moody, silent type finally speaks again. I thought you had lost your tongue," said Tan, shifting his gaze to him. "OK, shoot, Mr Bond—but not your gun. I just meant shoot with your question."

Kyle didn't laugh. "If you took out this rogue unit that wanted the Potentials killed but you don't know if the others want them dead, why do think you'll be able to take us somewhere safe now?"

"Good question—someone has been paying attention." Tan smiled. "Because, dear boy, I'm not going to take you to any sanctuary the Followers or even the Disciples know about. I'll take you where Mira will be with her mother and my brother."

"And where is that, exactly?" said Kyle.

Tan half smiled. "If I were to tell you, then it wouldn't be a safe place."

Mira watched Kyle's grip tighten on his gun. "OK," he said. "Mira recognises you, and if you are Dr Alextopolis' brother—even though I now have doubts about him—I guess I'll have to trust you, for now. But when Mira told you what happened to us back at that island, and then what Pyrrha told her, it didn't look like you believed her. So, I need to know. Do you believe in the gods, or are you just a gun for hire?"

Tan threw back his head and laughed. "Gun for hire? Really? That's how I come across? Listen, I was raised a Disciple. But when I got older and saw more of the world, I started to look at things differently. So, here's what I believe now. Mira's great, great, great ancestors had a terrible thing done to them, but what Pyrrha told her about the vases having special herbs to bind Pandora and Epimetheus is utter horse-twaddle. They are jars of poison, toxin, or whatever you want to call it that will explode if the coffins are opened, that's all. You know, it happened all the time back then, more than you think."

"That's what I told them," said Josh.

Tan nodded in agreement. "Yes. For the ancient Egyptians, it was like stuffing a turkey."

"What?" Josh laughed. "They filled up turkeys with explosive poisons? I didn't read that bit."

Mira held her hand over Josh's mouth. "But if you and Pyrrha are both Disciples, why is it you believe they're jars of poison, but Pyrrha believes that Pandora and Epimetheus are cursed and waiting to be freed so that they can basically wipe out mankind?"

Tan howled with laughter. "Are you kidding? Is that what Pyrrha told you? I would have thought that they'd have at least moved into the twentieth century by now, if not the twenty-first. Then again, there is one sanctuary that believes the gods were simply aliens who came here thousands of years ago and left some of their people behind, and when they died the bodies turned poisonous."

"That's what I think," said Josh. "Aliens crash-landed, and because they were superior to us, they were worshipped as gods."

Tan blew out his cheeks. "I should have known you would think that. Now, what was I saying... Oh yes. Granted, I didn't know about Epimetheus until you told me, but even if my Elders know about him, and all the other Elders from the various orders, it seems to me you only have to think about it logically. How could mortals survive this long, even if they were cursed? I mean, really. Now, we can't let those idiot 'Followers' open them, so when they move the boy, my order and I will go and kill them all, and pish-posh done, and we can all go back to doing whatever we want."

"Wait," said Kyle. "What about the dreams Mira and I have been having? The woman in white we both saw? All these strange creatures? Surely they must convince you."

"Convince me of what? That there's a higher power?" Tan laughed. "Do you know how many creatures have yet to be discovered? They find a different type of spider and flower every two minutes. Look, I've travelled all the seas of the world, and I can tell you there are things beneath the oceans of this planet that have yet to be discovered by the scientific community that would terrify you. And these flying rodents—well, they're just another thing waiting to be found. Trust me, in a year or so they'll probably be performing tricks in a circus somewhere, or they'll be backing singers for Kylie Minogue in Las Vegas."

Kyle's face turned blood red. Mira could see he was about to erupt at any moment.

"Then what about these islands that disappeared but have now reappeared?" he continued. "Surely satellites would have at least picked them up? And what about the comet of doom that has reappeared after *thousands* of years?"

"Pish, posh, comets and satellites," Tan scoffed. "I can't get the bloody satellite dish in my garden to work half the time. And those boffins at NASA, they're only interested in outer space. Whereas all the agencies and governments of the world with satellites are only interested in knowing what you had for breakfast and if you're someone who will cause them trouble. They're not interested in islands covered in fog. Trust me, there are other islands yet to be discovered and there will always be new comets or old comets flying around the sky. Halley's Comet, anyone?"

"Yeah, but that comet doesn't hang around for years," Josh mumbled.

"He's right, Tan," said Mira.

Tan rested his hand in his chin to contemplate this. "OK, not a great example… Umm, let me think…"

It was taking too long. "Then what about the dreams, premonitions we've been having? Like the storm that sunk the cruise ship. Can you explain that?" Mira pressed.

"I'll admit that there are people that see things either before they happen or things from long past," said Tan. "But does that mean it's the gods showing them, or is it simply science? How much do they really know at the moment about the human brain, or any brain for that matter?

"Look at a shark. They give birth and move on, yet the babies seem to know instinctually what to do without their mothers teaching them. Millions of years of evolution passed down through the DNA. Don't think too hard about whether it's God or the gods that are doing all this—all you really need to know is that you don't open the coffins."

"So, Pandora and Epimetheus may not be in them, then?" Mira asked.

"No. I mean, what's left of their bodies is probably still in there, but still alive? That's ridiculous. No, it's just jars of poison. But I do believe the gods are influencing these creatures to do what they want."

Kyle shook his head and covered his face with his hands. "So, if you *do* believe in the gods, what was all that about being logical and what the brain is capable of and shark DNA, and well, basically everything you just said?"

"Yeah," said Josh. "You rolled your eyes at me when I said it could have been aliens. My reason makes more sense."

"I just meant you're concerning yourselves too much on whether it's the gods that are doing all this, or if there are toxic zombie bodies locked away just waiting to be released. Don't worry about any of that. Just don't open the coffins."

Mira knew what Kyle was thinking. She was thinking the same thing. Tan had either been in the sun too long, or he'd been dropped on his head as a child and was probably Josh's real father and there had been a mix-up at the hospital.

Josh grinned. "You've been talking to Jo, haven't you, Tan?"

"A little, yes. Seems like a smart girl. A bit too much of a know-it-all for me, though. So, are there any more questions?"

Josh raised his hand. "Yes, can I ask you something?"

"Sure, why not? Hang on—can you open any of the tombs?"

"No," said Josh. "Unless are there other tombs you wish to share with us?"

Tan stroked his beard. "Not that I know of, but who really knows. So, ask away, boy."

"Can I be your apprentice?"

Tan stared back coldly. "No. You're too old, and you're too weird, if I'm being totally honest. Now, don't get me wrong, I like you. Well, maybe like is not the right word. I can tolerate you, for now, which, for you, is good. So, any other questions before we go and rescue Punchy and Miss Know-it-all?"

"Punchy?" Josh laughed. "Don't you mean Slappy?"

"No, Punchy seems right," said Tan. "It always starts with slaps, but soon she'll be punching you, trust me. But to be fair to her, after listening to you for two days, I won't blame her for it. Not that I condone it for others, of course. The only people I think should be slapped are the ones who schedule the adverts on TV. They always come on when I'm in the middle of a good show, or a movie. Put the bloody adverts on for an hour after the show, just not during! Take last Christmas, for instance, when I stayed in Cardiff. There I was, totally immersed in the classic black-and-white 1940s film, *Scrooge*, and the Ghost of Christmas Past has taken him back to Fizzy-drink's party—"

"Fezziwig," said Josh.

Mira cast Josh, who had his head lowered and was laughing to himself, a steely glare. The last thing she wanted was for Tan to get off topic.

"OK, Fezziwig," Tan continued. "When out of blue, I'm watching someone whining about why her hair isn't bouncy enough! I thought, I don't remember this the last time I saw this film. Is it the director's cut, perchance? It was only when the DFS Boxing Day sale advert came on next that I realised what had happened. It's enough to drive you to drink."

Mira had had enough. "OK, can we get back to what's important, please?"

Tan nodded. "She's right. But first, I need you to wait here and let me check that the coast is still clear."

And, quickly climbing the ladder and opening the hatch, he was gone.

Kyle took a deep breath and rubbed the sides of his head. "So, can we trust him? Because it's like having two of him now," he said, pointing to Josh.

Mira smiled and let out a slight chuckle. She couldn't stay angry with Josh. Not when he'd selflessly taken the blame for the harpy attack. "Yes, I think we can trust him, but we'll still keep an eye on him, if you know what I mean."

Josh grinned. "Well, I like him. He makes no sense at all—he's my kind of psycho. And you would be lucky to have two of me."

They waited for ten minutes and were about to follow Tan outside when he reappeared, climbed back down the ladder and slumped to the ground. "It would be a bad idea to leave right now. I wouldn't have believed it if I hadn't seen it with my own eyes," he said, rubbing his red hands together.

"Seen what, Tan?" Mira asked, fearing the next words to come out of his mouth.

"It's snowing. This part of the world, and it's snowing a blizzard."

"Snow?" Josh leapt to his feet, grinning wildly. "No way!"

"Oh God, he's gonna want to build a snowman," said Kyle, massaging his temples again.

"Oh, c'mon, I gotta see it and then sing it!" said Josh, bouncing up and down.

"You could," said Tan, "but just be careful. The bears have entered the town, looking for cover."

"Do you mean one big bear and her two cubs?" Josh asked, no longer bouncing.

Tan took a seat on the floor. "No. I saw eight big, male brown bears. The females won't be with them; they will take the cubs somewhere safe."

Josh's shoulders slumped. "But it is snowing though, right?"

"Yes—don't you ever listen? It's snowing, and it's hard to see or move about, and there are bears!"

"Yeah, yeah, it's just I like snow, that's all," said Josh, dropping to the floor.

"Go then," said Tan. "Have fun. Get eaten. One less person for me to worry about."

Mira shot a look to Kyle, who was now staring off into space.

I know what you're thinking, she thought. *I'm thinking about Ted, too. Nice one, Tan. Kyle is back on Pandora's island.*

So, what are we going to do, Mira? she thought to herself. *How do I get the old Kyle back for good?* She then noticed that Josh was also staring at his brother. *Come on, Josh. If anyone can get Kyle to think of something else, it's you...*

CHAPTER THIRTY-FOUR

MEMORIES

An hour had passed in total silence, and Mira still couldn't think of a way to snap Kyle out of playing the events of the last island over and over in his mind. Part of her wanted to slap him out of it, another to wrap her arms around him—something she would often do with her brother when he was upset. But deep down she wanted him to be the one reassuring *her*. She wanted the person who had made her feel safe on Pandora's island to tell her everything would be OK. And yet, she knew how he was feeling. She, too, wanted to curl up and cry, but she couldn't fall apart now. That was the last thing the group needed. She held back her tears and was relieved when, finally, Josh spoke up.

"You know, this reminds me of the last time it snowed, and I was stuck underground."

Everyone tilted their heads toward to him.

"I'm sorry, what?" said Kyle. "When were you ever stuck underground?"

"When we had that heavy snowfall two years ago," said Josh. "Sorry, that would be five years ago now. Anyway, I was with Belinda Harrington and we got stuck in her grandfather's bomb shelter. You must remember, Kaiboy. Mum had the police out looking for me?"

"Oh yeah, that I remember," said Kyle.

Josh's eyes narrowed. "Speaking of which, you know about Belinda, don't you?"

Kyle dropped his head into his hands. "No, what about Belinda?"

"What, you haven't heard?"

"No, Josh, I haven't heard."

"Well, I thought at least you knew about Belinda?"

"Why would I be asking now if I knew?"

"She's pregnant." Josh grinned.

Kyle sat up straight. "Belinda Harrington is pregnant? We're talking about the same Belinda Harrington? She was going to be a nun, wasn't she?"

"Yeah, and you know who the father is, don't you?"

"Oh, dear God, it's not you, is it?" said Mira.

Josh laughed. "No, it's Alex Regis."

Kyle took a moment, then emitted a deep groan that told Mira he was close to breaking point with his brother. "Alex is gay. He goes to aikido and he's a friend of mine."

"That's what he tells all the girls." Josh smirked. "He makes friends with them, tells them he's gay, puts on a sob story, they invite him for sleepovers and then miraculously turn him straight. This will be his third kid. Looks like his parents will have to move house again."

Mira looked to Kyle. He was totally immersed in what Josh was telling him. She had to keep herself from smiling. *That's it, Josh—you're giving him a chance to regroup.*

"Although," Josh added, "the father is also rumoured to be Paul Williamson Deggs."

Kyle's eyes widened. "The drug dealer? He's doing five to ten years, isn't he?"

"Ten, to be precise. Bet there was fun at his house when his girlfriend Gemma Muston found out he could be having a kid with someone else. Then again, she was arrested for posting horrible stuff about someone on Talk till You Drop. Simply because they'd disagreed with Gemma's own ideals on… Oh, I can't remember what it was now. But to do that to the person who had got her a job? What a truly nasty piece of work Gemma has turned out to be."

"When did this happen?" said Kyle.

"Just before we left for the cruise. Hey, maybe the guards have put Gemma and Deggsy in a cell together for the entertainment factor—"

"I didn't hear about that," said Kyle. "Are you making this up?"

"No, I swear. Graham Byrne told Steven Stillward. Graham was going to have Gemma in his next low-budget horror movie, but she told him she couldn't be-cause of the upcoming court case."

"Graham is in the entertainment industry? No way. He's only a year older than us. In fact, his birthday is next week, which will make him seventeen—"

"Yeah, I know." Josh grinned. "He's been doing it a year. Goes by the name After-Byrne now. Or is that his production company…?"

"Production company?" Kyle cried.

"Yeah, he's got his own production company. He's doing really well by all accounts. He asked if I wanted a summer job, but we had this holiday, so I couldn't do it, sadly."

"Doing what?"

Josh shrugged. "He said I couldn't go on the set, but I would run messages, bring the tea, coffee and biscuits to the stars' rooms."

"Hold on, doesn't he live with his parents in Amer-ica?"

"No, he's back, and asked his sister Wendy to ask me."

"How do you know Wendy Byrne? She's twenty-five at least."

"I know, she goes to my gym. She's a really good boxer. I used to spar with her. Anyway, he's doing the movie not far from where we live. The old Burton house."

Kyle blew out his cheeks and finally seemed relaxed, and as he stared at the floor, shaking his head, Mira gave Josh a wink and mouthed the words *thank you.*

"So, I take it apart from sharing a room, you two don't bother with each other at home?" she asked.

"No!" they said together.

At that moment, there was a loud thud above their heads. Mira's heart began to beat faster. *Oh no. Are the harpies or the bears waiting for us to make an appearance?* Her eyes drifted to the hatch. *Hang on—are those snow-flakes fluttering through the cracks?*

At the thought that the snow had entered the room above and they were slowly being buried alive, Mira had to clench her hands together to stop them from shaking. *Do not show the others how scared you are!*

Slowly, she turned to Kyle. His eyes were closed, but his face was red and he was sweating profusely.

Has he seen it too?

She looked to Tan, who had his cowboy hat pulled down over his face.

Should I warn him?

Her eyes flashed back to the hatch.

That's it, I can't take any more! I have to get out of here!

Before she could leap to her feet and run up the ladder, however, Josh opened his eyes.

"So, is it still snowing, Kaiboy?" he asked chirpily.

Kyle sighed. "I don't know, I haven't got X-ray vision."

"Oh, yeah, course you don't. Hey, remember last year's holiday in the snow? I mean, three years ago?" Josh laughed.

"Yes, Josh, I remember. It's forever burned into my brain, as well as Mum and Dad's."

Mira eyes widened. "Why, what happened?" She was desperate to take her mind off what was happening above their heads while also trying to control the wild thumping in her chest.

Kyle shot Josh a glare. "We went on a skiing holiday, and it snowed so bad that we were stuck in the hotel for five days, and Josh had only brought one pair of socks. And we couldn't open the window because Josh had somehow managed to break the handle. And, of course, we couldn't change rooms because the hotel was full, so my mother had to wash his socks in the sink every night because the laundry room refused to do it due to the foul odour. Oh, and to top it off we could never get rid of the smell in the room."

"It wasn't that bad." Josh smirked. "And it was Mum's perfume we could smell. It was like essence of cat pee, and you know full well that Dad has never bought it for her again. Anyway, talking of bad holidays, remember two years ago? Or should I say, five years ago. Ah-ha, tell Mira what happened then, Kaiboy?"

Mira knew she shouldn't, but now she had to ask. "Kyle?"

"You mean the holiday in America where you jumped up and down in the elevator so hard that we were all stuck in it for four hours? Or when you decided to go for a walk on your own and Mum had the New York police out looking for you? Or when you raided the mini fridge and cost Dad hundreds of pounds? Or was it when you snuck off and managed to get yourself locked in the Statue of Liberty? Is that the holiday you're on about?" Kyle seethed.

Josh shrugged. "The year before that, then. But let me just say, for everyone's information, the elevator said it would hold—oh, I can't remember the weight—but I did them a favour proving it couldn't. And the mini fridge wasn't my fault because nobody told me you get charged; I thought it was complimentary with the room. And the New York police were brilliant. They told Mum she'd overreacted. They actually took me on a ride-along before they brought me back. They had to arrest that guy from that show, um, *Law & Order*, I think it was. Hey, how ironic is that? He was really nice, though. He gave me his autograph and said if I was ever in New York again to look him up. Said his daughter was single and would love my accent. As for the Statue of Liberty incident, well, that was completely Mum's fault."

"How was it Mum's fault?" Kyle growled.

"Because she trusted me not to get locked in, that's why."

"So, what happened five years ago?" said Tan, raising his cowboy hat above his eyes.

"Oh, nothing," said Josh. "Just that Rocky Balboa over there laid out three boys and got us kicked out of the summer camp after—how long was it, Kaiboy? Oh, that's right—one hour. And Mum and Dad had to come all the way back and pick us up. One hundred miles they had to come, mind you, in Bank Holiday traffic."

An alarm went off in Mira's head. "Why did you hit them?" she asked. She knew that Kyle had got into fights before, but he had sworn to her he'd never started any trouble. Was he not the person she had fallen so deeply for?

"They were bullying someone younger than them," Kyle said, scowling, his eyes fixed on Josh.

"But they weren't, were they?" said Josh. "*Nooo.* They were trying to see to their younger brother, who was screaming after being stung by a wasp."

"Well, I didn't know," said Kyle, cringing at the thought of it. "They were crowding him, and he was crying. What else do you do?"

"Oh, I dunno, maybe ask the kid first? That would have been the smart thing to do."

"OK, I ruined one holiday, but how many others have been ruined by—"

Josh broke into a big grin. "None," he interjected. "I've enjoyed them all."

Again, there was silence. Even though Mira was happy that Josh had successfully taken Kyle's mind off Pandora's island, and that he'd stopped her from freaking out and giving away their location to any predators that could be waiting for them, she soon realised her mistake in not stopping Josh from going too far.

"So, is it still snowing, Kaiboy?" he asked with a straight face.

Kyle leapt to his feet. "That's it! I don't care if I freeze to death, get chased by flying monkeys, or get eaten by bears—I'm going to get Rachel!"

And as he took his first steps up the ladder, Mira leapt from her spot and held on to his leg.

"Look, if he carries on, I'll do what Rachel does, only harder, but you can't go out there yet!" she begged.

Taking a deep breath, Kyle then turned to Josh. "I swear, Josh, ask me again if it's snowing and I'll hit you!"

"And I will!" said Mira.

"Jeez… Take a chill pill. I won't ask if it's snowing again," Josh promised.

Kyle climbed off the ladder, took another deep breath and, with Mira holding his hand tightly, returned to sit next to Tan. But at the very moment Kyle slumped back against the wall, Josh took a big sniff and wiped his nose on his sleeve. He then looked to Mira and, with a wicked glint in his eye, said, "Is frozen water still falling then, Kaiboy?"

Before Kyle could get to his brother, Tan held out his arms and stopped him. "I had a younger sibling, and you know what—she bugged me. But they feel it's their job, being the youngest. Now, get some sleep, because we don't know how long it will be till we get another chance." He then turned to Josh. "And you, funny man—any more from you tonight and I'll cut little things off you and use them to lure the bears away."

"Then can I just say one more thing and then I promise I'll sleep?" Josh asked.

He looks serious now, Mira thought, praying he actually was.

"OK, one more thing, so make it really good," said Tan.

Josh looked at all the stern faces staring back at him. He grinned, and before anyone could stop him, he broke into song.

CHAPTER THIRTY-FIVE

A SHINING LIGHT ON A DARK WINTRY NIGHT

Josh's hands were tied and his mouth gagged. Kyle took off his jacket and placed it around Mira's shoulders. Snuggling against him, she closed her eyes.

"Sorry, I brought sleeping bags," said Tan. "Enough for the three of you. All I could get in the time I had, but they are big enough to fit two people inside. Sadly, they're on my boat right now. But as long as the snow doesn't get into the room above, it will be cold in here tonight, but not freezing."

Mira sneaked a look to the hatch. She let out an inner sigh of relief when all she saw fluttering down between the cracks was dust.

"Actually, these uniforms that Pyrrha gave us are really warm," said Kyle.

"Lucky she gave you those boots as well," said Tan. "Tomorrow, your feet would have frozen, and we wouldn't have got very far. It's just a shame they didn't give him clean socks." Tan pointed to Josh, who was already sound asleep. "I've never smelled anything like it."

"Only once have they been this bad," said Kyle. "Ironically, it was snowing then as well, as I told you."

Tan scrunched up his nose. "Good grief. Maybe we should cut them off and stick them above the hatch. It would definitely keep the bears away for sure…" His eyes then narrowed as they turned to Kyle. "So, what's the story with you and my niece?"

Mira kept her eyes closed and waited.

"Story?" said Kyle.

"Yes, story. I see by the way you are holding each other that you are a couple. You'd better be treating her well."

Enough of that! Mira thought. *You may be my uncle, but you have no idea what we have been through and you don't know how I feel about him!* "He is!" she snarled. "So, leave him alone!"

"OK then, that's good. That's all I wanted to hear." Tan settled back and closed his eyes.

Kyle wasn't finished. "Wait, can I ask you something?"

Tan yawned and sat back up. "Sure, we've got all night, and I don't need to sleep—I mean, I've only been awake for four days straight. So, what's up?"

"Do you really think we are going to just stroll into that pyramid like Josh and Rachel did, and then walk out safely?"

"Sure, why not… If Funny Man, Punchy and Miss Know-it-all were allowed to leave, why not us?"

"So, you don't think those things are simply waiting for the rest of us to turn up? We all dreamed we were in the sepulchre."

Good question, Mira thought.

"Perhaps, perhaps not." Tan yawned again. "Maybe I'm wrong about them. Perhaps they're just trying to protect the girls. Some accounts I've read say that certain creatures will protect the females of the different species. Look, worry about it if or when it happens."

"Fine," said Kyle curtly.

Mira could sense he'd thought of something else.

He proved her right. "So, you met Linus in the pyramid then?"

She felt him tense as he said Linus' name.

"Yes, and I took him to my ship. Why?"

"Took him to your ship?" Kyle cried in alarm. "Oh, great. I'll be surprised if the boat is still there when we go for it. He's not entirely trustworthy."

"I know he killed his mother and brother. And before you ask, he told me, and he'll get what's coming to him, but not from me. I don't kill children. Anyway, he can't start the boat, trust me."

"Do you have radio on board?" Kyle asked.

Mira knew where he going with his train of thought. She started to panic.

"I do."

"Does it work—since you arrived?"

"On and off. Mainly off, why?"

"I saw the Followers here, on this island, in my dream. We all did," said Kyle. "Linus will do anything to survive. What if he calls them here, hoping that, as a reward, they will take him home?"

Mira's breathing quickened. She opened her eyes.

"There you go again, worrying before it happens. How would he know the phone number or channel to call them? Not that my phone works, mind you. But even if they do come, I'll kill them all—simple. And when we leave, you can be the ones to throw him overboard, if you like. But get some sleep first!" Tan lay on his back and placed his hands behind his head.

Mira gave Kyle's hand a squeeze. But when he closed his eyes, she began to wonder. Was Tan correct? Was it really only jars of poison inside the coffins? And if it wasn't—surely even the Followers weren't stupid enough to release Epimetheus. Even if he did want to wipe out the Disciples, the risk would surely be too great. Who, or what, would stop him from turning his anger upon them as well?

After one last look to the hatch, Mira looked around at all the peaceful faces. She was thankful about one thing: even though they were trapped, Josh wasn't one to fall to pieces in a crisis, and more importantly, he wasn't selfish. He had stopped her from making a fool of herself; he had annoyed his brother for Kyle's own good and got tied up and gagged for it. She now saw him in a completely different light. He had been a shining star. But as she closed her eyes, she still prayed that even though Kyle needed a rest from all the fighting, he would be back to his normal self soon, for all their sakes.

CHAPTER THIRTY-SIX

AN ELEMENT OF TRUTH

A bright light was shining in her face. Mira opened her eyes. Instinctively, she threw out her hand and knocked the bright object away. There, before her, holding a small torch, was Tan. Inhaling deeply, she wiped the tears from her cheeks.

"What are you doing?" she hissed.

Tan raised a finger to his lips. Turning her head in the direction in which his arm was now extended, her gaze fell upon Kyle and Josh, still sleeping.

Quietly, Tan slipped beside her. "You were calling out in your sleep," he said, keeping his voice low. "It sounded like you were dreaming about your brother."

"I was…" Her breathing quickened. Thoughts of what Jacen had told her in her last dream were like pinpricks to her scalp. "Hey, we need to get a message to your people somehow. I think I know a way to get to him."

Tan's beady eyes narrowed further. "I can do that. Is there anything else?"

Why aren't we leaving? We should be leaving! We should be doing something! "Like what? We don't have time!" she said, pressing her trembling hands tightly together.

"Time, we have," he said. "Now, is there anything else you want to tell me?"

She wanted to run and scream. "Tell you what?"

"About the dream you just had?"

Mira stared at the floor. Her heart was still racing. *Trust no one, Jacen said.* "Would you be angry if I said 'Not yet'?"

"I'm not angry, dreams are private," he said. "But if I'm going to help your brother, I need to know what I, or my order, could be walking into."

He was right, of course.

She drew away from the wall. "Alright," she said, slightly frustrated, but now resigned to sharing her vision. "I was standing on the street below the Acropolis in Athens. A coffee house or restaurant was there. The sun was setting on my right, so I must have been heading south. As I walked along the street, I suddenly saw Jacen enter a red, scorched building. I think it was once a bakery. I can still smell the burnt bread. It had a sign above the door in the shape of a diamond. I can't remember what the insignia inside it looked like now, but there was a basement and a cupboard with a hidden door behind that led down to a canal and then on to a circular chamber under the Parthenon with only one set of stairs. There were armed people walking about. But at the top of a set of stairs, Jacen was at the end of a winding tunnel."

Tan shook his head. He spoke softly. "I didn't mean that... I need to know, did Jacen tell you anything?"

He asked if I was still his sister. Why did he say that? Oh, what has Mr Tripp done to you?

She could feel Tan's gaze intensifying. *Don't tell him anything,* her inner voice suddenly told her. "I—I can't. I'm sorry."

She looked to Kyle. She trusted him with her life. She wanted to drag him out of their tomb, take him anywhere where they could be alone and she could tell him.

"We need a sign of trust here, so I'll go first," said Tan. "I've just had an interesting conversation with him, too. Nice kid. Likes to jump up and down a lot, especially on the bed I have at home." He half smiled. "He told me to trust you with what you have to do. Would you care to elaborate?"

"He was jumping up and down on your bed?" she asked.

Tan nodded.

The same thing he used to do with our stepfather. "How old did he look?"

"Like any happy six-year-old, I guess."

Mira was confused—he'd looked at least twelve in her dream. Her reasoning then took over. *It was a dream, Mira.* But what if it was the future, she saw? *Damn it! That means he may not be in Athens yet... But what if he is there and you don't try to rescue him?*

"Well?" said Tan. "Is there something you want to tell me?"

Doubt again crept into her mind. *Will you go along with what Jacen wants me to do?* "Do you know of a place called Haven?"

Tan shook his head. "Never heard of it."

"Then what about the Desolate One?"

Tan's face turned ashen. "Never say that name again," he whispered. "I mean it. It's cursed."

"But who is it?" Mira pressed.

Again, Tan shook his head. "What did I just say?!" His tone was not only one of anger, but fear.

Fine, Mira decided. *I'll ask Pyrrha, if we ever get out of here.*

It was then that Kyle opened his eyes. Before she could ask him to take a walk with her, Josh also awoke. He immediately, and noisily, attempted to free himself from the restraints, so Tan removed his gag and untied his hands.

"You're not going to believe this," said Josh, his face filled with delight. "I just dreamed of Jacen. We were standing in one of the rows of the Colosseum in Rome, and he knew all the history of the place."

Mira pulled on her bottom lip. "What did he look like?"

Josh's face scrunched up. "Umm—weird question to ask," he said. "He looked like, err, Jacen."

Mira decided to change tack. "What was he wearing, Josh?"

"Jeans and a T-shirt that was way too big for him. It had an *Olympus Has Fallen* logo on it, if I recall. Hey, Kaiboy, didn't Dad have one of those?"

Kyle nodded. "But I just dreamed that Jacen and I were in the London Museum. And he was dressed—and I know this is going to sound weird—he was wearing an *Assassin's Creed* T-shirt. Little young for those games, isn't he?"

Mira nodded. "He is. My stepfather won't let him play them."

"Maybe the Followers are allowing it to pacify him…" said Josh. "Remember, three years have passed. He's nine years old now."

Mira slammed her hand down onto the hard, cold stone. "Damn it. I hoped that with me in the dream and the fact he was wearing the T-shirt I brought back for him from Athens, it was a sign… But if you dreamed that he was in Rome and in London, it just confirms what Pyrrha told me: he is probably in one of those three Follower sanctuaries."

Tan looked to each of them. "So, he didn't jump up and down on anyone else's bed—just mine?"

"Wait," said Kyle excitedly. "Before I woke up, we stopped at one particular section of the museum—now what was it called… That's it—the Elgin Marbles. And the T-shirt he was wearing was *Assassin's Creed: Odyssey*."

Mira's excitement rose. "Josh, did he show or tell you anything?"

"Wait. So, he jumped on nobody else's bed, just mine?" Tan reiterated. "How unfair is that?"

Josh rolled his eyes. "He said to trust you with what you have seen and what you must do. But I have no idea what the film *Olympus Has Fallen* has to do with anything…"

"Olympus, Josh…" Tan grunted. "Think about it. Take your time, we have all night."

"Oh, right. Now I get it." Josh beamed. "Hey, come to think of it, he did keep going on about some Greek gladiator that fought in the arena. Now, what was the name… Harry? No, wait. Hairy Iglesias, I think it was?"

Tan gave him a withering look. "Hairy Iglesias? Really? Was it Ares-Enyalios, by any chance?"

"That's it!"

Tan scratched his beard. "Ares-Enyalios is the god Ares. Enyalios means warlike. We have writings that say in AD 401, when Emperor Arcadius held the gladiatorial games in the Colosseum, he prayed to the old gods for their help. He wanted it to be the best spectacle Rome had ever seen. Even though Zeus had decreed that no Olympian have any contact with any more humans, especially after what happened to his beloved Pandora, Ares disobeyed his father.

"Early in the day, Ares put on a magnificent show, raising the bloodlust of the crowd to a fever pitch. When a young, Greek Christian, Telemachus, charged onto the field of battle and tried to stop the fights, Ares took his life with a single swing of his sword."

"That's not what I've read," said Kyle, who was fascinated with the history of the Roman Empire. "Telemachus was stoned to death by the crowd. Because he was martyred, he became Saint Telemachus."

"From the writings *we* have," Tan continued, "Ares killed him. And, having already incurred Zeus' wrath for his many heinous acts, Zeus destroyed nearly all the records of his son's victories in the arena."

"What happened to Ares?" Mira asked.

"I don't know."

Josh threw his hand into the air. "Go back," he said. "If Zeus forbade the other gods from interfering in mortal affairs, are you implying that he is the same god Christians now worship?"

Tan shrugged. "I don't know. Maybe. The Romans seemed to think he was the same, but they called him Jupiter. And if you read the Old Testament, the Christian God was wrathful. Just like Zeus. Yet, in the New Testament, God is an all-loving deity. If Zeus did indeed forbid the other gods from interfering in mortal affairs... if he did banish one of his sons from Olympus and into Hell... then yes, maybe he is the Lord God, Jehovah."

"What son did he send to Hell?" Mira asked, hoping Tan would break his silence on who the Desolate One truly was. "In the Christian Bible it was one of God's angels, Lucifer, also known as the Fallen One. But in Greek mythology, I can't recall ever reading of anyone being known as the Devil. OK, Hades was the master of the Underworld, yes, but he wasn't regarded as Satan. Or was he? Wait... Was Ares the son he sentenced? Is he the Desolate One?"

"No," said Tan, and he gave Mira a look that made it clear she should never mention that name again.

"Wait a minute," said Josh. "What if Mr Tripp is the Devil in disguise? And if Zeus is the same god Christians now worship, then that's going to cause quite the religious backlash if it ever comes out. If we were characters in a book right now, we'd be tossed upon an open bonfire at this point in the story, I reckon."

"Look, Mr Tripp is *not* the Devil in disguise," said Tan angrily. "And I don't know if Zeus is the same god Christians worship. I'm just speculating. No one has come forward with any actual proof of who or what God—or the Devil, for that matter—truly is, or what is out there in the cosmos, have they? But unlike some, I have never, and will never, try to disprove anyone else's beliefs. As I said, I'm just giving my simple thoughts on it—something that seems to be frowned upon today. That's the problem with the world now and with you kids. Us older folk are shut down and cancelled because—"

"Maybe it's because we kids today also have opinions," Josh interjected. "In fact, we've always had something to say. Too long we've been kept quiet. Kept down. Finally, the old saying 'kids should be seen and not heard' has at last gone the way of the emu."

"Dodo, Josh," Kyle corrected him.

Tan's face turned blood red, and Mira held out her hand to stop him from lashing out at Josh. The last thing they needed, in this confined space, was for a fight to occur.

"OK, everyone has the right to an opinion," she said. "Can we all agree on that? Now, can we please just get back to the matter in hand?" She cast a steely eye at both Tan and Josh.

Tan shook his head. "Fine. So, where was I…? Oh yes, it looks like Jacen *is* guiding us to Greece. Why he couldn't have just told me instead of jumping up and down on my bed, though, is anyone's guess." He raised his eyes to meet Mira's. "So, big sis, what do we trust you with, and what have you seen?"

"Before I tell you," Mira said, "Pyrrha said that only the descendants have dreams. Does that mean you are one?"

Tan slapped his forehead. "What?" he scoffed. "Is that what her crazy order is teaching them all? Boy oh boy… Look, everyone has dreams and anyone can have visions. Now, listen. The only reason that you can open the tombs is because of some clever locksmith. How, I don't know. They were a lot cleverer back in those days, I can tell you that. But as I keep pointing out, all you lot need to know is that you shouldn't open the coffins. And now that has been made abundantly clear and hopefully has *finally* sunk in, I know we won't be doing that. So, Mira, what does your brother want us to trust you with?"

OK, you asked! "To take the coffin from this island to the desert where Pandora was cursed, open all the coffins, and then I'll know what to do when the time comes," she said plainly.

Tan's jaw hit his chest. "I did not see that coming. So now we're opening them?"

"No, not you, just us," Mira replied. "You're just here to help us achieve it."

"But you're not really going to open them, are you?" Tan broke into a smile. "*Nooo*, this is just a way to get your brother back, right? Pretend to do what they want and then you spring a trap, right?"

"I don't know yet," said Mira. "Maybe I am going to open them, maybe not. First, I have to finish this journey we appear to be on, whatever that entails. Then we, and by that I mean me, Kyle and Josh, along with Rachel and Jo, need to take this coffin to Egypt, and then I'll do what I'm supposed to do. Except, I don't know what that is yet."

"Wait, what about Jo?" Kyle whispered.

"Guess I'll know what to do when the time comes."

"Hang on. What's this about Jo?" Tan asked.

"Doesn't matter for now. All we need to do now is get Rachel and Jo back and find a way into the sepulchre."

Tan scratched his beard. "Are you sure you're not a Follower?"

"Quite sure." Mira smirked. "And I'm also sure that nothing is going to go the way we plan it, but you will get to kill lots of Followers before all of this is over."

"No, this is too dangerous," said Tan, folding his arms across his chest. "They could have hypnotised your brother into saying what he said. I'm sorry, but whatever is inside those things cannot be allowed to get out!"

"You're right, but if I can't figure out a solution, then you'll have to, right?" said Mira.

"I could do that right now. I could shoot you all and be home in time to watch the new season of *Love Island*."

Mira smiled. "But you're not going to, are you?"

"What, shoot my niece? No. Shoot the other two? Err… Damn it, no, I couldn't do that either; they're around the same age as my son and daughter. Very well, we'll do it your way, for now. So, what's the plan?"

Yes, what is the plan? Mira thought. "I have absolutely no idea. Except that we need to rescue Rachel and Jo first, then we worry about everything else as it happens."

Tan rose to his feet. "Good philosophy to have. Who taught you that—Daniel?"

"No, you," said Mira.

He beamed.

As Tan began to climb the ladder, Josh got to his feet. "Hey, before we go, I've been thinking a lot about all that's happened and I have two questions. Now, bear with me. Pyrrha said that Pandora will release a plague upon the earth if her coffin is opened, right?"

Everyone nodded.

"And that if Epipotomus' coffin is opened—"

"Epimetheus, Josh," Mira sighed.

"That's what I said. And if *his* coffin is opened, *he* will wipe out the Disciples, right? Which would explain why the Followers would want it."

"Yes, that's right," said Tan. "Now what point are you trying to make, Josh?"

"Who, or what, is in the third coffin? Mira, you said you saw three coffins."

Mira's eyes widened. "I don't know. I've never thought about it until now, to be honest with you."

"OK," said Josh. "Fair enough. Then let me tell you my theory. What if there isn't poison inside any of the vases? What if the original story about Pandora is true, but the box she possessed was actually a coffin that contained her son, who had become infected with a deadly virus? What if Pandora and Epipotomus' coffins need to be joined with the third for them all to open?"

Silence struck the group.

"Too far-fetched?" said Josh. "OK. Then here's something else to consider. What if Pandora and Epididdly are actually real gods? It would explain how they survived this long inside the tombs and why Pyrrha believes the vases contain elixirs that are binding them to their coffins.

"*OH*, and if that is the case, and you and Jacen really are their descendants, wouldn't that then make you gods, too? *Or*, if Pandora was indeed the first woman, like Eve, and Epimethane was a god, then wouldn't it make you and Jacen demigods?" His eyes widened further. "And if

Rachel and Jo are also related, as our dreams seem to be telling us, wouldn't they be, too?"

Something else then struck him. "*Oh, oh, oh,* and if the third one requires me and Kyle to open it, that would make us demigods, wouldn't it?"

Everyone simply stared, open-mouthed.

"No? OK, I just thought I'd put it out there. But still, food for thought."

"Let me see if I got this right," said Tan. "You're saying the box that contained all the evils of the world was actually Pandora's son?"

"Why not?" said Josh. "Every story has an element of truth to it, and it would explain, in the original story, Pandora wanting to open it, being his mother and all. Obviously, not realising what he had become, of course." He winked. "Think about it. Pyrrha told Mira that he came down with a terrible affliction and was trapped beyond the wall. Makes sense then that he was the one placed inside the box—because he was infected—and the screaming we heard was Pandora warning us to leave?"

"I saw Pandora being buried, Josh," said Mira flatly.

"Oh, yeah—that means there was someone else telling us to open it. Hmm, maybe it's not her son who's the problem... Oh well, I thought I'd just throw it out there."

Tan let out an exasperated sigh and, with a shake of his head, disappeared into the room above.

Josh pulled Mira and Kyle into a huddle. "I think it would be wise if we kept the fact that we've been missing for three years a secret from Rachel and Jo. They are freaked out enough as it is. To find this out on top... Who knows what they'll do."

Josh began to climb up the ladder but stopped halfway and looked down at Mira and Kyle. "Then again," he said, "what if the Followers want to recreate what happened?"

Kyle's shoulders dropped. "Recreate what, Josh?"

"What if they hope to infect Jacen, just as Pandora's son was cursed? Perhaps that's the only way the infection can spread, through human contact? Then again, maybe the whole Pandora kerfuffle is just a ghost story to stop anyone from finding out what really is inside the coffins, and everything that has occurred has been a smokescreen for what truly lies ahead of us?"

Josh disappeared through the hatch, and Mira and Kyle took a moment to contemplate what he'd said.

"He's right about not telling Rachel and Jo," said Mira. "But don't you find it scary the way he keeps coming out with all these other things? It's like he knows everything already and is just toying with us, or he's waiting for the rest of us to catch up."

Kyle could only shrug.

CHAPTER THIRTY-SEVEN

ORDERS COLLIDE

Mira, Kyle and Josh finally left their hiding place and followed Tan up onto the roof. Leaping across the short gaps between the tops of the buildings, they reached the last derelict shell, which was now mainly rubble, and dropped into a snowdrift. As they sped out of town, Mira cast a look back over her shoulder. Seeing the bears returning to the forest, and no sign of the harpies out on the hunt, she breathed a sigh of relief.

Tan led the group along the same route Josh and Rachel had taken, keeping a wide distance from the river—claiming he had seen something huge lurking in the water, with many teeth—until the pyramid came into view. As the sun had only just started to rise, he brought the company to a stop.

"Best to go in when it's a bit lighter—that's when they sleep."

"That's probably how you were able to get Jo out the first time, Josh," said Mira.

"No, I'm pretty sure they saw us leave." Josh shrugged. "They were hanging from the trees, deep within the foliage, with those scary, yellow eyes of theirs following us. With the shadow from the trees blocking out the sun, they could have snatched us up in a heartbeat."

Kyle scratched his head. "So, why would they let Jo and Rachel leave, only to then bring them back?" he asked. "Wait a minute… Was Linus there before Jo was brought in, Tan?"

"No. I told you, I met him later. Why?"

"He was definitely alone with them after we left," said Josh.

Kyle slapped his forehead. "Then it's obvious—he told those things who Rachel and Jo are!"

Josh raised an eyebrow. "Oh, so now he's Dr Doolittle, is he? And how would he know anyway?"

"Oh, I dunno, maybe some goddess told him—it's not like it hasn't happened before, is it!"

Josh ground his teeth. "Hmm… Maybe he had the dream as well… You know what? You think you know someone. You run around like a headless chicken making sure he's alright, then *bam!*, he stabs you in the back. Then you let him go, wish him the best of luck, and *bam!*, he pushes the knife in again."

"Look, we don't know if Linus has done anything yet, so before you go and do something you'll regret, just be sure first, yeah?" Mira paused. "No, on second thoughts, don't do anything. If he *has* told those creatures, then we'll leave him here to his fate. Life has a funny way of getting back on those that deserve it."

"Yeah, I suppose," said Josh. "But, in saying that, before we go, can I at least hit him?"

"Get in line," said Kyle.

"No, you can't hit him," Mira growled. "What did I just say? Let life deal with him!"

"Can I kick him, then?"

Mira's blood was starting to boil. "Josh, carry on and Rachel's hand will be the least of your worries!"

"See: 'No, Josh, you can't hit him—let life deal with him.' But it's OK for you to hit me." He sulked.

Mira took a deep breath. "If I do hit you, Josh—that *is* life dealing with you!"

"Are you lot like this all the time?" said Tan, staring dubiously at them all.

"Like what?" Josh smiled.

Tan gave a heavy sigh. "When we get out of here, I'm taking you to see a shrink," he said. "Now look, that boy hasn't told them anything, and from what you told me, his part in all of this is over, so let's just concentrate on getting your friends, shall we?"

The snow had started to fall heavily again. Getting to his feet, Tan clapped his hands to gain their attention. "We can't wait any longer, I'm afraid. If we don't move now, we'll all become snowmen. I mean, snowpeople. Persons. Whatever."

But after he'd taken only a few steps, the ground ahead of him moved. Before Tan could steady himself, Pyrrha and two of her guards appeared from beneath snow-covers, weapons at the ready and aimed directly at him.

"I've got to be honest, I did not see this coming," Tan said, raising his arms high into the air. "How did you know we'd be here?"

"We'd not long left the pyramid. We saw and heard you coming." Pyrrha stomped forward. "Mira, what the hell were you thinking? I told you we would get Jo and Rachel together and then go and get Laurie. As it is, my brother has had to go to the sepulchre alone! And who the hell is this?"

Tan removed a glove and held out an outstretched hand. "How is Sherme?"

Pyrrha took a few steps back and raised her gun at him. "You know my brother? Or did they tell you about him?"

"I know Sherme very well, as it so happens," said Tan calmly. "Big guy, bushy beard. Likes to hit people when he's angry. Which seems to be all the time."

"How do you know him?"

"Met him last year at the Elders' get-together party, and boy can he drink." Tan chuckled.

Pyrrha shook her head. "Elders' party?"

Mira's doubts began to grow. She gripped her gun tightly. "You both claim to be members of the Disciples, and yet you don't know each other or that these Elders apparently go to parties? Would one of you care to elaborate why that is?" She waited as they both stared at one another. "Tan? Pyrrha?"

Pyrrha's cheeks, red from the cold, turned sharply back to white. She gulped. "Your name is Tan? Not… Tandigo Sing?"

Tan bowed his head. "The very same."

She lowered her gun. "There were rumours you were dead."

He broke into a wry smile. "Not yet." He then turned to Mira who was staring worriedly back at him. "Don't worry, we're not your enemies. She knows only my name because I am nothing more than a shadow to the other Disciples. As for me being dead, I started the rumour. I was on a special mission that I'm afraid I cannot discuss." He turned his attention back to Pyrrha. "But I am surprised that, with your rank, you knew nothing about the parties."

The wind had picked up and was now driving the snow into their faces.

Josh's teeth were chattering. "How about we get Rachel and Jo first," he said, "then, on our way to the sepulchre to get Laurie, you can talk all you like about the why and the why not of knowing anything?"

"There's no safe way into that place," said Pyrrha. "Those creatures are guarding it. We're all that's left—they killed everyone else—and Sherme is probably inside the sepulchre by now, so I have to go get him. As for you, you will go back to the ship and lock yourselves in."

"No—we have to get Rachel and Jo first!" Mira insisted.

As Pyrrha's cheeks turned red again, Tan stepped between them. "I know how you feel," he told her. "They're just like my own kids. They don't listen, they're stubborn, but what're you gonna do, shoot them?"

"Oh, don't tempt her," said Josh, looking at the way Pyrrha was now gripping her gun.

"Look, Pyrrha, I wouldn't go to the sepulchre, at least not yet," said Tan.

"He's my brother and our captain, and I don't care who you are—I take orders from my leader only!"

Tan raised his open palms in a sign of friendship. "Please, just listen to me. We've just left the town. There are hungry bears roaming. If Sherme has got through unscathed, which I'm certain he has, and is now inside the sepulchre, I know he'll be OK. He's as tough as they come. But, at your own leader's request, I was sent to sort out the rogue Madrid order that was planning to kill all the Potentials. It's done. But then my brother, Mira's stepfather, called me. I have simply come here to get my niece. But as you can see, it's not working out like I thought it would as she will not leave until her friends are rescued.

"Now, if you say those yellow-eyed, flying geriatrics are feeling touchy about letting the girls go, and have also killed your group, then we need to go plan. And as it's snowing and I hate getting wet, what do you say to going back to your ship, getting dry and a change of clothes?

Which, may I say, I like what you're wearing, it looks really warm and waterproof, and I like the way the colour coordinates with the snow." He smiled.

Her eyes like an eagle's, ready to swoop for the kill, Pyrrha cocked her weapon. "Before we go anywhere, you should know the procedure?"

"Oh, right, the mark," said Tan, rolling up his sleeve.

"Mark? What mark?" Mira asked.

"It's more like a bloody cattle brand. It shows you're a member of the Disciples and can be trusted," said Tan, displaying his arm.

The brand that had been burnt into his skin was a bolt of lightning escaping from the tip of a trident encased inside what looked like, to Mira at least, an underground mountain. It was surrounded by a circle with ancient writing around its edge. The same writing, she believed, that was around the seal in the palace on Pandora's island.

Mira froze, wondering whether to tell the group.

Instead, it was Josh who announced it. He, too, had awoken upon the cold, hard floor by the seal when Peter had rendered him and Rachel unconscious.

"The seal in the palace wasn't there when we first entered," he said.

"You probably weren't paying attention, that's all," said Tan. "Not surprising, when you have giant wolves chasing after you. As for the writing, it just says that we are guardians of the tomb."

"So, why did the emblem inside Pandora's palace have a hooded cloak?" Mira asked.

"I can answer that," said Pyrrha. "It was the first symbol that was created by the Disciples. When the Disciples then split into various groups, each sanctuary came up with a different design so that the Followers would find it harder to infiltrate."

Satisfied that Tan was a member of the Rhodes order, and after Tan convinced them all that trying to rescue Rachel and Jo with the few weapons they had was suicide, Pyrrha finally agreed to return to the ship.

But as she started toward the town, Tan called her back. "Hey, where are you lot going? Your ship is south of here, isn't it?"

"There's a giant croc in the river, and piranhas apparently," Josh explained, rubbing his ears against the cold. "Plus, there's no other way to cross unless we go back to the bridge near the town."

The sides of Tan's mouth twisted. "Then pull the drawbridge up."

"What bridge?"

Pyrrha lowered her head. Her cheeks were once again red as Tan trudged through the snow, reached down and pulled a rope from under the snow near the river. With one tug, a plastic bridge appeared. After securing the rope tight, Tan hurried across.

"What the bloody hell do they teach you lot about survival at your sanctuary? You always bring a portable bridge with you!"

"Fine," said Kyle. "She should have brought one. No need to get snippy about it. But for us laymen, how did you get the bridge over to the other side?"

"Crossbow," said Tan. "You keep a firm hold of one end, then fire the other across using the special arrow—simple. When the arrow hits the ground and you pull the rope, the head then opens up into claws. Now let's get a move on, shall we?"

The group crossed the bridge and ploughed on through the snow. Mira took the opportunity to drop back and speak with Pyrrha alone.

"Do you know a place called Haven?" she asked.

Pyrrha's eyes widened. "Where did you hear that name? Was it Tan who told you?"

"No. I heard it in a dream." She could sense Pyrrha's panic, so added, "Only I dreamed it, if that makes you feel better."

Pyrrha leaned in close. "It's where I'm taking you. Do not tell the others. It must remain a secret until we get there."

That's one riddle answered. "Then what about the Desolate One?"

At first, Pyrrha's whole body seemed to stiffen. But then she laughed. "An old wives' tale. Nothing more. Something to scare the children into going to bed early if they're naughty or if it's past their bedtime. *'The Desolate One will come and get you unless you do as I say.'* " She laughed again. "Do you not have them from where you come from?"

"Where I come from, the Desolate One is the Devil," Mira replied seriously.

"The Devil?" Pyrrha laughed again. "We don't believe in those stories."

Mira lowered her eyes. She had been raised to respect other beliefs.

Sensing her discomfort, Pyrrha placed her arm around Mira's shoulder. "I'm sorry, Mira. That was insensitive of me. It is an interesting concept, God and the Devil doing battle for the souls of mankind."

Mira jumped on that. "Did the ancient Greeks or your Disciples ever write about Hell, or someone we— and I mean Christians—would now consider to be the Desolate One? Or the Devil?"

"Erebus," Pyrrha corrected her. "The Hell you speak of is what we call Erebus." She took a moment. "As for a Devil-like character, I'm not sure. There were plenty of beast-like characters that could appear to be 'devilish' to a human, but if my memory serves... I would have to say no. There was never anyone who was known by that name."

"What about Ares?"

"Never speak that name out loud again, Mira. It's cursed. Now, let's pick up the pace."

Cursed? That's what Tan said! Mira refused to move.

"Fine," said Pyrrha impatiently. "To us, he is simply the god of war."

"What about Mr Tripp?"

Pyrrha burst into laughter. "Him? No. Definitely not." Her expression, just as Tan's had, hardened. "And this is the last time we shall speak on the matter. Some things should never be spoken about, Mira. Even an old wives' tale can bring about misfortune."

Mira now knew that there was more to the Pandora story than Pyrrha had let on. And she was convinced the god Ares, even if he wasn't the Desolate One, *was* somehow part of it. But the snow was getting deeper, and each step was becoming a mammoth undertaking. As the flurries of snowflakes in the grey sky were threatening to once again progress into a blizzard, Mira decided to let it go and hopefully find out the truth once they were safely at this so-called Haven.

CHAPTER THIRTY-EIGHT

PARTY PLANNER

After the group had all taken warm showers and dressed in clean uniforms, Pyrrha brought them freshly cooked meals.

"Now, would you mind telling me about this Elders' party?" she asked, taking a seat next to Tan.

"Once a year, the senior Elders of each sanctuary get together to discuss everything from finances, uniforms, new recruits—you know, things like that, the boring stuff. But really, they come for the meal, drinks and entertainment. Take last year for instance, I had to stand and watch some so-called comedian tell the worst jokes ever while operating a camel puppet. Boy, I won't get those hours back, I can tell you," he said, shaking his head.

"How come you were there?" Pyrrha asked.

"It was held in Rhodes, and I organised the security."

"But how have I never heard of this?"

"I'm guessing because they never hold it at your place, and because it seems you're a mushroom. I am surprised that Sherme didn't tell you though." Tan bit into a slice of bread. "Being your brother and all."

"Sherme was there as well? And what exactly do mean by *mushroom*?" Pyrrha growled.

"You know, fed full of sh—" Tan caught himself. "Oh, I can't say the word in front of my niece. Umm, basically you're fed full of manure and kept in the dark. As for Sherme, he knows because he was your leader's security. Anyway, after the leaders were tucked up safely in bed, Sherme and I, well, we had a few drinks together."

Pyrrha's mouth was now hanging in disbelief.

"I can see by your expression that this has hit you hard, but it's the way of the world," Tan continued. "And think about it, there hasn't been a sign for thousands of years, so what else are they gonna do but hold parties? But now all this has happened… well, now they'll have to prove their worth, won't they?" he added with a wink.

Pyrrha glared at the table, and with the colour of her cheeks reddening by the second, it became obvious that Josh was about to be the one she would unleash her anger upon. Quite oblivious to her steely gaze now fixed upon him, Josh finished his meal and slumped down on his bed, already drifting off to dreamland.

Unfortunately for him, this would have to wait; he was suddenly jerked back into consciousness by Pyrrha's shrill voice. "And don't think I have forgiven you for entering the women's showers and taking the weapons bag!"

Kyle was quick to defend him. "If you hadn't locked him away and had agreed to go after Rachel and Jo to begin with, then he wouldn't have had to!"

"Excuse me," Pyrrha retorted, "but it was your idea to lock him away, not mine!"

With tension mounting, Tan again intervened. "Talking of weapons—what's your ammo situation? Do you have enough?"

Pyrrha shifted her gaze toward him. "Yes, for the moment. But the bullets don't have much effect on those things unless you hit them directly in the mouth. It seems to be their only weak spot. But now the harpies know that, it's almost impossible."

"Good to know. Then, I'll have to return to my boat. I have rounds that will cut them in two. Do you have a 50 cal rifle here?"

"No."

"I'll bring that as well. Now, what about personnel? How many are left?"

"Not including Sherme and Laurie… five," said Pyrrha solemnly.

The room fell silent. Sixteen reduced to five. Nobody had expected that news.

"Five? Not including you?" Tan asked.

"Five in total."

The gasp was even louder this time.

"Oh, that's not good. I was hoping for more," said Tan. "Right then, I'll go back to my boat and get what we need, and when I return, we'll go kill those things, get the two young ladies back and then all go to the tomb."

Pyrrha flew out of her seat. "Go to the tomb? I hope you mean just me and you go after Sherme and Laurie, right? Not any of them."

"No, we all need to go. My niece needs to get the coffin out of the tomb so she can save her brother, and the world."

"I really hope you're joking."

"No, I'm serious. Her brother spoke to us. Actually, he spoke more to them. With me he just kept jumping up and down on my bed. It was really annoying, to be honest with you. I'm surprised my brother wants him back—"

Mira slammed her hand down upon the table. "I know he's not blood-related, but that's still your nephew, and my stepfather thinks the world of him—us!"

"I know! Surely you know a joke when you hear one?" Tan laughed. "Right, Funny-man?"

"They say it's the way you tell them," said Josh drily.

Pyrrha removed the empty dishes from the room and soon returned with two armed guards. "I'm sorry, but they're not going anywhere near that place!" she said, aiming her gun at Tan.

Tan's eyes widened. "You know what—I did not see this coming," he said, raising his hands into the air again.

"Do you really want to risk unleashing them?" Pyrrha shouted.

"Who's them?" Tan asked, slowly lowering his arms as nobody else had raised theirs.

"You know full well who! Do you know what they will do if they are released now?"

Tan dropped his head forward. "Oh, for the love of… Are you kidding me? Look, the only thing that resides in those coffins is jars of poison. OK, there may be mummified victims slowly decomposing, too, but it's only the poison that we need to be concerned about. Crikey, I thought all that nonsense was done away with years ago. Now, if the children are right and the Followers are looking for Epimetheus, then it must mean the poisons need to come together to be potent, and I agree with you one hundred per cent that they can't be let out, but I trust my niece to do the right thing when the time comes—"

"What do you mean, the Followers are looking for Epimetheus?"

Tan shot a look of concern toward Mira. "She doesn't know, does she?"

Mira gave a slight shake of her head.

"OK, forget what I said," he said, turning back to face Pyrrha. "I probably dreamed they were here. Anyway, just put the guns down, help us get Punch and Judy

away from the flying chipmunks, get inside the sepulchre, get your brother Sherme and hopefully his wife
Laurie, and the coffin, just to be on the safe side, leave
this place, arrange a meeting of all the orders, gather
all the troops we can and then go kill some Followers—agreed?" He smiled expectantly.

***

The door to the cargo hold was closed and the bolt bar
slid across, locking the company inside.

Tan flopped to the ground and stared at the door.
"*Wow*, I did not see that coming. Talk about love
among the orders. You know, I'm sure I outrank her,
and if that is the case, then I could have her shot."

"Well, that's just great," said Kyle. "We're locked
in the cargo hold, again. Rachel and Jo are MIA. Now
what do we do?"

"Relax, pretty boy," said Tan. "I'll get us out of
this. OK, Sir Talks-a-lot, hand me the knife I slipped
you before we were brought here," he said, looking to
Josh.

"Knife? What knife?"

"The one I put in your pocket. I really thought
they were going frisk us, and I'd rather you get caught
with it than me. Pyrrha really seems to like you and
she may have only shot you in the leg. Whereas me…
I'm guessing right between the eyes."

Josh reached into his pocket, pulled out a Swiss
army knife and thrust it into Tan's hand. "That's not
funny. And will everyone stop putting things in my
pockets without my knowledge, please!"

Tan grinned. "It's a little funny," he chuckled. "Now, just give me some room and I'll have us out of here in no time."

As Tan worked on trying to release the door, Josh removed the air vent cover at the rear of the hold and crept inside the ducting. After many twists, turns and a steep climb, he reached the hatch above the galley. Again, he could hear muffled voices coming from below, so he waited.

This time, there were no conversations of malcontent, and when the light finally went out, he dropped down and carefully opened the door. Peering out into the corridor, he was relieved to see there was nobody about. He crept down the stairwell until he was once again outside the cargo hold. He pulled on the bar and slid the door open.

"How in the…? Never mind, good job, Funny-man," said Tan. "Right then, I'll go back to my boat and get what we need."

"Why can't we all go?" Mira whispered.

"There are too many of us to not be seen in daylight, and if Pyrrha comes back and we're all gone, she may take matters too far, but if I go alone, I'm certain she won't follow. So, stay here and talk loudly so they know that someone is still in here. When I come back, I'll be more prepared to deal with her if things go wrong."

"You'll never get off this ship now," said Josh simply. "She'll be expecting it."

"Wanna bet?" Tan grinned.

"Your funeral." Josh shrugged, acting as though he knew something the others didn't.

"Look, take Josh with you; he'll only come after you, anyway," said Kyle. "He can't stay still for a minute. The rest of us will stay here."

Tan pressed his lips tightly together. "Fine," he said resignedly. "But are you going to be talking the whole way? Because if you are, I'm going to need that gag."

"I promise, I won't say a word," Josh whispered.

The slide bolt was replaced and Josh led Tan up the stairwell and through to the outside. With Pyrrha on the deck, talking loudly to what remained of her troops about boarding up the broken window on the bridge, Josh and Tan were able to slip over the railing and drop into the water.

"Right, follow me and stay low," said Josh.

Tan pulled Josh's arm back. "Follow you? Why? Do you know where my boat is, then?"

"No, I just meant follow me until we're clear of the ship, then you can lead the way. I've done this more times now than I care to remember."

"But if you don't know where my boat is, how are you going to lead us clear?" said Tan. "We may need to go a way that's not clear."

Josh crinkled his nose. "Are you related to Rachel by chance?" he hissed.

"OK, Einstein, which way were you going to lead us then?"

"Through the forest, across the field to the river, then across the bridge you built, and then I was going to pass it over to you."

Tan's eyes narrowed as he silently motioned for Josh to lead the way.

CHAPTER THIRTY-NINE

NOT PART OF THE PLAN

The snow was falling heavily once again, making it difficult for Josh and Tan to not only see ahead, but also walk in a straight line. Yet, even with the swirling wind whipping at their frozen hands and faces, with Tan's keen ear, they were able to find the river, and further on, the drawbridge.

Tan began to walk across first, but Josh had seen movement in the water.

Taking a tight hold of Tan's coat, Josh yanked his new friend back to the safety of land. "If what I just saw is what I think it was, Tan…" He gulped. "Then we're going to need a bigger bridge!"

The snout of the crocodile below was now bobbing above the waterline.

"Come on, it won't harm you, and we haven't got all day!" Tan shouted, and pulling himself away from Josh's grip, he smartly dashed to the other side of the bank.

"This wasn't part of the plan, Tan!" Josh yelled back. "It's alright for you—you're wearing a crocodile-skin coat. It probably thinks you're related!"

Josh took a deep breath and tentatively stepped onto the plastic slats, his focus now firmly set on the murky depths. But just as he reached the halfway point, a dark shadow appeared below. Seeing the flash of a giant tail disappearing beneath the water, Josh started to run.

The land was within his reach when the crocodile lunged out of the river. Paralysed, Josh could only watch open-mouthed as the giant reptile bore down upon him.

The enormous jaws snapped shut, missing Josh by inches. But the crunch of bone-shattering teeth piercing the plastic walkway sent a quiver through Josh's entire core. Spurred into action, he took hold of the guide-rope to steady him as the bridge began to buckle and roll.

The giant crocodile shook its gargantuan head. Josh held on tighter to the rail.

Annoyed that Josh was proving to be a difficult meal, the croc, using its greater weight, pulled the bridge below the waterline. But when it released its grip and the bridge sprung back, instead of Josh flying into its open jaws, he landed with his legs straddling its muscular snout.

Instinctively, Josh gripped the huge crocodile around the side of its head and tried to cover its eyes, a manoeuvre he'd seen on a wildlife show that claimed it would calm the crocodile. But it only infuriated it even more.

"Jump, you idiot!" Tan screamed, pushing himself forward against the rising gale.

But the creature's jaws had once again snapped shut on the bridge. And as it twisted and turned its immense head, all Josh could do was hold on tighter.

"It's not a bloody rodeo, you idiot! You don't have to impress me!" Tan wailed.

Josh prepared to jump. But in that very moment, the giant crocodile, sensing Josh's intentions, suddenly stopped thrashing. Its reptile gaze stared deep into Josh's frightened eyes. Then, with a swing of its powerful tail, it drove its huge body backwards and forwards until the plastic slats began to crack and break.

With his only escape to freedom at the rear of the crocodile, Josh pushed his head down onto the croc's brow and lifted into a headstand. Incensed, the crocodile gave a violent shake of its head, sending Josh tumbling forward. Again, it was foiled. Instead of throwing Josh into the water, as planned, the croc suddenly found him sat astride its tail.

The crocodile thrashed, and Josh squeezed his legs tighter against the massive frame of the beast.

"It's not a bloody wild horse!" Tan screamed from the bank. "You are not going to tame it! Now let go before—"

Josh didn't need to let go. A mighty slap of its immense tail, and he was flipped into the air. He landed face first in the freezing water.

The cold snap tore through Josh's senses, blinding him for a moment. As his vision cleared, desperately, he tried to swim for the bank, but his clothes were weighing him down, his arms flailing. The crocodile flew into a frenzy. Tearing itself from the plastic debris, it drove its body forward under the water.

Josh had managed, with a great deal of effort, to reach the bank. But the soft mud slipped beneath his grip, and sensing that the crocodile was getting nearer, he turned to face his nemesis.

Helpless, he watched the riverbed mud swirl as the crocodile prepared its assault from below. Even when Tan appeared above him and took a firm hold of his arm, Josh realised that he'd finally given up hope. Yet strangely, he had no sense of panic. It was as if an angelic voice was whispering to him, and he suddenly felt calm. He kept his eyes firmly fixed on the river until, as anticipated, the crocodile launched out of the water toward its victim.

Josh could only watch and wait for his end as the jaws of death snapped closed.

CHAPTER FORTY

CURSED LUCK

It was only when Josh opened his eyes that he realised, to his amazement, that the croc had somehow missed him and was now swimming off into the murky shadows.

Dragged to shore and then to his feet, Josh was ushered through the deep snow, and only when they were far enough away from the river did Tan let them both collapse into a heap.

Lying on his back, Tan began to laugh hysterically. "If I live to be a hundred, I'll never see anything that funny again in my life!" he hooted.

"Oh, I'm so glad you found it funny," Josh said, gasping. With his heart finally restarting, it began to hammer away like a thrash-metal guitarist.

"You definitely have someone watching over you, lad!" Tan wiped away tears. "It was like watching someone breakdance for the first time."

"You think that's funny?" said Josh, regaining his breath. "Have you ever stared into the eyes of something that could swallow you whole? And you took your bloody time getting to me! What were you doing, booking a train ticket?"

"Oh, lighten up, Lucky Jack. You made it," said Tan, getting to his feet. "You've done something none of the rest of us have. Be proud of yourself, boy. Tomorrow, you may have to ride a bear or one of those giant flying gerbils. Look, you lived, and you still have your giblets, so no more sulking. Now, come on, before you freeze to death." And lifting Josh to his feet, they pressed on through the deepening snow.

Finally, the pyramid was in sight. But as Tan began to veer west toward the ocean, Josh was finding that, with each step, his own pace was slowing dramatically as the cold caught up with him and sank into his bones. And when they started their descent through a small ravine, with his eyelids encrusted with ice, unable to take one more stride, finally, he collapsed.

***

Through the blizzard, Tan could just see his boat anchored in a small cove. He gave a loud call for help, and Linus appeared on deck. Immediately, seeing Tan struggling to carry Josh, he dived into the water and swam toward the shore.

It was quite an undertaking, getting Josh aboard, but once inside the cabin, he was stripped to his underwear and his feet were lowered into a bowl of hot water. A heating blanket was placed around his shoulders.

But as Linus dried himself, Tan's eyes suddenly widened. "This looks bad," he said, noticing a deep gash on Josh's leg. "I thought it was too close. That crocodile's tooth did catch him, by the looks of it." As he set about cleaning the wound, a rank-smelling pus-like substance began to seep out. Tan knew it was poison. "Oh no, I did not see this coming."

"Didn't see what coming?" Linus asked. Even out of the icy water, he couldn't stop shivering. His teeth chattered.

Tan sniffed the leg again. "It's definitely toxic. I've heard crocodile bites are venomous, but I never thought it would smell the same as a Komodo dragon's. They bite the victim and then just follow behind, waiting for the end. The bacteria they carry is lethal. Oh my, this is bad. I don't have anything to give him."

"What about the other ship? Would they have anything?" said Linus, already donning clean clothes to go back out and check.

"Possibly. Maybe. But to get there and back…" Tan checked his watch. "I'm sorry, there's not enough time."

"I'll go, I'm faster than you." Linus finished tying his bootlaces and leapt from the chair.

"It's too dangerous," said Tan. "The bridge is gone, which means you'd have to go all the way around, back to the town. No, I think I'll have to cut his leg off and pray the poison hasn't spread too far."

"Sail the boat then!"

"Are you crazy? With that thing patrolling the ocean, we'll all die!"

"No, listen. There's another cove the *other* side of the river. That *thing* out there is just watching their ship now!"

"Really? I did not see that coming," said Tan, rushing to start the boat.

It was a fight to navigate the boat through the blizzard, but with Linus at his side, pointing the way, Tan found and entered the small cove.

"Now, I'll go get help!" said Linus, leaping into the dinghy. "Keep him alive!"

"They'll kill you on sight," Tan called after him.

"I don't care, as long as you can save my friend!" Linus hollered back.

Tan watched Linus disappear into the swirling, white haze, then hastily returned to the cabin.

Josh was pale, and sweat was pouring down his feverish face. Lifting Josh's legs onto the sofa, Tan inspected the wound again. The green pus seeped from the bloody gash.

Tan opened one of the cupboards above Josh's head and reached inside to retrieve his katana. He then poured whiskey from a decanter over the festering wound and positioned Josh's leg so he could take it clean with one swing.

"What the bloody hell are you doing?" Josh whimpered, suddenly opening his eyes.

Tan whipped the sword behind his back. "Ah, you're awake. Good. OK, um, here goes. I've got kind of a good news, bad news situation going on. Which do you want to know first?"

"Seeing you hide a sword behind your back is telling me that's the bad news," said Josh, glaring at the tip of the blade sticking out over Tan's shoulder.

Tan had to think quickly. "Here's the thing. The pus coming from your leg tells me that croc was carrying some kind of venom. I'm afraid that your leg is badly infected. Linus has gone to see if the other ship has an antidote, but I don't think he's going to make it in time, so I need to take your leg now to stop the poison from spreading. Now, it's really, *really* going to really hurt, so try not to move."

Josh's jaw hit his chest. His mouth was open wider than the Grand Canyon.

"Try not to move—are you freaking kidding me?! Besides, you know it's too late. Unless you take it straight away, the poison spreads in minutes, if not seconds. I've watched enough wildlife shows to know that. But if I'm going to die, which I'm not, I'll go to heaven fully intact, thank you very much!"

"I did not see that coming. But—"

"No buts and no cutting," Josh interjected. "Now what's the bloody good news?"

"I lied; there's no good news." Tan half smiled. "I just wanted to give you some hope."

Josh glared back. "You know, your bedside manner really needs working on!"

"Funny, my wife says exactly the same thing." Tan shrugged. "You know, for someone who's going to die, you're really taking it well. Better than most, I can tell you."

Josh shook his head. "Look, stop saying that! I'm not going to die. Linus will make it, you'll see!"

Tan pulled a chair from beneath the table in the small galley and sat. "Of course, he will. But—he won't really. The snow's too bad and Pyrrha will probably kill him on sight. And even if she doesn't and they do have a cure, just looking at how pale you are now… Ah, I would say you haven't got long. So, any last words? Anything you want me to tell Punchy, or your brother?"

Josh was now biting his bottom lip. "Yes. Please tell Punchy and my brother to take you to the river, let that croc bite you and see if you're willing to have bits of you removed. That's my last request!"

"Good for you," said Tan. "Go out fighting, that's my motto."

They sat for a while and stared at one another, but with the colour draining from Josh's face, Tan again reached for the decanter. "Do you want a drink? It's good whiskey."

Josh wiped the perspiration from his forehead and looked at the gash in his leg. Only blood was seeping out now.

He took the glass that Tan had poured him. "They say it's the worst thing you can do—drink thins the blood. But what the hell, I'm on holiday."

"That's the spirit. Look death in the eye and smile," Tan said. "You know, it's a shame—I was just starting to find you amusing."

"Oh good, that's a huge worry off my mind," said Josh. "I'd really hate to die thinking you didn't like me."

"Well, you're a strong, young man. I was sure you'd be gone by now."

"Sure I'd be gone by now?" Josh gasped. "Sorry to disappoint you, but I've no intention of going anywhere." He took a sip. His whole face turned crimson, and he coughed. "Wow, this *is* good stuff."

"Yes, I know. Cost a fortune, mind you, so you're honoured, but you taste the price, I guess—so, how are you feeling? Do you need another blanket or another tot of whiskey?"

"How am I feeling?" Josh stared at him in disbelief. "Let's see, shall we. Apart from a hole in my leg and a burning fever—I suddenly feel pretty good actually." Then he laughed.

Tan took the glass out of Josh's hand. "Oh, right. Nearing the end then, I see."

Josh's smile evaporated. "Excuse me—what do you mean, nearing the end?"

"They say that you normally start to feel better before you die," said Tan. "It's funny how many people say, 'Hey, you know what, I feel better' and then two minutes later, *poof*, they're gone. Never been able to understand it, to be honest with you."

"Thanks for that," said Josh. Then it hit him. "Wait, are you saying I've only got two minutes left to live?"

Tan checked his watch. "No, no—if you'd only had two minutes left when you said 'I feel pretty good', then you'd be dead already. And the time for me to just tell you what I told you has probably been another two minutes, so hey, good news at last—you've lived longer than I thought you would. That's the way to do it. Be different than everyone else and prove me wrong."

Josh wiped his brow and snatched the glass of whiskey off the small table beside him. In one gulp he finished the drink and rested his head back against the pillow. "Promise me you'll keep Rachel and the others safe till I'm better, because I'm starting to feel really tired, and I just need to shut my eyes for a moment..." He trailed off and closed his eyes.

Tan could see that Josh's breathing had slowed down dramatically. Sensing the end was near, he leaned in and pulled the blanket up around Josh's shoulders. "I promise. Now, shut your eyes, lad, and rest. You need to conserve your strength." But then, taking Josh's hand into his own and feeling his pulse, he knew it was too late. The slow beat of Josh's heart had come to a final stop. "Here's to you, brave boy. May the angels guide you on to a better place than the hell I am yet again about to face."

Tan poured himself another drink and raised the glass in a toast. But as he caught his own reflection in the mirror behind Josh's head, the glass slipped from his hand. To his amazement, his eyes had filled with tears.

CHAPTER FORTY-ONE

OUT OF TIME

Pyrrha watched Linus approach out of the treeline. Deliberately, she cast the ship's spotlight into his face, blinding him for a moment.

"Stupid boy, you had a way out," she growled, stepping off the boat. "Why did you have to come back?"

Linus was breathing hard. "Josh is really sick, and he needs an antidote for a crocodile bite."

Pyrrha shook her head. "That's the best you can come up with? You were hoping to either hide aboard or steal some food, weren't you?"

Linus covered his eyes against the piercing beam of light and staggered forward. "Look, we don't have much time—do you have an antidote or not? Tan said that it smells like Komodo dragon toxin."

"Oh, so now Tan is with him, too, is he?"

"Yes. Please, Pyrrha, Josh is dying!" Linus begged.

Pyrrha stood motionless for a moment, her eyes narrowed. Suddenly, she lunged forward, grabbing him roughly by the scruff.

"So be it," she snarled, dragging him on board. "We shall go and see Josh and Tan now, and then I'll deal with you later."

"Pyrrha, please, there's no time!" Linus hollered in desperation. "Please don't let my friend die!"

Pyrrha was deaf to his cries, and when they reached the cargo hold, she slid the door open and thrust him inside. "Your friend here was stupid enough to…" Her voice trailed off as she scanned the room. "Where the hell is Josh? And Tan, for that matter?"

"I told you…" Linus spoke calmly, but something in his tone implied he was anything but composed. He took a slow intake of breath before continuing. "Josh got bitten by a crocodile. He needs an antidote. Otherwise, he is going TO DIE!"

There followed a stunned silence, before it was broken by Kyle swiftly racing past Pyrrha, grabbing Linus by his throat and pinning him against the wall. "What have you done to my brother?!"

"Wasn't me," Linus choked out while fighting for air. "He got bit by a crocodile and he's not got long, if I don't get back to him with something to save him. He's… he's on Tan's boat," he managed to croak.

Kyle spun to face Pyrrha. "Do you have an antidote?"

Pyrrha was stood frozen, her glare fixed upon Linus. "No, and I'm sorry," she finally said.

Kyle felt as though he'd been struck in the stomach with a sledgehammer. His breathing had become so rapid, red spots had appeared before his eyes. "Then what can we do?" he screamed out.

Pyrrha could only stare back at him. "Nothing. If Laurie was here, she'd know what to do, but I don't. I'm sorry."

Kyle made for the open door. "I have to see him," he said. "Linus, show me the way."

Pyrrha pulled at his arm. "I can't let you do that."

At that instant, two burly guards appeared and blocked his exit.

Mira shot in front of Kyle to shield him. "Pyrrha, you've got to let him see his brother," she pleaded.

"I can't, it's… it's much too dangerous."

But this decision was no longer hers to make as, in one fluid motion, Kyle had disarmed her and placed the gun to her head.

"If you don't allow me to go, you and I will die!"

"Pyrrha," said Mira. "You were willing to go after your brother—let him do the same." Slowly, she reached out and took the gun from Kyle.

"If that bite is toxic, you won't want to see him, trust me," Pyrrha said. "It will stay with you forever."

Kyle suddenly couldn't breathe. *Did she just say that?* He desperately held back his tears. "He's my brother and if he's going to die, he's not going to be alone!"

"He wasn't alone," said another voice.

All eyes shot to the door. There, standing behind the guards, holding guns to each of their heads, was Tan.

"I held his hand, and he went peacefully. Bravest kid I've ever met, and his last wish was for me to keep you lot safe. So, Pyrrha, if you don't want to lose any more of your crew, order them to drop their weapons now and allow us to leave to save their friends." His eyes displayed a cold, fearsome intensity none of them had seen before.

With no other option left to her, Pyrrha reluctantly gave the order. The guards withdrew their weapons, and only then did Tan lower his guns.

"Where's my brother now?" Kyle asked. His whole body was shaking uncontrollably.

"He's on my boat," Tan whispered, placing his arm around Kyle's shoulder. "Don't worry, he'll not be left behind. He'll come back with us, trust me. But first, we have to find Rachel and Jo."

***

Once the situation had calmed, everyone headed back to the cabin. Pyrrha sent for thermal coats and a fresh uniform for Linus, and Kyle sat on the bed where his brother had slept.

"Was he in much pain, Tan?" It was a question he'd never dreamed he would have to ask. He feared the answer.

"No, not really. And if he was, he never let on," said Tan, keeping his head low while he filled the magazines for his weapons.

At that moment, everything seemed to move in slow motion for Kyle. *I was supposed to look after him. I let him down, let Mum, Dad and Rachel… I've let everyone down.* "What do I tell my parents?" he asked.

"The truth. He died saving his friends." Mira sniffed.

Once the company were given the coats, Tan took Mira's arm and led her outside for a crash course on using a crossbow. Pyrrha sat beside Kyle.

"I know what you're going through. Deep down, I know my brother is… you know. But I'm going to need your help when we get Rachel and Jo back. I'm going to trust you with these weapons, but you have to promise me that you won't let them open the tomb. The Followers having one coffin is bad enough—two will be disastrous."

Kyle stared at the floor. At that moment he didn't care if the tomb was opened or not. *I have failed. They chose me to lead, but what have I achieved? Rachel and Jo are missing, and my brother is dead. This is my fault. I should never have allowed Josh to go. I should have done more to keep them all away from the first island. Maybe Lyssa and Peter would still be alive as well. I've failed Mum and Dad. I promised them I would always look out for him. Oh God, how do I tell them?*

"I'm sorry, Pyrrha. I can't promise you that," he said finally. "I swore I'd do whatever Mira wants me to do, and I'm not going to let her down again. But ask yourself this: why are you trying to stop it? Just look at the state of the world. It's only a matter of time before we make ourselves extinct. Maybe releasing what's in those coffins will be a good thing."

Pyrrha removed her arm from his shoulder and stood up. "Do you really believe that?"

Kyle took a moment before he shook his head. "No—no, I don't. If I had my way, I'd drop those things to the bottom of the ocean, but like I said, I'll do whatever Mira wants. But I have another question. Why do you believe Pandora and Epimetheus are still alive in there, yet Tan believes it's just jars of poison? In fact, he said one of the orders believes they were aliens?"

Pyrrha stared at him for a moment, then sat back down next to him. "My order is the oldest, Kyle. We were the ones that saved Pandora's daughter and fought and captured Epimetheus. And I don't care what Tan or any of the other orders believe—I know it in my heart that they are both still alive, and there are things that will be revealed to you all when we leave this place. Please, you have to trust me."

"Why don't we just open the tomb and blow the coffins to hell?"

"Do you know for sure it would work?" she asked. "I don't know how many times I have thought of it myself."

"You know what, that's a great idea, kid," said Tan, re-entering the room alone.

Kyle took a deep breath to steady his nerves. "What's a great idea? And where's Mira?"

"Still practising," said Tan, scratching his beard. "As for your idea, we'll take the coffin to Egypt. Once they are all together, and after we rescue Jacen, obviously, we blow the lot under the ground and seal it tight. Those pyramids go down pretty deep. And that place is a lot further away from Cairo, hiding away under the sand, so as long as there isn't a crosswind, that could work." He grinned.

"But what if Pandora and Epimetheus are alive inside them?" Kyle asked. "What then?"

"I told you, it's only jars of poison. Do you really believe in this day and age that mortals could survive for thousands of years simply because of a curse?"

"And what if they are gods, like Josh said?"

"Then they'll be buried as well when we blow it up, so win-win, I say."

"You can't kill a god!" Pyrrha cried. "All you will do is anger them!"

"Actually, you can kill them," said Tan. "Granted, it's virtually impossible for a mere mortal to kill one due to their strength and speed, but it has been known."

"How do you know?" Pyrrha asked.

"Your order may be the oldest, but you don't have all the rights on what has happened throughout the ages. My order in Rhodes knows for a fact that a mortal defeated the mighty Ares in battle."

"The god of war... Impossible!"

"Not impossible," Tan replied calmly. "From the scrolls I have read, Zeus ordered Ares' death. But when a mortal, Hercules, chosen by Zeus, defeated Ares in battle, he felt pity for him. He couldn't deliver the final, fatal blow. Instead, Zeus punished his son in another way. The point I'm making is that it is possible. Sometimes, life throws a curveball. A mortal that is equal to the gods in all respects. They were called the demigods, once…"

"I know what they were called." Pyrrha scowled. "But their kind died out long ago."

"That may be true," said Tan. "But who's to say they can't come back? Now, let's get Rachel and Jo back, shall we, before our chance has gone."

When Mira returned to the cabin and sat beside Kyle, she took his hand into hers. "You can stay here if you like?" she suggested.

Kyle stared out the window. "No. I've let you all down as it is. I'm coming. It's what Josh would have done. He'd never have stayed behind."

"We can't go now," said Pyrrha. "The sun is setting, and the harpies will surely be coming. We can't fight both sets, there are not enough of us. And to think we'd thought there were only three—according to our writings at least."

"But will the harpies come out of the forest or the pyramid in daylight? You saw what happened when you turned the light on," said Kyle, eager to get going.

"And what if they were just waiting for it to stop snowing before taking them to that place?" Tan added. "Or, what if they are just waiting for the other flying squirrels to attack here? It would give them clearance to the sepulchre then."

It was at that moment that Linus raised his hand. "I know this isn't my place, but isn't that what you want? To open the tomb to take the coffin to a safer place? If you truly believe that the yellow-eyed harpies are going to take Rachel and Jo to the sepulchre, why don't we go there now and simply wait for them to turn up?"

"No, we can't risk that," said Kyle. "They were under the harpies' influence. It's the only explanation as to why they'd let themselves be taken so easily. And if we have to fight all those things at the sepulchre... well, Rachel and Jo might just open the coffin as well as the tomb, and then we are really screwed. No, we have to be with them at all times."

"Look, I'll help in getting Rachel and Jo back, but there's no way that coffin is being opened, or moved," said Pyrrha. "Unless you can give me a surefire reason for doing so?"

Mira paced the cabin. "Didn't you say that a ritual had to be performed first before Pandora's coffin could be opened, though?"

"Honestly, I don't know if it has to be performed," said Pyrrha, "or whether it's just Follower beliefs, but we know that's what they are going to do. Now, if they haven't noticed it needs a second key and take it to Egypt, then by the time they find out it will be too late and the comet will have gone. But if Jacen has told them and they find the second key, then they are going to try and find you. I say we leave this one where it is, leave this hellhole, find the second key ourselves and take it, and you, out of the equation. My order will then come back and move this coffin to a safer place when we are certain the Followers are no longer a threat."

Mira looked to Kyle, who gave her an approving nod.

"I have the key already," she said.

Pyrrha shook her head. "I should have known. Then, all the more reason to take you, Rachel and Jo away from here, now."

"You know full well we are not leaving this place," Mira insisted. "Remember the other island? The bronze gates wouldn't open until the coffin was released. And I'm damned sure that thing out there in the ocean will not allow us to go until we retrieve it. Why else did it bring us here? Look, we now have the chance to move it somewhere safer before the Followers come. And you know they will, Pyrrha. We've all dreamed it. As for the comet, you said it would be gone in four weeks—it's been here three years!"

Pyrrha's gaping mouth showed she'd had no clue what Tan had revealed to them already. She looked to Tan, who gave a simple nod of acknowledgement.

"This is dangerous, Mira, but it seems we have no choice now," she said. "We'll leave as soon as I prepare what's left of my people."

When Pyrrha left the room, Linus took the opportunity to use the toilet, naïvely assuming that he wouldn't miss anything further said about the mission.

It was then that Kyle leaned in close to Mira. "You didn't tell her about us taking it to Egypt. How are you going swing it, or have you changed your mind?"

"No, I haven't changed my mind—but, one thing at a time."

Kyle scratched his head. "You know, for someone who didn't want us going anywhere near the tomb, Pyrrha seems to have given in pretty quick, don't you think?"

Mira shrugged. "I guess. Perhaps she's finally realised that she doesn't have all the answers that she was brought up to believe in. Or that there are some things you can't change, no matter how hard you fight against it."

***

All weapons and rucksacks inspected, and the four remaining guards left on the ship to deal with another possible attack, the small company once again departed the ship.

As Pyrrha forged ahead, Kyle just behind her, Mira noticed Tan cast a furtive glance over his shoulder toward her.

Oh no—either he wants to share or ask me something. She braced herself before approaching his side. Leaning in toward him, she whispered, "What's the matter?"

Tan opened his mouth, then closed it again. "Nothing," he said, refusing to look her in the eye.

"It is something," she said. "C'mon, you can tell me."

Tan opened his mouth again but then stopped himself. "It's not important."

Now she was fully convinced that whatever it was Tan was reluctant to share, she would have to winkle it out of him, and soon. The last thing they needed was Tan getting killed and taking the information to the grave.

With the prospect of a long trek ahead of them, Mira began to consider how she could elicit this information before they reached the pyramid, preferably without Tan realising she'd obtained it from right under his nose.

CHAPTER FORTY-TWO

A FREUDIAN SLIP

They had just reached the edge of the forest when they became aware of the great, shadowy mass of harpies appearing like a cloud across the face of the moon. The group immediately dived inside the tents for cover and anxiously waited. When gunshots were heard from the ship, Mira and Tan had to physically stop Pyrrha from returning to her crew.

The company sped through the trench that Linus had carved through the snow and approached the river. Then, keeping their distance from the water's edge, they veered away from the track and headed toward the bear forest.

With no sign of the harpies returning, or the huge brown bear with its cubs, and the ravine now impassable due to the great depth of snow that had fallen, the group rushed through the trees, across the open field and over the first bridge without any issues.

Upon approaching the second bridge, however, the head of a giant crocodile rose out of the water, made eye contact with the group and slowly sank beneath the muddy surface.

"Is that the croc that attacked Josh?" Kyle asked, his eyes remaining firmly fixed on the river.

"I... I think so," said Tan. "It waited for him to get halfway across, then, without warning, attacked..." Suddenly realising the impact this statement would have upon the group, Tan turned to look back and was met with a row of stunned expressions. Some with jaws ajar, others watery-eyed. "But my bridge was nowhere near as strong as this one," he added, with what Mira thought was an attempt at a reassuring smile.

"If it is the same crocodile, how is it now in this river?" Pyrrha asked shakily. "You don't think it picked up our scent and followed us on land, do you?"

"The rivers join further downstream," said Mira, remembering what Kyle had told her. Not wanting the group to panic any more, she added, "It's not following us. This is probably just part of his territory. That's all."

Pyrrha edged onto the bridge. "We can't just stand here and hope it goes away," she said. "Those harpies could return at any moment. Now, what I suggest is this: run as fast as you can, but do not look to the water. I'll stay here, and if I see as much as a nostril of that croc, I'll put a bullet between its eyes."

Mira steadied her nerves and stepped forward. Then, before anyone could stop her, she bolted across.

Her feet hardly touched the wooden slats, and once she was safely on the other side, Kyle hastily followed, then Linus and Tan.

Finally, it was Pyrrha's turn to cross. Taking a deep breath, she stepped forward, slowly.

"What's she playing at?" said Kyle. "Come on! Pick up your pace before Killer Croc has you for a snack!"

Suddenly, Mira noticed a path of ripples moving through a bed of weeds. "It's seen her!" she cried, pointing to the increasing undulation through the water. "Hurry, Pyrrha!"

Pyrrha, in the meantime, had stopped and was gazing, as though in a trance, at something else in the river. Kyle and Mira were now jumping up and down, shouting and waving to her, but Pyrrha seemed completely unaware of the approaching danger. Unable to just allow the inevitable to happen, Mira forced her way past Tan, who was blocking her access to the bridge, and raced across to the now paralysed figure.

She was at Pyrrha's side in a moment. But when Pyrrha still refused to move, she grabbed her by both shoulders and furiously shook her until her head was bobbing around like a float. Suddenly, the veil was lifted and Pyrrha was released from her trancelike state. Immediately aware of the impending danger, both she and Mira started to run.

The rotting planks beneath their feet bowed and cracked as they took their weight, but there was no time to worry about falling through to the watery darkness below them. The sound of rushing water at their heels let them know that they had to do something NOW to avoid being torn apart by the monster that was launching itself, with jaws wide open, out of the water behind them.

When they were within a hair's breadth of the land, the wood beneath them disintegrated. Mira instinctually grabbed a tight hold of Pyrrha's hand, and with an almighty effort, they leapt.

A gunshot rang out above them as they landed heavily on the grass, and Mira breathed a huge sigh of relief when she saw the now-lifeless mass slowly disappearing beneath the water, leaving a muddy red trail behind.

"My goodness. Talk about a cliffhanger," Tan laughed, and calmly wiped his sweaty, blood-speckled face with the sleeve of his shirt.

Mira was far from composed. "What the hell happened? What were you thinking, Pyrrha?"

Pyrrha dusted herself down, refusing to look Mira in the eye. "I thought I saw someone I knew, that's all."

Even Tan appeared confused by this statement. "And that would make you stop in the middle of a rickety bridge with death stalking below you…?"

"Who did you see?" Kyle asked.

Again, Pyrrha kept her eyes down. "Someone I cared about very deeply appeared to be sailing a boat up the river toward me. But it couldn't have been him, because he's dead. Now, if you don't mind, I'd rather not talk about it—we have Rachel and Jo to rescue."

Conscious of the time ticking by, the company decided that although Pyrrha was right, and Rachel and Jo were the priority, they accepted Tan's suggestion that a 'timeout' was needed to calm down and gather their breaths. So, instead of heading straight for the pyramid, they entered the first building they came to in the town.

"Fifteen-minute break max," said Tan. "Make sure you all fill up on food and fluids. It's never wise to go into battle on an empty stomach. And no talking from now on. We don't know what else could be out there listening."

Everyone sat quietly with their backs to the wall, but all eyes were fixed on the entrance. Linus greedily gulped the juice from his flask, and Pyrrha opened her tin of peaches, but when Tan pulled a Mars bar from his rucksack, Mira couldn't stay silent any longer.

"You know, with everything that's happened, Josh was the only one that never truly lost hope, or his sense of humour. And out of everyone, I truly thought he would be the one to survive it all." She wiped away another tear. "And I really thought I'd be a bridesmaid at his and Rachel's wedding… *Oh, no!* What do we tell her?"

"Nothing, until this is over," said Pyrrha.

"We have to say something," said Linus. "She'll notice straight away he's not with us."

"Tell her the truth," said Tan. "No good ever comes from lying. She's going to find out at some point—better to be upfront and honest, I say."

Mira knew this was her moment to find out what Tan had wanted to tell her. "I'll do it. She's my best friend. You're so right, Tan—no good ever comes from lying, or holding back things that you wished you had told someone." She looked directly at him.

Tan's eyes met hers. He was about to speak, but to Mira's dismay, Kyle interjected. "Did he have any other last requests?"

Tan scratched his beard. "No, not really. Just to take care of you lot… OK, he did have one other request, but he was joking."

Mira's heart began to race. "What was it?"

"He wanted Kyle and Rachel to—"

She gasped. "Don't say he wanted Kyle and Rach to be together?" *Please don't say that's what you wanted to tell me!*

"No, no, no—although that would be better for me." Tan smiled. "No, he wanted Kyle and Punchy to take me to the river, let the croc bite me and then one of you cut off the infected bit, that's all. But, like I said, he was joking."

Everyone stared.

"Did I just hear you right?" said Kyle.

Tan looked around at all their faces. "Hey, he was joking. OK, he was serious at the time when he said it, but then we laughed about it. No, that's a lie, we didn't laugh. But he was joking."

Pyrrha looked aghast. "Why on earth would you tell them that?"

"Honesty is the best medicine." His eyes then rested on Mira.

Here it comes! Mira thought. She tensed, ready for the bad news about to come her way.

"Yes," Tan relented. "I lied to you."

"About what?"

"When I said I didn't know where your real father was."

Mira reached for Kyle's hand and squeezed. "He's dead, isn't he?"

Tan's mouth fell open. "No, why would you think that? You kids today can be awfully morbid at times. No, he's not dead."

Butterflies rose up through her stomach. "So, where is he?"

Then she noticed Pyrrha glaring at him.

No, no, no. You have to tell me, Mira willed him.

Tan got to his feet. "I shouldn't have said anything, but trust me, he's alive and is very, very well."

Mira couldn't swallow. "No, Tan—you have to tell me!" she insisted.

Tan dropped his head forward and let out a sigh. "If we live through all this and get off the island, I'll take you to him, I promise."

Her mind was now in overdrive. "Why can't you tell me now?"

"Because you need to be focused on the task at hand, so don't ask again or I won't take you," he said firmly.

Is he crazy? "What if you die? How will I find him, then?"

Tan's whole face drooped. "Die? Who said I'll die? You haven't had a vision, have you?"

Mira thought for a moment. Her eyes narrowed. "Let me see... maybe I have."

Sweat began to trickle down Tan's forehead. "That's bad form, Mira. That's a right dirty trick... How's this— I'll tell Pyrrha, and if I die, she'll be able to tell you, agreed? But, you now have to tell me, have you had a vision?"

Mira silently fumed. *Why won't he tell me?* "Not agreed. But tell Kyle, and we have a deal." She offered out her hand to shake.

"No, he'll tell you as soon as my back is turned."

"I could tell her to your face if you'd prefer?" Kyle cut in.

Tan looked wearily to the sky. "Me and my big mouth," he mumbled. "Let me think... Right, I've got it. I'll write it down and put it in my pocket, and I'll tell Pyrrha to give it to you if anything happens to me. Agreed?"

Mira's hands began to shake. "Oh, for goodness' sake, just tell me!"

"No, I can't. Not yet. So, let's make a move."

Mira regained her composure, then narrowed her eyes further. "Don't you want to know what happens to you?"

"To be honest with you—no, not really. But don't worry, you'll see him again, I promise," said Tan, striding away.

If he knows, Pyrrha surely already does, too. "I know you know where he is," Mira told her. "Are you going to tell me?"

Pyrrha also got to her feet. "I'm sorry, Mira, I can't. But Tan is right—you will see him again, I swear."

Mira watched Pyrrha leave the building with Tan, and then a dishevelled, possibly reprieved Linus (she hadn't wanted to ask Pyrrha what she was going to do to him once they'd found Rachel and Jo, fearing her response) running to catch them up. Mira could only follow behind with Kyle, praying that at least one of them would survive the night.

CHAPTER FORTY-THREE

TIME FOR A TALK

Finally, the pyramid was in sight. As Pyrrha and Kyle headed toward the lake, Tan turned back and handed Mira the crossbow she'd been attempting to master only a few hours earlier.

"Now remember, the arrows with the yellow tips go bang," he said. "The arrows with the blue tips don't. Even then, be sure not to hit any of us, because they will penetrate anything, even a thick sheet of steel, and will do lasting damage if we live. Although, I can't see anyone surviving being hit with one of those, so on caution's side, do not hit anyone other than the flying mongooses."

Mira snatched the crossbow and retrieved a blue arrow from the quiver.

"That's it, see if they work first," Tan instructed. "Don't want to waste the others, we may need them later. Linus, I need you to stand near the entrance. If you see any of those flying hamsters, simply run toward us and we'll take care of the rest."

Linus gulped. "Where are you going to be?"

"My niece and I are going to be near the river, hiding. The weapons we have are more suitable for silent ambush, rather than all-out war." Tan patted Linus on the shoulder. "Don't worry, we're both excellent marksmen.

Just run in our direction and we shall make sure none of those things get anywhere near you."

Linus gave a slow nod of his head and half-heartedly made his way toward the lake, all the while keeping one eye on Tan and Mira as they slowly walked off together.

***

Mira and Tan had reached the edge of the river. Nagging thoughts of where her father was were still buzzing around in Mira's mind, which prompted her to pull on Tan's arm and say, "Does my mother know where my real father is?"

Tan dropped his head forward. "For once, I saw this coming. Listen, all you need to know right now is that they are all safe. Now, I need you to remain focused. I'm going to keep my eye on the river in case that crocodile had any mates who may decide to sneak out and ambush us. You just keep your eyes forward for anything that flies. Remember, if you hit one with a blue arrow and it doesn't take it out of the sky, don't wait around. Reach for the yellow arrow immediately. But, if it does take it to the ground alive, tell me and I'll deal with it and you move on to your next target."

Mira lay in the snow and stared out toward the pyramid. "You know, Tan, they are still alive in those coffins. We heard Pandora calling out to us. And with the visions I was given when I looked inside her tomb—well, they just have to be alive."

Tan kept his head low. "Fine, they're alive," he said, loading the rifle.

"You still don't believe me, do you?" Mira asked, looking back to him.

"Does it matter what I believe? Look, whatever is in them—gods, cheesed-off ancestors or vases filled with poison—just be sure you know what needs to be done before they're opened, that's all I ask. If you can do that, then I'm with you till the end. And don't always trust what visions show you. They can always change, and they don't always show you everything. Sometimes, they are just guidance, what *could* happen. Other times it's the gods having a laugh at your expense."

Mira thought for a moment. *Trust.* "Speaking of which, do you trust Pyrrha?"

"Trust her to do what?"

"To let us go to Egypt and do what we need to do."

"Look, what she told you about being your aunt, she did it to protect you and your brother. She's also loyal to her order and will do anything to protect it. I can respect that. Now, do I trust her…? Yes, absolutely, and now that she knows that the Followers know about this place, I'm ninety-nine per cent certain she'll do what she can to get the sarcophagus out of here."

"What about after, when we need to take it to Egypt?" said Mira, testing his reaction.

"When we get out of here, I'm going to gather all the Disciples together and explain the situation. If they refuse to go to war or help to retrieve Jacen, then I shall go and get him myself. But that is something to worry about later."

Mira smiled. At last, she felt a small sense of relief. Tan, at least, would do anything for her and Jacen, even knowing all the risks it brought.

CHAPTER FORTY-FOUR

THE RESCUE

Kyle and Pyrrha approached the entrance to the pyramid. But as they stepped inside the giant doorway, Kyle realised a flaw in the plan just by seeing the layout and remembering what Josh had described.

"You know, unless you can fly, this is the only way in and out, don't you?" he said. "If those things block the entrance, we don't have the firepower to fight our way out. This could be another massacre."

Pyrrha opened her rucksack, pulled out a torch and handed it to him. "This should buy us some time. It's really powerful, trust me. They don't seem to like light, remember."

"What about you? What are you going to use if we get separated?" Kyle asked, anxiously looking at the small device and seriously doubting its capability.

Pyrrha grabbed his holster belt tight. "Now we won't get separated." She laughed nervously. "But I need to know—are you ready for this? Are you alright?"

"If you're talking about what happened to Josh... No. I'm not alright. I'll never be alright. But two friends need me now. So, let's just get this done."

A gentle nod of her head, and warily, they entered the pyramid.

Darkness wrapped its cloak around them. Kyle shakily held out the torch and turned it on. The beam of light proved to be as powerful as Pyrrha had claimed. With the way ahead clearly lit, Pyrrha rested her gun upon Kyle's shoulder but instructed him to place a finger in his ear as the firing of the weapon could potentially deafen him.

After what felt like an eternity of turning corners, they arrived in the centre of the compound. Kyle's initial gut feeling was to turn back as they surveyed the lifeless bodies of all the yellow-eyed harpies, some speared to the walls with tree branches, others lying in a heap in the centre of the chamber, their throats slit, but then he noticed smoke billowing from the second tunnel. Were Rachel and Jo OK? Had they arrived too late?

Kyle ran through the thick, choking cloud, and again, remembering what Josh had described, he coughed his way to the chimney and removed the dead, yellow-eyed harpy blocking the fumes' escape.

The chamber began to clear. Through the last of the haze, Kyle saw Rachel and Jo huddled together in the shadows, their noses and mouths hidden inside their jumpsuits.

Rachel ran forward and threw her arms around his neck. "The red-eyed ones came, and we had to hide," she said. "They could come back at any moment."

"Yeah, it was horrible," said Jo, gingerly getting to her feet. "They came so fast that it was over before we knew what was really going on. One of the yellow-eyes came back and told us to hide in that crevice." She pointed. "Lucky it did, cos a red-eye came shortly after, killed the yellow-eye and stuffed it up the chimney."

"Before it was killed," Rachel added, "it also said that whatever we do, we must not go to the sepulchre."

"It told you?" Kyle asked, wondering if he'd heard right. "Are you saying… you could understand it?"

"Rachel could," said Jo. "I couldn't."

"It might have something to do with the amount of toxin that was spat in my face compared to Jo," said Rachel. "At least, that's Jo's explanation. She believes it opened up pathways in my brain that made me understand them. We think that some of the yellow-eyed harpies have survived but are now in hiding."

Kyle closed his eyes, anticipating what was about to happen. "Oh dear."

"What? What's, oh dear?" Rachel gulped.

"Mira, Tan and Linus are outside, ready to kill them all. We thought that after they killed Pyrrha's people, they were going to take you to the tomb."

"They can't kill them, they're friendly. They tried to protect us!" Jo squealed.

"They are not friendly!" Pyrrha snarled, entering the chamber. "If you saw what they did to my people, you would think differently!"

"Look, she just said they haven't hurt us," Rachel fumed. "It must have been the red-eye ones that attacked you." Her eyes drifted to the entrance. "And where the hell is Josh? I would have thought he would have at least come to see if I was alright!"

Kyle's insides immediately flipped over. He had hoped to delay telling her until later, much later, when the risk of them all dying had reduced. "He couldn't come," he said, and started back toward the entrance. "Now, we need to get out of here. Mira needs you to open the tomb."

"Oh, so now we're opening it, are we, just because Mira says so?" Jo shouted after him.

"Yes, and because Jacen says so as well," said Kyle, turning to face them.

"What do you mean, Jacen says so?" Rachel's face lit up. "Has he been found?"

Great, more heartbreaking news to tell her. "He visited us in our dreams and told us to do what Mira says."

"So, he's OK. Right then, I'm with you," said Rachel. "And wait till I see Josh—my hand is itching for his arm now. Couldn't come. I'll give him *couldn't come!*"

"Rachel, don't," Pyrrha called after her, her eyes filled with tears.

Rachel ran to the entrance; her eyes were wide, hopeful. "Kyle, where is he?"

Kyle's mouth and throat were dry. He could hardly get the words out. "He got bitten by a crocodile and… and it carried a lethal toxin. He… he didn't make it."

For a brief moment, it was as if all the oxygen in the chamber had been sucked out.

Until Rachel screamed. "No! No way! He wouldn't leave me! You're lying! Please tell me you're lying?!" She collapsed to the ground.

Kyle lifted her up, throwing his arms around her as she wept. Pyrrha and Jo looked on, tears pouring down their faces.

Rachel's whole body trembled. "So, where is he now?"

"Tan's boat. I was going to see him when we got you back."

Rachel released herself from Kyle's embrace and started down the tunnel. "I want to see him now!" she said and broke into a sprint back toward the centre chamber.

"Great. We've only just found her and she's off again," said Kyle, chasing after her.

Rachel had already arrived at the second chamber. Just as he was about to call out and ask her to slow down, he heard a spine-wrenching shriek.

The now-familiar sound of flapping wings and a gust of cold air enveloping them confirmed their fears. The harpies were swooping in from the opening above.

Kyle pushed Pyrrha and Jo into the second tunnel after Rachel. His heart leapt into his mouth. Their only means of escape was blocked by a wall of leathery wings and snarling pointy teeth.

"See—red eyes!" Rachel roared. "Give me a gun! They won't stop me from seeing Josh!"

From her rucksack, Pyrrha handed Rachel and Jo two handguns apiece. "It will save time having to re-load," she added.

"Wait," said Jo. "Maybe they will listen if we tell them we have no intention of entering the temple."

And before they could stop her, bravely, she stepped forward.

Everyone held their breaths as Jo held out her open hand, showing she meant no harm. "We don't want to go to the temple." She smiled. "Can you help us leave this island...?"

Slowly, one harpy tilted its head toward her. A long, deep inhale of Jo's scent, and the harpy returned to its pack. Jo turned back to the company, a huge grin stretched across her face. But just as she was about to say something, the harpy lunged.

Kyle's reaction was quicker. He pulled Jo out of the harpy's grasp, but one of its talons connected with his arm instead. The smell of fresh blood drove the harpy into a crazed delirium. And as it tried to bite Kyle, Rachel stepped forward and fired into its snarling mouth.

For a moment, there was complete silence as everyone watched the creature's limp body flop to the ground.

"Oh, this is going to be bad," said Kyle, and as he backed further into the tunnel, the deafening shrieks from the harpies began to bounce around the walls.

The harpies entered the corridor en masse, teeth and claws bared. Then, to everyone's surprise, suddenly, they came to a stop.

"What are they waiting for?" Rachel asked, shuffling into the middle of the group.

It was at that precise moment that they heard the frightful hisses and growls of more harpies approaching from behind them.

"Never mind," said Rachel. "If I were to make a guess, I'd say this is going to be a coordinated attack. OK, anyone with an idea on what we are going to do would be nice right now!"

Pyrrha stepped forward. "We fight!" she cried. "You and Jo take up the rear defence. Remember, short bursts! Hit as many as you can in the mouth and they will flee!"

Her confidence wasn't as inspiring as she'd hoped.

"And what if they don't?" Jo whimpered.

"Then we shall die fighting!" she said, handing out the spare ammo clips to each of them. When it was Kyle's turn, she added, "You're with me. Now make your brother proud!"

CHAPTER FORTY-FIVE

OUTNUMBERED

The harpies were attacking in force. From the front, Kyle and Pyrrha could see the tunnel was piling up with dead bodies, and the route to the exit was becoming almost impossible to reach.

Suddenly, another war cry from the harpies came from behind. Rachel, having already taken up defence at the rear, shouted, "They're coming this way now, more of them! What do we do? There's nowhere to go!"

Wave after wave, the harpies attacked. And wave after wave, the company fought them back until finally, there was silence.

Pyrrha climbed the pile of dead bodies and peered over the top. "It looks like they're regrouping," she called out. Her eyes widened. "And with the backup that has just arrived, it looks like the next attack will be a full-on onslaught!" She checked her pouch for ammunition. "I have enough for one more attack and then I'm out," she said, dropping back.

"Same back here!" said Rachel. "Oh, I can see them gathering now. And I have only one full clip left, too!"

"Why don't Mira and Tan do something?" said Jo, breathing heavily.

"Perhaps they are under attack as well," said Pyrrha. "OK, let's not panic just yet. Kyle, how much ammo do you have left?"

Kyle could hear her, he just couldn't answer. From the moment the attack had ceased, he'd been enduring the image of his parents standing before him.

His father had fire in his eyes, and his mother was sobbing. *"You promised us, Kyle. You promised you would always take care of him,"* said Mrs M. *"It should have been you that died! Not my son. Not Josh!"*

"Kyle!" Pyrrha shouted again.

Kyle rubbed his eyes. Yet, even though his parents were gone, Mrs Mooney had now appeared.

"You failed them!" Her face hardened further. *"You were no match for my son!"* She pointed. *"He could have protected them!"*

Kyle shifted his gaze. From out of the darkness, Peter strode forward. His face was filled with twisted aggression and his huge, shovel-sized hands were clenched. But just as Peter raised his sledgehammer fist to strike, Kyle heard Rachel's screams.

Wrenched back to reality, he raised his weapon. He was too late. The battle had already recommenced, and one harpy had him firmly in its sights.

The force of the harpy's blow sent Kyle reeling. It felt as if he'd been hit by an articulated truck. Knocked onto his back, gasping for air, Kyle still tried to move. But the harpy held him firm to the ground, and he could only stare into the red eyes of death and wait for his end as the harpy opened its mouth wide, baring razor teeth.

The creature salivated in its moment of victory. Then, from out of nowhere, Rachel was upon it. Her weapon pressed into the creature's throat, she fired twice and the harpy was dead.

"That's it, I'm out," she said. "Kyle! Get your head out of your arse and fight!" She yanked him to his feet and, using her own weapons as a battering tool, began to fend off more of the incoming beasts.

The attack was coming from all sides. A mass of dead bodies and a river of blood cascaded across the floor. Kyle knew it was now only a matter of minutes before they would be finally overrun. He checked his gun's clip.

Only three bullets left.

He looked to his group, all fighting valiantly to the bitter end. He remembered Pelenna's screams as she was carried away to the harpies' nest, and the guard who had been torn in half before their eyes. He looked to his gun again.

Should he use the bullets on them? Save them the agonising death that he would then receive?

Slowly, he raised his weapon.

CHAPTER FORTY-SIX

HANDS OF RED

The attack had come so swiftly, and in greater numbers than anyone had anticipated, that Linus hadn't had time to call out a warning. Instead, he had hidden in the undergrowth. But with the harpies now piling into the pyramid, he slipped from his cover and ran.

"They're being overrun! There are more than we thought!" he bellowed, not noticing that four harpies had heard his cries and were now gunning for him.

As he ran in circles, desperately ducking and weaving through the harpies' attacks from above, even with her little knowledge of the crossbow, Mira realised that she was too far away for the arrows to have a critical effect.

Leaving her sniping position, with Tan hot on her heels, she ran toward Linus. But as she neared him, four more harpies suddenly zipped over their heads. With a standing twirl, Mira lined up her target and unleashed the first arrow. But Linus' yelling had caught the attention of the harpy. It swooped into a dive and the bolt missed its target by inches. The harpy's claws closed around Linus and lifted him into the air.

Mira tried to reload. But the arrow had caught in the hood of the quiver. Tan fired instead. The bullet struck the creature's leg. Stung by the blow, the harpy released Linus, dropping him face first into the snow.

With the arrow finally released from its pouch, and the harpy still stunned from Tan's shot, Mira fired her second bolt. This time, the arrow simply ricocheted off the harpy's torso, so she did as Tan had instructed and pulled out a yellow bolt.

Mira lined up her shot, then hesitated. Three more harpies were closing in on Linus. Coolly, she waited. Then, when the harpies were all together, she fired. This time, when the arrow struck, it exploded on impact, causing the creatures to spiral to the ground. Another arrow pulled from its quiver, Mira set up her next target.

With two harpies taken out of the sky by Tan's skilful shooting, Mira fired again. The explosion killed the harpies instantly, before they could take to the sky.

Blood and guts scattered the battlefield. One harpy had returned to the pyramid, but one remained. It had Linus running in circles again, and as he avoided the swooping claws, Mira called out, and he shone his torch upon the harpy. The target in her sight, blinded by the light, Mira unleashed another arrow. It struck the harpy in the mouth, immediately killing it.

The sky clear of harpies, Mira and Tan ran toward the entrance of the pyramid, leaving Linus lying exhausted in the snow.

They entered the labyrinth. Seeing a chaotic wall of harpies ahead, Mira fired another explosive arrow.

Sprays of blood and body parts instantly decorated the walls, and rock dust filled the tunnel. Then, from out of the haze, Mira and Tan were suddenly greeted by Pyrrha and Rachel, stumbling over the debris.

"What the hell happened in here?" Tan asked, aghast, stepping over the mass of lifeless bodies.

"Thank God you came when you did," Rachel choked. "They had us completely surrounded, and we were all out of bullets—except for Kyle. I think he's lost his mind, Mira. It looked like he was about to shoot us."

Tan picked up a discarded gun. "If this was his, then I know what he was thinking, crazy fool."

"What was he thinking?" Rachel spluttered.

"He was going to save you all the agony of a terrible death. And by the looks of it, outnumbered and with only three rounds remaining, I would say he was going to allow them to tear him to pieces rather than let it be done to you." Tan looked at the mass of dead bodies again and then to Pyrrha. "My god… did you know there would be this many? The ancient writings we have claimed there were only three."

"That's what I thought." Pyrrha coughed. "And there was only a dozen that took my men out."

"Where are Kyle and Jo now?" said Mira, panicked that she may have inadvertently killed them with her rash actions.

"When the explosion came, I saw one of those bitches grab Jo," said Rachel. "Kyle went after her. I wanted to go after him, but I need some fresh air. It feels like my lungs are about to burst. I'm so sorry, but I can't go back in there. Not yet." Rachel ran out to the edge of the lake, where Linus was now standing.

Mira and Tan followed Pyrrha deeper into the structure to find Jo and Kyle.

Mira entered the centre chamber. There she could see Kyle, knelt over the body of a harpy, a large knife gripped in his hand. She ran toward him, but seeing that his hair, uniform and hands were soaked in blood, she slowed her approach, fearing he could instinctively lash out at her by mistake. Suddenly, she could hear Jo's cries echoing from the second tunnel.

"You get Jo," said Pyrrha. "I'm out of ammo and no good with a crossbow. I'll see to Kyle."

Torn between wanting to stay with Kyle and not wanting Tan to enter the second chamber alone, Mira reluctantly followed her uncle.

The fire was still burning brightly. As Mira cautiously went left of the chimney, and Tan went right, she could see that Jo was being held roughly by a harpy, larger in size than those they had already faced.

She aimed her crossbow directly at the harpy's head. Mira waited for Tan to get into position, then called to Jo. "When I say go, stamp your foot on its talons and then drop to the ground."

Jo's eyes widened. "You do realise it can probably understand you, don't you?" she squeaked.

The harpy did appear to understand. It wrapped its wings tightly around Jo's body, holding her legs firm. But it left its head unprotected. Mira smiled. It had fallen into her trap. She fired.

The blue arrow penetrated the harpy's eye. Its vice-like grip released, enabling Jo to dive to the ground. Tan took his shot.

Initially, Jo was too scared to move, but seeing the large figure of the harpy fall prostrate before her, she scrambled to her feet and ran from the chamber.

"Clever girl," Tan beamed, patting Mira on the back. "I couldn't have done it better if I had planned it myself."

They returned to the main chamber, where Pyrrha and Tan led Jo outside. Mira joined Kyle and wiped the blood from his face.

Kyle stood motionless. His eyes were wide and watery. "It was like Lyssa all over again, but this time, I couldn't stop stabbing it," he said. "Even after it was dead."

Mira continued to clean the blood away. "It was you or them. I've just wiped out half a dozen. But we can't dwell on it. This isn't our fault."

Kyle finally made eye contact. "What happens the next time? What if there's more killing to be done? What if I can't stop killing when all this is over?"

Mira gently stroked his cheek. "You will stop. I promise you will. You are not a bad person, Kyle. Hey, I need you to be strong. I can't do this alone. But if you really can't take any more, if want to go home, I'll understand. And when this is over, I'll come find you, I swear."

Kyle pulled her close. "I want you to promise me something."

Mira wrapped her arms tightly around him. "Anything."

"Promise me that if I can't stop killing... then you will kill me."

Mira didn't want to think of such a thing. How could she kill the only boy she'd ever felt this strongly for? But when Kyle asked her again, reluctantly, she agreed.

***

Once Kyle's arm had been bandaged, they joined up with Pyrrha, Tan and Jo and departed the pyramid. Linus was lying near the river, unconscious in the snow, and Rachel was nearby, shivering with the cold.

Mira took off her coat and threw it around her best friend's shoulders.

Kyle checked on Linus. "What happened?" he asked.

"He saved my life," Rachel croaked. "One of those flying things attacked me; he threw himself in front of it. A crocodile came out of the water and grabbed the harpy's wing. It dragged the harpy and Linus into the water. Thank goodness that croc has a taste for harpies, or I wouldn't have been able to get Linus out." Rachel pointed to the river, where the crocodile was still performing a death roll. "Was that the one that killed, Josh?" she snarled.

As Mira restrained Rachel from hunting down the crocodile, Kyle removed Linus' drenched coat and threw his own around him. The air bit at his skin, a thousand tiny ice picks, but he fought the cold and checked for bite marks on Linus' body. When he found nothing, Tan gave Linus a hard slap around the face.

"Was there any need for that?" Rachel shouted.

"Look, his eyes are open now," said Tan. "Would you have preferred to carry him?"

The icy wind was rising, and the snow was falling heavily. The company had to find cover quickly, so, staggering across the bank, Rachel approached Kyle with what he assumed would be a hand to help him up off the ground. With one mighty swing, she slapped him across the face, then immediately threw her arms around him.

"I know what you were going to do," she said, kissing him on the red mark. "But in the future, if we fight together then we shall die together." She turned to the whole group. "And that goes for the rest of you. From now on we work and act as a bloody team. Now, I want to see Josh!"

"Our ship is closer, and you need to get warm first," said Pyrrha.

Tan shook his head. "I think you'll find my boat is closer."

"No, it's not—not now the bridge is gone. And by the time we walk around, it will be quicker to my ship."

Kyle knew whichever way they took, the temperature was dropping, and Linus was in serious trouble. "Pick one! Or he'll never make it to either!"

"That's his fate then," said Pyrrha, storming away.

"She's right, Kyle. Just leave me here," said Linus, his body shaking and teeth chattering. "I deserve it."

"We're not leaving you," said Mira. "Rachel's right—we're a team. You've saved Rachel and you tried to save Josh. You also found Jo. And until you've saved a million more people, you're not dying on us." She looked back to the pyramid. "The only chance we have is to go back to the fire!"

There was a moment of stunned silence.

"My niece is right," said Tan, his tone filled with pride. "But, just to check, how many boom-boom arrows have you got left?"

"Enough. Now instead of talking, let's get these two warm!" said Mira, and grabbing Rachel's arm, she led her friend back toward the pyramid.

"Are you freaking kidding me? You're going back in there?" Jo bellowed.

"Unless you want to freeze to death, we have to," said Kyle, hauling Linus onto his feet.

Pyrrha insisted on returning to her ship to check on her crew, which left Kyle with a dilemma. He wouldn't leave Mira, or the others. Yet, for some reason, he was feeling strangely concerned for Pyrrha's well-being.

"I'll be fine, Kyle. I've been trained for this." She half smiled. "Keep them safe."

Reluctantly, Kyle followed behind the group, back to the uncertainty of whatever the pyramid had in store for them.

"I'm sorry I misjudged you," Pyrrha suddenly yelled out to him. "And just so you know, I would have done the same to those I care about."

Kyle turned to answer, but she'd already disappeared into the swirling blizzard.

CHAPTER FORTY-SEVEN

A TIME TO MOURN

There was no sign of the harpies returning to the pyramid.

Linus was stripped to his underwear and instructed to lie by the fire. While Mira and Kyle took the first watch at the entrance, Tan and Jo tried to sleep. But with Rachel pacing, her feet scuffing the stone floor, Tan sat back up.

"It's OK to mourn, Rach," he whispered. "Now is as good a time as any."

"So, how did he get bitten?" Rachel said through her sobs.

"He crossed the bridge too slowly," said Tan. "It came out the water and bit down on the slats, and I guess Josh felt like having a challenge because he decided to ride it. He did really well, too. A natural. You would have been really proud of him."

"Felt like a challenge? Are you kidding me!?"

Tan shrugged. "Why else would he have jumped on its nose?"

"He jumped on its nose? Oh! This just keeps getting better. If I die, I'm going to spend an eternity slapping that arm of his!" She was weeping now. "So how did he look? According to Mira, Pyrrha told Kyle it's not the nicest of things to see."

"How did he look?" said Tan, rubbing his chin thoughtfully. "Umm, like a young, handsome movie star that bit the bullet at the end of a film. How's that?"

Rachel began sobbing even louder, and when it escalated to loud, long, soulful wailing, Mira ran to comfort her, realising it was going to be a very long night.

Tan joined Kyle at the entrance. "Who needs sleep anyway?" he murmured to himself. "So, how are you feeling?" he asked Kyle.

"How am I feeling?" Kyle repeated. "Dead inside. Like… like I don't think I'll ever be happy again. And yet I can't cry. What the hell is wrong with me?"

"Nothing," said Tan. "And you will feel happiness again, I promise. I had a younger sister that died. Way too young, she was, and I, too, couldn't cry. Then one day, out of the blue, it hit me like a ton of bricks, and I thought I'd never be able to stop crying. Then I met my wife and things got better."

"What happened to your sister?"

"She went for a stroll with her husband in the jungles of India at night on their honeymoon. They never saw the tiger coming."

Kyle wasn't sure he'd heard right. "I'm sorry? Why— why on earth would they do that?"

"Some people like to live life on the edge. Like your brother. But now they are asleep, waiting for the day the dead rise."

Kyle shook his head, placed his fingers in his ears and wiggled them about. "I'm sorry—did you say when the dead rise? Have you been watching *The Walking Dead*?" he asked. It had been one of Josh's favourite shows.

"Actually, I was talking about a book I once read. It says that at the end of days the dead shall rise up. Some believe the dead are only sleeping."

"That's not comforting," said Kyle. "You do know that, don't you? Do we really want all the psychos from history walking around again?"

"I don't believe *they* will. Only those that deserve it shall live again. Don't you want to believe that Josh will one day rise again?"

Kyle's heart again began to ache. "I'd like to think Josh is sat in the great hall in Valhalla right now. *Vikings* was another of his favourite shows."

Tan nodded in agreement. "Mine too. Look, go get some sleep, if you can. I'll keep watch."

***

Kyle joined Mira, who had managed to get Rachel to lie down by the fire next to Linus.

"I think she's all cried out, hence the heavy breathing," she whispered, moving him to a quieter spot in the chamber.

"I hope Pyrrha is OK," he said softly.

Mira raised an eyebrow. "I got the impression you didn't like her?"

"I don't dislike her. And I kind of get where's she coming from—opening the tomb, I mean—but she told me she doesn't trust me. I know I wanted the gates open on Pandora's island, but…" He paused. "Hang on, didn't Josh say something about her not trusting him either?"

Mira didn't answer. Instead, she rested her head on his shoulder.

Yet, despite her calm appearance, Kyle could feel the tenseness of her body leaning against his. "Has she said anything to you?" he asked.

Mira shook her head and again said nothing. And when she held him tighter and closed her eyes, as Kyle kept a watchful eye on the entrance, he began to wonder if Mira was once again keeping something to herself.

CHAPTER FORTY-EIGHT

A TIME TO SHINE

The sun was shining into the tunnel ahead, and Tan yelled to make sure everyone was awake. Linus' clothes were now dry, so once he'd dressed, the party took one last look at the fire still burning and left the pyramid.

Pyrrha was already on the other side of the river, waiting. Wearily, the company approached. It was then they noticed that a new bridge had been secured. Tan took a position in the middle, aiming his crossbow at the water's edge, and once they were all safely across, he hastened to the other side.

"Remembered we had one on board," said Pyrrha.

"Is everyone OK your end?" Tan asked.

"No. Another of my guards was taken. Don't ask how. Only the three brothers are left."

"I'm sorry for your loss," said Rachel. "Truly. But I want to see Josh, like right now!"

With that fire in her eyes, nobody dared to argue, and they all followed Tan to the cove.

With only three people able to fit safely in the dinghy, Kyle rowed Mira and Rachel to Tan's boat and climbed on board. They stood in the doorway for a moment, looking at the motionless body on the sofa. Then Kyle placed his arm around Rachel's shoulders, and together they entered the cabin.

"He looks so peaceful," Rachel sobbed. "Damn you, Josh Michaels. You just had to ride a giant bloody crocodile!"

Kyle lowered his arm and placed his hand into Rachel's. Mira came to his other side and cupped her arm through his. "Do either of you want to spend some time alone with him?" she whispered.

Both Kyle and Rachel shook their heads.

"He always said we're a team," said Rachel.

They stood for a while, all hugging each other, and when Rachel finally kissed Josh goodbye and gently pulled the blanket up over his head, they left.

It was only a short boat ride to the shore, but Kyle felt it was the longest journey of his life.

Mira and Rachel stepped off the boat first. Kyle slowly followed, keeping his head low. No one said a word as they began the long walk back to Pyrrha's ship. But just as they reached the top of the ravine, Linus, who had stayed well back from the group, ran forward and brought them all to a stop.

"Look!" he cried.

Everyone, except Kyle, spun around to see what he was pointing at.

Loud gasps echoed along the narrow gorge, and Kyle finally turned back to see what all the fuss was about.

The sun was still low in the sky, and with its orange glow casting glistening sparkles across the water, Kyle was blinded for a moment. Then, as his eyes slowly adjusted, his gaze was drawn to a lone silhouette standing on the bow of Tan's ship. Instantly, he dropped to his knees.

"Excuse me, where the hell do you lot think you're going?" cried the figure. "And which of you tried to suffocate me? Come on, admit to it!"

The shock of seeing Josh alive had also brought Mira down to Kyle's level. Rachel was rooted to the spot with her mouth wide open. Only Linus had found the power of movement, fist punching the air as he dashed back down the slope. He leapt into the dinghy and rowed back to the boat.

When Linus brought Josh to shore, Rachel, at last finding the will to move, ran and threw herself on top of him and covered him in kisses. It took Tan to finally drag her off.

Meanwhile, Kyle and Mira scrambled to their feet and rushed to the shore.

"Bloody hell, you can't take a nap anymore without someone trying to kill you," said Josh, removing a rucksack from his back. "And why are you all now staring at me like that? Did you draw something on my face, Tan?"

"How…? You were dead!" Kyle gasped.

"Dead tired, yes," said Josh. "You ever ridden a giant crocodile? Takes it out of you, Kaiboy."

"But—but the bite?" Mira inhaled sharply. "Tan, you said it was infected?"

Josh also looked to Tan. "Yeah, you said that to me. Yet, when I woke up and checked, there was no gash."

"So, what did you do?" Rachel asked, prodding his arm to make sure he really was in front of her, alive.

Josh shrugged. "I just thought I must have banged my head and dreamed it all. And with nobody here, I thought I'd catch up on the sleep I've sorely needed."

"Catch up on some sleep?!" said Rachel, and she released an eye-watering slap. "Do you know what we've been through?!"

"*Oww!* No! So, what have you been through now?" said Josh, vigorously rubbing the inflamed spot on his crimson arm.

"It doesn't matter," Kyle laughed.

Pyrrha edged forward, and with Rachel's approval, she threw her arms around Josh. "You never cease to amaze me, Josh Michaels. Never," she said, tears once again rolling down her cheeks.

Tan finally spoke. "Show me your leg, boy?" he asked.

Josh opened the tear in his trousers. "See—no gash." He then turned back toward the ship inquisitively. "Hang on, am I dreaming now?"

Tan studied the calf thoroughly. "Well, miracles do happen, because I've never seen a dead person come back to life before." He laughed and, grabbing Josh's hand, checked his pulse.

"I wasn't dead, I was sleeping," said Josh, pulling his hand away.

"No, boy. You were dead. I checked. Your pulse had definitely gone to ground."

"Perhaps the venom just slowed his pulse so much that you couldn't detect it?" said Pyrrha.

"Look, I know when someone is dead," said Tan. "It's my job to know, and this young man was as dead as Speedos!"

"Will you stop saying I was dead, please," Josh groaned. "And more importantly, does anyone have anything to eat? I'm famished."

Pyrrha reached into her rucksack and produced something that brought a smile back to Josh's face.

"A Mars bar," he said, wiping a tear from his eye.

"They were Sherme's favourite, too." She almost smiled.

Josh slipped it inside his suit with a grin. "There is a God after all."

Mira, who had been staring at both Kyle and Josh, suddenly burst into a nervous laugh. "Don't you all see?" she said. "Josh is right. The ancient scholars were right—Epimetheus was a god. One of the Titans, if I recall. Heck, Pandora could have been one, too, for all we know…"

"What are you trying to say, Mira?" asked Jo.

"It's why we're all here," Mira continued. "If me and Jacen can open Pandora's tomb and coffin, and you and Rachel can open Epimetheus', and with Kyle healing so quickly, and Josh's leg showing no signs of a wound, it must mean we're all descended from the gods—especially as there's a third tomb we need to find."

Pyrrha gasped. "A third tomb?!"

Before Mira could respond, Josh slapped his thighs. "I bloody knew I was a demigod," he said, smiling from ear to ear. "So, come on, Pegasus, I'm ready and able to do some flying. You know, it wouldn't surprise me if we're all demigods. The Children of the Gods, everyone will call us." He then looked to Tan. "Maybe they'll refer to you as Grandpa of the Gods."

Rachel shook her head. "Josh, get this into your head. *You* are not a demigod."

"But Mira just said I was. And you saw for yourself how fast Kyle healed, so I must be special as well." Josh grinned.

"Oh, you're special alright," Tan groaned.

Pyrrha paced back and forth. "You are not demigods," she said, scowling. "Be very careful, Josh. The gods do not like it when you speak of such things. Now, what's this about a third tomb?"

Josh stared at Pyrrha, as if he was the one who was going to reveal Mira's secret. But instead, he said, "Wonder who I'm related to?"

It was as if he had poked a shark in the eye. "Did you just hear what I said? Do not upset the gods!" Pyrrha reiterated. "Now, tell me about this third tomb, damn it!"

Josh slowly nodded, but then said, "I wonder if it's Apollo?"

Rachel blew out her cheeks and hastily intervened. "Josh, listen to me. You are not a demigod."

"Or Athena, she's cool," said Josh, not seeming to have heard her either. "*Ooo*, what if it's Zeus himself, or Poseidon? I've always loved the ocean. Well, I did, before a storm almost made me soil myself, and of course seeing that thing that brought us here. Oh, and seeing the movie *Jaws*, and *Deep Blue Sea*, and the one with that woman stranded on a floaty bell thingy."

Rachel held his face firmly in her hands. "Josh, I know it's hard for you, but try and listen to me very carefully. You are not a demigod. We are not demigods. I understand where Mira is coming from, but there has to be another explanation we haven't yet thought of."

"She's right," said Tan. "And I would hate to be a demigod. If you read the stories, it never ends well for any of them. Then again, I also wouldn't want to be a god. I reckon they're miserable in their immortality and would secretly love to be mortal."

"Perseus had a good life," said Jo. "He lived to a ripe old age. He had many children and grandchildren, if you believe in all that nonsense. Hercules is from his line."

"There is always the exception to the rule!" Rachel growled. "But like Tan just said, the rest were miserable! You hear that, Josh? Miserable!"

Josh stared blankly back. "Not Poseidon then. Why am I only thinking of the Greek gods? Pyrrha, didn't you say the gods were all over the place and just appeared differently to everyone, even though they were the same gods, if you take my meaning? So, what about Thor or Odin? They're gods. Hey, I can hear it now: 'Josh, son of Thor'. Has a cool ring to it, don't you think?"

"Sounds to me like the croc had healing saliva, that's all," said Jo. "You know, like dogs. And the strange backward way the sun seems to set and rise on this island, it wouldn't surprise me if the crocodile's venom simply acted in the same way."

Tan clapped his hands together. "See, there is always a rational explanation for everything. Nice one, Jo. Glad to have you with us." He smiled.

Josh's shoulders slumped. "You always have to ruin it, don't you, Jo?" he grumbled. "Couldn't bloody give me five minutes of feeling special."

"Better that than you waiting for a mystical bloody horse to turn up." She glowered back at him. "Now, are we staying here to get attacked by that thing out there in the sea next, or are we going back to Pyrrha's ship?"

"She's right," said Rachel. "We can't stay this close to the ocean."

Linus, who had been stood apart from the group, silently listening, now raised his hand. "Sorry to be the harbinger of bad news, but if there *is* a third tomb that only Kyle and Josh can open—is it also hidden away somewhere on this island?"

"There is no other tomb!" said Pyrrha defiantly.

"She's right," said Tan. "I've never heard of a third tomb either."

"You didn't know about the second tomb until Mira told you," Josh reminded him.

"Touché."

Mira, who had joined Kyle at the water's edge, knew it was time to finally come clean. "I believe it's in Egypt," she admitted. "Where Pandora suffered her fate."

"In your vision, was the coffin from this place there as well?" Pyrrha demanded.

Mira replied with a simple nod of her head.

"That settles it then—we have to move it to a safer location now," said Tan.

"No, no. I'm sorry, we can't risk going for it now," Pyrrha insisted. "We have to get out of here. I need—I need to find out what's going on."

Mira sensed this wasn't the first time Pyrrha had experienced a complete feeling of uncertainty in what she'd been taught.

"Are you gonna leave Jacen with the Followers as well?" Rachel cried.

"And what about your brother, Sherme?" Tan asked. "And Laurie. Are you really gonna leave them in that place? We know that the Followers are probably on their way. Mira's vision was a warning for us to move it, I reckon. Look, let's just get the coffin and Sherme and Laurie, get off this island, get these kids to safety, and then I will go and get my nephew back."

Her head in her hands, Pyrrha kept pacing. "If we do this, then you all should know there is no going back to your old lives, for any of you, ever. It will be far too dangerous. Now, we'd better prepare ourselves better this time, because who knows what we are going to face in that place."

Tan grabbed Linus' arm and stepped back into the dinghy. "We'll catch you up. Going to fill some bags with things we may need."

CHAPTER FORTY-NINE

A CHANGE OF PLAN

The sky was crystal blue and the air crisp. The sun reflected brightly off the snow, and the company had to cover their eyes as they struggled to march back to Pyrrha's ship through Linus' half-buried trench.

Once inside the cabin, everyone took separate bunks, and a quiet, sombre mood suddenly filled the room.

"Is there really no going home for us, Pyrrha?" Jo asked tearfully.

Pyrrha shared a momentary glance with Mira, then shook her head. "I'm sorry, Jo, but no. We will try to retrieve your parents, I give you my word. Listen, our home is a very nice place to live. It's peaceful, everyone helps one another, and there are no rules or any judgement given on who you can, or should, love." She smiled.

"So, we're definitely going to your sanctuary?" Jo asked. "No lies this time?"

"Yes. I promise."

"Then we should leave now," said Jo, clapping her hands together.

"We've already decided, Jo," said Mira. "We can't risk the Followers finding Epimetheus' tomb. What if there's a map or something engraved on it that gives the exact location of the third? I saw markings on Pandora's."

"But what about that thing we saw in our dream?" Jo said sharply. "There's something huge in that place. Look, without us, they can't open them, so I want a show of hands first. Who believes it *would* be better to go to Pyrrha's sanctuary right now?"

When only Pyrrha raised her hand, and knowing that Tan and Linus would vote with Mira, Jo excused herself from the cabin, slamming the door behind her.

Tan and Linus finally returned. Along with Pyrrha's weapons and ammo, the contents of their bags were emptied onto one of the free beds. Everyone gathered around the bunk.

"This isn't good," said Tan. "I was hoping you would have more." He motioned to Pyrrha. "I forgot that I had to use more ammo at that rogue sanctuary than I would have liked. Right then, let's see what we have altogether. OK, we have only three boom-boom arrows left, so unless we can get all those flying mice to pose together for a group photo, I say we keep these as a last resort."

Tan then continued to list what was remaining from their firearm booty. The intermittent tuts, puffs and sighs that he emitted only confirmed what the rest of the group had already suspected: they had to make every shot count if they were to survive.

Finally, Tan perked up and said, "But I do have some good news. I have these sticky bombs—and they will stick to anything, wet or dry. Now, they have a wide blast range, so it's possible to take out more than one of those harpies, but remember, as soon as the pin is pulled, throw it, because it doesn't have a long fuse time."

"We can't go to the sepulchre without the proper firepower," said Kyle. "God knows how many of those flying things are still out there."

"Harpies, Kaiboy. They're called harpies," Josh reminded him.

"They could be called fluffy bunnies for all I care. I still don't think we can go with only the weapons we have now."

"I've had a rethink, too," Pyrrha said. "Our only options are to either wait for help to arrive or set a diversion for that thing out there in the sea and try and escape on Tan's boat. If we're not on the island, then maybe the Followers won't be able to traverse the fog. And before you say it, Josh, it's not the kraken out there. Perseus killed it."

Josh's eyes twinkled. "Maybe it's the kraken's wife, or one of the kids. But if you had studied the legend of Perseus properly, then you would know that the kraken wasn't actually named. A 'marine beast' was sent forth to claim Andromeda."

Pyrrha gave no response, but with a shake of her head, she left the cabin.

"So, Tan, you're the expert," said Kyle. "What do you think we should do?"

"I'll be honest with you, with the situation we now find ourselves in, I think Pyrrha and Jo are right—we should try and leave this place. But before we do anything, let's all have something to eat. The mind works better when the body is fed."

***

It was quite late when everyone had finally finished eating. No one made a move to get some sleep, partly due to the general sense of melancholy filling the room, but mainly because they were all quietly contemplating their next course of action as they remained seated around the table.

Mira cast a glance in Josh's direction. She could see that his mind was in overdrive. *Here it comes. Any moment now he'll convince the others to stay, I just know he will.*

"I've been thinking," he said, proving her right. "Do we have any traps?"

"Traps?" Pyrrha repeated, a sigh in her voice.

"Yeah, the town is full of big brown bears."

"You're not thinking of killing the bears, are you?" Jo said, returning from the toilet for the third time in quick succession.

"No," Josh groaned. "Hence the word *trap*."

"No. We don't have traps," said Pyrrha. "Hey, maybe you can wrestle them into submission, seeing as you're an invincible demigod now?"

"Oh, don't give him any more ideas, please," said Rachel.

"Maybe you can put a leash on that crocodile and take it for a walk through the town and scare the harpies away," Jo laughed. "Hey, everyone, meet the next P. T. Barnum: Josh Michaels."

Mira was amazed how Josh's composure wasn't slipping. Jo had a way of making you feel stupid, even when it seemed to all be in good fun.

"If I was the new P. T. Barnum, Jo, you would definitely be the star attraction," Josh retorted. "The Continually Weeping Lady, the punters will call you... But what I was thinking was this. If we could trap the bears, when the harpies attack, we could unleash them."

"I like where your head is at, Josh," said Tan. "But I thought we were all thinking of ways to escape the island now?"

"That's right," said Jo. "If Pyrrha is telling the truth about her sanctuary, then I for one am eager to see it. Besides, bears are deceptively quick, and I don't think even the fastest of us could outrun one, or is stupid enough to even try and trap one."

Then, abruptly, she leapt from her seat. "I have it!" she squealed. "This ship has an autopilot function. We wait until the krak—" She paused and shook her head. "We wait until that thing moves around the island, then we set this ship on a course in one direction, and while the thing is chasing after it, we escape on Tan's boat in the other direction."

Tan stroked his beard and a big smile appeared beneath. "I think you have the answer, Jo. Well done."

"You're not actually going to leave without opening the tomb, are you?" said Mira. "We have to! Remember what Jacen told me?"

After everything they had been through, she couldn't believe that they were contemplating the idea of simply leaving. She understood that they were scared, but she had also witnessed first-hand their courage in the face of adversity.

Kyle gripped her hand. "You're probably right, but we have to try. Look, I'm not happy about this, but I can't lose you, Mira. Or anyone else. When I thought I'd lost Josh…" He took a deep breath. "So, when do we put Jo's plan into motion then?"

At first, Mira wanted to yell at him. Kyle had promised to do whatever she asked of him, but as she looked into his eyes, she knew it wasn't just the thought of the voices starting up again once they entered the temple— he was terrified that he would again have to kill again.

"It's too late in the day now," said Tan. "We'll leave for my boat in the morning."

Mira shook her head. "Fine—I'll go alone!"

"I'll go with you," said Josh.

"What good would that do?" said Tan. "You can't open the outer tomb and there's no way just the two of you can move it."

Mira realised her mistake. "We'll find a way or... or we'll protect it until Pyrrha's people arrive. Right, Josh?"

"Too right we will." He nodded. "We'll show 'em."

"Oh, if you are staying, then I'm staying," said Rachel. "But for a change, can we please have a plan that actually works?" And she left the table to lie on her bunk.

Kyle dropped onto another bunk. "If that's what you want to do, we'll do it." But behind his soft smile, Mira could see that he was concerned.

"Right," she said. "Everyone, this is my plan—"

"Oh, please, Mira." Jo dropped her head into her hands. "Can we have one night without having to think of the mess we are in?"

"We need to be prepared, Jo," Mira reiterated.

"Then, let's just do it tomorrow. I would like to have at least one full night's sleep. In fact, can I suggest we stagger our sleep times? I'll take the first watch, if you like."

Mira took a deep breath. Perhaps Jo was right; they needed to rest. "Fine. If that's what you all want?"

"Yes, let's do it tomorrow," said Rachel. "It will give my nerves a chance to calm down."

Tired faces slowly rose out of their seats and flopped down on the beds, leaving only Josh and Mira at the table.

"Do you think we should open the tomb?" she whispered.

Josh took a moment. "Truthfully? No. I think we should leave it well alone and get off this island. But I'm going to trust in your judgement—Jacen's as well. But you know what we have to do now, don't you? We have to prepare."

As Josh snuggled up next to Rachel, Mira sat for a while longer.

To finish this journey and get Jacen back, we have to open that tomb. But if this has to happen, please, let them all live. If a life is needed, take mine and mine alone.

And lowering her head onto the table, she closed her eyes.

CHAPTER FIFTY

OUT FROM THE DEPTHS

Mira opened her eyes, slowly raised her head off the table and wiped the drool from her mouth. The cabin was in near darkness and everyone was soundly asleep. She didn't know why, but her gut was telling her something was wrong. It was *too* quiet.

She crept to the door. The handle firmly in her grasp, she tried to open it.

Her instincts were right; it was locked. A quick glance over her shoulder, and she was surprised to see Pyrrha on one of the bunks, curled into a ball with her eyes firmly shut and the satchel of bombs in her arms.

Was she afraid to be alone? Did she lock the door for safety reasons?

Suddenly, the ship's engines kicked into life and Pyrrha awoke. Her eyes displayed sheer panic. Instantly, Mira knew she'd had no knowledge of what was about to happen. She cursed herself for not being prepared.

She turned on the light and proceeded to wake everyone else up. But her attention was brought to the now empty bed where all the weapons and ammo had been neatly laid out.

"Idiots!" Pyrrha screamed. "They're trying to leave! They'll kill us all!"

Pyrrha placed the grenades into her rucksack, leapt from the bed and ran toward the door. But with Mira shaking her head, she about turned and ran to the window instead.

"I didn't see this coming," said Tan, lifting the crossbow and the remaining bolts he'd stashed under his pillow.

"Do you ever see anything coming?" said Josh, rolling from his bunk.

"Yes! Just not your bullshit!"

The ship was moving now. As it made a sudden sharp turn, they were all thrown about the cabin.

"Anyone got any bright ideas?" Kyle shouted.

"Yes, I'll climb out of the window, get to the bridge and kill them!" Pyrrha growled.

"Oh, I wouldn't," Linus shouted. "That thing is rising out of the water and—and those flying banshees are back as well!"

Everyone stared helplessly out through the Perspex sheeting over the broken window. Along with the glow of the moon, the ship's high-intensity spotlights finally revealed the full size and height of the creature from the deep.

Jo had seen enough. She dived back onto her bunk and covered her head with her hands. "I'm going to die!" she kept repeating.

"That's got to be over four hundred feet tall at least," Josh gasped, his eyes remaining glued to the immense creature. "Come on, Pegasus. It's time to make your appearance and carry me into action!"

"What bloody good would you and a flying horse do against that?" Jo screamed.

"When Pegasus turns up," said Josh, "for the good of everyone, I'll fly you in front of that thing, show it your face and our problems are solved."

It was the spur Jo needed. "How about I remove your head from where the sun doesn't shine, Josh! With all the horseshit you've been speaking lately, just talking to that thing will make it pass out!"

"I got it," said Tan, who was surprisingly calm. "Josh, take off your shoes and wave your socks around. That will kill them all out there."

"Rach, where's that bottle of perfume that worked on that ginormous wolf?" said Josh, trying to steady himself as the ship turned sharply again.

"Never mind my bloody perfume, where the hell is my bag?" said Rachel, now crawling around on her hands and knees, desperately searching for it.

Unable to believe the conversations going on around her, Mira leapt onto the bed and kicked open the recently repaired window. But as she climbed out and dropped to the deck, quickly followed by Kyle, the ship violently rocked again.

Losing their footing, Mira and Kyle slid on their backsides hard into the railing. But they were up on their feet in a moment and, steadying themselves, they hastily made for the metal stairs that led up to the bridge.

The ship was gaining speed, and as Mira began to ascend the steps, a large shadow appeared above her head. The stench of death filled her nostrils. Pre-empting an attack, she dived to the ground, and when she rolled onto her back, razor claws whooshed past her face.

As the harpy dived for her again, Kyle aimed his gun, but the creature swooped away and instead joined a large contingent of harpies in an attack on the creature from the deep.

The bridge was within Mira's reach. But as she scrambled up the stairs, Kyle grabbed her arm and pointed to what he could now see.

The colossal, webbed hand of the monster had reached down into the water and was now somewhere under the ship.

"Jump—before it lifts us out!" he yelled.

Mira could see the company were still inside the cabin. "What about the others?"

"I'll get them out, but you have to jump now. Swim for the shore and head for the forest!"

Instead, Mira looked back to the bridge. The three brothers were still inside. *I'm sorry, Kyle. I can't let anyone die, no matter what they've done!*

Mira yanked her arm free from his grasp and ran to the top of the steps. Finding the door locked, she pulled out the small dagger hidden in her boot, sliced open the clear plastic sheeting that had replaced the glass window, and leapt inside.

"Turn us around!" she said, aiming her handgun at the man steering.

His wide eyes told Mira that she was too late.

A loud bang, and the ship was lifted clear of the water at just the moment Kyle burst through the locked door. "We have to go—now!" he commanded, like the old Kyle.

Two of the brothers bolted past him. But when they jumped over the railing, four harpies appeared from above in a swift dive. The guards were caught by their ankles and lifted high into the air.

Mira could only watch as the brothers' screams vanished with the swarm of harpies over the treetops.

Mira turned to the remaining brother. "Please, you have to let go and come with us now!"

But the guard's hands were locked to the wheel and throttle in terror.

Mira tried to remove his hands from the controls, but the boat suddenly tilted, sending her crashing to the far side of the bridge.

Kyle was up on his feet in a moment. He reached out his hand for Mira to take. "That's it," he said. "You tried. But if we don't go now, we're both done for."

The ship rocked again, and Mira and Kyle clambered to the door. They could see Josh and Rachel leaping over the side, hastily followed by Pyrrha and Linus, while Tan had to physically carry Jo to the railing before blindly tossing her overboard and joining her in the long drop.

Mira gave one last look to the final brother, who was still staring wide-eyed ahead, too petrified to move.

"Please!" she cried. "Come with us!"

The ship was now well clear of the water and close to the salivating mouth of the monster. Mira and Kyle stumbled from the bridge.

The huge teeth of the ocean beast were but a hair's breadth away when they made it to the railing. Without looking down, they both jumped.

Mira landed heavily in the water. When she opened her eyes underwater, she couldn't see Kyle, only the faintest ray of moonlight. But with a momentous push to the surface, as the rolling waves tumbled her body toward the shoreline, she felt his hand grab hers.

Gasping for air, they dragged their bruised bodies unsteadily up the bank, where Pyrrha led them to the rest of their weary companions, standing just inside the treeline.

"How the hell did you survive a fall from that height?" Jo gasped.

Before Mira could answer, there came a horrific scream. She ran back to the water's edge, not really knowing what she could do to help the third brother, but knowing she had to try, when the monster brought the ship down hard against the rocks.

The vessel erupted into a bright ball of flame. And even though Mira was clear of the explosion, the sudden shock wave threw her clean off her feet.

CHAPTER FIFTY-ONE

PLAN Z

Apart from aching limbs and sore heads, surprisingly, no one in the company had been badly hurt. Dejected, they stood at the edge of the forest and watched the creature from the deep slowly lower itself back into the ocean. When it had finally disappeared below the rolling waves, the sudden realisation that they now had little ammo and no food or water brought the survivors once more to their knees.

"It's like it waited for us to get off," Jo spluttered.

"Oh, well spotted, Sherlock," Josh said. "And—oh look, it's starting to snow. It's like someone up there doesn't like us. OK, anyone with a Plan Z, this would be a good time to tell the rest of us."

"It's too far to go to my ship, even if that thing hasn't already destroyed it," said Tan. "We'd all freeze to death long before then."

"It will have to be the tents then," said Pyrrha. "There should still be food and water there, and we'll have shelter from the blizzard I sense is building."

Josh, still struggling to gather his breath after having gulped what he claimed was half the ocean when he'd landed head first in the water, threw his hand into the air. But the others had already started to follow Pyrrha through the forest. Slowly and silently, he trudged after them.

***

The survivors of the monster attack exited the treeline. Sullen faces stared gloomily at the campsite. Not only had the tents been torn to shreds, the food and water had been taken.

"I have a suggestion—so don't bite my head off," said Jo. "What if we go back to that pyramid with the lovely warm fire?"

"Are you having a—!" Rachel lowered her tone. "Are you having a laugh? Besides, it's further than Tan's boat."

"Let's go there then?"

"And what if Tan's boat isn't there?" said Kyle.

"Then we go to the pyramid. If Rachel talks to those things, I'm sure they will allow you all to stay as well." Jo smiled. "We have to try."

"Yeah, right," said Josh. "It's not like you killed half their family members, probably just by being there to begin with. Yes, I'm sure they will welcome us all with open mouths and knives and forks at the ready."

"So, we just freeze then, is it?" Jo snapped. "Mira, you seem to be giving the orders now since *he* lost his nerve." She pointed at Kyle. "What'd you say?"

With the spite in Jo's tone, Mira hoped that Kyle would get angry, but when he flopped onto his backside and rested his head in his hands, she knew he still hadn't got over the incident at the pyramid.

"Listen," said Linus. "I saw a documentary once where a group of people were caught unawares by a sudden snowstorm. They dug a hole beneath the snow, and keeping an airway for the smoke to clear, they lit a fire and managed to survive. As long as we are out of the wind and use our body heat to keep ourselves warm, we should be OK."

Josh raised his hand. "Or, we could just go to the cave near the shoreline."

Everyone turned to him, then to each other, then back to Josh.

"There is no cave near the shore," said Pyrrha.

"Yeah, there is," said Josh.

"No, Josh, there isn't. We checked everywhere when we landed."

Josh turned his back to the group. "Righto, but I'm going there now. So, if anyone wants to come, follow me," he called out, and headed back into the forest.

"I bloody hate it when he does this," Pyrrha moaned, but she followed behind him all the same.

When they reached the shore, they found Josh staring across to a giant rock that stood high and alone, now lit up by the flames of the ship, still burning brightly.

"So, where's the cave?" Pyrrha said, shivering.

Josh pointed to the rock face. "Right in front of you."

"There's nothing there, Josh," said Rachel. "Except for a giant rock that looks like a… Fabergé egg?"

Josh started to laugh. "It's right in front of you. Are you all winding me up?"

"Now, you do know the basic concept of what a cave is, don't you, Josh?" Jo said, her teeth chattering.

"Yes, it's a gaping hole that nothing good comes out of. A bit like your mouth, in that regard."

"I have to say, lad, dying has made you see things that aren't there," said Tan. "You don't happen to see dead people as well, do you?" he asked, looking nervously about.

With a shake of his head, Josh walked along the shore alone and stood in front of the giant rock. Then, when he turned to face the group, who were silently transfixed, with a wave of his hand he took a step to the side and disappeared.

"What in the name of everything holy just happened?" said Tan, open-mouthed.

"Optical illusion," Kyle laughed. "Just like the last island we left."

"But how the hell did he know?" Pyrrha cried out.

"He sees the world differently from us, obviously," said Rachel, running to join him.

"Yeah, he's bloody Rain Man. Doesn't play poker as well, does he?" Tan chuckled and ran after her.

"Jo, shall we?" Pyrrha asked.

Jo shrugged. "I'm never going to hear the end of this."

Mira watched them leave and smiled. "I'm so glad he's on our side." And taking Kyle's hand, she ran with him toward the rock.

When they entered the cave, Josh was already sat rubbing his hands in front of a fire, with his socks laid out to dry on stones.

"How did you light a fire?" Kyle asked, rushing to warm himself. Following Josh's lead, he removed his boots and socks. "And where did you get all the wood?"

"Jo dropped the lighter that Ted gave you." Josh grinned. "And I had already gathered wood just in case we needed a place to stay or hide."

"And why in the hell did you think we would need a place to hide?" Pyrrha pressed.

"I had a feeling something like this was going to happen."

"What do you mean, you had a feeling?" Rachel asked.

"I overhead one of the crew trying to get others to agree to leave—mutiny even—and I thought, hey, that doesn't sound good, maybe I should be prepared."

"Did you bring anything other than chocolate this time?" Kyle asked.

Josh pointed to a tarpaulin in the corner. "Of course I did. There's a container filled with water, a crate of apples, tinned fruit, and I filled a box with bread rolls that should really be eaten now before they go stale. Oh, and I brought butter and Pyrrha's butter knife, in case you all wanted to make toast."

Rachel, like the rest of the company, was now completely bewildered. "When did you do all this?"

"Couple of hours ago. When I saw what little ammo we had, I figured if something like this happened, then at least we wouldn't starve."

"Hang on. Why didn't you tell me what my crew were planning?" Pyrrha asked. "And how the hell did you get past a locked door?"

"I didn't think you would believe me, to be honest. They said they were working for a Captain Brann...?"

Pyrrha's whole body stiffened. Before Mira could ask who this Captain Brann was, Josh continued.

"...And I certainly didn't think they would try something stupid like sailing a boat into the kraken's mouth," he said. "And the door was locked?"

"Why do you think we all climbed out of the window?" asked Jo incredulously.

Josh shrugged. "I dunno. I thought you all wanted to feel like me for a change."

"Wait," said Rachel, still shaking her head in disbelief. "If you went outside, how did you get back in? The outer door was locked, wasn't it?"

"That door was locked, yes," said Josh. "But did you really think that plastic sheeting you placed over the window on the bridge was going to keep anyone out?" he asked Pyrrha.

"Hold on," said Rachel, not finished with her questioning. "You climbed out the window, crept back in, walked past our cabin door on the way to the galley and grabbed what you wanted, then left the way you came, without checking to see if our cabin door *was* locked?"

"Well, yeah," said Josh, looking baffled.

"Why would you go to all that bother, Josh?" said Pyrrha, appearing to have regained her composure. "You saw I hadn't locked it."

"But it was locked. You just said it was."

Pyrrha began to massage her temples. "You know what, I don't care. Well done, good thinking, glad you're with us."

Everyone, other than Rachel, had a few toasted rolls each, and having already slept, they all stared quietly into the fire and listened to the wailing wind shriek through the cave mouth.

As Rachel sat with her head bowed, Josh placed his arm around her shoulder. "You alright?" he asked.

Tears welled in her eyes. "I can't believe I lost my bag. I'll never ever forgive myself." She began to sob.

Jo looked to the ceiling of the cave with contempt written across her face. "I'm sure Pyrrha will have make-up back at her place."

Everyone held their breath, fearing Rachel's reprisal.

"Is that what you really think of me?" Scowling, she looked between them all. "I don't care what was inside it. I'm not that superficial. That bag was given to me by my mother, who had been given it by my grandmother before she died."

To everyone's surprise, Jo reached across and placed her hand on Rachel's shoulder. "I'm sorry. I was out of order. If you hadn't been with me at the pyramid, I don't think I would have made it out of that place alive."

As Rachel and Jo hugged, Mira leaned across to Tan. "I guess leaving on your boat is out now, then?"

"Was going to be hard anyway," he replied. "But now, you're right—without a diversion, there's just no way."

"I guess we have to go to the sepulchre then," said Josh. "Otherwise, we are definitely stuck here."

There were exasperated sighs all round.

Linus raised his hand. "I have an idea—if it's OK with you, Rach?"

"Sure, why not," said Rachel, buttering a toasted roll that Josh had insisted she eat.

"You said that the yellow-eyed harpies spoke with you, so, while the rest of us go there and wait, why don't you ask if they can take you and Jo to the sep—temple thingy. Maybe with their help against the red-eyed ones, it will be enough to get us in?"

Kyle glared. "Your idea, Linus? Or is someone telling you to do it? You seem awfully keen to get in there."

Linus gulped. "I'm sorry, I didn't mean… Look, I'll do whatever the rest of you want, and no, nobody speaks to me, and I promise, if they do, you'll be the first to know, I swear. I just don't want to lose you lot again. You're… you're all I've got left in this world," he said sheepishly.

"I can't ask the harpies to help," said Rachel. "They specifically said to stay away."

"It's that or wait for the Followers to turn up," said Jo. "They'll probably have enough firepower to deal with those things." She turned to Mira. "What do you want to do?"

But Mira's attention was now firmly fixed upon the cave entrance.

CHAPTER FIFTY-TWO

NEW PLAYERS ON THE FIELD

Since they had entered the cave, Mira had felt a presence. Someone was watching them. As she turned her eyes to the opening, two teenagers suddenly appeared and beckoned to her to follow. Unafraid, Mira stood up and left the cave; she knew this was only a vision. But there was something familiar about the boy and girl, too. The girl was like looking in a mirror, even down to the colour of her eyes, except that her hair was blonde. The boy, however—even though he did facially resemble Jacen a little, his hair was black and his eyes were a darker shade of blue with a hint of green.

"Who—who are you?" Mira asked.

"We are the past," said the girl.

"And your future," said the boy. *"Come, we don't have much time."*

Mira froze. *Oh, my. Could they be who I suspect?* "Is your name Pandora?" she tentatively asked. "Are you Epimetheus?"

The girl remained silent, and the boy held out his hand. *"Come,"* he repeated.

Mira followed them along the shoreline and out through the forest. When they came out under the giant archway, Mira noticed that all of the strange glyphs scorched into the rock were now making sense.

"You do not need to fear the one that lies in eternal sleep," said the girl. *"For he now needs your help."*

It was then that the boy took Mira's hand into his, and in a blink of an eye, Mira found herself standing high on the edge of the mountains, looking out at the approaching ships.

"There's a storm coming," he said. *"They are coming. They know, Mira. They know everything now. He has been watching. Listening. You have to leave this place. But first, you must recover the coffin. If you ever want to see your brother again, you and the others must fulfil your destinies. Remain strong, Mira. They will need your strength in the long days ahead."*

"Who is this 'he'?" Mira asked.

"The one who started all this madness," said the girl. *"But once again, he is playing a dangerous game. When all seems lost, you must seek out Asia. She has some of the answers you seek. But it will not be for some time. Your brother needs you."*

Tears rolled down Mira's cheeks as she watched them walk away hand in hand.

"If you are not Pandora and Epimetheus, can you at least tell me your names?" she called out.

"When the time comes, you will already know them," they called back.

***

Jo's voice brought Mira back to where she was: sat beside Kyle in front of the fire. As she stared at the cave mouth, tears welled up in her eyes.

"Mira, what do we do now?" Rachel asked this time.

Mira didn't so much as flinch.

"We can't wait for a rescue that may never come," said Tan. "Forget what I said, there's no other option left to us. I say we head for my boat. As long it's still there, maybe the grenades and my boom-boom arrows will divert that thing's attention. Hopefully, long enough for us to make a run for it."

"That thing could give us a ten-mile head start and still catch us with a few strokes of its tail," said Josh.

"We've got no food, other than apples and tinned fruit, and that's not going to last us long," said Pyrrha. "Guess we could kill some deer, but what then? Grizzly-bear soup or harpy pie?"

"No killing of bears or deer!" Jo shouted. "Look, we have three choices. Either we stay in this cave and wait for a miracle to happen, we go to the sepulchre and hope that the harpies' stomachs are finally full, or we make a run for it on Tan's boat. Now let's just decide and get on with it, please! I vote for going to Tan's boat."

Everyone had an opinion on what they should and shouldn't do, and with her heart thumping and mind racing, Mira finally leapt to her feet. "We can't stay in here, and we can't leave this island!" she exclaimed. "Not yet. We have to open the tomb. They know everything now. The Followers are definitely coming!"

Open mouths and wide eyes stared back. Mira retook her seat and placed her head in her hands.

"And how do you know this?" Tan asked.

"She's had a vision," said Kyle. "I know that look all too well."

Mira was now in a quandary about whether to tell the group who she had seen and what the children had told her.

How will they all react to having two more players on the field?

She made a decision. "Jacen came to me," she lied. "He showed me that the Followers are coming. They know the location of the tomb. They have equipment that can carry it."

Then she decided to change tack. She would have to guilt the others into going with her. "Jacen wants us to leave this place. He wants us all to forget him. But I can't do that. If getting the coffin is the only way that I will see my brother again, then I have to get inside the sepulchre! You all know I can't do this alone, and I feel terrible that I have to ask, but... are you with me?" Her gaze rested on Jo and Rachel.

"You know this means some, if not all, of us are going to die?" said Pyrrha.

"That's why I'm going to suggest that you, Linus and Tan stay here and keep a close eye on the fog and leave the rest to us."

It was Linus' turn to stand up. "If I'm going to die, I'll do it protecting my friends. I have a lot to make up for, so I'm coming," he insisted. "Mira, you will see your brother again, I swear."

"Hear, hear," said Rachel. "He's like my little brother, too, so of course, I'll go with you."

"And I can't let you go without me," said Pyrrha. "OK, I'm in."

"Wow, I did not see this coming," said Tan. "And you know there's no way I'm leaving my niece to face whatever is in there without me, so I'm in as well."

Mira looked hopefully to Kyle.

He smiled. "Of course, I'm with you."

Josh raised his hand. "As we are all on the same page at last, before we go, can I ask a serious question first? It's been bugging me for a while now."

Everyone waited in anticipation.

"The Followers already have a coffin, so my question is this. With the technology we have today—diamond-cut drills, saws and the like—why can't they just open it? Why the need for the key that Mira has? Why hasn't someone just X-rayed the coffins to see what exactly is inside? Because we're all going to look like right idiots if we go to all the trouble of moving it and there's only a stuffed turkey or chicken inside. I can see it now…

"*'Hey, I'm bored,'* said the pharaoh to his trusted bodyguard. *'I know, for a laugh, what if we place some coffins inside some tombs and start a rumour that some are filled with poison and the others have cursed people trapped inside. I bet those who find them thousands of years from now are going to have a right shock when they discover we removed the bodies and that all that is in them is our leftover KFC. The rank smell alone with have them running for their lives!'*"

There was a stunned silence.

"He's absolutely right," said Rachel, eventually. "What if this was just a prank by the ancient Egyptians?"

It took a moment before anyone else could speak.

"As for why they want it open, you already know," said Pyrrha. "Mira's dream. The reason they can't be opened is because the locks and coffin were created by a god."

"What do you say, Tan?" asked Kyle.

"I'm sorry, I've got this picture in my head of a turkey with irritable bowel syndrome waiting to explode… OK, I know Pandora's outer tomb was constructed from marble, but the coffin was lead-lined—according to the writings we have, anyway. As for the locking mechanism, I hadn't given it much thought until now."

"I saw what happened to Jo when she tried to open the tomb, and I can tell you it was not something the ancient Egyptians could have conjured up," said Mira, certain there were gods trapped inside the coffins.

"Yeah, and I felt it," said Jo.

"So, is that all the questions, Josh?" asked Pyrrha.

"No, I have one more… Um, what are we doing, exactly?"

CHAPTER FIFTY-THREE

NO ESCAPE FROM ONE'S OWN DESTINY

The company was standing silently at the entrance to the cave, their sense of purpose crushed. A sombre mood had once again enveloped the group. Even though they were relieved it had finally stopped snowing, and that the crashing waves together with the rain now lashing down were making light work of erasing any evidence of an icy landscape, there was now an ever-increasing flood of water surrounding their hiding place, blocking their exit, forcing them to return to the fire.

"That's put a stop to us going for the time being," said Pyrrha.

"I dunno. If the water level gets any higher, we could find ourselves trapped in here," said Tan.

"Yeah, but do you really want to go out there to get wet and squidgy again?" said Jo.

Tan crinkled his nose. "What the hell is squidgy? Is it a relative of a squid?"

"No—squidgy, squelchy. What happens when the insides of your shoes get wet," said Jo, squirming at the thought. "And my socks have only just dried."

"Oh, mine, too. I don't like squelchy shoes either."

Mira felt a familiar frustration creeping over her already tense frame. *Has everyone got amnesia?* "We have to leave now!" she said at a volume loud enough to cause Jo to flinch and draw looks of concern from the rest of the party. "If the Followers landed in the night, they could be making their way there now!"

"She's right," said Josh.

"Yes, but I really do hate squishy shoes," said Tan. "And it's going to be murder to get to the sepulchre in this weather without passing through the town, because the mountain will be too dangerous to cross."

This is it. Time to tell them. "We're not going to the sepulchre. I mean, we are, but not yet."

"We're not?" Tan's eyebrows were attempting to make contact with his cowboy hat. "Have I missed something? I could have, I suppose. I have this terrible smell of burning, sweaty socks fogging up my senses."

Pyrrha looked around the group, gauging their reactions, before asking, "So, where are we going, Mira?"

"We're going to the river first, then the forest, then the town—and lastly, the sepulchre." Mira braced herself for the objections she knew would soon follow.

"What's the difference?" said Pyrrha. "We have to do that anyway to get there."

"No, I mean some of us need go to the river to get that crocodile to follow. At the same time, the others will go to the forest and get the bears to follow them. If we can time it right, when those harpies attack, they'll have the shock of their lives. If they're all fighting each other, maybe we can slip through into the burial chamber."

Josh raised his hand. "But the bears are in the town?"

"Some are, maybe," Mira replied. "But I definitely saw others returning to the forest."

All eyes were now sharing worried looks, searching for assurance that this was going to succeed and that, somehow, they would all survive.

"Hold on, you want to get the giant croc that killed Josh to follow us?" said Rachel, visibly alarmed. "And you want to get bears, that are potentially either starving or hibernating, to also follow us and hope they have some grudge with the harpies and join up together? Wouldn't it be better to have just one species after us rather than three?" This last remark had come out a little higher than she intended, so after taking a breath to calm herself and sound like she was still in control of the situation, she continued, "And what if the yellow-eyed harpies want to join in as well? We could have four groups against just the eight of us!"

"You know what, my niece has a point," said Tan. "We can't beat the red-eyes now, not with the little ammo we have, but if we could get that giant croc to follow... I mean, the size of it alone would take a lot of those things to beat it. And with that tough, armoured skin, it may be impossible to beat, so yes, that could work. And if those bears are hungry, or tired, they are highly formidable when mad. Yes, yes, but how to do it?" he said, pacing back and forth.

"With the rolls we have left, I could make a picnic basket for the bears?" Josh smirked.

"Picnic basket? I don't follow."

"Oh, for Pete's sake, ignore him!" said Kyle. "Josh, we need you, just for once, to be serious."

"That crocodile seemed to like Josh," said Jo, with a wide, supercilious grin in Josh's direction. "Let's dangle him over the river to entice it, then drag him to town."

"Or maybe you could just talk to the red-eyed harpies? That should send them right off to sleep," said Josh.

Mira gave them both a steely glare. "Enough, you two, the adults need to think."

"What if we capture one harpy?" said Kyle. "You've heard how they screech. That should attract the bears."

"Yes, that could work," said Tan, patting him on the shoulder.

"And that croc seemed to like the taste of the one that came for Rachel and me," said Linus.

"Oh, so now we have to catch two of those flying things as well?" said Rachel.

"And would the croc follow us to town?" asked Josh. "It gave up pretty quickly after it attacked me."

"I could shoot a deer in the leg," said Tan. "If we then drag it toward the sepulchre—"

"No—no shooting of deer," said Mira. "I've never got over Bambi's mum…"

"Right, so the plan is to catch two harpies, now all we need to do is figure out how. Any thoughts?" said Kyle, desperately hoping that someone would have at least one sensible suggestion. His hopes were temporarily dashed when Josh raised his hand, but fortunately it was slapped down by Rachel.

"You, say nothing," she said.

"If we can shoot the boom-boom arrows into their wings, that will make it easier," said Tan.

Again, Josh raised his hand. Again, Rachel slapped it down, only this time she aimed a threatening glare directly at him as well. Josh sat cross-legged and lowered his head onto his hands.

"What if we lead them into this cave?" Linus suggested. "The ceiling isn't high enough for them to fly around in here."

Everyone stared.

"And then what?" said Rachel. "Get them to join us in a singalong around the fire, or perhaps we could invite them to a game of poker? Loser has to leave the island. Win-win, for us."

"No, but I could lasso them," said Linus, holding on to the last remnants of his patience.

Rachel rolled her eyes. "Oh, so you just happen to have a lasso on you, then?"

"No, but Tan does, on his boat."

Josh half-heartedly raised his hand in a third attempt to garner attention, but again, everyone ignored him.

"If there is still a boat," said Mira.

"And you know how to lasso?" Kyle asked.

"Hell yeah." Linus beamed. "I was brought up in Texas, remember. I'll have it down and hog-tied in no time."

"Why do you have a lasso, Tan?" asked Mira. "Do you also have the skill?"

"No, I don't. I have a boomerang, too, and that also defies whatever I want it to do."

"Right, so if we can lure them one at a time in here, we'll have our bait," said Kyle.

"Oh right, I'm sure they'll just queue up outside in an orderly fashion. Maybe we can sell tickets as well, while we're at it!" said Jo, getting up to stand by the entrance.

"No, I do realise we need a diversion, Jo," said Kyle.

"This is getting us nowhere," said Mira.

"It was your idea to lure Doc Croc, Yogi and Boo-Boo," Jo called back.

"Hey, wait, picnic basket, I get it now," said Tan, laughing. "Ha ha, very good, Josh. Yogi Bear, I like it."

"Surely the safest way is to capture deer and then use them as bait for the croc and the bears?" said Pyrrha.

"Before all that, shouldn't you check you still have a boat first?" Rachel reminded them. "But I still say we might as well continue to hide here and wait for things to unfold, because all this planning will come to nothing. Trust me."

"Goldilocks is right about the boat," said Tan. "So, I'll go with Linus and check to see if it's still there, and you lot decide how to lure the flying mongoose in here."

"Wait—what's with the Goldilocks crack?" Rachel huffed.

Tan didn't answer. Instead, he shuffled Linus toward the entrance. "Right, I'm going to need a hand and you're it."

Again, Josh raised his hand. This time, he coughed as well.

But everyone shook their heads and joined Jo at the entrance. When Linus and Tan disappeared among the trees, Kyle began to scratch his head. "If they do bring back the lasso, does anyone have any sensible suggestions on how we get only two harpies to enter?"

Josh raised both hands this time.

Pyrrha began to pace back and forth. "If we had a smoke grenade, maybe we could separate them that way, but they were on the ship."

Josh lowered his arms and pointed to the rear of the cave. "There's some in the corner over there."

Pyrrha stopped in her tracks. "How did you—? Never mind. Well done, Josh. Right then, how to separate one from the group before tossing it at the others? What we need is a decoy, someone who is willing to stand in the open, then run in here. Someone they'll notice. Someone who can't stay still and likes seeking attention. Now… who could that be?" She smiled.

"There's no way you're sending my Rach out there," said Josh. "Besides—"

"No, sweetie," Rachel interjected. "She means you. But I keep telling you all, there's no point in planning."

"I'll do it," said Kyle.

Listening to him offer to risk his life, Mira suddenly regretted saying anything. "No, if anyone should do it, it's me," she insisted. "It was my idea, and I'm as fast as any of you."

Pyrrha shook her head. "No. I'm the fastest and better with a sword, so I'll go, and that's final."

As the water began to flow into the cave, the small group moved away from the entrance and back to the fire, and when Josh raised his hand, Kyle finally acknowledged him. "What is it, Josh?"

"As I've been trying to tell you, the lasso is already in the rucksack, along with the smoke grenades and the boomerang."

There was a stunned silence.

CHAPTER FIFTY-FOUR

MONSTER BAIT

By the time Tan and Linus returned, the rain had stopped and the sun had at last shown its warming face.

"So, how bad was it out there?" Kyle asked.

"Tan's boat was still there," said Linus. "But that thing in the sea is watching it now, I'm afraid. Tan's brought his swords, but we couldn't find the lasso, and there's more bad news: the fields are soaked in mud and it's slippery as hell, and… and lightning is flashing like crazy over the sepulchre."

"Plus," said Tan, "it appears to still be snowing in the very area we need to get to. Which means I very much doubt the flying hedgehogs will make an appearance. And with no lasso, I think we will just have to go there and improvise."

All eyes turned to Josh.

"Oh, what's he done now?" said Tan.

***

The plan was set. Linus was going to try and lasso a deer to lure the crocodiles. With Pyrrha admitting to the group that she had experience dealing with bears and knew exactly how to get them to follow her, it was decided the rest of them would split into two groups. One would keep close to Linus but remain hidden with weapons drawn, in case anything went wrong, while the second group would keep a watchful eye on Pyrrha. Everything that was needed was packed into rucksacks, and the group left the cave.

The fields were as Linus had said, muddy and slippery, and by the time the company had reached the river, each one of them had slipped at least once and ended up covered head to foot in mud.

With the crocodile basking on the other side of the bank, but no sign of any deer, the first group ignored Pyrrha's plastic bridge and followed the second group along the river upstream. But the giant croc had seen them, and it slipped into the water to follow.

Jo laughed nervously. "I think that croc is in love with you, Josh."

"Yeah, well, I don't want to alarm you, but that isn't the croc I gave my phone to."

"How the hell can you tell?" said Kyle refusing to take his eyes off it.

"I got pretty up close and personal with it, and that one is smaller."

"So, you're saying there's definitely more than one croc?" said Jo.

"If I had to put money on it, I would say there's at least three."

"I know I'm going to regret asking," said Rachel, "but why three?"

Josh pointed. "Because there's another two watching us on the bank over there. I know we wanted one to follow us, but as there are now three, if you don't mind, I'm going to give the river a much wider berth."

As the group followed Josh, everyone kept a firm eye on the river, but when finally they came to the forest and found it still covered in deep snow, panic ensued when the bear with her cubs appeared between the trees.

"If that bear thinks we're a danger to its cubs and comes at us now, we're screwed," said Jo, trembling. "And if those crocodiles come now, we're screwed. Look, let's forget about the tomb and make a run for it on Tan's boat, yeah?"

"Oh, Jo, where's your sense of adventure?" Josh smiled. "Look at the wildlife and the scenery. I mean, what else would you be doing now if you weren't here, other than whacking people over the head, looking for treasure?"

"I'd be home, bashing little boys like you for their cheek!" she snarled.

With the only other way to the bridge through the forest, the group cautiously followed the bear at a safe distance, and behind Tan, who had his assault rifle at the ready. But, not wanting the mother and its cubs to get harmed, and with no sign of any of the other bears, they decided it would be safer for them all to simply stay together and hope they could sneak into the sepulchre unseen.

Safely through the forest and across the open field, Kyle brought them to a stop at the first bridge. "I thought you said there was lightning in the sky?" he asked.

"There was. Just ask Tan, he saw it, too," said Linus. "Hey, maybe things are looking up. It's also stopped snowing."

Kyle looked warily to the sky and then to his watch. "It's also becoming darker, even though it's only…" His eyes widened. "Six p.m.? How is that possible? It's never taken us eleven hours just to get to this point before."

Everyone raised their eyes skywards, then, in unison, looked toward each other and finally toward the bridge. Suddenly, it dawned on them what Kyle's statement meant for them.

"Don't ask me how," Tan said, "but it seems that Mr or Mrs Time is playing tricks with us again, and I think we are almost out of it." He pulled the group into a huddle. "Look, we're going to have to make a run for it. Everybody stay close to one another, and on the count of three we go—agreed?"

Without even waiting for the count of one, Rachel and Josh dashed across the first bridge and out into the open field, soon followed by Linus and Jo.

"Does anybody know how to count?" Tan shouted as Mira grabbed Kyle's hand and they both sprinted across.

However, at the second bridge, although most of them had crossed to the other side, Josh refused.

"Go on, boy. What are you waiting for?" Tan asked him, catching up at last.

"Oh, I dunno, fond memories of the last time I crossed a bridge seeing a giant crocodile staring at me!" Josh screamed back. "And not only that, but I can now see the three other crocodiles that were following us up the first river have found a way into this one!"

Tan turned to where Josh was pointing, just as three tails whipped in the air and disappeared beneath the surface of the murky water. He spun Josh to face him. "Now there are six of them? I have to say it, lad, it's got to be your feet that's attracting them! Oh, brother. It'll be almost impossible to keep an eye on all of them if the harpies and bears also decide to make an appearance right now!"

He took a firm hold of Josh, and they both started to run. But as soon as they reached the middle of the bridge, one crocodile leapt from the water ahead of them. As it began tearing at the wooden slats, another crocodile appeared from behind and joined in, trapping Josh and Tan in the middle. When a third crocodile disappeared under the bridge and began ramming against the rotten wooden boards under their feet, with nowhere to go, Tan aimed the crossbow and fired an explosive bolt. The arrow struck the wide snout of the croc ahead and exploded on impact. The crocodile released its hold and dived back into the river, taking a huge section of the bridge with it. This left a long jump between Josh and Tan and a safe landing on the other side.

The attack was now coming on all sides. Removing his assault rifle from his shoulder, Tan tossed it to Rachel, and the crossbow to Mira. He then reached for Josh's hand. "It's now or never, boy. Are you ready?"

The slats had begun to splinter under Josh's feet, leaving them with only a short run-up. Seeing its opportunity, the crocodile with a burnt face launched from the water and into the air space that Josh and Tan were about enter.

But Mira was prepared. Steadying her aim and slowly exhaling, she released the arrow, sending it flying straight into the crocodile's open jaws. It exploded, and the croc once again disappeared under the water.

Even though Josh and Tan had successfully made contact safely with the land, the other crocodiles now began to swarm from the water.

The company entered the town, somewhat slower than they would have liked due to some sprained ankles and injured toes, a result of desperately trying to put as much distance between them and the water monsters. But just at the moment they began to feel some relief that they'd managed to all escape the crocodiles, the cry of harpies sounded overhead.

Diving and swooping, the harpies split the company into three separate groups. While Josh, Rachel and Linus dived into one building, and Mira, Kyle and Jo into another, Pyrrha and Tan, who were bringing up the rear, were forced to seek cover in the narrow streets.

But there would be no hiding for any of them now; the attack was upon them.

CHAPTER FIFTY-FIVE

CROCODILES, HARPIES AND BEARS, OH MY!

There was no suitable hiding place to be found on the ground floor of the derelict building. Josh, Rachel and Linus crept up the stone staircase and entered a large room. The small window had no shutters to keep the harpies out.

Suddenly, creaks could be heard coming from the tiles above their heads. Josh and Rachel dived to either side of the window while Linus disappeared into the shadows.

The hairs on Josh's arm stood to attention like soldiers on parade. But it wasn't the sound of talons scraping the tiles that concerned him—it was the fearsome head of one harpy, hanging upside down outside of the window, its red, terrifying eyes scanning the room for its prey.

The harpy's long claws gripped the window frame, and the foul stench of rotting flesh permeated from its open mouth into the room.

Frozen, Josh could only look to Rachel. He expected her to run. But to his surprise, for once, she appeared calm. In fact, she was so focused on the harpy that he feared what she would do.

Bloodstained nails dug deep into the beams of the ceiling, and folding its wings tight to its body, the harpy slowly began to pull itself through the narrow gap.

Josh sensed Rachel was preparing a stealth attack. But just as was she about to lunge, from out of the darkness, Josh heard the *whooping* of rope.

The lasso whipped out from the shadows and wrapped tightly around the creature's neck. Linus pulled it down to the ground. Josh immediately threw himself on top before it could open its wings. He struggled to hold the creature, but as it unleashed a high-pitched scream, Rachel rammed her gun into its mouth and pulled the trigger.

The harpy was dead. But the sound of claws scratching on the stone steps below was steadily getting louder.

While Linus tied the lasso around one of the roof beams and tossed the end out of the window, Josh crept to the door and peered over the railing into the darkness below.

It was then he witnessed what was coming up the stairs. His heart dropped to the pit of his stomach, and he sprang back inside the room.

"Rach, you go first," he said, taking the assault rifle from her.

Rachel's eyes widened. "Why? Wait. How many are coming?"

He shot a look back to the stairs. "All of them, I think," he said, pushing her to the window.

She climbed out first, and once she'd lowered herself to the ground, Josh pushed Linus forward.

"No, you go next," said Linus.

"You ever see the film *Aliens*?" said Josh, thrusting the rope into his friend's hand.

"Yeah?"

Josh shook his head. "Do I need to say any more?"

Linus' mouth fell open. "Holy shit! That many?"

He swiftly flew through the window to join Rachel. Josh began to follow, but the horde of harpies had entered the room.

"Josh, c'mon!" Rachel screamed from the street below.

Josh had to delay the harpies, or they would be upon them in seconds.

"RUN!" he yelled, leaping back inside. Frantically, he fired the machine gun. But the harpies simply shielded themselves with their bulletproof wings and continued to advance.

Josh's only option was to climb down the rope. But as he backed toward the exit, another harpy appeared at the window, and suddenly, he found he had nowhere to go.

***

Meanwhile, across the street, Mira, Kyle and Jo had found refuge in the same cellar where Mira and Kyle had hidden before. But as the rope had been cut and was now not long enough to tie to the hook, Kyle had to wrap it around his hand to keep the hatch closed.

The chilling sound of the multitude of harpies, and the distant echo of bullets ringing out, sent a blood-curdling shiver through the unlit room.

Mira turned on her flashlight. "We can't stay in here," she said. "It sounds like the others need our help."

Jo was quick to respond. "And we can't go out there because we will get torn to pieces!"

Mira looked to Kyle. "What do you think?"

His face had turned ashen. "Turn off the light," he whispered. And motioning with his finger, he pointed to what he could now hear above their heads.

At first, there was only the faint sound of talons scraping on stone. But as the *tap-tap-tap* of the harpy's razor claws neared, Jo dropped to the floor, held her hands over her head and let out a squeal. Mira loaded the crossbow with a blue arrow and, holding her breath, aimed at their only exit.

There followed an eerie silence above. Kyle peered through the gap in the hatch, trying to see if they were safe, when suddenly, a claw exploded through the wood. Splinters rained onto his face, and he lost his footing, left hanging by the rope wrapped around his hand.

The hatch began to open.

"Jo! For goodness' sake get up and help Kyle!" Mira yelled, trying to see her target.

Jo sprang to her feet and guided Kyle's legs to the ladder. But at the very moment he let go of the rope, the hatch flew fully open, and the harpy burst inside.

Mira fired. The bolt took the harpy directly through the eye, and it fell forward. But it wasn't dead. Kyle thrust his pistol into its mouth and pulled the trigger. The harpy fell through the hole, and as it landed on top of him, two more appeared above.

Mira reached inside the rucksack and withdrew a sticky bomb. She tossed it directly at one of the creatures.

A blast of white light illuminated the cellar, and blood and chunks of flesh were sent flying around the basement and the room above.

The small hatch was now a gaping hole, and smoke billowed into the basement. But even with her ears ringing, Mira dragged the carcass of the harpy that had saved Kyle's life off his body, and lifted Jo to her feet.

They climbed the ladder and blindly ran out into the unknown.

***

Across the street, Pyrrha and Tan had been shepherded into a narrow alley behind the buildings.

Two harpies had swooped down and blocked their exit, and when another two landed behind, they were left with no way out. Then came the chilling squeals as three harpies descended the wall from above.

Tan reached for his assault rifle. But when he heard a sudden blast of bullets ringing out within a building, he remembered he'd tossed it to Rachel.

"I hope she's having more luck than we will with these peashooters!" he said, pulling out his handgun.

Pyrrha, instead, reached for her sword. "Stand back to back!" she ordered. "The three hundred Spartans at Thermopylae bottlenecked the Persians at the Hot Gates and survived for almost three days against insurmountable odds. We only have to survive till the sun comes back out!"

Tan looked warily up at the three harpies, now only metres away. "Yeah, but the Spartans didn't have to fend off the enemy from above as well." Turning and pressing his back to her, he drew his katana. "And it doesn't look like this alley ever gets any sun."

From all three sides, the harpies began to move in on their prey.

But only inches away from a fresh meal, suddenly, they came to an abrupt stop. There then came an ear-splitting screech from one harpy at the rear of the street where Pyrrha and Tan were trapped, and a low, rumbling roar. They knew what that meant immediately; the giant crocodiles had entered the town.

The harpies above fled, along with the ones in front, but those that had come from behind were dragged back along the street and torn mercilessly to pieces by the giant crocodiles.

As Pyrrha and Tan prepared to run, another huge crocodile appeared, blocking their path forward. It was then that Tan noticed a boarded-up window above their heads.

As she was the lighter of the two, Tan lifted Pyrrha to a small ledge, but as she punched at the wooden cover, the crocodile with the severely burned snout began to make its way toward Tan.

"I hope you're not going to be long, Pyrrha," he called out. "I think crocodiles hold grudges…"

The attack was swift. Giant jaws snapped closed. But Pyrrha had already kicked her way inside the building and grabbed Tan's outstretched hand. The crocodile missed his feet by inches.

***

The building was thankfully deserted, and Pyrrha and Tan ran through the rooms and down the stairs out into the street, spying Kyle, Mira and Jo running toward them from one direction and Rachel and Linus appearing from another. As they all joined up in the centre of the street, more of the harpies swooped from above and surrounded them.

"Where the hell is Josh?" Kyle cried.

"He stayed behind to give us time to get away," Rachel said, weeping. "We tried to go back for him, but these ugly bitches had already swarmed into the building."

Prepared for the assault, Mira handed out the last of the bombs, and they were tossed in all directions. Again, the harpies formed a protective shield, and when the bombs exploded, only four lay dead.

"Anyone with a brilliant plan of escape is more than welcome to share it right now!" Tan yelled.

When none came, the group formed a tight circle.

The harpies advanced like velociraptors: claws extended, ready to tear flesh from bone. Mira reached for the last explosive arrow. To her dismay, not only was the shaft bent, rendering it useless, she quickly discovered the crossbow itself had been damaged after she'd caught it on the ladder of the larder during the escape. And then, to make matters worse, from the corner of her eye she saw not only Josh running toward them, but a slew of bears following closely behind.

Mira waited for the attack that would bring her painful death, but instead, the bears and the crocodiles engaged the harpies in a frenzied onslaught. It was then she spied an opening in the harpies' flank. Hastily, she directed the group into one of the side streets.

Not stopping to see if they were being followed, they ran from the town. The field was crossed in seconds, and when they reached the top of the hill, with the roars and screeches echoing back to them, but an absence of harpies flying above, everyone collapsed into the snow with loud sighs of relief.

"OK," said Josh. "Next time we need to plan something, let me be the one to come up with it, yeah? Cos I have to say it, this is the second time in only a week I've felt like I'm in a bloody *Jurassic Park* movie! You know, I never thought going on holiday would end up as a training course for the London Marathon."

Rachel threw her arms around his neck. "How in the hell did you escape that room? And how did you get the bears to follow you?" she said, planting numerous kisses upon his cheeks.

"Promise you won't laugh?" Josh said, panting for breath. "I fell through the floorboards. But let me say first that they *were* rotten."

"OK, so you fell through the rotting floorboards," said Rachel. "But how did you get out of the building? They were coming in through the doors and the window when we tried to get to you."

"Oh, right," said Josh. "Funny story. I, ah, kind of landed on top of one harpy coming through the window, and knocked it clean out, preventing any more of them coming in. You know, I thought with all this running around, I'd have at least lost this holiday weight by now—"

Jo slapped her forehead. "For the last time, Josh. How did you get out of the building and then get the bears to follow you?"

"Oh, right." Josh smiled. "Rach, you're right, the house was full of harpies. But when I landed on the one, I noticed a way out through the rear. The only problem—it led into the next building, where the bears were beginning to hibernate. You know, they look really cute when they're sleeping—"

"Josh!" Rachel screamed. "How did you get the bloody bears to follow you?"

"Oh, right," said Josh. "Remember when I mentioned a picnic basket? It, ah, kind of worked. You see, I had filled my rucksack with some, err…" He hesitated.

"Filled it with what, Josh?" asked Pyrrha, eyeing him closely.

Josh reached inside his rucksack and, after a moment of contemplation, pulled out a multipack of mini Mars bars. "I guess bears love them, too." He smiled. "I know what you are going to say, Pyrrha. But if I had left them in your safe, then we wouldn't have them now to enjoy," he said, dishing them out.

For once, Pyrrha didn't berate him, but instead, graciously accepted her Mars bar.

"I don't know about the rest of you," said Jo, "but I hate running. I hate ships and I hate bloody islands, temples and pyramids, and if I ever manage to get home, my holidays in the future will be me sitting in the back garden reading *The Wind in the Willows*."

Tan levered himself heavily to his feet. "We can't stay here any longer. Any one of those things could come for us at any moment, and by the looks of it, we've lost the crossbow and my beloved assault rifle. We need to find shelter, quickly."

"Ah, do we have to go?" Josh grumbled. "I mean, look at the view from here. Can we at least wait till the sun comes up? I'm sure it will be a perfect picture moment."

"Does anybody still have a phone that works?" said Rachel. Everyone shook their heads. "Then I agree with Jo. We should get to Tan's boat and get the hell out of here. Let the bloody Followers have what they want. As everyone keeps pointing out, without us, they're screwed. I say we go to Pyrrha's sanctuary, gather as many troops as we can and go to Egypt to kick the Followers' teeth in and then get Jacen back."

Mira understood how Rachel was feeling. If it wasn't for her brother being kidnapped, she, too, would find any excuse not to enter the sepulchre. But this was the only way she was going to see Jacen again.

"Rach, I need you," she said. "Jacen needs you."

Rachel looked embarrassed and hugged Mira tightly. Without a word, she then stormed down the bank, heading directly for the temple.

Tan looked between them. "Right then, if everyone is ready—"

"Don't say it," Josh interrupted.

"Don't say what?"

"*'Let's do this.'* Every time they say it in the films, it makes my butt cheeks squeeze tight together. It's almost as bad as *'It's time to kick ass.'* I mean, who talks like that, really? And if you do speak that way—please, don't!"

Tan rubbed his temples. "Fine. It's never bothered me, but then I'm not crazy. OK, everyone, could we all make our way to the sepulchre, pretty please, with sugar on top," he said sarcastically.

Everyone got to their feet, and even though Mira was eager to get it over with, as she looked around at the tired faces, Rachel's words sprang to mind.

"I don't want violence to become just a normal thing in my life!"

As none of the group appeared to show any signs of the fear they had all felt only days earlier on Pandora's island, it was Mira who was suddenly afraid. Not of the challenges they could possibly encounter next, but of what was happening to her and her friends' psyches. Had all this violence and death really become the norm? Could any of them truly go back to their old lives after what they had already bravely faced? Would they ever feel safe again? Was she being selfish, putting them through another possibly horrid ordeal, all for the sake of her brother?

All eyes now upon her, downhearted and reluctant, Mira caught up with Rachel and led the exhausted company toward the foreboding presence she suspected was awaiting their arrival with ardent anticipation.

CHAPTER FIFTY-SIX

HEADS UP

The enormous monument stood out ahead, above the colonnade. They entered beneath its shadowy umbrella.

Mira leaned in to Kyle. "How do you feel? Is your breathing OK?" she whispered.

"Funnily enough, I feel fine now," he said. "But I have to be honest with you, I still think this is a bad idea."

"I know, and if anything bad happens, I'll take full responsibility for it. But I wouldn't go in if I thought there was another way."

Kyle stroked her hand with his thumb. "And that's why I'm coming with you. I can't really see another way either."

"Nor can I," said Rachel, joining her side. "But I just feel I have to point out that in my dream, that statue appeared smaller. And where has all the grass gone? What could have done this?"

"It wasn't like this when Kyle and I came here earlier," said Mira, looking out at the now barren wasteland.

"Maybe the tomb is leaking poison and has killed everything," Jo suggested.

"Well, thanks for that, Jo," said Josh. "Now doesn't everyone feel better? We're all walking to our doom."

"It was the lightning storm that caused it," said Tan. "Most probably."

"Oh, great," said Rachel, looking up at the black clouds covering the starlit sky. "Not only should we be worried about leaking poison, we also have the concern that lightning could strike again now! Does anyone else have any theories that will lighten the mood?"

"Well, you started it," said Jo, thrusting her hands into her pockets.

"Perhaps some building firm cleared it last night, ready for some fancy new towers or a theme park to be built," said Josh. "But the workmen were called away onto another job and will have to come back at a later date. Although, if that is the case, then this mess has to be the work of the water board. Which means it could be years before they return. They were supposed to be repairing a leak in my street. Two years it's taken, mind you, and still we haven't seen any bloody workmen. And before Kyle and I left for this holiday, they still had the poxy traffic lights set up."

Tan prodded Josh's arm, hard. "Do you take anything seriously, boy?"

"I am being serious," said Josh. "The electricity company dug it up first, but instead of the water board fixing the leak there and then—and there was one—they waited for the hole to be filled back in, then turned up a few days later to re-dig it up. And it *has* been two years. It took less time to build the Statue of Liberty."

"OK, OK," said Tan. "I'll let you off this time. But as for all the other times, and the fact we don't know what we could be walking into, I shall repeat my question. Do you take anything seriously?"

Josh stared him straight in the eye. "Umm… No. No, not really."

Mira again found herself smiling inside. She liked the way Josh had an uncanny knack for making every potential nightmare less stressful. And the last thing they needed right now was Jo freaking out and refusing to enter the sepulchre. "He's right. No point in worrying until it happens," she said.

"Yeah, we've faced the worst of it," said Josh, upbeat.

The entrance to the sepulchre was just ahead. Rachel grabbed Josh's hand and the two rushed up the steps and disappeared inside, closely followed by Kyle. But Jo remained at the bottom.

"I don't think it's wise, going in there," she said, slowly backing away.

Mira could see Jo's breathing was quickening, so she placed her arm around her shoulder and gave it an encouraging squeeze. "The sooner we go in and grab the coffin, the sooner we can leave this island."

"If you want, Jo," said Linus, "see if you and Rachel can open the way first, and then I'll wait out here with you while the others do a bit of exploring?" He winked at Mira.

"Would you mind, Mira?" Jo asked.

"No one will force you to do anything, Jo. I promise." Mira smiled. But inside she was in turmoil; she hated lying to anyone. But if this was the only way of reuniting with her brother, then Jo would have to do what was needed, whether she wanted to or not.

Inside, there was no sign of a way in except for a slim crack in the rock face, but when Rachel and Jo edged toward it, with Kyle at the ready to pull them clear if there was something bad hidden beyond, the cleft began to widen. Then, with a sudden blast of wind to envelop them, the wall fell away.

"I did not see that coming," said Tan, staring wide-eyed.

With the wall nothing more than crumbling dust, Jo stepped away from the entrance. "I know I'm going to have to, but I don't want to go in just yet."

"Then we'll stay here, like we agreed," said Linus. He turned to Mira. "If she's needed, I'll bring her through."

Mira simply smiled and gave Jo's arm a reassuring squeeze. She really hoped she wouldn't have to drag her inside when the time came.

Josh and Rachel clambered through the gap first. When the oil-filled lanterns hanging from the walls suddenly burst into life, Josh turned back to the group.

"That's a cool trick. I bet Mr Tripp couldn't do that." He gave a beaming smile. "Can't be bad inside if whoever or whatever wants us to see where we're going."

When Pyrrha and Tan followed, to Mira's surprise, Kyle stepped back. "Jo's right," he whispered. "I don't think we should go in. *I* shouldn't go in. Those other things in there—"

"Wait. What things?" Linus asked.

"We saw bones around the tomb. A lot of deaths occurred in this place. I have the feeling their spirits are not at rest."

Mira smiled and stroked his arm. "That's OK. I'll take it from here."

Cautiously, she followed the others inside, but as she reached the bottom of a long tunnel, deep underground, a fierce blast of freezing air suddenly blew up from nowhere, driving the group into retreat.

"OK, I was wrong. Someone doesn't want us to be here," said Josh, picking himself up off the ground, having received the worst of the impact.

"That's great," Pyrrha said, smiling. "If we can't get in, then the Followers won't be able to enter either."

Kyle suddenly appeared behind them, out of breath. "Is everyone OK? We felt the gust from outside."

"Gust… I thought I was in yet another remake of the movie *Twister*," said Josh.

Tan ushered the group into a huddle. "I think it's finally time to try option two," he said. "Let's get to my boat and try our luck in getting away from this island before we get trapped in here forever. What do you all say?"

Kyle edged ahead, right up to where the wind was still blowing. "No, Mira is right. We have to get it away from here." And before Mira could stop him, he stepped into the path of the storm.

To everyone's surprise, the raging whirlwind immediately subsided.

"Now, that's a neat trick," said Tan, peering around the wall.

"Perhaps it just doesn't want me and Josh here," said Rachel.

Josh stepped out next and stood by his brother. Mira was next, followed by Tan and then Pyrrha. Rachel remained where she was.

"Only you, it seems," Josh told her. "It must be you who can open the tomb."

"Well, that's just great," she said, stamping her foot. "If this is the tomb's defence mechanism, they haven't thought it through very well, have they? I mean, what's the point if anyone else can enter and remove it?"

Josh rejoined her side. "Hang on, I've got an idea," he said. "Try going now, Rach."

Rachel stepped forward. This time, nothing happened.

Josh stroked his chin. "Hmm. Interesting."

"What's interesting? What do you know that we don't?" Rachel said, her tone rising with her anger.

"I don't know anything," he said. "I just thought it was interesting. Don't you?"

"Never bloody mind interesting!" Tan barked. "Run, before whatever regains its breath blows us all to kingdom come!"

Everyone sped along the tunnel until they were looking out into a vast open chamber. In the ceiling, a large hole allowed plenty of light. A hundred yards in front of them was a high wall, and at the centre, a waterfall, which was gushing forth its life-force down into a large lake that disappeared beneath the rock face. Behind the cascade lay the tunnel that led to the tomb.

But something else was now occupying their attention. The long arm of a dead tree that stretched out over the pool.

"Oh, I'm going to be sick," said Rachel.

"Too late, I beat you to it," said Josh, straightening up and wiping his mouth. "Oh, you don't think there's something in the pool that did that, do you?"

Ahead, dangled by their feet from vines, were the missing crew, minus their heads, distributed evenly along the branch.

Pyrrha rushed to the edge of the lake. "I can't see Sherme, or Laurie! That means they could have got out, right?" She looked hopeful.

Mira didn't want to look again or think what the probable alternative was, so Kyle looked into the pool instead. After only a brief moment, he stumbled back, almost falling to the ground.

"Are you OK?" Mira asked, taking his arm.

"No," he gasped. "I saw—I saw myself. I mean, I saw someone who looks like me take Epimetheus in chains through the tunnel to where the tomb…" Suddenly, his words trailed off. He paused. "Listen, everyone, be on your guard. Mira was right: this place is going to play tricks with our minds!" he called out. "Like it did with Pyrrha at the bridge."

"We have to cut the bodies down first, surely?" said Rachel. "If Jo has to come in here, she'll freak out big time. She could still be the one who has to open the tomb—"

"Hold on," said an agitated Pyrrha. "What exactly do you all know that I don't?"

"You'll find out when we leave this place and get to where we're going, I swear," said Mira, turning the tables on her.

Slowly, a wry smile appeared, and Pyrrha mouthed, "Bravo."

"So, who's the best climber?" Tan asked.

"Josh," said Mira and Kyle in unison.

Tan handed Josh his sword, and Josh reluctantly began to climb the tree. "I don't remember having to do this in my dream," he grumbled. "And do we really want these bodies floating around when we swim across?"

"Swim?" Tan squawked. "You mean we have to swim it? Nobody said anything about swimming. Are you sure there isn't a lever somewhere that'll make stepping stones magically appear?"

"Can't you swim, Tan?" said Mira, taking his arm.

Tan shook his head and laughed. "Who said I can't swim? I didn't say I couldn't swim—I just said do we *have* to swim!"

She sighed. "You can't swim, can you?"

His laughter grew louder, until it abruptly stopped. "No. No, I can't."

"So why would you sail a boat alone?" Kyle asked.

Tan's face contorted. "Because I'm not in the water, I'm in a boat."

"Yes, but what if something happens to the boat?"

"I've got a dinghy. Is it too hard to understand what I'm saying?"

"No, but what happens if the dinghy sinks?"

Tan paced back and forth near the edge of the pool. "That's what life jackets are for. And why would a boat sink, anyway, or the dinghy for that matter? Besides, if it's a storm that capsizes my boat, armbands are not gonna be much good in rolling waves. Anyway, can you fly a plane?"

Kyle shook his head. "No."

"Well, I can, but if you can't, why on earth get on one?"

Kyle was now scratching his head. "Well, umm... huh?"

"What happens if the pilot suddenly can't fly, what would you do?"

"I guess we'd crash."

"And knowing that, you would still get on a plane, wouldn't you?"

"I suppose so."

"There you go." Tan nodded. "I sail alone. If the boat and dinghy sink, and the life jacket doesn't work, I drown."

Josh was now above the hanging corpses. With a single cut to each of the vines, the mutilated bodies fell into the water. But as they slowly sank, Josh saw something to make him close his eyes.

"Oh, Pyrrha, I'm so sorry, but I think I see your brother from here," he called out, blindly pointing into the pool. "I recognise the jumper he was wearing."

Pyrrha slowly leaned over and stared. Spying the headless body of her brother, released from a lightless crevice by a fallen body, she dropped to her knees and screamed.

Rachel and Mira were at her side in a moment. Lifting her to her feet, they escorted her away from the pool. But Mira's sixth sense was suddenly ignited. And just at the moment she grabbed Pyrrha's sword from its sheath, there was a huge eruption from the pool.

Pyrrha and Tan took the full force of the sudden expulsion of water, sending them tumbling to the far side of the cavern. And as Josh wrapped his arms tightly around the branch, the largest snake any of them had ever seen rose up from the lake.

Frozen in fear, everyone watched the white-scaled snake with its yellow, reptilian eyes uncoil its immense body and slowly rise, seemingly endlessly, toward Josh.

Now only a metre away from swallowing Josh whole, the serpent opened its hood like a cobra, and then, extending large wings from its slithery back, it moved in for the kill.

Without thought for her own safety, Mira ran toward the pool and sprang high into the air. She drove Pyrrha's sword deep into the snake's huge body.

The serpent thrashed in pain, forcing her to release the weapon, but as she dropped into the pool, the body of the snake coiled, trapping her against the wall of rock. Unable to move, Mira looked desperately to Kyle for help. But he was stood stock-still, unmoving, and with the snake writhing in pain, she was pushed further and further down, inch by inch, until only her head was above the waterline.

She gasped for air. But as she fought to release herself, her body wilted. Crumpled under the hideous, scaly weight, with her last breath, she called his name, "Kyle…", before disappearing into the murky darkness.

CHAPTER FIFTY-SEVEN

BUTO

Kyle was in torment. Invisible hands were holding him firm; he was paralysed.

There was only one person it could be. The boy who had beaten him to a bloody pulp, the boy he'd been seeing since he'd arrived on this cursed island.

Do you want her to join you in the afterlife, Peter? he thought as he struggled. *Is that why you're holding me back?*

His vision was becoming blurred, and Mira was calling for help.

Please, Peter, if you truly love her, then let me help!

Blearily, he watched as Mira slipped into the watery darkness.

But suddenly, he was free. His senses were returning, assaulting him all at once. He had to fight to focus through his newborn eyes.

At last, Kyle's vision was crystal clear. But there was no sign of Mira, and his brother was still in serious trouble. He called out to Josh to throw him the sword.

Kyle caught it with one hand.

The head of the snake was the size of an African elephant. With fangs like giant stalactites bearing down upon him, Kyle stood his ground. He didn't care anymore. If this was to be his death, he would drive the blade through the serpent's gaping mouth, into its brain, before he left this world, he promised.

The snake was almost upon him, ready to strike. But to Kyle's surprise, at the last moment, the serpent flipped its head sideways.

Rachel had tossed the boomerang, grazing the monster's eye.

Kyle took the moment to thrust his sword forward. The steel pierced through the serpent's lower jaw like a needle through satin, but as the reptile flailed about, Kyle was struck by one of its wings and sent careering into the wall of rock and then into the blood-curdled pool of death.

He slipped beneath the water, but amazingly, he could now see Mira, floating weightless, lifeless. A short breaststroke, and he pulled her into his arms and placed his mouth over hers. He would give her his last breath, if he could just see her violet eyes once more.

Slowly, Mira's lids opened and with a mammoth effort, the two of them kicked to the surface and climbed onto the bank. But there was not a moment to relax. Out from the deep, a second giant snake head appeared.

"Are you kidding me?" Josh bellowed. "A two-headed, humongous bloody flying cobra, now?! And look—the head is where the tail should be! Where the hell am I? I know—does anyone speak any Parcelforce?"

"For heaven's sake, Josh!" Rachel yelled, desperately trying to avoid the snake's attention. "It's called Parseltongue! And no, I don't know any! Can't you be serious just once in your life?"

"I am being bloody serious!" But as he attempted to pull himself onto the branch, at the sound of his moans and grunts, the second head spun toward him. A warning cry sounded from Rachel, and Josh's and the snake's eyes locked together.

Josh was transfixed. He could only stare at the scaly body as it rose higher.

The snake was almost upon him, its mouth open wide, with teeth the length of Josh's body ready to inflict a killer strike. But from below, Rachel launched the boomerang again and caught the snake directly in the centre of its forehead. With the boomerang embedded deep in its skull, it recoiled.

Pulled free from the monster's trance, Josh heaved his body up and onto the branch. But the snake's attention had been broken for only a second, and turning its giant head, it spat venom.

The thick, woody arm of the tree was now soaked in a substance with a horrendous stench. Josh attempted to slide his body away, but he slipped, leaving him dangling precariously above the hooded serpent by only one hand.

"That's just great! Why is everything bigger? Can't we for once meet a friendly, miniature creature?" he called out.

The snake once more moved in for the kill.

***

Spying his brother in trouble, Kyle leapt to his feet, but he had lost his sword. It was then he noticed Josh was eyeing Mira's blade, which was still protruding from the snake's bloodied body. Kyle instinctively knew what Josh was about to do. Before he could call out to him not to do it, however, Josh released his hold of the branch.

He dropped like a stone. But at the last second, he caught the hilt of the sword with both hands. The force and weight of his fall allowed the blade to slice open the snake's body with ease. But as the serpent shrank back into the lake, it took the sword, and Josh, into the void with it.

Without thinking, Kyle dived back into the water to retrieve his brother and, hopefully, the weapon.

He resurfaced. Josh was gone, but the first snake's head was bearing down on Mira. With no time to get out of the water, he threw her the sword he'd retrieved from the snake's body.

The giant cobra attacked, but with sword firmly in hand and a balletic twirl of her body, Mira raised the instrument of death high over her head. One swing, and the sharpened steel sliced through the serpent's scaly armour, sending a river of blood gushing forth.

As the hooded menace disappeared into the murky depths, the second head dropped limply to the bank. Devoid of pity, Mira drove the blade down through its skull, deep into its brain.

***

The giant, two-headed cobra was dead. Everyone, for the moment, was safe.

Kyle scrambled out of the pool and fell into Mira's loving embrace.

"And for my next trick, I shall perform a tightrope walk over a lake of boiling tar, blindfolded," Josh spluttered, tossing the other sword he'd retrieved onto the bank before clambering out of the water and collapsing onto his back.

"How in the hell did you four accomplish that?" Tan shouted, staring wide-eyed at them.

"It's true!" said Pyrrha, dropping to her knees in wonderment. "It explains how they survived the fall from the ship. They are the children of the gods! The ones fated to bring order out of chaos!"

"That's ridiculous!" said Tan.

"Then can you explain how they killed a goddess?"

Still cradling Kyle, Mira turned her head to Pyrrha. "You mind explaining what you just said? That snake was a... goddess?"

Pyrrha took a moment to answer. "That was Buto. One of the lesser-known gods. It was the protector of the Pharaohs of old." She turned to Tan. "Read your history!"

Tan took off his cowboy hat and ran his hands through his mop of curly hair. "I have. I've just never read that one. But, OK, if you say so."

"See—I told you, Rach." Josh winked. "Hey, maybe I am descended from Perseus."

Rachel dropped beside him, also out of breath. "Fine... Just don't let it go to your head. And as for bringing order out of chaos, sweetie, could you try to cause less of the pandemonium, please?"

Josh simply grinned.

Linus and Jo appeared shortly after, but both stepped back into the tunnel when they saw the colossal, lifeless body of the snake.

"What in the Sam Hell is that?" Linus cried out.

"We came to see if you needed help, but seeing that thing, I'll just go back and wait outside, if you don't mind," said Jo, turning away.

"Jo, it's dead," Rachel shouted. "It should be OK to go through now."

"Wait. Is that what you saw past the waterfall?" said Josh. "Or is there something bigger or, more importantly, worse behind there?"

"Yes, it makes sense now," said Rachel. "I saw something slithering around the tomb. Although, the second time it wasn't there, but we had to walk through thousands of bones."

Mira nodded. "I saw the bones as well. But was it this that pulled us under the water the first time we had the dream?" She pointed to the head of the serpent.

"I thought it was hands, but perhaps it was the snake," said Kyle.

"Well, good news, Tan, at least we have a bridge for you to walk across now," Josh said with a grin, looking at how the torso of the snake had fallen across the lake.

Mira stepped onto the monster's large body first, but Tan pulled her back and stared at the waterfall. "Did you see me, Pyrrha, or Linus even, in there with you in your dream?" he asked.

"No. Why?"

"Then, I think it would be wise for us three to stay out here," he said, caution in his tone.

"Why? It should be plain sailing now," said Josh. "What else could go wrong?"

Rachel shook her head and lashed out at her favourite target. "You just had to say it, didn't you?"

Tan continued. "You said when you opened the first tomb, a thick mist came out and rendered you all unconscious. After seeing Josh's leg heal, and coming back from the dead, and from what you say about Kyle healing fast, and what I just saw you lot achieve, I believe something has been awakened in each of you, and I don't think that mist will affect you now. But we three don't have protective masks, and if something goes wrong in there, you're going to need us out here. We will come as far as the entrance to ensure you're safe, but before you open that thing, Pyrrha and I will rejoin Linus out here."

"I was thinking of doing the same thing," said Jo. "But I'll wait all the way outside, if you don't mind."

But Linus blocked her exit, shaking his head, so Jo reluctantly turned back and began walking across the dead snake's body.

"And I really, really hate snakes as well!"

CHAPTER FIFTY-EIGHT

MIST AND BONES

Mira and Rachel followed Jo through the waterfall, which had suddenly ceased flowing the moment they approached it. With Kyle and Josh close behind, and Pyrrha and Tan bringing up the rear, the company proceeded along a terracotta-tiled oval passageway.

"I like what they've done with this," said Josh. "And I especially like the colour. What do you say we ask Dad to do something like this in our back garden, Kaiboy?"

Kyle gave him a heartfelt smile. He didn't want to remind Josh that there would be no going home for either of them now. "Sure. Whatever you want."

When they came out into another vast chamber, Kyle looked at the ground, which was illuminated by narrow beams of red light spilling through hundreds of tiny holes in the rocky ceiling.

"This looks different to what I remember," said Josh glumly.

"There's the red and white tree, and the tomb in the centre. Looks exactly like what I dreamed," said Kyle, wiping the sweat from his brow.

"Yes, but there's something missing, or something different?"

"It's the ground around the tomb," Rachel pointed out. "Look, it's full of a thick, red mist—not skeletons."

"Oh, yeah, right, there are no skeletons. That's what's missing." Josh smiled. It soon faded. "But why is the fog glowing red?"

"It's an eclipse," said Tan, looking ominously to Pyrrha. "The sun and the moon have converged."

"Shouldn't everything go dark, then?" said Josh. "Not red?"

"It's a blood moon. That means…" Pyrrha trailed off.

"Means what?" Josh pressed.

"By the look on Pyrrha's face," said Tan, "I'd say it means we must hurry."

"Oh, here we go. Look, if you're both going to be secret squirrels about this, then I'm not taking another bloody step."

"He's right," said Rachel. "Just look at the way that mist is hovering and glowing—something's not right about all this."

"Oh, what if there are eggs underneath the fog?" Josh asked.

"Eggs?" Pyrrha repeated.

"Yes, eggs," said Josh, folding his arms across his chest. "Tell her what happens if there are eggs, Kaiboy?"

Kyle was sweating profusely. Mira took his hand. "You don't have to go any further," she said softly. "So, what is this blood moon, Pyrrha?"

"The prophecy says that when this place is opened, the sun and the moon shall become as one. The moon shall turn red, and the dead shall rise up."

Everyone other than Pyrrha turned to face Jo, expecting her to debunk the theory and offer up her own thoughts. But to their surprise, she remained silent. Her focus was firmly on the tomb.

"So, how many bloody prophecies are there altogether?" Rachel said.

"Never mind prophecies. Tell her about the eggs, Kaiboy," Josh insisted. "And what happens when they open."

All eyes turned to Kyle.

They look scared, he thought. *Now, pull yourself together!* "Giant chickens appear?" he said, hoping to lighten the mood.

Mira started to laugh.

"Oh, what if they are golden eggs?" said Rachel excitedly, breaking into a smile.

"If they were golden, I'm pretty sure Jo would have bashed us all around the heads by now and already be carrying them to Tan's boat," said Josh. "No, if there are eggs, just make sure you don't put your face near them, because if they open—"

"You get yolk on your face, or the chick will follow you, thinking you're its mother?" Kyle interrupted, remembering a *Tom and Jerry* cartoon he'd seen as a child.

"Oh, come on," said Josh. "You must have seen this film? It's one of the all-time classics, for Pete's sake. I definitely know you've seen it, Kaiboy. We took Uncle Trevor's DVD box set and we haven't given it back yet."

"Right, now I remember, sorry. *Puss in Boots*, yeah?" said Kyle, looking at the green patch of land where the tomb rested beneath the tree.

"Screw you, Kaiboy," said Josh, sulking. "I told you before, you're not funny. I'm the funny one, so just do your thing and stand there looking pretty!"

"Are you going tell us or not?" said Jo, glaring at the mist.

"No, you're all taking the mick. You all know what it is!"

"No, really, Josh," said Mira. "You know I wouldn't have seen it."

"Fine, but if you say I'm kidding, you're carrying that thing out of here by yourselves. It was *Alien*."

"Oh, I have seen little bits of that film," said Mira, staring up at the shafts of light. "My stepfather was a huge fan. Oh, I wish I hadn't asked now."

"And me," said Rachel. "But wasn't it a bluish-grey light around the eggs? You know, after my boyfriend saw the third film in the series, and then the news broke that weird lights were seen above Moreland Hill a few miles from where we live, he thought it was going to happen to him when he got sent to prison."

"Um, excuse me?" said Josh. "So, it's OK for you to talk about other men, is it, but as soon as I mention any woman, I get lightning hand, Rach?"

"So, what did he get sent down for?" Mira asked, ignoring Josh's rant.

"Tax evasion. He wasn't very bright," said Rachel, shaking her head.

"That was the footballer, right?"

"Yes. Funnily enough he was training to be a human resource manager, but was so good at football, and the money was so much better, he did that instead."

"Err, hello? I'm still here you know!" said Josh, waving his arms around.

"So, why did you break up with him?" Jo asked, finally looking away from the green patch of land.

"I haven't. Not officially yet, anyway."

"What! You still have a boyfriend!?" Josh cried.

"Technically, yes. But I was going to break up with him when I got home." Rachel shrugged. "Honest, I was."

"Umm, don't want to interrupt girls' night..." said Kyle, squeezing his trembling hands together. "But shouldn't we be opening that thing? The sooner we do this, the sooner we can get the hell out of here."

"He's right," said Mira. "Let's get this over with."

"To be honest with you, Mira," said Rachel, "I don't fancy walking across there since Josh mentioned *Alien*." She pushed Josh forward instead. "Would you and Kyle mind going and checking it out for us first?"

"What about equal rights and all that?" Josh shouted.

"Mira just killed a humongous two-headed snake. And Jo and I had to fight an army of the flying trade unionists while you were taking a snooze, so now it's your turn to do something!" said Rachel, motioning for him to cross to the other side.

Josh threw his head back. "If you recall, so did I, back at the town. And I don't know if you noticed, not only did I get chased by eight angry bears, but I just jumped out of a bloody tree, caught the handle of a sword mid-flight and ripped open the belly of that humongous two-headed snake, which enabled Mira to kill it. And not only did I ride a bloody giant crocodile, I did a headstand on the head of a giant bloody crocodile, and then died, apparently—all in the search for you. So, it's your turn to go have a look!"

"Josh!"

"Fine." Josh pouted. "I'll go have a bloody look, but no more talk of boyfriends!"

As Tan and Pyrrha, shaking their heads, left the chamber, Josh waited for Kyle to join him. They both walked cagily through the mist, the sound of bones crunching beneath their feet confirming that the skeletons were there.

"No need to panic—there are no eggs!" Josh called back. "But, umm, there are bones."

"Then come back and you can lead us through," Rachel shouted.

"You just watched us walk through," said Josh. "C'mon, there's nothing to worry about."

"Josh!"

"Fine, I'll come back now," he huffed, and walked back.

Kyle held out his hand for Mira to take.

She didn't. "If you don't mind, I think I should wait here," she said. "Remember the dream and where we were all standing?"

Instead, Kyle offered his hand to Jo and started to lead her through the mist. With Rachel refusing to walk, Josh was forced to give her a piggyback ride.

"Would you like me to carry you, Jo?" Kyle smiled.

"No, just don't let go of my hand, because I'm going to keep my eyes closed," she said, covering her face.

Upon reaching the small, green patch of land, Rachel jumped off Josh's back, and Kyle released Jo's hand.

"You're standing on the grass now," Kyle said.

Jo removed her other hand from her eyes and, without being asked, stepped forward and reached into a small notch in the tree and withdrew a key. Silently, she stared at it with curiosity. "Don't ask me how I knew where it was, because I have no idea. But if I die, promise me you won't bury me at sea?" she said nervously.

Jo's hand was trembling so badly that Kyle had to help guide the key into the lock. Hearing the click of the mechanism, they all stepped away. But as the lid opened, this time there was no appearance from the feared thick miasma.

"So far, so good," said Rachel, but as she and Jo then tried to lift the coffin, it refused to move. "It's too heavy!" she said, grunting in frustration.

Kyle passed his sword to Rachel and, together with Josh, reached in and grabbed the handles.

"Gently now, Salah," Josh said with a smile.

He's unbelievable. "Josh. Now is not the time to be quoting *Raiders of the Lost* bloody *Ark*," Kyle growled.

The coffin was lifted clear of the tomb. But as they all began to walk back toward Mira, a familiar gust of cold wind swirled around the chamber. Suddenly, the ceiling above crumbled away, leaving a large hole. Kyle, still with a firm hold on the coffin, leaned back and peered up through the gap.

Through the swirling red cloud hovering above his head, he could see electric sparks begin to crackle. Without a moment to spare, Kyle and the group dived for cover, just at the moment a bolt of purple and silver lightning fired down through the opening.

Silence engulfed the chamber. Warily, the company pushed their tired bodies to their feet. The tree was burning, and a low, deep hum could be heard coming from inside the tomb.

Transfixed, they watched as the marble enclosure began to slowly expand.

"Everyone, hit the deck!" Kyle yelled.

An explosion of blue light, and needle-like splinters of marble flew over their heads in all directions. It was only once the tumult had stopped that Kyle released his hands from his head and got to his feet.

"I've got a bad feeling about this, Kaiboy," said Josh, reaching down and taking hold of the handle again.

Kyle had to agree. "Me too."

Rachel and Jo, who had tiptoed on ahead, suddenly came to a stop.

"Do you hear that?" Rachel asked.

"I do," said Jo, closing her eyes again.

Out of the mist, a skeleton sat up and turned to face them. Decayed flesh hung from its bones like Spanish moss.

Rachel and Jo briskly power-walked back to the coffin.

"See what happens, Josh?" Rachel threw him a steely glare. "You had to say there would be nothing to worry about, didn't you!"

Jo threw her hands over her head. "This isn't happening," she said aloud. "This isn't real. Now pull yourself together, Jo. There are no skeletons. There are no harpies, giant crocodiles, bears or gods. Any minute now, you are going to wake up in your own bed and find that this has all been a terrible dream."

Slowly, she removed her one hand from her eye. Seeing more skeletons rise from the mist, she doubled over and began to hyperventilate.

"There are no skeletons, there are no skeletons!" she said over and over. "You're in the shopping mall aboard the cruise ship. This is all just fancy dress!"

"If this is fancy dress," said Josh, "could you ask those extremely malnourished security guards to let us through then please, seeing as you're nearer to them?"

Kyle and Josh staggered clumsily across the floor with the cumbersome coffin, but before they could reach the other side, yet more skeletons stood up and blocked their path with their swords. Surrounded, Kyle and Josh accepted defeat.

"Oh my God, I'm going to pee myself," said Jo.

"Relax," said Kyle. "Just don't make any sudden movements."

"OK," said Jo. "But if they start to scream, then I'm not going to be held responsible for what happens next."

"Trust me, Jo," Josh whispered, "if they start screaming, there will be more than pee running down my leg, I can assure you of that."

Kyle watched the skeletons closely. "Right. They're not attacking us. Mira, see what happens if you move toward them."

The sword held tight in her hand, Mira edged forward until she was stood behind three skeletons blocking their exit.

"Josh… When I give Mira the signal, drop the coffin and run as fast as you can," said Kyle.

"I can't speak for you, Kaiboy, but my upper-body motor functions don't seem to be doing what I want at the moment," said Josh, as yet more skeletons suddenly appeared out of the mist.

Kyle turned to Rachel and Jo. "How about you two try reaching Mira?"

"Funny thing is, Kyle," Rachel squeaked, "my bottom half doesn't seem to want to move now."

When even more skeletons got to their feet, Kyle knew there was only one thing for it. He looked to Mira. "Ready?"

Mira adjusted her stance as if she'd been born to wield a blade. "Ready when you are."

Josh turned his head to look at her. "You're not actually going to—"

Before Josh could finish his sentence, Mira swung the sword. Three skeletal skulls were removed with one swing, and as the bodies dropped to the floor, the way ahead opened up.

"Run!" Kyle cried, pushing the coffin against Josh.

As the fleeing group reached the exit, high-pitched cries behind them confirmed Jo's fears, and frozen in fear, she could only stare at the fast-approaching cascade of skeletons, waving swords and bows, wailing and screeching like banshees.

Jo closed her eyes, waiting for the darkness to descend. But today wasn't her time, and as Kyle and Josh entered the tunnel, Mira and Rachel swooped her up and took up the defence at the rear.

CHAPTER FIFTY-NINE

THE COLD HANDS OF DEATH

The corridor echoed with the horrendous cries of the skeletons, and the coffin was getting heavier by the second. Kyle and Josh had to place the sarcophagus down. Mira and Rachel, who had managed to repel the first assault, slowly backed into the tunnel.

"I don't want to alarm you," said Rachel, "but if you two don't move your arses, then—"

Her next words were abruptly cut short as there was a sudden surge forward and two skeletons broke their valiant defence.

As if their minds had become one, Kyle and Josh lifted the coffin, turned it sideways, then ran directly at the sword-wielding skeletons. Driven back hard against the wall, their fleshless frames broke apart.

It was then that Pyrrha and Tan came running along the tunnel from behind.

"Where are Jo and Linus?" Kyle cried. "We need some help here!"

"Jo took off past us like a cruise missile, and Linus ran after her to bring her back," said Tan.

"We can't carry this all the way—it weighs a bloody ton!" Josh gasped.

"Right, don't panic," said Tan. "Pyrrha and I will take it as far as the bridge, then we'll swap. You two pick up the swords and bow the skeletons have dropped and help those wonderful, brave girls!"

As Tan and Pyrrha made their way back down the tunnel with the coffin, Kyle and Josh rushed forward to help Rachel and Mira.

The passageway was now full of skeletons, all stood with wide, gaping smiles, waiting.

"Why do you think they've stopped?" said Rachel, taking the bow from Josh and handing him her sword.

"Perhaps they can't go any further," said Mira, looking hopefully for some kind of magic forcefield that would have appeared if this were a movie.

"Or maybe they're just waiting for the ones with spears," said Josh. "And what the hell are you planning to do with the bow, Rach? The arrows will fly straight through them."

In a flash, Rachel aimed the bow and fired a shot. The arrow's clean strike on a skull took it completely off the skeleton's shoulders.

"That's what I'm going to do with it!" she growled. "Finally, Dad's insistence on me taking archery has paid off!"

Pulling on Josh's arm, Kyle spun him around. "I know I'm going to regret asking, but why did you say 'the ones with spears'?"

As if on cue, there was a clatter of bone on stone. There ahead, marching in formation toward them, were the spear-wielding skeletons.

Mira's heart sank. "Oh, I don't believe it! Look what's coming from behind the tomb!" she cried, pointing to another group appearing from around the great tree. "Are you making this happen, Josh?"

"No, but when you're in a situation like this, I find keeping your eyes open and alert is the best thing to do," he said. "Now, let me think what our next move is, cos when they get close enough, not only are we screwed, but we'll be skewered." Josh looked back to the pool and snapped his fingers. "I think I've got it. Can skeletons swim?"

"How the hell do I know?" Mira snarled. "They don't appear to be in a talkative enough mood for me to ask them!"

"OK, OK, just asking. Then, what if me and Rach go back and remove the snake bridge, and when those things get too close, you run and dive into the water?"

"No way, that's what pulled me under, a bony hand!" exclaimed Kyle. "I remember now!"

Mira closed her eyes. "Yes, me too."

"Then unless someone can think of a better way… Oh! What if we reverse who goes where?"

"It's too bloody big to move, Josh!" Rachel yelled. "How about we all stay and fight or we all make a run for it? Maybe they'll be scared of the dead snake?"

"Do they look like they would be scared of anything?" said Josh.

"Shame we don't have any of those sticky bombs left," said Kyle.

Josh began bouncing up and down, beaming. "We do! I took two out of Pyrrha's rucksack and put them in Jo's in case of an emergency. Problem is, she's probably on her way to Brazil by now."

"Perhaps Linus has caught her and brought her back?" said Mira.

"Well, unless someone goes and looks, we won't know, and the skinless ones with very long spears are nearly here!" Rachel shouted.

"So, which of you is going to check?" Mira asked.

"You're the fastest, you go," said Kyle.

"I'm not leaving any of you here!"

"I think it's time for us all to run now!" Rachel cried, pointing to the sword-wielding skeletons, which had now parted, forming two lines.

The spearmen marched through the gap, and turning on their heels, the four teens ran.

High-pitched screams were closing in from behind. Mira shot a look over her shoulder. "Can we run a little faster?" she cried. "Faster would be better right now!"

But as the skeletons swarmed the tunnel like an army of ants, Kyle suddenly stopped and turned to face the horde. "Mira, get them out!" Before she could stop him, Kyle was running at the skeletons, cutting through them like light through shadow.

Mira kept running and ushered Rachel and Josh across the body of the snake. But with Pyrrha and Tan struggling to get to the other side, and the skeletons that had managed to bypass Kyle closing in fast, they were now stuck in the middle, and as Mira turned to face the skeletons, a spear was thrust toward her.

With lightning reflexes, she dodged. But as the snake began to shake beneath her, thanks to the numbers now upon it, she stumbled into Rachel, causing them to lose their balance. Both Rachel and Josh tumbled head first into the water.

Mira was now alone, and she knew it was up to her to stop the skeletons from getting to the sarcophagus. Raising her sword, she struck one square across the ribcage. It fell into the water, taking two others with it.

But already, more of them were trying to cross the bridge.

***

Rachel swam to the opposite bank. But as she pulled herself out and reached out for Josh, cadaverous hands burst out from the depths and pulled him under.

Frantically, Rachel attempted to clear the debris floating in the murky water. It was then she spied Josh below. Skeletal fingers were clawing at his body, dragging him further into the darkness. Without thinking, she plunged head first into the icy water. Her waving arms caught hold of something. It was Josh's sweater. Grasping hold of the material, she managed to drag him toward her as she lifted herself out of the water.

Gasping heavily, she dragged Josh's limp body up onto the bank.

Just then, Linus entered the cave with a distraught Jo in tow.

"I just want to go home!" Jo wailed. "Please, just let me go home!"

Still breathing heavily, Rachel left Josh on the bank and completed the hundred-yard dash to the entrance of the cave in Olympic time. She reached inside Jo's rucksack, pulled out a sticky bomb and, without saying a word, but taking another dramatic inhale of breath, ran back toward the snake bridge.

***

Meanwhile, Mira had driven the remaining skeletons back inside the tunnel. There was still no sign of Kyle, but before Mira could stop her, Rachel had removed the protective tape and lobbed the bomb at the rock face above the entrance to the tunnel.

The explosion rocked the entire chamber. Rocks tumbled and more of the skeletons were tossed into the water. Then, through the smoke and dust, Kyle appeared. But as he leapt through the avalanche of falling stone, suddenly, a boulder caught him squarely in the back and he, too, was sent careering into the depths of the lake.

Mira waited for him to surface. But as the ripples began to settle, she spied the hands of the dead dragging him deeper into the void. Without thought for her own safety, she dived in after him.

CHAPTER SIXTY

WHAT'S IN A NAME?

The entrance to the tunnel had been completely sealed, and Tan and Pyrrha had smashed the remaining skeletons into dust. When Mira finally surfaced, gasping for air, Rachel leapt into the water, and together they pulled Kyle's body to the bank.

Tense, nervous minutes followed. But Kyle finally opened his eyes and spat out a mouthful of water. Mira swept him up into a tight embrace and kissed him. Unable to contain her emotions any longer, she let the tears spill down her cheeks. "What the hell were you thinking?!"

But Kyle was breathing hard and he couldn't answer.

Tan laughed with relief. "You see, that's why I don't swim."

"I swear, one was trying to kiss me," Josh gasped, falling onto his back in exhaustion.

Rachel was quick to apologise. "I'm so sorry, Kyle. I don't know what came over me."

Kyle at last found his voice. "You did the right thing. It was a lot bigger inside than we thought, and there were more of them coming. It was like the terracotta army back there."

"Can someone please explain how in the hell they could scream with no vocal cords?" Josh asked. "Or see us with no eyes? In fact, how in the hell could they bloody move at all? Am I in a *Sinbad* movie by any chance?"

"Actually, the screaming that you heard might have been me," said Tan. "As for them seeing us, and everything else, I have no idea."

"Who cares who was screaming, or how they could see us—can we please all leave this place now?" said Rachel, hugging Josh even tighter.

"Where's Jo?" said Mira, suddenly conscious of her absence.

Linus said, hesitantly, "She took off when she saw—and, am I right in saying?—walking, screaming, sword- and spear-wielding skeletons?"

"Oh, you missed all the fun, Linus," said Josh. "You both should have stuck around and watched the show."

"Well, you lot can't go outside yet," said Tan. "Two soakings in a day and you'll catch your death. Linus, would you mind bringing Jo back inside, and I'll go gather the wood to start a fire."

***

Fortunately, due to the abundance of dead tree branches lying around the cavern, by the time Tan had finished building the pyre, there was still enough wood to put a 5th of November bonfire to shame. Once Linus finally convinced Jo to re-enter the cave, they all sat around the flames, enjoying the warmth.

"You know, I never thought in all my life, I'd see what I just saw," said Tan. "Enormous creatures of the deep, I can accept. Giant flying bats that resemble my grandmother after a night out on the town? Again, why not. But a huge, two-headed snake with wings, and walking, running, sword- and spear-carrying skeletons? I have to say I did not see that coming. Maybe the gods are making things happen after all."

As Pyrrha stoked the fire, Mira could see by her expression that she was contemplating whether to reveal something to the group. It wasn't long before she proved her right.

"Before we go any further, do you all now believe that there is more to all this than just vases filled with poison?" she asked.

Tan blew out his cheeks. "Pretty hard for us not to now, especially after explaining who Buto really was."

Pyrrha scanned everyone else's concerned faces. "Then, before we leave, there's something you all should know. There's a reason I didn't want us to come here. There's a chance that if we remove the coffin from this sepulchre completely, we may incur the same curse that befell all those poor souls. As I have become fond of you all, I now have to ask if you want to risk it. None of you asked for this, so it's only right that you all have the choice in what you do next."

Mira expected Jo, at least, to jump to her feet and flee. But Jo was to surprise her.

"If we leave it here the Followers will claim it and we will lose our only bargaining chip to get Jacen back," Jo said. "I for one don't believe we will be cursed if we remove it. I think we are meant to take it to your sanctuary. But I'm with Mira and whatever she wants to do."

"What about the rest of you?" Pyrrha asked.

Rachel looked around the company, smiled and took Mira's hand. "I think I speak for everyone when I say, we're with Mira."

"Damn right we are," said Linus.

Mira looked to Kyle, who simply gave her a wink and a nod.

"Right, now that's sorted," said Josh. "There's just one problem. There's no way we are going to be able to carry that thing all the way back to Tan's boat—it would take a week. So, if anyone has any idea what we can do, speak now, because just like Pandora's island, the Followers could be here at any moment."

"He's right," said Kyle. "There's only one thing for it. Tan, you'll have to sail your boat to the edge of the town."

"What about the crocodiles and the bears?" said Tan. "And if the sun hasn't come out and the harpies are still there...?"

Everyone fell silent and stared into the flames.

Mira could feel the sombre mood beginning to rise among them once more. "We shall deal with it when, or if, the time comes," she said. "For now, we just concern ourselves with getting the coffin to the town. But that's for later. First things first—let's make sure we're all rested and, more importantly, dry."

Everyone was still staring miserably into the flames.

She needed to change the topic. *What can I say that will lighten the mood?* It then struck her. "Tan, I've been thinking, if you don't mind me asking—Tandigo, is quite an unusual name. Where does it, umm, originate from?"

Mira watched all the lowered heads rise, now in wonder, and when Josh snorted through his nose, she could see that none of the company were thinking of the next trial they would have to face.

"What's so funny, Josh?" Rachel snarled.

Josh shook his head. "Nothing."

"Your boyfriend finds my name funny because to him it sounds like dancing," Tan remarked. "But to answer your question, my dear niece... Mama liked to make up names. You know, so I'd be different and not just another—oh, what's a popular name… err… John. So I wouldn't be another John."

"I didn't think John would be that popular in Greece?" said Rachel. "Then again, you don't sound Greek. Where are you from exactly?"

"I was born in Ontario." Tan winked. "Beautiful part of the country. When my parents divorced, my mother relocated us to her homeland of Greece. Rhodes, to be precise."

"Hang on," said Josh. "Are you saying Tan, or Tandigo, is a popular name in California? Although, I'm not surprised if it is. Especially with all the freaky movie stars and weird music moguls that live there."

Jo shot from her seat. "California? Canada, Josh! Ontario is in Canada."

"There's also an Ontario in Los Angeles," said Josh. "Isn't there?"

Jo shook her head. "No, there isn't. There's one in Oregon."

"Well, that's just up the road from Los Angeles." Josh shrugged.

"Just up the road, he says!" Jo shrieked. "About eight hundred and seventy miles up the road!"

"Oh, don't be so pedantic, Jo." Josh turned back to Tan. "So, is your name popular in *Canada* then?"

"What did he just say, Josh?" Jo hollered. "His mother liked to make up names. Right, that's it… Does anyone have anything intelligent to say about how we get out of this bloody mess?! In fact, I'm sorry, everyone, but if I'm going to stay on this bloody crazy train till the end then can you please do something about him?" She thrust a finger directly at Josh, who was now grinning wildly.

"No one can change him, Jo," said Pyrrha. "Look, once we reach our destination, I swear that you three girls shall have a room all to yourselves. In fact, you won't have to see him at all, if that's what you want, Jo."

Jo beamed a wide, toothy grin at Josh.

"Oh, come on, Hanna," he said. "All for one and all that?"

"Who the heck is Hanna?" asked Linus.

"Jo," said Josh. "As in, Johanna. But I like Hanna. And I reckon you have a middle name as well, don't you?"

"I told you before, Josh. I like Jo. And no, I don't have a middle name!"

"Yes, you do," said Rachel. "Come on, tell us. My real name is Phoebe Martise-Hayes. Martise is my mother's maiden name."

Everyone was left open-mouthed.

"So why did you tell me your name was Rachel?" Mira asked.

"Because my father has always called me Rachel. Actually, it's his little Rachey-Wachey. You see, I had a sister called Rachel who died a year before I was born. When people would ask him what my name was, he would always reply, 'Rachel.' I guess he has never got over her death. Oh… Now that I think on it rationally, how utterly morbid and depressing is that…?"

"And your mother is OK with it?" Mira asked, more than a little confused by Rachel's sudden admission.

"Yes. I guess. She's never said anything to me."

"So do we call you Phoebe from now on?" asked Pyrrha.

Rachel shook her head. "No. I prefer Rachel. I hate Phoebe. And before anyone asks, I don't want to go into why I hate it, OK!"

As everyone exchanged silent looks, Mira suddenly remembered that Jacen had mentioned a Phoebe in her vision. *Was he talking about Rachel? He loved her dearly, I know that. But how would he know that her real name is Phoebe? Did she tell him when they were together on Pandora's island? Must have. They shared a strong bond pretty much immediately…*

Josh, who was still smirking, finally broke into laughter. "Wouldn't Ray-Ray be better than Rachey-Wachey?"

Rachel scowled. "No, it wouldn't, Joshua. And I will only tolerate my father calling me Rachey-Wachey, got it?"

"OK, Phoebe-Ray," said Josh, still smiling.

"No, not Phoebe-Ray. Rachel!"

Her hand clenched, and Josh became serious. "Oo…kay, then. So, anyone else want to share?"

Linus raised his hand. "I'll lighten the mood," he said. "My full name is Linus Montague Cutter." He laughed. "So c'mon, Jo—yours can't be worse than that?"

Everyone now started to clap and chant in unison. "Come on, Jo, tell us your name."

After six bars of this, finally Jo stood up and smiled. "Fine. I was named after my aunts, and they all had posh names," she said proudly.

"Calling yourself Jo is not very posh, but Johanna, or Hanna, on the other hand?" said Josh.

Jo cast Josh yet another steely glare. "It's, Johanna Angelica Elizabetta Giselle Anna-Maria Rosemary-Loris."

"Wow, that's so cool." Mira smiled. "I don't even have one middle name. Don't you think that, too, Ray?"

Rachel tilted her head side to side and pursed her lips. "I guess."

"Hey!" said Josh. "How come she can call you Ray and not Rachel?"

"She didn't do it with the intention of winding me up, Josh!"

Josh quickly turned his attention back to Jo. "Are you sure you were named after your aunts?" He sniggered, and rising to his feet, he returned to the lake to wash the snake's blood from his hands, leaving the group to ponder what he'd actually meant by his comment.

"Yes!" Jo snapped. "And just like Rachel, I will only tolerate being addressed as Jo."

Silence fell once more upon the group. It was then that they heard the distant sound of metal scraping against rock. Josh, who had been noisily splashing his hands around in the water and whistling to himself, turned glumly toward the collapsed rock face. What was once solid rock was now just rubble.

"You know," he said. "It really wouldn't surprise me if that twister came back through here right now and blew those boulders—"

As if he'd conjured it himself, an icy wind suddenly surged through the opening in the tunnel.

Mira leapt to her feet. "Right then, is everyone dry and ready to make a move?" she asked and eagerly dragged Rachel toward the exit.

**

Kyle and Tan lifted the coffin, and everyone followed them out of the temple into the bright sunshine.

They had all carried the coffin at least once by the time they reached the base of the hill, and a team effort was necessary to pull and push the heavy vessel to the summit.

"Oh no, I just remembered something!" said Jo, on reaching the top and looking anxiously back to the temple. "The other key. We forgot about the other key!"

"Forget the key," said Mira, breathing heavily. "We just have to hide this thing. And even if the Followers dig through that rubble and defeat the remaining dead, hopefully we'll be long gone."

"Right," said Tan. "I'll go back to my boat. Now, just carry this thing to the edge of town, and we'll figure something out once I've docked. But if you see any bears or crocodiles, drop it and run. No use killing yourselves for it."

"I'll go with you, if you want?" said Linus, nervously looking at Pyrrha, who was glaring at him.

"You'll have to keep up," said Tan. "We may not have much time. The Followers are close. I can feel it in my old bones."

As Tan and Linus disappeared over the brow of the hill, and the rest of the team headed for the town, Mira noticed that all faces were now looking toward Linus. She could only guess what everyone must be thinking. With the end in sight, what was Pyrrha going to do with him? She'd hoped that, if they did indeed make it off the island, everything Linus had done to help them would somehow convince Pyrrha to grant him some leniency.

But as Mira tried to think of a way of broaching the subject, in case she hadn't changed her mind about killing him, Pyrrha suddenly ran toward the town, insisting that she would scout ahead.

CHAPTER SIXTY-ONE

A DIFFERENT PERSPECTIVE

The companions had reached the edge of town. Blood and guts stained the street where some of the harpy corpses had been dragged either back toward the river or the house that Josh had unwittingly discovered full of bears.

Thankful that there was no sign of the bears or crocodiles, Kyle and Josh placed the coffin down.

"Until we see Tan's boat, I'm not carrying this thing an inch further!" said Josh. "I want biceps like Arnold Schwarzenegger, yes, but not permanent backache!"

"We can't wait here in the open," said Jo. "And I need a pee."

Pyrrha, who had returned to the group, once again scanned the area. "She's right. We need to get it under cover." And taking hold of the box, with Mira's help, she dragged it inside the nearest building. When Kyle and Josh again took over, they carried it up the stairs to the top floor.

Sat inside a small room with their backs to the wall, they each took a sip from the bottle of water hidden in Jo's rucksack. Unable to sit still, Josh left the building to see if Tan's boat was coming. Exhausted, but insisting he shouldn't go alone, Rachel allowed Pyrrha to go with him.

Josh and Pyrrha cautiously walked the street, checking every side alley for signs of bears or crocodiles that could impede their progress when Tan docked. When they arrived at the building with the best view of the river, Josh skipped over the gruesome remains of several harpies and up the stairs. As he was standing by the window, watching the sun rise higher over the rolling hills, dispelling all the shadows of the town, Pyrrha tapped him gently on the shoulder.

"Can I ask you something?" she said. "About Linus, I mean?"

Josh knew what she was going to ask, but didn't want to talk about it. "Do you have to?" he said flatly, thinking he could see a large shape in the distance traversing the river. But with Pyrrha shuffling her feet, he knew it was coming whether he wanted it to or not.

"Do you trust him?"

Josh knew he would have to answer her. "Yes. No. I don't know. I thought he was my friend, and what he did I can't forget, or forgive. But then I see what he's done for us here and think maybe he was pushed to it. You didn't know Barry like we did. He was a thief, a bully and almost a rapist. Hell, for all I know he could have been one anyway, and he deserved what he got. But his mother, well, she was an alcoholic, yes, but she didn't deserve to die like that. But again, I don't know what else she may have put Linus through. Look, I'm not the one to judge him, or anyone else, but until all the facts about Linus are in—I say give him a chance."

"Do a few good deeds erase murder, though?" she asked. "Back at the palace on Pandora's island, I saw the face of a killer."

"No, they don't excuse it, but get the whole story first. Heck, I'm sure there are drugs that will make him tell the whole truth."

Pyrrha stepped back and stared. Josh wondered what he had said now.

"There are drugs, and yes, we have them. Did you know that already?"

"No. I had no idea. But the way Tan speaks, well, I'm guessing he's what they call in the trade a 'cleaner', or 'plumber'. Technically, he's an assassin. And if the movies have taught me anything, people like him always have drugs that make people talk."

"You're very perceptive, aren't you?" said Pyrrha. "That's why I wanted your opinion. You're one who sees things—oh, how can I say it—differently from the rest of them," she laughed.

Josh shook his head. "I don't know what Kyle, or Rachel, or even Mira for that matter have told you, but I'm not a bloody alien. I don't see things differently from the rest of them. OK, maybe I see things differently from Jo, but she's a bloody know-it-all. Look, you say you saw the face of a killer back at the palace, well, I saw a killer when you fought that giant wolf. But now I consider you a friend. Not girlfriend, not your toy boy, just friend. Anyway, as I've already pointed out, who am I to judge; but what I will say is, just be sure some god didn't screw with his mind to make him a killer and then make him confess to the crimes before you sentence him."

"So, you do truly believe in the gods then?"

"Well, if this is just some gameshow that we've been duped into playing, I'm going to be really pissed off…" Josh trailed off for a moment, then pointed to the looming shape approaching down the river. "Is that what I think it is?"

Pyrrha looked to where Josh was directing her. "That's not one of ours," she whispered. "It must be a Follower ship. We don't have anything that new."

Josh let out a deep sigh. "Good to know. So basically, they're the Empire and we're the Rebel Alliance?"

"As usual, I have no idea what the hell you are on about, Josh. But we need to get back to the others and get that coffin away from here," said Pyrrha, heading for the exit.

Josh shook his head. "I'm going to stay here, keep watch and buy you the time you're going to need."

"If they get you, they could seriously hurt you," Pyrrha stressed.

"But they can't kill me because they think they may need me. I've got the feeling they don't know who can open the coffins, and that's why they didn't kill us on Pandora's island." He winked.

Pyrrha took a moment, then exhaled. "Good point. So, what's your plan?"

He looked out through the window and studied the layout of the town. "I'll lead them away and you head around the rear of the buildings and make for the pyramid. Hopefully, Tan will be making his way up the river, and if he is, get him to take you back to the first cove he landed in, and I'll catch you up."

"What if they catch you, Josh?"

"Then go to the British government and get them to send the SBS or SAS to come rescue me. Trust me, they're the very best in the world and they will have me home before you can watch the entire special edition of *The Lord of the Rings*. But if they're busy, tell them to send the Paras or the Royal Marine Commandos. They're all mean and tough as hell as well. But can you also tell them to bring plenty of Mars bars? I don't think the Followers are people who appreciate them."

Pyrrha crossed the room, held his face with both hands and planted a quick kiss on his lips. "Don't you bloody die again, and for God's sake, don't tell Rachel that I just kissed you. That was only a friendly, you're-out-of-your-mind kiss."

Then she disappeared around the rear of the buildings. Once she was out of sight, Josh took a deep breath.

***

The ship had docked. When heavily armed guards disembarked, Josh leaned out of the top-floor window. "Excuse me, do you have a reservation? If you do, sorry about the mess, but the cleaning staff are on holiday, and I've been too busy to do it myself. In fact, I've really had a bitch of a week."

Hearing the troops enter the building, Josh ran to the next room and climbed out of a window. It was a long drop to the ground, but he landed safely and headed for the river. Seeing more troops lined up on the ship, all snarling, Josh gave them a cheeky grin and wave as he ran past.

CHAPTER SIXTY-TWO

DIVIDED

When Pyrrha rushed into the room, her eyes wide and breathing heavy, Mira leapt to her feet. "Where's Josh?"

"Where's Jo?" Pyrrha said, gasping for breath.

"Nature called. But where is Josh?" Mira asked again.

Pyrrha grabbed one handle of the coffin and looked hopefully to Kyle. "The Followers are here. We need to move, now!"

"Not until you tell us where Josh is," said Kyle, frantically getting to his feet.

"He's going to lead them away while we get to Tan's boat!"

Kyle dropped his head into his hands, and Mira rushed to his side.

"Like heck he is," said Rachel, her teeth gritted tightly together.

"Look, we have to get out now, Rach!" said Pyrrha, kicking Jo's rucksack across the floor toward her.

"I'm not going anywhere without Josh!" said Kyle, rushing to the window.

"Nor me." Rachel ignored the bag. "Now, where is he exactly?"

"He said he will meet us at the cove where Tan first had his boat," said Pyrrha, struggling to lift the coffin alone. "Now, do you really think they are going to catch him? This is Josh we're talking about."

Kyle took a long, deep breath. He then spun around and heaved up the other handle. "Does this mean more to you than his life?"

"No—of course not!" Pyrrha growled. "But if we don't get it out of here, then Josh will have put his life on the line for nothing. I won't allow that!"

"What about Jo?" Rachel cried.

"Do you know where she went?"

Despite everything, Mira knew Pyrrha was right—the coffin couldn't fall into the Followers' hands. "We'll find her. You and Kyle get that thing away!" she said and rushed down the stairs.

As she and Rachel left the building in search of Jo, Kyle and Pyrrha carried the coffin out through the rear of the building and back to the open field.

***

Troops were walking the centre of the town. Mira and Rachel were unable to find Jo, and time was running out before the enemy were upon them.

They headed through a side alley they hoped would bring them out to the open field. But with more troops entering the side streets, they found they were being shepherded toward the ship. With only one last building to hide in before they found themselves at the river, Mira and Rachel ran inside and upstairs to peer out of the window.

"Where the hell could Jo be?" Rachel whispered. Her teeth and bottom jaw had begun to ache due to the duration she'd had it clenched so tightly.

Mira's thoughts raced. Her insides felt like they were about to explode. She closed her eyes and held her head. "I don't know. I'm so sorry, Rach. All I wanted was to find my father and for him to hold me and tell me everything would be OK. That Jacen would be OK, and that you, Kyle and Josh would be OK. But every time I begin to hope, the Followers turn up like a bad dream. I'm tired, Rach, and sometimes I feel so alone, even with Kyle holding me. I just want my family back."

"Look, Mira," said Rachel. "I don't have any real friends back home. I have girls that hang out with me because I'm popular, and the boys like me because of the way I look and want to be the 'first', if you get my meaning. But when I met you, I liked you from the very start. There's no bullshit with you about what the latest fashion trends are or what makeup has to be worn. And you've become the closest friend to me in the shortest time. But I now consider you not just my truest, bestest friend, but my sister, and Jacen is the little brother I always wanted. I guess what I'm trying to say is, we are part of your family, too, now, and if you need to talk, or need a hug, then we are here for you and we are with you till the end. And Mira, you are not alone."

As her eyes filled with tears, Rachel grabbed Mira into a hug. "Now, let's go find my crazy boyfriend, Little Miss Know-it-all, Xena, warrior goddess, and your sexy hunk, shall we?" She smiled.

***

Kyle and Pyrrha had reached the open field. But realising that none of their group were coming anytime soon, Kyle dropped the coffin. "I'm sorry, Pyrrha. I know what this means, but if anything happens to any of them, then I don't care what happens afterward!"

Pyrrha attempted to drag the coffin on her own, but it was just too heavy. Reluctantly, she had to drop it. As she threw her head to the heavens, Kyle could see tears welling in her eyes.

"I agree," she said. "You are all like my family now."

Kyle led the way back to the edge of the town, but seeing the Followers patrolling, they had to hide behind the first building they came to. He pressed his body to the corner of the wall and listened closely to the tramping of boots as he prepared to take a weapon off the first soldier that appeared. But suddenly, he heard Josh laughing and whooping. Without warning, the armed troops about-turned and joined the multitude that were already chasing after him. Kyle prepared to run after his brother, but Pyrrha grabbed his arm.

"Your brother is crazy," she said. "Brave, but totally crazy. But they're not going to catch him... Now, isn't that Rachel's perfume I can smell?"

This time, taking Kyle's hand, she led him in the direction of the aroma.

Josh was now singing, with almost all of the troops chasing him, and as Kyle and Pyrrha ran through the alley, they could see Jo being escorted toward the ship. Another detour, and they found the alley where Rachel's perfume was strongest. They entered the building and joined Mira and Rachel, who had been readying themselves to leave.

The group watched silently from the upstairs window. They could see Jo, her hands tied behind her back, tears rolling down her cheeks, being escorted up the ramp to the ship by two soldiers in heavy armours.

"Now what do we do?" Kyle whispered.

Rachel tearfully pulled at his arm. "They have Josh as well now," she said, holding her hand to her mouth to stop herself from screaming out his name.

Kyle watched his brother, bound, dragged along the street, but when Josh raised his head, took a deep inhale of breath, looked up slyly to the window and winked, Kyle knew they hadn't caught him.

"He let himself get caught," he said proudly. "He's not going to leave Jo alone with them."

"You three have to get out of here," said Pyrrha. "Otherwise, it's all over." She placed her hand on Kyle's shoulder. "I'll see what I can do to get him back."

"No! There's got to be a way without you putting your life at risk as well."

"I'm sorry, but the danger you place us in is too high now. Please, will you all just try and get to Tan's boat!" Pyrrha pleaded.

"We are not leaving them or you," said Mira. "They know they need me, right? Well, let's see if we can use that to our advantage."

Pyrrha stared at the ship. "I still have a sticky bomb as a last resort, which is now upon us. I'm going to try and blow that coffin up—that should send most of the troops running to my location. We're not going to be able to get that sarcophagus to a safe place now anyway. You think how we can get Josh and Jo back, but please, I know it's a lot to ask—don't let the Followers take you alive. The outcome will be hell on earth!"

Pyrrha turned to leave but had to step back into the room as Tan entered, carrying a high-powered rifle. "If you want to remain incognito, Rach," he said, "don't wear perfume that the enemy can smell from five miles away. Now, I'm sorry, but we couldn't get the boat here.

I've had to leave it where I first docked. Lucky we did go back, though, because I forgot I had this rifle. Unfortunately, I have only three rounds. So, before anyone tries to do anything heroic, let's hear what Tripp has to say before I kill him."

Kyle's hands were clenched and the veins in his neck were beginning to throb. "Mr Tripp is here as well?" he growled.

"He is. We saw him. And, if I'm not mistaken, he's about to make an announcement," said Tan, lining up his shot.

"Wait—where the hell is Linus?" Kyle asked.

"He's about to do something that will get him killed if you don't let me concentrate!"

CHAPTER SIXTY-THREE

DID YOU SEE THIS COMING?

Forced to stand on the deck of the ship, Josh and Jo waited as their hands were untied and the door to the bridge opened. When a hooded figure stepped out carrying a bullhorn, Josh pushed himself to his full height and glared at the approaching adversary.

Eyes like sunken tombstones looked out from under its cowl. "Well, well. If it isn't my favourite Michaels boy." Mr Tripp smiled a thin, dry smile.

Josh watched him close in. His timing had to be precise. But before he could grab Mr Tripp and use him as an escape route, Mr Tripp skipped around to his rear and held a gun to the back of his head.

"I always know what you are thinking, Josh, even before you do. Please, do not make the mistake others have. I didn't become a leader just for my knowledge. Now, your hands have been untied as a show of good faith. I don't want to hurt any of you. I want you all with me when we open these coffins. I want you to be a part of the new world."

Josh's insides turned over. "No, not for me, thank you. And I'm pretty sure the others don't want to be a part of your new Eden, either. But I do have a piece of advice for you. If you open those things, you're going to unleash something that you're not going to be able to control."

Mr Tripp placed one hand on Josh's shoulder and gently squeezed. Josh shuddered as if the Devil had left an imprint upon him.

"I sense you have grown up these last few days, Josh my boy." Mr Tripp smiled. "Shame you're on the wrong side. But I still have high hopes for you, and your brother." At a wave of his hand, one trooper opened the door to the bridge. "I have a surprise for you, Josh. Someone who wishes to say hello."

Suddenly, another hooded person stepped out. Josh had to take a step back. And as the figure strode across the deck, his hands began to shake.

Josh stared into the face; it looked different. The woman before him was standing tall, and there was an elegant beauty to her he'd never seen before.

"Mum?"

Saying it out loud, Josh felt as if he'd been shot through the stomach.

"Bet you didn't see this coming," Mr Tripp whispered into Josh's ear.

Clare Michaels held out her arms to embrace her son. "You need to come with me, sweetheart. There is so much you need to know. We are not the real enemy." She smiled.

Josh fell into her arms. "Please, tell me you are not really with them?" he whispered.

"Where's your brother and the sarcophagus, Josh?" she asked.

Josh pushed her away. "Where's Dad?"

Mrs M looked to Mr Tripp.

"He... he is taking care of some things for me," he said. "Tasks I would trust to no one else. Now, listen to your mother and tell me where it is, Josh."

"What, the playing card?" Josh smirked. "Oh, I'm sorry. I lost it. Hope it didn't have sentimental value?" he added defiantly.

Mr Tripp laughed, a vile laugh. "Still funny and very brave. I like that. No, I want the location of the sarcophagus, your brother, and your friends."

Josh let out an exasperated sigh. "A long way from here. I'm the one you want. I can open the coffin. But I'm afraid you will just have to keep looking for it, cos it isn't on this island."

As he said it, he caught sight of troops carrying the sarcophagus along the street. His insides shrank, but there was no way he would give Mr Tripp the satisfaction of seeing it.

He pointed to his chest. "Did I say I could open it? Oh dear, I can't, sorry. But if you enter the sepulchre, I think you will find what you are really looking for in there." He grinned. "You might have to do a bit of digging, though."

Mr Tripp's smile held a sinister edge, and turning Josh to face the buildings, while still keeping himself hidden, he placed the bullhorn to his mouth.

"I know you are watching us, but I am not the monster you think I am," he called out. "The ones you travel with are the ones you should fear. They tell lies and will continue to do so. But if you come with me, I will tell you the whole truth."

When no one appeared, William Tripp waited for five minutes, then signalled to his guard. The cabin door opened, and Jo's and Rachel's fathers were led out at gunpoint.

"Very well… then I want you all to listen very carefully. If you don't come out, these two will pay for your mistake. But I give you my word that if you come peacefully, then I will let everyone else go. Choose wisely, children. If you don't… I would say your goodbyes now!"

Josh was infuriated. "And you say you're not a monster?"

***

Kyle and Rachel immediately rushed to the door. Pyrrha swung out her arm and blocked their path. "Please, don't be foolish. They knew this could happen and are prepared to die to save everyone!"

Rachel almost fell onto her backside. "They knew this could happen? Are you saying my father is one of you and you never had the decency to tell me?" she said, spitting fire.

Pyrrha lowered her gaze. "Yes. He has been undercover for a very long time. He didn't want you to know. I'm sorry."

"What about Jo's father? Is he one of you, too?" said Mira.

Pyrrha looked to the bound man. "No, I don't know who he is. They must have him simply because of Jo. Wrong place at the wrong time."

Kyle again attempted to push past. "My mother is there. I have to speak with Mr Tripp. I'll tell him I can open the coffin and negotiate my mother, Josh and Jo's release." But when Pyrrha refused to move out of the way, he turned back to his mother. And seeing that she was in no peril, it suddenly all made sense to him.

"My mother is a member of the Followers, isn't she? That's why you don't trust me and Josh?"

"Yes!" Pyrrha spat, pulling a knife from her belt. "And if you go to her, then not only will the Followers know about this third tomb, they will use you to get to Mira! I want to believe that you knew nothing of this, Kyle, truly, but if you try to leave this room—I will have to kill you!"

Kyle looked to Mira, who was staring at the floor. "You knew, didn't you?"

Mira raised her eyes and looked tearfully back. "I'm so sorry. I wanted to tell you…"

He dropped his head, and Rachel reluctantly returned to the window, where they could see Mr Tripp whispering into Josh's ear before moving behind Jo's father.

A single shot rang out. Time itself seemed to come to a stop. But then Jo's father fell forward into the river, and Mr Tripp sidled behind Mr Hayes.

"Please, don't force me to do this."

Jo's screams echoed around the room, and with tears streaming down her face, Rachel returned to the exit. "I have to go, I'm sorry. I won't let him kill my father, or take Josh away."

"Listen to me—I know that man," said Pyrrha. "Tripp will not let them live, even if you go to them now."

"She's right," said Tan. "Now, we have to give Linus time, or they will die for nothing."

They watched as Mr Tripp pulled back the hammer of the gun and held it to Rachel's father's head. But then he hesitated. "Oh, that's right," he called out. "You're probably being forced not to do what I've asked. So, I have one more surprise. We have never met, but I have heard about your reputation, so this one's for you, Tandigo Sing!"

Another woman was brought out and lined up beside Mr Hayes. Tan threw his head in his hands.

Tan was breathing heavily, and Mira placed her arm around his shoulder. "Is that your wife?" she whispered.

"No. It's my mother."

Wide-eyed, Mira couldn't believe that the raven-haired beauty could be who he said she was. Surely she was too young?

"You know, this woman was the finest spy we had, and yet she threw it away for love," Mr Tripp called out. "Such a disappointment. But I give you my solemn vow that I will even let this traitorous bitch go if you come with me now!"

"So, do you feel the same now?" Kyle asked Tan. "Are you willing to let her die?"

Tan glared out the window. A tear trickled down his cheek as he lined up his shot. "I am, and she means more to me than life itself. But she taught me to be strong, and I promise you, we shall have vengeance on them all!"

Mr Tripp peered out from behind Tan's mother and held the gun to her temple.

Tan adjusted his telescopic sight. "Pyrrha, you know what needs to be done."

Pyrrha whipped out of the room and was down the stairs in seconds. Mira followed behind. But when she had reached the entrance to the building, where Pyrrha had stopped and was peering around the door, it suddenly dawned on her what Tan was about to do. Why he'd adjusted his weapon's sight.

She pulled on Pyrrha's arm to gain her attention. "He's not actually going to—"

Three rapid shots rang out.

CHAPTER SIXTY-FOUR

A NOBLE END

Two soldiers lay dead at Josh's feet. The third bullet struck Tan's mother in the chest, killing her instantly. The force of the blow sent Mr Tripp tumbling backwards.

In all the confusion, Linus leapt over the railing and, grabbing Mr Tripp around the throat, pressed a gun to the side of his head. "If you don't mind, William, I'd appreciate it if you let my friends and family go!"

Mr Tripp clawed at Linus' arm to get breath. "You want to die, boy, is that it?" he gasped.

"At this moment, the question's more, do you want to die?" Linus chuckled, holding him firm. As the troops edged closer, he cocked the gun. "Now, do we really want to be putting your leader's life at risk?"

"I am just a simple nobody, boy. So go ahead, kill me," said Mr Tripp. "But know that everyone that doesn't matter will die here and now!"

"Now the truth comes out, finally." Linus laughed. "You hear that, Josh? He's going to kill us anyway. Well, William, I'm prepared to die with my friend. Heck, there's no better way to go. But ask yourself... Are you ready to face the Devil?"

The soldiers closed in, and Linus pressed the gun tighter to Mr Tripp's head.

Mr Tripp raised a shaky hand, and the troops stopped their advance.

"Well, shucks, looks like you're not ready to die after all, William," said Linus. "Now if you don't mind, Josh, would you be so kind and take everyone that *does* matter off the ship?"

Josh picked Jo up off the deck and instructed Mr Hayes to take her to Pyrrha, who was standing just outside the building. Josh then returned to his mother and held out his hand.

"C'mon, now's your chance to get away from them!" He smiled. It was a hopeful smile.

Mrs M stood her ground. "You don't understand, Josh. You have to come with me."

"You want to release a poison that will kill millions of innocent people, Mum. If not billions." Josh scowled. "How can you expect me to be a part of that?"

"It's not poison that will be released," she said. "We are going to free something far more powerful—weapons, which will finally turn the tide in this unholy war—"

Mr Tripp coughed into his hand. A signal to stop her from revealing any more.

Josh couldn't grasp what was happening. "And Kyle? Have you forgotten about him?"

Mrs M's expression hardened. "He's chosen his side. He wants to be with her. Now, come with me, Joshua, before he gets you killed!"

Josh stepped further away from his mother just as Kyle appeared at his side. Mira, on the other hand, threw herself at Mr Tripp and slapped him hard around the face. "Where is my brother, you monster?!"

"A long way from here, child." Mr Tripp glared. "You don't think I would be stupid enough to bring him to this godawful place, do you?"

Mira bolted toward the bridge. Josh threw both his arms around her waist and lifted her off her feet to hold her back. "He's not lying," he whispered. "Jacen isn't here. Remember, three years have passed. Maybe six, if this island is as loopy as the other one. Think about it. If Jacen was aboard this vessel, then he wouldn't have appeared to you in your dream looking older. Now, we need to get away if we're to have any chance of getting him back."

Kyle wrenched a gun from one of Tripp's troops and aimed directly at Mr Tripp's face. "Is he aboard? Don't lie to me, William! I swear I'll kill you here and now if you do!"

Mr Tripp glared back with cold, dead eyes. "William? I expected more from you, Kyle. How about you show some respect for your elders. It's impolite to use someone's first name unless invited to do so! That's the problem with you know-it-all youngsters today—no respect for those that have fought and died to give you an easier ride in life!"

Kyle cocked the hammer. "Don't make me ask you again, William. After what you did to us back on Pandora's island, I have no qualms about pulling this trigger now!"

"Yes. I can see that," said Mr Tripp. "So be it. No, Jacen is not aboard this vessel. But he is safe. And he will remain that way. I am not the monster you think I am, Kyle. But there are things that you should know—"

Kyle cut him off. "I don't want to hear any more lies, thanks. Linus, time for you to go. I'll take it from here. Josh, take Mum and Mira with you."

"Mum's not leaving, Kyle," said Josh. "She and Dad are... with them."

Kyle looked despairingly to his mother. "So, it's true... Why didn't you tell us?"

"There are a lot of things I haven't told you, Kyle!" she said harshly. "But if you are willing to leave *her* and come with me, then I shall tell you everything."

Josh took his brother's arm. "C'mon, Kai, we can't stay here," he said. "I hope you know what you're doing, Mum."

"He's right, Kyle. You need to go now," said Linus. "You have to keep them all safe. Don't you worry about me—Mr Tripp and I have a lot to discuss, don't we, William? Promise me, Kyle, promise that you will take care of them all. And Josh, don't do anything too stupid, yeah?"

As Linus dragged Mr Tripp further away from his troops, Mira took Kyle's arm.

Josh looked to his mother, one last time. "I'm sorry, but my place is with them," he said. "I can't be a part of what you are going to do."

Mrs M's face softened. "We are going to stop the religious zealots and dictators from ending this world, Josh."

"No," said Josh. "You are going to unleash things that *will* bring about the end. You have to believe me, Mum. The gods are real, and I can tell you, they have no love for us."

"Then go," she said. "But remember my words, Josh. Not all is as it seems. The Disciples cannot be trusted." And with an elegant twirl, she returned to the bridge.

Kyle placed his arm around Josh's shoulder to guide him away. "Time to go. She's made her decision. We have to go now, or Linus did this for nothing."

They ran from the boat to the building where the others were waiting.

Tan rushed down the stairs. "Mira, please take Jo— she needs your friendship now more than ever. The rest of you, follow me." He turned to Pyrrha, still standing in the doorway. "And you, dear child, make sure you make it back to us, alive."

***

Tan led the group back through the street and out across the field, but Mira was unable to leave Pyrrha behind. She turned tail and rushed back. "What the hell are you planning to do?" she whispered, catching up with her.

"I need you to remain here," Pyrrha answered, and while she slowly walked toward the river, Mira watched from inside the doorway.

Nobody saw Pyrrha approach the ship. But when Mira saw Linus give Pyrrha a smile and a nod, she realised what Pyrrha was about to do.

"Guess we're going to see the Devil now, Mr Tripp!" Linus called out.

Pyrrha removed two grenades from her coat and tossed them at the ship. The smoke grenade erupted first, and with a thick, white smog covering their escape, she dragged Mira back through the building, out into the street and across the field to where the others were waiting.

The sticky bomb exploded, and the shock wave sent Mira and Pyrrha tumbling to the ground.

"I hope that at least one of the coffins will no longer be a threat!" said Pyrrha, lifting her head out of the long grass.

While Kyle had to restrain a distraught Josh from running toward the river, Mira silently watched the burning ship sail past. But when she saw the sarcophagus aboard the deck, unscathed, along with Mrs M standing beside it, staring at her sons, her heart sank. Even though she was relieved that Kyle and Josh had chosen to stay with her, they'd made an enemy of their parents. And even if Mr Tripp was dead, once again, he had got the better of them.

As Mira sat in the long, damp grass, and the ship limped out into the ocean, Tan, Kyle and Josh headed toward Tan's boat.

Pyrrha got to her feet and held out her hand for Mira to take. "I guess you were right, Mira. There is a traitor in our ranks," she said, looking back to the departing vessel, her face contorted with hatred.

Mira's heart sank once again. "How Mr Tripp knew about this island, you mean? Or do you still believe Kyle and Josh are spies?"

"Only a select few of my order knew about this place and what was contained here," said Pyrrha.

"What are you going to do?"

"What else? Get you to safety, find the one responsible for betraying us—and I now have a fair idea of where to start looking—and kill them. But I'm also going to find out how Rachel and Jo are able to open the tomb and coffin, when I know for a fact they are not descended from Pandora and Epimetheus. I will also discover what this third tomb you saw actually contains, and I swear you shall hear the truth of it."

Mira began to panic. "Kyle seemed to recognise parts of this island. If his mother and father are Followers, do you think he's been here before? Josh, too? What if the Followers discovered they needed Jo to open the tomb, and had their memories erased somehow to make it appear natural when we met aboard the cruise ship?"

Pyrrha tucked her hand under Mira's arm. "I saw Clare Michaels' reaction when she saw them. They were never meant to be here. I fear there's something else at play. What exactly Kyle and Josh have to do with all this, I will, however, do my best to uncover. But let me add, as of this moment, you all here with me now are the only ones I do completely trust."

CHAPTER SIXTY-FIVE

A LOOK TO THE HORIZON

After the continual bad luck they'd been having, Mira was not surprised to find that Tan's boat had been scuppered and was sinking fast. With Tan already on the radio he'd managed to rescue, calling for help, Mira looked for Kyle. He was standing alone at the edge of the water.

She was about to join him when Josh gently placed a hand on her arm.

"Did you see Linus?" he asked.

Mira couldn't answer.

Pyrrha patted him on the shoulder. "He's dead."

"Did he know what you were going to do?"

"Yes, he knew," Tan called out. "It was his plan. He knew he couldn't go with us after what he had done. In the end, he wanted to save the only real friends he ever had."

"How long before our people can get here, Tan?" Pyrrha asked. "And did you do what we spoke about?"

"They shouldn't be long. And yes, everything is now in motion. But I have more bad news. Apparently, just like on the other island, we've been here for three years. We were lucky that our people were testing a new ship they've acquired and were in the vicinity to pick up my call."

"That explains why we've had a full moon for the past week then," said Josh.

Yes, Mira thought to herself. *It explains that. But who has been playing with the timing of the rise and setting of the sun?*

"Hold on!" Rachel cried. "Three years! What the hell? And we were on the last island for the same length of time? Are you saying that I have been away from home for six bloody years?"

Mira wrapped her arm around Rachel's shoulder. "We should have told you, I know, but we didn't want you to worry. These islands seem to have an effect on time. One day spent on them is actually a year or two in the outside world."

"So, when you said you got word out to your people, you lied?" Rachel exclaimed, spinning around to face Pyrrha.

"No, we got word out, but they were too late in getting to us. When they arrived at the coordinates, this island was gone."

"Oh, great," said Josh. "I know I've shown delight at not being able to go back to school, but if this keeps up, me and Kyle are going to be the oldest students they've ever had!"

Rachel placed her hand over Josh's mouth. "It also means that the Followers must have been hiding here on this island with us all this time, just waiting for the tomb to be opened. To them it's only been a couple of days as well. And if that is the case, then your mother must have been on Pandora's island with Tripp the whole time."

Josh bit his bottom lip. "Yup—nice, isn't it. Makes me feel warm inside to know that she was willing to sit by while me and Kyle were almost eaten by giant wolves, a two-headed snake, and then almost turned

into shish kebabs by an army of extremely peeved skeletons."

Rachel shook her head. "You're missing the point,
sweetie. Why did they follow us to begin with if they had
no idea about Epimetheus?" She turned to face Pyrrha.
"There was a traitor aboard your ship, wasn't there?"

"It must have been the ones that mutinied," said Josh.

Pyrrha slowly nodded. "Looks that way," she said, not
disclosing the fact that she and Mira now believed that
the true traitors were yet to be found.

"So, would you mind revealing why Epimetheus is so
important to them now?" Rachel added. "Cos I for one
don't believe the Followers are stupid enough to believe
they are going to be able to control him so that he only
comes after you."

Pyrrha simply hung her head.

Josh sighed. "Then what about the third sarcophagus?
Any idea where it is, or do we just have to wait and see?"

"I... I don't know. Truly I don't," said Pyrrha. "Only
Mira seems to know the answer to that, but it appears
that it is locked away in her subconscious."

Everyone looked to Mira, who had her eyes tightly
closed.

*Three years you've been gone, little brother. No wonder
you were angry with me. Why you asked if I was still your
sister. What decent sister would have left you this long?*

"You may be right," she replied.

Another thought then came to her. She shot Tan a
concerned look.

"I know what you are going to ask," he said. "No, your
parents were not with them. While the Followers did have
a ship waiting for them after the storm struck, Daniel en-
sured they got on the rescue helicopter that had been sent
out from the cruise liner that received the distress call."

Rachel looked to her father. "Why couldn't you and Mum have gotten on the same helicopter?"

Mr Hayes lowered his head. "Your mother and I have been undercover in the Follower camp for quite some time."

Rachel's eyebrows jerked upwards. "What! Why didn't you tell me? Or at least give me some warning of what to expect? Do you know what we've been through?"

"I'm sorry, duckling," said Mr Hayes. "We didn't know what was going to happen, I swear. Tripp insisted we bring you along to get close to Mira. That's all."

"Or maybe it's because he knew either you or your wife is actually descended from Epimetheus," said Josh.

Mr Hayes' face contorted in confusion. "I'm sorry—say that again?"

"Oh, wait till you hear what I've got to tell you," said Rachel.

"I think it would be best if we did all this later, when we're away from here," said Tan.

"What about Jo's parents? Were they undercover as well?" Mira asked. "And are Josh and Kyle's parents really undercover, too?"

Mr Hayes shook his head. "I have no idea. If they are then I have no knowledge of it."

"Smart move," said Tan. "If they don't know each other, then it's harder for their cover to get blown."

"So, now what happens?" asked Josh.

"Like I told you, I've given the code to call all the orders together and then we'll decide what's to be done. Look to the horizon, kids. It's not as bad as it seems."

"Not as bad as it seems?" Rachel repeated. "What if they want to do nothing? Are our families expendable?"

"No," said Tan. "They might have two of the coffins now, but we still hold all the cards. So, let's take one step at a time, plan our next move, and not do anything rash that will get them killed."

As Pyrrha assisted Tan in recovering items from the boat, Rachel left Mira's side to comfort Jo, who was in shock, sitting upon a rock.

Josh pulled Mira out of earshot. "I think when they hear what I've got to say, they're going to do everything they can to stop what's going to happen!" he snarled.

Mira stroked his cheek. "Whatever it is you know, whatever Mr Tripp has told you, keep it to yourself for now, yeah?" she whispered. "But about your parents—"

"I know what you're going to say," Josh interjected. "What if they aren't double agents? Well, Luke Skywalker had to deal with his father who had turned to the dark side, but he brought him back to the light, so I reckon I can do the same with my mum and dad." He smiled.

Not for first time, Mira couldn't help but be impressed with the way Josh handled traumatic events. In contrast, Kyle was standing alone, staring out to the skyline. She began to wonder how much more he could take.

"Can you hear that?" he asked as she reached his side.

Mira strained to listen. "I can't hear anything."

Kyle took her hand into his and squeezed it gently. "I can hear singing. There is something waiting for us out there, beyond the horizon. I can feel it." He turned to face her. "I'm so sorry you had to carry me through this nightmare, but I swear, I won't let you down again."

"You have never let me down, Kyle. I'm just so sorry about your parents. I should have told you."

"We all make choices in life. They chose their path, Josh and I have chosen ours." He took a moment. "I swear I'm going to get Jacen back, Mira, and if the Followers want a fight—then I'll give them a fight they won't forget!"

This frightened her. Yes, Kyle wouldn't back down from a fight if he thought his friends, or even someone he didn't know, were in danger—that is what she loved about him. But he was now threatening to go looking for a battle.

Will I get the time to talk him out of it? Or is history about to repeat itself? In his anger to keep me safe, will he, too, end up locked away, just like Epimetheus?

She felt exhausted and afraid.

Were the girl and boy who visited me in that vision siblings? Or the real Pandora and Epimetheus? Will they come to me again, only this time with the answers I seek? Or will they convince me to give up on my brother? Or even, Kyle?

No. I will never give up on either of them.

Strangely, a sudden tingle of excitement ran through her body. She would soon see her father.

He will have all the answers, I'm sure of it. He will know who the Desolate One is. He will also know the true reason Pandora and Epimetheus were so cruelly locked away. He must!

Mira and Kyle were shortly joined by Rachel and Josh. But as they stared silently out at the horizon, waiting and praying for any signs of a rescue, Mira looked to their gloomy expressions. Her heart again sank. She knew what they must all be now thinking and feeling.

When they had left Pandora's island, they had a sense of purpose. Find a way to rescue Jacen and stop the Followers from releasing Pandora's curse. But now, nothing truly made sense. There was more to Pandora's story than Pyrrha and Tan were letting on, or they, too, were just as much in the dark as the rest of their company.

One thing was certain. The brutal murder of Jo's father and Tan's mother had crossed the line. Sides had now been taken. There was no going back to their old lives for any of them. And if they were to rescue Jacen, a war was going to have to be fought. A war that, she now believed, had placed the fate of the world in all their hands.

...to be continued...

Author Profile

P. H. Townsend is the author of the *A Dream of Destiny* series. It was during the Covid outbreak of 2020, a dark time for the world, that he awoke in the early hours of the morning. One line of text permeated for the rest of the night:

'Finding the key, they went to where it was hidden.'

The next morning, he put fingers to keyboard.

A Dream of Destiny: Children of the Fates is the second book in a planned series of four. He currently lives in the picturesque region of the Brecon Beacons, Wales, United Kingdom, working on Book 3.

What Did You Think of
A Dream of Destiny:
Children of the Fates?

A big thank you for purchasing this book. It means a lot that you chose this book specifically from such a wide range on offer. I do hope you enjoyed it.

Book reviews are incredibly important for an author. All feedback helps them improve their writing for future projects and for developing this edition. If you are able to spare a few minutes to post a review on Amazon, that would be much appreciated.

Publisher Information

Rowanvale Books provides publishing services to independent authors, writers and poets all over the globe. We deliver a personal, honest and efficient service that allows authors to see their work published, while remaining in control of the process and retaining their creativity. By making publishing services available to authors in a cost-effective and ethical way, we at Rowanvale Books hope to ensure that the local, national and international community benefits from a steady stream of good quality literature.

For more information about us, our authors or our publications, please get in touch.

www.rowanvalebooks.com
info@rowanvalebooks.com